Popular Library
Detroit Public Library
5201 Woodward Ave.
Detroit, MI 48202

DETROIT PUBLIC LIBRARY

W9-BXD-948

PRAISE FOR **GHOST FLEET**

"It's like the *Battlestar Galactica* reboot meets *Band of Brothers* meets *Hunt for Red October* meets *Call of Duty*." — Yahoo News

"*Ghost Fleet* delivers a realistic and sweeping vision of the future of war with a story that reveals that the secrets to victory on tomorrow's battle-fields will be nothing like we expect."
— **Steven Pressfield, author *Gates of Fire* and *The Profession***

"A harrowing, realistic future of world war . . . Every single military tech-nology, 'sci-fi' weapon and geopolitical trend mentioned in the book is grounded in reality. That's why, rather than simply a good read, *Ghost Fleet* can come across as a 400-page warning." — *Wired*

"If you've been looking for a smart update to Tom Clancy, this is for you."
— *Foreign Policy*

"What makes *Ghost Fleet* so scary — and so compelling — is how real it feels. Want to see the future of national security? Get ready."
— **Brad Meltzer, author of *The Fifth Assassin***

"An absolute pleasure to read. It contains much of the same storytelling as a work by someone like Tom Clancy, but with an intensity, depth of knowledge, and vision infrequently found in those books. It is an expan-sive work in its scope, and one that will undoubtedly retain its relevance for years to come." — *Medium*

"*Ghost Fleet* nails the perfect vision of World War III . . . A futuristic techno-thriller that's as plausible as it is entertaining. Make no mistake, however, this is no technical slog — it's a highly readable and engaging thriller that sets a new standard for techno-thrillers." — *io9*

"I couldn't put this one down. *Ghost Fleet* reads like the very best of clas-sic Tom Clancy, updated for the twenty-first century, persuasive in its detail, simultaneously thrilling and terrifying."
— **Philipp Meyer, author of *The Son*, Pulitzer Prize for fiction finalist**

APR 1 2 2019

PL

"This page-turning marvel is the best source of high-tech geopolitical visioneering since Tom Clancy's *Red Storm Rising* and Sir John Hackett's *The Third World War*. A startling blueprint for the wars of the future, and therefore needs to be read now!"

— Admiral James Stavridis, U.S. Navy (Ret.), supreme allied commander of NATO, 2009–2013, and dean of the Fletcher School of Law and Diplomacy, Tufts University

"It's a page-turner . . . Thoughtful, strategic, and relevant."
— Admiral Jonathan Greenert, 30th chief of naval operations, U.S. Navy

"A ripped-from-the-headlines novel about war that's just around the corner . . . Exciting." — *Buzzfeed*

"*Ghost Fleet* is what *Call of Duty* would be like if it put on a tie and went to Capitol Hill." — *Playboy*

"*Ghost Fleet* is an ambitious blend of fact and fiction, Herman Wouk meets William Gibson, with a dash of *Brave New World* and *In Harm's Way* for good measure." — *American Conservative*

"The first 'post-Snowden' techno-thriller." — *Intercept*

"It's Tom Clancy for the twenty-first century, a rip-roaring, 'near-futuristic' thriller . . . The book is peppered with real-life military facts and figures, but it moves so briskly you may hardly notice that you're learning as you go." — *Business Insider*

"Tom Clancy fans will relish Singer and Cole's first novel, a chilling vision of what might happen in a world war." — *Publishers Weekly*

"*Ghost Fleet* is a page-turner filled with thrills and chills, but it is also more than that. Drawn from real-world trends in cyber tech, intelligence, and defense, *Ghost Fleet* offers a haunting glimpse into our future that you'll find hard to forget."
— Nina Jacobson, producer of *The Hunger Games*

"Too realistic for comfort . . . Tom Clancy–esque." — *Fast Company*

"A great book." — *Fox News*

"Some may compare this thriller to those of Tom Clancy, but in addition to packing a hefty punch of adrenaline, it is much more accurate."

— *Military Times*

"Whether on a commute to the Pentagon or relaxing on a beach . . . readers will find *Ghost Fleet* a highly enjoyable, at times uncomfortable, and always thought-provoking read."

— U.S. Naval Institute

"*Ghost Fleet* is not only a riveting novel, it is science fiction at its best. It helps us ask the right questions about our future — questions whose answers might help us take advantage of technology while minimizing risk to humanity."

— H. R. McMaster, author of *Dereliction of Duty;* lieutenant general, U.S. Army; director, Army Capabilities Integration Center, and deputy commanding general, Futures, U.S. Army Training and Doctrine Command

"The next great military techno-thriller has finally arrived."

— *Task & Purpose*

"Every Army officer should read it — and it's fun . . . It's one of those books that is the perfect companion to a cold beer in a beach chair. It will also help you imagine a future of war that is very different from our experiences in Afghanistan and Iraq."

— *Best Defense*

"If you are an avid reader of fiction or suspense, love Ian Fleming and his famous Agent Bond, or are an academic interested in science, technology, military affairs, strategy, war, or moral philosophy, this is a great book."

— *Huffington Post*

"In addition to being a page-turning read, this is a clarion call to get our act together before fiction becomes fact."

— Vint Cerf, coinventor of the Internet

"An unforgettable techno-thriller that turns the classic Clancy formula upside-down. As I turned the pages of my review copy of *Ghost Fleet,* I found myself in all-too-familiar territory: unable to set the book aside, devouring it with a voracious appetite for more. I read when I should have been working, I read when I should have been sleeping . . . This book is everything you look for in a techno-thriller, and more."

— *Pendulum*

"Action packed."   —*Sydney Morning Herald*

"Throughout the story, as venues change, the reader gasps for breath and delves back in as the action continues. Thriller readers will find this a welcome addition to their collections. Thinkers, advocates, policy wonks, geeks, and nerds will all find something to chew on that will confirm or challenge their own biases . . . This highly recommended story is a daring look at the fusion of traditional and modern warfare, delivered at 'machine speed.'"   —*Black Five*

"A scarily plausible techno-thriller for the twenty-first century; expect to be reading headlines ripped from this book in the coming decades."
                                                    —*Aerospace*

"Important on the substance but also highly entertaining and a great summer read . . . It is also scary. It's scary because the whole thing is not implausible."   —*National Interest*

"Go out and get *Ghost Fleet*. Enjoy the read. Recommend it to your friends. Argue about it over beers. The novel's power lies in its ability to spur conversations about the future of conflict with people who might not otherwise be engaged."   —*Leading Edge*

"*Neuromancer* meets *Red Storm Rising* . . . A rattling good read."
                                                    —*South London Books*

"Terrifying, futuristic, and also entertaining and plausible . . . A novel that reads like science fiction but bristles with rich detail about how the next world war could be fought."   —*Vice*

"A highly realistic portrayal . . . A tremendous book."   —*Defense News*

"A sizzler." —*Charlotte Observer*

"Scary, accessible, entertaining, and plausible."   —*Cyber Defense Review*

"This year's defense 'must-read' . . . Their cautionary message should resonate powerfully with Marines."   —*Marine Corps Gazette*

"A perfect summer read. If what you like is edge-of-the-seat action, you'll have trouble putting it down."   —*Bloomberg*

GHOST FLEET

A NOVEL OF THE NEXT
WORLD WAR

P. W. SINGER

AND

AUGUST COLE

AN EAMON DOLAN BOOK

MARINER BOOKS

HOUGHTON MIFFLIN HARCOURT

BOSTON   NEW YORK

First Mariner Books edition 2016

Copyright © 2015 by P. W. Singer and August Cole

All rights reserved

For information about permission to reproduce selections from
this book, write to trade.permissions@hmhco.com or to Permissions,
Houghton Mifflin Harcourt Publishing Company, 3 Park Avenue,
19th Floor, New York, New York 10016.

www.hmhco.com

Library of Congress Cataloging-in-Publication Data
Singer, P. W. (Peter Warren)
Ghost fleet : a novel of the next world war / P.W. Singer and August Cole.
pages cm
"An Eamon Dolan Book."
ISBN 978-0-544-14284-8 (hardback) — ISBN 978-0-544-14597-9 (ebook) —
ISBN 978-0-544-70505-0 (pbk)
1. World War III — Fiction. 2. Operational art (Military science) — Fiction.
3. Asymmetric warfare — Fiction. I. Cole, August. II. Title.
PS3619.I572455G48 2015
813'.6 — dc23
2014039678

Book design by Brian Moore

Printed in the United States of America
DOC 10
4500754417

Lyrics from "Space Pirates" by David Pierce and Steve Hammond, copyright
© 1975 (renewed 2003) by Chrysalis Music Ltd., are reprinted by permission of Hal
Leonard Corporation. All rights reserved by BMG Rights Management (U.S.) LLC.
All rights reserved. Used by permission.

The following was inspired by real-world trends and technologies. But, ultimately, it is a work of fiction, not prediction.

243 Miles Above the Earth's Surface

"I am so sorry."

What did Vitaly mean by that? As the sole American astronaut on the International Space Station, U.S. Air Force Colonel Rick Farmer was used to being the target of the Russian crew's practical jokes. The most recent had involved their sewing him shut inside his sleeping bag and then wide-casting his reaction for the whole net to see.

Now, that had been funny. But this was outside. Different rules when you're floating outside, only a thin tether keeping you hooked to the station.

The odd thing was that Cosmonaut Vitaly Simakov's voice had been unaccompanied by his usual booming laugh.

Farmer rechecked his tether, more for mental reassurance than any need. It had been twenty-four minutes since he'd been able to raise Vitaly or anyone else in the station on his suit's radio. That message was the last Farmer had heard from the mission commander after he'd made his way out of the station to repair the fluky number four solar panel. Even Houston was offline. He chalked up the silence to another one of those technical problems that made daily life in space so difficult, rather than the romance NASA still spun for the media.

With a PhD from Caltech in systems engineering and over four thousand flight hours in everything from T-38 trainers to F-22 stealth fighter jets, Farmer knew that big, complicated things sometimes just did not work as they were supposed to. He remembered the time his twin boys had played around with his flight gear on the eve of his first deployment to Afghanistan, half a lifetime ago. "Daddy needs a helmet because sometimes his job can be really hard." He hadn't told them that in his line of work, the mundane stuff was the hardest.

Farmer approached the hatch to reenter the space station.

"Farmer, validate. Open hatch," he commanded the system.

Nothing.

He said it again, emphasizing each word this time to allow the voice-recognition software to lock on.

"Farmer. Validate. Open. Hatch."

It was as if the system couldn't hear him.

He reached for the manual override and lifted the cover that protected the emergency-open button. Well, he thought as he pressed it, this was fast on its way to becoming one.

Nothing.

He pressed again, harder, the force of his fingers against the bright red button pushing him backward in the weightless environment of space. If he hadn't been tethered to the station, that push would have sent him spinning off at a rate of ten feet per second on a trajectory toward Jupiter.

Nothing. What the hell?

The outside of his visor was gold-coated, the world's costliest sunglasses. Inside was an array of computer displays projecting everything from his location to the suit's internal temperature.

Farmer couldn't help noticing the red light flashing in the corner, as if he needed the computer to inform him that his heart rate was spiking. He paused to center himself with a deep breath, looking down at the sweeping span of blue beneath. He tried to ignore the black void ringing Earth, which seemed to widen menacingly. After half a minute of steady breathing from his core, just like the NASA yoga instructor back in Houston had taught him, he stared hard at the door, willing it to open.

He tried the button again, and then again. Nothing.

He reached down for his HEXPANDO. The expanding-head hexagonal tool had been designed by NASA's engineers to remove or install socket-head cap screws in hard-to-reach places. It was a glorified wrench.

The instructions explicitly said that the HEXPANDO was "not intended for application of torque."

Screw it.

Farmer banged the HEXPANDO on the hatch. He couldn't hear any sound in the vacuum of space, but the pounding might resonate within the station's artificial atmosphere on the other side of the hatch.

Then a hiss of static and Farmer's radio came back to life.

"Vitaly, you hear me? I was getting worried there. The comms are on the fritz again, and now the damn voice-command systems on the hatch aren't working," said Farmer. "Tell Gennady I am going to send him back to trade school in Siberia. His repair job yesterday actually broke everything. I need you to open manually from the inside."

"I cannot. It is no longer my decision," said Vitaly, his voice somber.

"Say again?" said Farmer. The red heart light pulsed just outside his field of vision, as if Mars were suddenly blinking over his shoulder.

"I am no longer authorized to open hatch," said Vitaly.

"Authorized? What does that mean? Get Houston, we are going to sort this out," said Farmer.

"Goodbye, my friend. I am truly sorry. It is orders," said Vitaly.

"I've got an order for you. Open the fucking hatch!" said Farmer.

The soft pulse of static that followed was the last sound Farmer would hear.

After five minutes of pounding on the hatch, Farmer turned from the station to stare down at the Earth beneath his feet. He could make out the Asian landmass wreathed in a white shroud, the cloud of smog stretching from Beijing southward toward Shanghai.

How much time did he have? The red light's urgent flashing indicated spiking respiration. He tried to calm himself by running calculations in his head of the Earth's rate of turn, the station's velocity, and his remaining oxygen. Would it be enough time for the Eastern Seaboard to come into view? His wife and grown boys were vacationing on Cape Cod, and he wanted to look down at them one last time.

PART 1

You can fight a war for a long time or you can make your nation strong.
You cannot do both.

— SUN-TZU, *THE ART OF WAR*

10,590 Meters Below Sea Level, Mariana Trench, Pacific Ocean

Sometimes history is made in the dark.

As he scanned the blackness, Zhu Jin thought about what his wife would be doing right now. He couldn't see her, but he knew that ten kilometers above, Liu Fang would be hunched over her keyboard, ritually tightening her ponytail to burn off the tension. He could imagine her rough sneeze, knowing how the cigarette smoke from the other geologists irritated her.

The screens inside the Jiaolong-3 Flood Dragon deep-water submersible were the only portholes that modern science could offer the mission's chief geologist. His title was truly meaningful in this case. Lo Wei, the Directorate officer sent to monitor them, had command, but ultimately, responsibility for the success or failure of the mission fell on Zhu.

So it was appropriate at this moment, he thought, that he alone was in control, deep below the COMRA (China Ocean Mineral Resources Research and Development Association) deep-sea exploration vessel *Xiang Yang Hong 18*. This particular pocket of the Mariana Trench belonged to him alone.

Zhu guided the course underwater with a series of gentle tilts of the softly glowing control-sleeve gloves he wore. He was moving too close to the sheer trench walls to consider using the autopilot. He exhaled to clear his mind. There was so much pressure, poised to crush his vessel and everyone's dreams at any moment.

He adjusted the headset with a nudge of his shoulder. There, just as he thought. Blinking, he leaned forward, as if proximity to the lightly glowing video screen and the crushing darkness beyond the sub's hull could make the moment any more real.

This dive was the last; it had to be.

A wave of his hands, and the sub backed away from the wall and paused, hovering. Zhu turned off the exterior lights. Then he turned off the red interior lighting. He savored the void.

The moment had come. It was the culmination of literally decades of research and investment. No other nation had even attempted to plumb the depths of the sea like Zhu and his comrades, which was why 96 percent of the ocean floor still remained unexplored and unexploited. Indeed, the training alone for the deep-sea dive had taken a full four years once the team at Tianjin University developed the submersible. Compared to that, the five days of searching on this mission was nothing.

This descent, with Zhu at the controls, was the mission's last shot. At some point soon, the team knew, the Americans would be paying them a "friendly" visit, or maybe they would have the Australians do it for them. The Chinese were too close to the big U.S. base in Guam; it was a wonder nobody had come to look into what they were doing yet. Either way, the clock was ticking, both for the COMRA vessel and, he worried, its crew.

He thought of Lieutenant Commander Lo Wei standing over Zhu's wife's shoulder, getting impatient, lighting cigarette after cigarette as she sneezed her way through the smoke. Zhu could almost feel the crew scrutinizing her face with the same intensity they viewed their monitors. They would think, but not say aloud, *How could he fail us, when he knew the consequences for us all?*

Zhu had not failed.

The discovery itself was anticlimactic. A screen near Zhu's right hand flashed a brief message in blue and then flipped into a map mode. There had been indicators of a gas field here, but as the data streamed in, he now knew why his gut had guided him to this spot. He nudged the submersible on, sorting the deployments of the sub's disposable autonomous underwater vehicles, which would allow the team to map the full extent of the discovery. Each vessel was, in effect, a mini-torpedo whose sonic explosion afforded the submersible's imaging-by-sound sensors a deeper understanding of the riches beneath the sea floor. The sound waves allowed the computer to "see" the entirety of the field buried kilometers below the crust. The mini-torpedo technology came from the latest submarine-hunting systems of the U.S. Navy; the resource-mapping software had originated with the dissertation research of a PhD student at Boston University. They would never know their roles in making history.

After thirty-five minutes of mapping, it was done.

Enough time in the dark, Zhu thought. The transition between the deep and the surface, he once confided to Liu, was the worst. To die there would be his hell, trapped in the void between the light of day and the marvels of the abyss. But this time it was his joy; the void filled with the sense of anticipation at sharing the news.

When he opened the submarine's hatch, he saw the entire crew peering over the port rail, staring down at him. Even the cook, with his scarred forearms and missing pointer finger on his left hand, had come to gape at the Jiaolong-3 bobbing on the surface.

He squinted against the bright Pacific sun, careful to keep his face expressionless. He searched for Liu among the crew gathered at the ship's railings. At the crowd's edge, Lieutenant Commander Lo stood staring at him with a sour face, an unspoken question in his eyes. Zhu locked eyes with his wife, and when he couldn't contain his discovery anymore, he smiled. She shouted uncharacteristically, leaping with both hands in the air.

The rest of the crew turned to stare at her and then began cheering. Just beyond them, a faint sea breeze lifted the Directorate flag hanging by the ship's stern; the yellow banner with red stars fluttered slightly. To Zhu, it seemed like perfection, fitting for the moment. When he looked back to the rail, he noticed that Lieutenant Commander Lo was gone, already on his way inside to report the mission results back to Hainan.

U.S. Navy P-8, Above the Mariana Trench, Pacific Ocean

Even from eight thousand feet up, they could see that the people on the deck were celebrating something.

"Maybe the captain announced a pool party," said Commander Bill "Sweetie" Darling from the controls.

Darling and his crew were on their way back from a check-out flight on the P-8 Poseidon's recent engine upgrades. The plane had been designed for warship hunting, but there were none in the quadrant, and they were bored. The Directorate research vessel offered some excitement, at least as much as could be had in this corner of the Pacific.

The copilot, Dave "Fang" Treehorn, sent a live feed of the *Xiang Yang Hong 18*'s deck from the P-8's sensor-pod cameras. The cockpit of the Poseidon, a Boeing 737 passenger jet modified to Navy specifications for sub hunting, was considered spacious by military standards. But military aviators always want more information, and Darling regularly flipped through the available sensor feeds on the cockpit screens to satisfy the craving.

"Time to head down and take a closer look?" asked Treehorn.

"No fair that they get to have all the fun today. If it's a party, we should have been invited," said Darling. "Make sure to zoom in and grab shots of that submersible; give the intel shop some busywork."

"Registry says it's a science expedition," said Treehorn.

The P-8 dove smoothly down to five hundred feet, Darling banking the plane in a steep turn that kept the vessel off the starboard wing. A plane that big, that fast, and that low roaring overhead was disconcerting to any observer. The crew of the *Xiang Yang Hong 18* would be on notice now.

"X-Ray Yankee Hotel 18, this is U.S. Navy Papa-8 asking if you need assistance," said Darling. "We noticed you are stopped just over a rather deep hole in the ocean, not the best place for snorkeling."

Treehorn started laughing, as did the rest of the P-8 crew listening in on the comms.

Darling brought the plane back up to a thousand feet. "That's good; now maybe they can actually hear their radio," said Treehorn.

"Got their attention, though," said Darling.

"I'll say. Check your screen. They're hoisting the submersible and trying to put a tarp over it at the same time," said Treehorn. "One guy just fell overboard."

Then a voice came on the radio. Darling instantly recognized the command tone of a fellow member of the military brotherhood.

"U.S. Navy P-8, this is Zhu Jin, chief scientist of an official expedition of the China Ocean Mineral Resources Research and Development Association. We are in international waters, operating under scientific charter. Do you copy?"

"We copy, XYH 18," said Darling. "I don't want to get into the legalities, but these waters are protected U.S. Exclusive Economic Zone, as designated by the Mariana Trench Marine National Monument. Stand by. We will be vectoring a U.S. Coast Guard vessel to ensure that you are not engaged in illegal fishing."

"Negative. This is a scientific mission. We do not need authorization. Any further interference with this peaceful mission will be considered a hostile act by the Directorate government," said the voice. "Do you copy?"

"Well, that got nasty pretty fast," said Treehorn to his pilot.

"Foreplay's for chumps," said Darling.

"Are we really calling in the Coasties?" asked Treehorn.

"Naw. I guarantee they aren't fishing, but no need to start a war over it," Darling responded.

"We copy, XYH 18," he said into the radio. "Papa-8 is leaving station. You lost one overboard, don't forget."

Darling brought the P-8 up to three thousand feet and powered back the engines, giving the big jet a near weightless moment. Then Darling brought the P-8 around and pointed the nose down at the Chinese ship's stern, backing off the twin engines' power even more, so that the almost ninety-ton jet's dive was nearly silent.

"We're not done yet. I'm going to take her low, and when they've got their heads down, we drop a Remora two thousand meters off the stern," said Darling.

"Aye, sir," said the weapons crewman. "Standing by."

Xiang Yang Hong 18, Mariana Trench, Pacific Ocean

Lieutenant Commander Lo handed the radio's mike back to the captain.

"This is taking too long," said Lo. "We need to be gone before their border-guard ship arrives. Dr. Zhu, do you have everything that your team needs?"

"Yes, we could do more surveys, but it is —"

A roar shook the entire ship. Zhu hit the deck with his hands over his ears. There was a flash of gray as the P-8 went overhead at full power less than a hundred feet off the starboard side.

Lo couldn't help but admire the move. Spiteful, yet audacious. The scientist felt like he might throw up.

As the jet's thunder receded, one of the crew shouted, "Something in the water, a torpedo behind us!"

"Calm down," said Lo, standing with his hands on his hips. "If it was a torpedo, we'd already be dead. It's just a sonobuoy, maybe one of their Remora underwater drones."

"Do they know?" said Zhu.

"No, there's nothing up here of interest. What matters for us is far below," said Lo, nonplussed, as he eyed the drone now following in their wake.

He turned back to the scientist. "And Zhu?" said Lo. "The leadership is aware of your success. Enjoy the moment with your wife. And make sure the submersible is secured."

It was the first kind word he had ever said to Zhu.

National Defense Reserve Fleet, Suisun Bay, California

The sun rising over the East Bay gave the fog a paper-lantern glow.

"Torres, you sleep at all last night?" said Mike Simmons. The contractor patiently scanned the water ahead of the battered aluminum launch, seeming to look right through the nineteen-year-old kid he shared it with. His fist enveloped the outboard motor's throttle, which he held with a loose grip, gentle despite his callused palms and barnacle-like knuckles. He sat with one knee resting just below his chin, the other leg sprawling lazily toward the bow, at ease but ready to kick the kid overboard at a moment's notice.

"No, but I'm compensated," said Seaman Gabriel Torres. "Took a stim before I came in."

Mike took a sip from a pitted steel sailor's mug. His right trigger finger had a permanent crook from decades of carrying his coffee with him eighteen hours a day. He shifted his weight slightly and the launch settled deeper to starboard, causing Torres to catch himself on his seat in the bow. The retired chief petty officer weighed a good eighty pounds more than Torres, the difference recognizable in their voices as much as in the way the launch accommodated them.

"Big group sim down at the Cow Palace again," said Torres. "Brazilian feed. Retro night. Carnival in Rio, back in the aughts."

"You know," Mike said, "I was in Rio once then. Not for Carnival, though. Unbelievable. More ass than a . . . how I got any of my guys back on the ship, I still do not know."

"Hmmm," Torres said. He nodded with absent-minded politeness, his attention fixed on his viz glasses. All these kids were the same once they put those damn things on, thought Mike. If they missed something important, they knew they could just watch it again. They could call up anything you'd ever said to them, yet they could never remember it.

The gold-rimmed Samsung glasses that Torres wore were definitely not Navy issue. Mike caught a flash of the Palo Alto A's @ logo in reverse on the lens. So Torres was watching a replay of Palo Alto's game against the Yankees from last night. Beneath the game's display, a news-ticker video pop-up updated viewers on the latest border clashes between Chinese and Russian forces in Siberia.

"Game was a blowout, but the no-hitter by Parsons fell apart at the bottom of the eighth," said Mike. "Too bad for the A's."

Torres, busted, took off the glasses and glared at Mike, whose eyes continued to pan across the steely water.

The young sailor knew not to say anything more. Shouting at a contractor was a quick path to another write-up. And more important, there was something about the old man that made it clear that, even though he was retired, he would like nothing more than to toss Torres overboard, and he'd do it without spilling a drop of coffee.

"Seaman, you're on duty. I may be a civilian now and out of your chain of command," said Mike, "but you work for the Navy. Do not disrespect the Navy by disappearing into those damn glasses."

"Yes, sir," said Torres.

"It's 'Chief,'" said Mike. "'Sir' is for officers. I actually work for a living."

He smiled at the old military joke, winking to let Torres know the situation was over as far as he was concerned. That was it, right there. The sly charm that had gotten him so far and simultaneously held him back. If Torres hadn't been aboard, the chief could have puttered across the bay at a leisurely seven knots and pulled up, if he had the tide right, at the St. Francis Yacht Club. Grab a seat at the bar and swap old sea stories. After a while, one of the divorcées who hung out there would send over a drink, maybe say something about how much he looked like that old Hollywood actor, the one with all the adopted kids from around the world. Mike would then crack the old line that he had kids around the world too, he just didn't know them, and the play would be on.

The rising sun began to reveal the outlines of the warships moored around them. The calls of a flight of gulls overhead made the silent, rusting vessels seem that much more lifeless.

"Used to be a bunch of scrap stuck in the Ghost Fleet," said Mike, giving a running commentary as they passed between an old fleet tanker from the 1980s and an Aegis cruiser retired after the first debt crisis. "But a lot of ships here were put down before their time. Retired all the same, though."

"I don't get why we're even here, Chief. These old ships, they're done. They don't need us," said Torres. "And we don't need them."

"That's where you're wrong," said Mike. "It may seem like putting lipstick on old whores in a retirement home, but you're looking at the Navy's insurance policy, small as it may now be. You know, they kept something like five hundred ships in the Ghost Fleet back during the Cold War, just in case."

"Floater, port side," said Torres.

"Thanks," said Mike, steering the launch around a faded blue plastic barrel bobbing in the water.

"And here's our newest arrival, the *Zumwalt*," Mike announced, pointing out the next ship anchored in line. "It didn't fit in with the fleet when they wasted champagne on that ugly bow, and it doesn't belong here now. Got no history, no credibility. They should have turned it into a reef, but all that fake composite crap would just kill all the fish."

"What's the deal with that bow?" said Torres. "It's going the wrong direction."

"*Reverse tumblehome* is the technical term," said Mike. "See how the chine of the hull angles toward the center of the ship, like a box-cutter blade? That's what happens when you go trying to grab the future while still being stuck two steps behind the present. DD(X) is what they called them at the start, as if the X made it special. Navy was going to build a new fleet of twenty-first-century stealthy battleships with electric guns and all that shit. Plan was to build thirty-two of them. But the ship ended up costing a mint, none of the ray guns they built for it worked for shit, and so the Navy bought just three. And then when the budget cuts came after the Dhahran crisis, the admirals couldn't wait to send the Z straight into the Ghost Fleet here."

"What happened to the other two ships?" said Torres.

"There are worse fates for a ship than being here," said Mike, thinking about the half-built sister ships being sold off for scrap during the last budget crisis.

"So what do we gotta do after we get aboard it?" asked Torres.

"Aboard *her*," said Mike. "Not *it*."

"Chief, you can't say that anymore," said Torres. "*Her.*"

"Jesus, Torres, you can call the ship *him* if you want," said Mike. "But don't ever, ever call any of these uglies *it*. No matter what the regs say."

"Well, she, he — whatever — looks like an LCS," said Torres. Officially designated FF for frigate, everyone in the Navy still called the LCS by its original name, Littoral Combat Ship. "That's where I wish I was."

"An LCS, huh? Dreaming of being off the coast of Bali in a 'little crappy ship,' wind blowing through your hair at fifty knots, throwing firecrackers at pirates?" said Mike. "Get the line ready."

"Didn't I hear your son was aboard an LCS?" asked Torres. "How does he like it?"

"I don't know," said Mike. "We're not in touch."

"Sorry, Chief."

"You know, Torres, you must have really pissed somebody off to get stuck with me and the Ghost Fleet." The old man was clearly changing the subject.

Torres fended the launch off from a small barge at the stern. Without looking, he tied a bowline knot that made the old chief suppress a smile.

"Nice knot there," said Mike. "You been practicing like I showed you?"

"No need," said Torres, tapping his glasses. "Just have to show me once and it's saved forever."

USS *Coronado,* Strait of Malacca

Each of the dark blue leather seats in the USS *Coronado*'s wardroom had a movie-theater chair's sensory suite, complete with viz-glasses chargers, lumbar support, and thermoforming heated cushions that seemed almost too comfortable for military life — until you were sitting through your second hour of briefings.

This briefer, the officer in charge of the ship's aviation detachment of three remote-piloted MQ-8 Fire Scout helicopters, thanked her audience and returned to her seat. A few side conversations abruptly stopped when the executive officer rose to give his ops intel brief.

When the XO, the ship's second in command, stood at the head of the room, you felt a little bit like you were back in elementary school with the gym teacher looking down at you. The twenty-first-century Navy was supposed to be all about brains. But physical presence still mattered, and the XO, Commander James "Jamie" Simmons, had it. He stood six four and still looked like the University of Washington varsity heavyweight rower he'd once been, projecting a physicality that had become rare among the increasingly technocratic officer corps.

"Good morning. We're doing this my way today," said Simmons. "No viz."

The crew groaned at the prospect of having to endure an entire brief without being able to multitask or have their viz glasses record the proceedings.

A young lieutenant in the back coughed into her fist: "Old school."

Coronado's captain, Commander Tom Riley, stood to the side holding a gleaming black ceramic-and-titanium-mesh coffee mug emblazoned with the shipbuilder's corporate logo. He couldn't help himself and smiled at the impertinent comment.

The display screen loaded the first image and projected it out into the room in a 3-D ripple: a heavily tattooed man on a matte-black electric waterbike firing an assault rifle one-handed up at the bridge of a container ship. Simmons had picked up this technique from an old admiral who'd lectured at the Naval War College: instead of the typical huge slide deck with immersive animations, he used just a single picture for each point he wanted to make.

"Now that I've got your attention," said Simmons, switching the image to a map of their position at the entry to the Strait of Malacca. A swath of red pulsing dots waited there, each marking where a pirate attack had taken place in the previous year. "More than half of the world's shipping passes through this channel, which make these red spots a global concern."

The roughly six-hundred-mile-long channel between the former Republic of Indonesia and Malaysia was less than two miles wide at its narrowest, barely dividing Malaysia's authoritarian society from the anarchy that Indonesia had sunk into after the second Timor war. Pirates were a distant memory for most of the world, but the red dots showed that this part of the Pacific was a gangland. The attackers used skiffs and homemade aerial drones to seize and sell what they could, mostly to fund the hundreds of militias throughout the archipelago.

None of the gangs bothered with hostages ever since Chinese special operations forces, at the behest of that country's largest shipping concern, had wiped out the population of three entire islands in a single night. It didn't end the attacks, though. There were six thousand inhabited islands left. Now the pirates just killed everyone when they seized a ship.

"This is *Coronado*'s focus during the next three days," said Simmons. "It's a standard presence patrol. But it connects to a bigger picture that Captain's asked me to brief you on: We will be linking up with the Directorate escort force at eighteen hundred, making this a true multinational convoy."

The XO then changed images, zooming out from the *Coronado*'s present position in its southeast corner to a larger map showing the strategic landscape of the entire Pacific.

"This leads me to the main brief this morning. It's a long one. But there's a bonus: if you don't fall asleep on me, I'll make sure you get double your PACE ed cred." That brought a few smiles; the Program for Afloat College Education, a quick way for sailors to earn college credits on the Navy's dime, was popular among the young crew.

"We're breaking some ground here on this multinational undertaking. It's the first joint mission with Directorate naval forces since Washington started the embargo threats," he said. "Which means our friends from Hainan are taking it seriously. As you can see on the screen, the Directorate will have one of their new oilers here for refueling, which it doesn't really need. They want us to see that in addition to having the world's biggest economy, they're buying their naval forces the range to operate anywhere on the planet.

"To understand why having a ship like an oiler is a big deal, you need to take a step back. Let's start with Dhahran three years ago. When the nuke — well, more technically, the radiological dirty bomb — went off, it made the Saudi house of cards fall down. Between Dhahran glowing and the fights over who comes in after the Al Saud family, the world economy's still reeling from the hub of the global oil industry effectively going offline," he said.

His next slide showed a graph of energy prices spiking. "Oil's finally coming off the two-hundred-ninety-dollar peak after the attack, but you don't want to know how much this cruise is costing the taxpayers. Put it this way: enjoy yourselves and all this sunshine because your grandkids are still going to be paying the tab."

"They'll be paying in ramen," said Lieutenant Gupal, one of the ship's newest officers. *Ramen* was slang for RMN, renminbi, the Chinese currency that, along with the euro, had joined the American dollar as the global reserve currency following the dollar's post-Dhahran crash.

"At least we can sail with our own oil now," said Captain Riley. "When I joined back in the Stone Age, Middle East oil owned the market."

"True enough," said Simmons. "And shale extraction is coming back at even higher levels than before the moratorium after the New York quake. Dhahran made people stop caring so much about groundwater seepage."

A new map of global energy reserves appeared on the screen. Simmons stepped closer to the crew and continued.

"The captain hit the key change to focus on. The scramble for new energy resources, heightening regional tensions here, here, and here, are sparking a series of border clashes around the world. The fact that the South China Sea oil fields were disappointments put new pressure on the Directorate. The hunt goes on," said Jamie. "The oilers are the Directorate's way of showing that their interest in this is now global."

A screen shot of a smoking mine in South Africa replaced the map.

"That's the Spiker mine, near South Africa's border with Mozambique. Remember that? These trends all connect. Even the renewed push toward alternative energy sources has caused more conflict than cooperation. Technologies like solar and deep-cycle batteries depend on rare-earth materials, *rare* being the operative word," said Simmons.

The picture shifted to the iconic photo of the green Chinese People's Liberation Army tank bulldozing into the Ministry of Public Security's riot-control truck as the crowd in Shanghai's People's Square cheered the soldiers on.

"This is important, so pay attention," said Simmons. "You all know the history of the Directorate. When the world economy cratered after Dhahran, the old Chinese Communist Party couldn't keep things humming. Their big mistake was calling in the military to put down the urban workers' riots, thinking that the troops would do their dirty work for them, just like back in '89. They failed to factor in that a new generation of more professional military and business elite saw the problem differently than they did. Turned out the new guard viewed the nepotism and corruption of those 'little princes' who had just inherited their power as a bigger threat to China's stability than the rioters. They booted them out, and instead you've got a Directorate regime that's more popular and more competent than the previous government, and technocratic to the extreme. The business magnates and the military have divided up rule and roles. Capitalism and nationalism working hand in hand, rather than the old contradictions they had back in the Communist days."

The image switched to one of the Directorate Navy's new aircraft carriers tied up next to a pier, Shanghai's skyline in the background.

"The bottom line is that the Directorate has changed China. They took a regime mired in corruption and on the brink of civil war and forged a locked-down country marching in the same direction, the nation's business leaders and the military joined at the hip.

"But net assessment, as they teach you back in the schoolhouse, isn't only about looking outward; it's also about knowing yourself and your own place in history."

A visual of two maps of the globe appeared, the first of British trading routes and colonies circa 1914, the second a current disposition of U.S. forces and bases, some eight hundred dots spread across the world.

"Some say we're fighting, or rather not fighting, a cold war with the Directorate, just like we did with the Soviet Union more than half a century ago. But that may not be the right case to learn from. About a hundred years back, the British Empire faced a problem much like ours today: How do you police an empire when you've got a shrinking economy relative to the world's and a population no longer so excited to meet those old commitments?"

A montage of U.S. Navy aircraft carriers in port appeared, the last shot a lingering image of CVN-80, the new USS *Enterprise*, still under construction.

"And, of course, if that is the case, you can't keep doing things the old way on the cheap. Take capital ships, the way navies back then, and even today, measured force. With the *Ford*-class carriers taking so long to build, although the U.S. Navy has nine CVNs, that actually means four in service to cover the entire globe. And with the cost of keeping our military in Afghanistan, Yemen, and, now, Kenya, well, we've had to get used to working without them."

"I'd rather be on this ship than a carrier anyway," said Gupal. "Just a bigger bull's-eye for an incoming Stonefish."

"Secure that mouth, Lieutenant, or you're not even gonna last one cruise on this ship," said Riley, jabbing a titanium e-cigar in the air.

"Aye, aye, Captain," said Gupal sheepishly.

Simmons, as the XO, was supposed to be the bad cop to Captain Riley's good cop, making the reversal of roles that much more amusing to the crew.

"Lieutenant, all jokes aside, you are making my point. You're right that the DF-21E, the Stonefish anti-ship ballistic missile, is not really about us," said Simmons. "But I want you to think about the various trends, the why, and then the what-next. So, what does the Stonefish offer the Chinese?"

"Well, sir, it's like a boxer stretching his arms out farther. Gives them the ability to target our big deck carriers before we can get in range of China," said Gupal.

"Right, it gives them freedom of action. So if you're Directorate, what do you do with that freedom? And why, or even when? These are the questions I want you asking. Just because you see the world one way today does not mean it will be that way tomorrow. It's pirates today. What will it be next?" asked Simmons.

Captain Riley stepped over to Simmons. He smiled, but his body language made it clear he was not completely pleased with the briefing. "Thank you, XO. The key, folks, is to assess these threats. There's dangers, but let's not build these guys up to be ten feet tall. And if it comes down to a boxing match, Big Navy's spent literally billions on the Air-Sea Battle concept, just for the Stonefish threat and more. In any case, given what's playing out on the Siberian border, it might be better for the XO to brief the next Russian ship we see rather than us. If anyone is going to war with the Directorate, it's Moscow."

"Yes, sir," said Simmons. "Any questions?" He looked around the room and chewed his cheek to keep from saying anything more.

Lieutenant Gupal raised his hand. "Sir, where does that leave us on the patrol? How should we think about the Directorate forces here? Friend or foe? Or frenemy?"

"Like I said, the Chinese are more likely to go to war with Russia than us," Riley replied. "And if the idea does cross their mind to tangle with us, well, they just don't have the experience to do it right. The XO's history lesson should've also mentioned that China hasn't fought a major war since the 1940s."

"Neither has the U.S. Navy," said Simmons quietly.

Silence followed. A few of the crew started fiddling with their glasses in their laps, trying to look busy. Lieutenant Gupal, though, was too green to understand that the silence wasn't another opportunity for him to gain notice. What worked at the Naval Academy was the wrong call in the wardroom.

"XO, do you think the captain's right about Russia and China, though?" asked Gupal.

Simmons glanced at Riley before looking at Gupal.

"The Directorate has been making claims about their guest-worker rights being abused by the Russians and how their government is not beholden to the old borders set in treaties signed by prior regimes on both sides," said Simmons. "So if I was in Moscow, I'd potentially come to the same conclusion the captain has. And the Russians seem to be acting on that belief. The latest satellite photos showed the Russian Pacific fleet has sortied from its base in Vladivostok, most likely to put some range between it and the Chinese air bases to complicate any potential sneak attack. It's the right move. The history supports it."

"And with that rare praise from the XO, dismissed," said Captain Riley. "We know where to get our sunshine when we need it."

U.S. Embassy, Beijing

The ambassador loved parties. So did Commander Jimmie Links, but for different reasons.

The truth was the parties were just an excuse. This farewell soiree was in his honor — he was finishing up two years in the defense attaché's office — but no matter the country the guest came from, no matter the rank, no matter the clout, everyone in the room was there to collect. Eyeglasses, jewelry, watches, whatever — all were constantly recording and analyzing. Suck it all up and let the filters sort it out. It was not much different from how the people back home did their shopping, wide-casting for discounts.

Links watched a beautiful Chinese woman in her late twenties glide by in a floor-length translucent SpecTran-fiber dress and noticed the telltale strip of stiff-looking skin at the base of her neck. The new folks joining the three-letter agencies didn't have a choice anymore. The human body, with the right technology, is an extraordinary antenna. Fortunately, as a U.S. Navy officer who'd joined before the policy shift, Links had gotten out of that one, at least for the moment. The Navy wasn't giving him a break; it was just that no one had figured out yet if the chips would interfere with sensitive avionics or ship systems. At some point, though, tradition would lose out to technology.

Someone tapped a glass, and the noise in the room hushed to a murmur. Links looked at his vodka martini and eyed the lemon twist. The question wasn't *whether* it was a recording device, but *whose*.

"Together, let us raise our glasses on this occasion to acknowledge our common interests and objectives," said General Wu Liao, a Directorate air force commander who Links knew was about to announce another wave of corruption purges. Links even knew the names of the men who would be executed in three days, all because Wu's driver had left a window cracked open to smoke. That's how good the collection was.

"It is in a navy officer's honor I toast. That is not something you often hear from an air force officer of any country's military."

Polite laughter from fifteen different nationalities followed the joke.

"The joint China-U.S. exercises to help bring order to the waters around the former Republic of Indonesia are a sign our future together will be a strong one," said General Wu. "As for our neighbors to the north, I cannot say the same."

Wu's angry glance at a Russian officer standing in the corner shifted the guests' gaze and cut off any remaining laughter. The Russian nodded indifferently and casually moved a highball glass from one hand to the other, as if he cared more about the temperature of his vodka than the speech.

After the toast, Links walked over to the Russian. Major General Sergei Sechin was a regular on the party circuit. He walked with the confidence of someone who'd been in uniform for most of his life, and he always smiled like he had just been told a bawdy joke. Sechin had been in Beijing for over a decade, so he must have been very good at his job if he was able to keep his own bosses happy while also riding out the Directorate's rise to power. Besides the violent purges of the old Communist Party leadership, there had been more than a few deadly traffic "accidents" involving the foreign intelligence community.

"Sorry about that," said Links. "Poorly done by Wu."

"The Directorate new guard, especially the core, like Wu, say they don't care what anyone thinks. But it makes them think only of their own plan," said Sechin. "The Communist Party had theirs too, and you can see how it ended for them . . ."

"I am going to miss our uplifting conversations, Sergei," said Links. "And the smog, and the winter."

A waiter passed with a tray of drinks, and Sechin deposited his and Links's empty glasses and snatched two more frosty vodkas.

"One day, we will all get past this unpleasantness," said Sechin, handing a glass to Links, downing his own vodka, and nodding for Links to do the same.

"*Za vas,*" said Links. The waiter reappeared with two new glasses, timing his return perfectly, likely another espionage professional at work collecting.

"Perhaps you will play a role in that . . ." Sechin focused on his glass. "Do you know what is America's greatest export?"

Links's eyes narrowed. "Biggest, or greatest? Sometimes they're not the same thing. Biggest by the numbers? Oil and gas. Greatest? Democracy," said Links.

"No, no, no," said Sechin. "It is an idea, really. A dream: *Star Trek.*"

He locked eyes with Links.

"If you say so." Links wondered what the computer analytics that parsed the transcripts would make of this conversation. Staring at his now empty glass, Sechin continued in a serious tone. "*Star Trek* was a television show watched by Americans during a time when my country and yours held each other, as you like to say in your nation's defense strategy, 'at risk.'"

"Can't say I ever watched it," said Links. "At least not the old ones. My dad took me to a couple of the newer movies."

"The vision was so positive, a crew from all nations sent out by a world federation. An American, Captain Kirk, was their leader. With him was a crew from around the world, from Europe, from Africa — notable in that time of racial tension in your country. Also, and perhaps relevant here, there was Mr. Sulu. He represented all of Asia, which, because of America's war in Vietnam, made this very capable man a symbol of the peace to come."

"Peaceful? Nobody like that here," said Links, tipping his glass at Wu.

"I give you that. But that is not what I want you to remember. Most important, just like you, an American officer, and I are friends," said Sechin, "the navigator was Pavel Andreievich Chekov, a Russian! Now, this Chekov was not a real man, of course," said Sechin. "But many believe that the character was named after a brilliant Russian scientist of the time, Pavel Alekseyevich Cherenkov. Do you know of him? He won a Nobel Prize in 1958, when my country was as sure of its destiny as Wu is of China's."

Sechin waved his glass to indicate the coterie around Wu. "My point is that without Chekov, what really could Captain Kirk have done out there in space? Our Cherenkov was the key to the future!"

Links caught the eye of the waiter, who brought another tray of vodka.

"It's coming back to me," said Links. "But in the story, didn't the Federation begin only after World War Three?"

"Yes, yes, I allow you this," said Sechin. "In any case, you should know that though we work for different sides, we are not all bad."

"There's work," said Links, placing their empty glasses on the waiter's tray, taking two full ones, and holding one out to Sechin. "And there's friends. You're a friend."

"Yes, please remember that. In a few months' time, when you are back in your warm office in the Pentagon, fourth corridor, D ring . . . Don't look surprised, we know these things. When you return to your friends in Naval Intelligence, think of me and think of Chekov. Promise me that."

USS *Coronado*, Strait of Malacca

Simmons sat at the small desk in his stateroom and watched the daily good-morning vid from his twins. While the *Coronado* sailed under a night sky, Claire and Martin, six years old, complained about school between bites of waffle. Their voices made his stomach tighten with sadness.

"Good luck today with Riley," said his wife. "It won't be easy, I know it. But we love you and can't wait to get you back."

His wife signed off, as she did every morning, with a kiss sent from around the corner after the kids said goodbye. Then he was alone again inside the ship's gray hull.

He pulled himself up and walked down the passageway to the bridge wing. Riley was there, smoking a real cigar. The bridge wing was not the officially designated smoking area, but the ship's captain could smoke where he damn well pleased.

"Freighter, Directorate, freighter, freighter, Directorate," said Riley, pointing to the mix of ships preparing to move through the Strait of Malacca tomorrow. "What do you see when you look at those ships?"

"Going to be tight in the channel, sir," said Simmons. "I think if the Directorate crews can actually handle their ships as well as we think they can, it'll be fine."

"That's not all I see," said Riley. "I see us and them. Working together. What was with the brief? You know how bad they need our oil. In the end, we each know that we have the other by the throat."

"By the balls, more like. But is that a good thing?" said Simmons.

"I see it like this convoy duty. They depend on us, and we depend on them. Maybe in different ways, but it's the same outcome. We're interlinked, even with the Directorate. Plus, China's holding, what, nine trillion dollars' worth of our debt?"

"And growing," said Simmons.

"Right. They're not our enemy, they're our largest investor. Each one of those ships out there," Riley said, waving his hand expansively, "is a reason not to go to war. People love making money. Especially the Directorate."

"Trade is just trade. You know how I made the comparison between us today and the Brits a hundred years back," said Simmons. "Well, who was Britain's biggest trading partner before World War One? Germany. Or if you prefer World War Two as a comparison, Germany's biggest trading partners just before the war were the very neighbors it soon invaded, while the U.S. was Japan's."

"I don't need another history lesson, Professor. The Directorate is the Russians' worry for now. We've got a few more weeks and then we'll be in Hawaii, which is an awful long way from whatever dustup starts in Siberia. Worry about sunburn instead," said Riley.

"Going to see John there?" said Simmons, changing the subject.

"Yeah, he's flying out," said Riley.

"That's good," said Simmons. "You guys going surfing?"

Riley paused and then wordlessly offered Jamie one of his precious cigars and helped him light it. *So now it will turn truly serious,* thought Jamie.

"Listen, make sure you hear this the right way: Do you understand what you are doing by turning down command and requesting the Pentagon job? I say this as a friend but also as your captain. If you don't fleet up, the entire Surface Warfare community will consider you dead. Your career will be crucified," said Riley.

Simmons took a deep draw from his cigar and exhaled.

"Lindsey's got a bad case of what she calls seasickness, as in she's sick of me going to sea. The kids are okay with it, but they don't know any different. And maybe that's the real problem."

Riley started to pull again from his cigar, then stopped and threw it overboard.

"Don't you think the whole crew miss their kids and spouses and dogs and all that shore shit? To do the job right, you have to give everything; that's how it's always been. You think my husband likes it? He hates it too," he said. "No technology we've invented shrinks the distance."

"I know," said Simmons. "I thought I could pull off the balancing act, maybe even had to, to prove I was better than my dad. But when I watch those vids of my kids growing up without me, all I think about is that I don't want to do to them what my dad did to me."

Riley's face reddened. "The Navy put you here as my XO for a reason. You have what it takes. And if you turn down command, you don't just screw your career over, you screw me over too. I burn my powder. I don't ever get to do that again for someone else."

The ship rolled to port, and Riley instinctively grabbed the rail.

"Jamie, you need to think this over one last time. You know where I'm coming from. I have to think about the ship and the Navy. I'm going to hold the paperwork until we get back to San Diego. You use the time until then to get your head on straight. Don't sink your career because you still have daddy issues."

Simmons nodded. "Aye, Captain."

He headed to his stateroom and brewed a fresh cup of coffee. The aroma and salt spray on his clothes reminded him of his father. That decided it; this cruise would be his last.

Yulin Naval Base, Hainan Island

Vice Admiral Wang Xiaoqian closed his eyes for a last moment of calm, running his thumb over the surface of the heavy coin in his palm. He could feel the eagle's wings and make out the texture of a tall ship's masts. By military custom, he would need to have the challenge coin from the U.S. Navy's chief of naval operations ready to show back to him when they next met.

The thump of the plane's wheels touching down brought him to a state of full alert. The four-engine Y-20 transport plane had been modified for VIP flights, but the long flight back from the United States had still been taxing. The question was why the trip had been cut short, and not knowing the answer worried him.

"Admiral, welcome home," said his aide, waiting at the bottom step.

"And?" said Admiral Wang.

"There will be a meeting, but nothing more for my eyes. Your pre-briefing is here," said the aide, tapping a metallic-white envelope. "Printed out."

"So is this a bull's-eye for me?" said Wang.

"Not for you," said the aide incredulously.

"I appreciate your confidence, but unfortunately you do not have a Presidium vote. At the very least, this meeting promises to be more exciting than my trip was. All the American admirals want is yet another 'strategic dialogue,' which betrays their inability to decide what they really want as a nation, and of us. You are lucky to have stayed home."

"Do you have any gifts for me to send along to your homes?" said the aide. With the dollar so weak, Admiral Wang usually bought small tokens for both his wife and his mistress.

"No, there was no time to shop," said Admiral Wang.

"Yes, sir, I'll take care of it," said the aide, hearing the unspoken order to find appropriate gifts for the women in the admiral's life.

The two climbed into the back of a Geely military SUV that drove with its lights off.

"And what news of General Feng?" said Wang.

"First, they took him to —" the aide began.

"I do not need those details. Did they kill him yet?" said Wang.

The aide nodded.

"Good," said Wang. "He thought that he could sell a hundred tons of small arms to that beast who runs North Sulawesi at twice the agreed price without us finding out. The perception of greed is what provides our Indonesian instability program's deniability. When Feng's greed became real, he became a liability . . . Let me see the papers they gave you," said Wang.

The SUV pulled up to a traffic circle just inside a cavernous hangar built into the side of the mountain. The island itself was now no more than a camouflage netting of dirt and stone above the Directorate's largest submarine and air base.

"They said not to open that until you are underground," said the aide.

"Did they?" said Wang, ripping open the envelope. "We are underground, by my definition. If I am going to be shot because General Feng wanted a second apartment, I deserve to know as soon as possible."

The aide fumbled to get a small red penlight out so Wang could read the message.

"The entire Presidium? Here?" said Wang.

The aide nodded. "The jets keep coming and coming," he said.

"And these others, whose are they?" said Wang. He couldn't help but notice that the parking area included eight new Chinese-modified versions of the IL-76 transport plane and a single older one, an original model of the Russian aircraft.

"I must apologize, the air force was not kind enough to share the manifests, *Admiral*," the aide responded, emphasizing Wang's naval title.

Wang chuckled at his aide's flash of frustration, warming up as the adrenaline that went with such uncertainty overcame the weariness of the long flight.

The SUV drew to a halt, and Wang got out. He looked back inside the vehicle at his aide, who hadn't budged.

"I'm sorry, sir. I was told I could not accompany you any farther."

"See what you can learn," said Wang. "I will find a way to bring you below. You deserve to be part of this . . . especially if they plan to shoot me."

"I doubt it will come to that," said the aide as Wang got out of the vehicle.

"We have fed the beast so long, at some point we have to set it off the leash," responded Wang. "Or it will bite us back."

Wang strode over to a waiting electric cart, barely glancing at the row of oversize diesel-electric military cargo trucks parked nearby. The shielding and blast-proofing of the subterranean base seemed to swallow all sound; not even his footsteps resonated.

The driver of the cart said, "Admiral, I am Lieutenant Ping Hai. It is an honor to escort you." He said it slowly, as if he had memorized it.

"Thank you, Lieutenant," said Wang. "But I'd prefer to walk. All I've done is sit for the past eighteen hours."

"Sir?" said Ping, confused by the admiral going off the planned script. "Walking here is very difficult."

"Why don't we give it a try?" said Wang.

Wang started following the luminescent markers at the edge of the four-lane road that curved gently downward. After he'd walked ten paces, the cart pulled alongside, its electric engine faintly humming. With the cart his sole command responsibility, the young officer apparently could not fathom leaving it behind. The admiral glared at the expectant lieutenant, who interpreted the look as a green light to begin chattering.

"Admiral, I read your 'Third Island Chain' essay with great interest last year," said Ping. "It was very bold. Visionary. I did not find it controversial at all."

Wang felt his desire for silence grow with every step. But he knew the nervous lieutenant would keep talking no matter his response.

"A welcome assessment," said Wang. If anyone ever needed a reason for why the Directorate had ended the one-child policy, this lieutenant was it, thought Wang. The young officer prattled on. His accent was at first difficult to place, but the more he talked, the more his country roots showed. Hubei Province. Was sending this idiot chaperone a message? Why was Wang's own aide kept aboveground while a fool like this was allowed to take him to the Directorate's inner sanctum?

"Just stop," said Wang. "I will get into the cart. You are right, there is no time to waste."

The lighting brightened to daylight levels as the electric cart entered a waiting elevator that could have swallowed two fighter jets.

"Admiral, our journey ends here," said Ping, capping a rambling disquisition on his strategic vision for force dispositions along the northern border.

"Thank you," said Wang. "You have given me much to think about. And for that, you deserve this."

The young officer took the challenge coin Wang had gotten from the U.S. chief of naval operations with reverence. He was, at last, speechless.

Wang remembered an old adage: In wartime, even idiots can be useful.

Presidium Briefing Room, Hainan Island

Wang discreetly allowed himself a single stim tab as he exited the elevator. He normally avoided taking such performance modifiers, knowing how they also tricked one's emotions. But the flight had left him exhausted, and he knew he needed to be as sharp as possible.

The quartet of naval commandos escorting him were assaulters, big-shouldered beasts in their signature formfitting blast-resistant uniforms. Their liquid body armor's exterior looked as if it were made from sharkskin. He took their presence as a positive, a reassuring sign the navy's influence remained strong here.

At the entry to the large briefing room, Wang began his scan, just as he would study the horizon for threats while on a ship's bridge. He saw Admiral Lin Boqiang with a cluster of other senior naval officers. Lin, the overall commander of the fleet, was among the most influential in the Presidium, the Directorate's joint civilian and military leadership council. At the other side of the room, a cluster of army officers stood around General Wei Ming, the land forces commander. The two services rarely interacted, even in meetings. To Wang, though, the difference was simple. Wei and the army had the numbers in China, but as part of a force that dealt with distance, Wang and his fellow navy officers understood politics and power better.

More notable was the number of civilian suits in the military command room. The Presidium members rarely met in person, the civilian and military sides protective of their respective turf. The original deal had been hastily hammered out in a hotel conference room during the Shanghai riots, but it had held firm since, each faction having autarchy to run its own economic and security spheres to maximum efficiency, with a mutual goal of growth with stability.

Admiral Lin approached and greeted Wang with a haphazard salute that had not changed since their academy days.

"I must apologize for cutting your trip short, but you can now see that this is the general meeting you have long sought."

"Yes, when I was first summoned, I thought I might come down here and never be seen again, like our friend General Feng," said Wang, speaking every word with a purpose, mentioning the executed officer to test the waters.

"While Feng's diversions were lamentable," Lin observed, "the goal of your operation to destabilize the south was met. But now, the Presidium needs to hear your larger message. Your views have been most persuasive inside our service, but the civilians need to hear from you now." He turned away from Wang and motioned to an aide to dim the lights, the signal for the meeting to begin. The Presidium members took their seats at a U-shaped table made from black marble.

The introduction was brief, focusing on Wang's key role in reorganizing the Directorate's command structure, clearly an attempt to establish his trustworthiness for the civilians. Wang knew that his efficiency at purging the old PLA's Communist Party apparatchiks in the General Political Department was what had gotten him to this position, but he wished Lin had highlighted his reputation as a leading thinker and a capable naval commander as well.

"I am an admiral, as you know," Wang said as he began his presentation, "but today I would like to begin with a quote from a general: 'On terrain from which there is no way out, take the battle to the enemy.'

"That is from Sun-Tzu's *Art of War*, written just before the Warring States period of our history. I first used that wisdom almost twenty-five hundred years after it was written, citing it in my thesis on Master Sun's texts at what used to be called PLA National Defense University."

The reminder of their ancient and recent past was another deliberate choice to set the scene for where he wanted to take them next.

Wang pulled an imaginary trigger with his right pointer finger, and the smart-ring on it transmitted a wireless signal that initiated the presentation visuals his aide had sent ahead. Behind him, a 3-D hologram map of the Pacific appeared. Glowing red lines moved across the map, marking the history of China's trade routes and military reach through the millennia. The lines moved out and then back in. Toward the end, a blue arc appeared, showing the spread of U.S. trade routes and military bases over the past two centuries. Eventually the blue lines reached across the globe. Then, as the decades closed in on the present, the red lines pushed back out, crossing with the blue. Wang didn't need to explain this graphic; everyone knew its import.

"I began with Master Sun's ancient wisdom to remind us that while we all would like to think that we have regained our historic greatness, in reality we face a situation in which there is 'no way out.' Indeed, the Americans had an apt phrase to describe a situation like ours, where your strength grows but your options become ever more limited: Manifest Destiny.

"Destiny drives you forward but ties your hands. Indeed, their own great naval thinker Alfred Thayer Mahan foretold how their rise to great power gave them no choice. As their economy and then their military began to grow to world status, he told his people that, whether they liked it or not, 'Americans must now begin to look outward. The growing production of the country demands it.'

"*Must. Demands.* These are words of power, but also responsibility. We must now face the demands that shape our own destiny. The Americans' destiny led them to seek land, then trade, then oil, but they refuse to understand that the new demands of the age are now upon us as well. Even though they no longer need the foreign energy resources they once reached out and grasped, we must still endure their interference in our interests in Transjordan, Venezuela, Sudan, the Emirates, and the former Indonesia.

"We most recently experienced this in our waters to the east, where they interfered in matters that are far from them, but close to us."

The map zoomed down to the South China Sea, and an image appeared of a U.S. Navy warship escorting a Philippine coast guard vessel that had been damaged in the Red Line skirmishes right after the Dhahran bombing.

"As you will recall, we debated then how to respond to their navy interposing itself into a regional matter, daring us to act. But for all our arguments, it was a situation of 'no way out,' as Master Sun said in his text. That it took place in the midst of our own domestic transition meant we had no choice but to acquiesce."

The image then shifted to scenes of the Dalai Lama speaking at the Lincoln Memorial to a cheering crowd and then to the new U.S. president shaking hands with the last Communist Party foreign minister, who in exile had somehow transformed himself into a human rights activist.

"But their interference does not stop at the water's edge. Their failure to understand our new strategic and domestic reality gives us no choice, as it threatens what we in this room have built. Even now that we are once more whole, their Congress threatens energy sanctions at the slightest whim, waving about an economic sword like a drunken sailor."

The image plunged deep into a projection of the Mariana Trench, then drove straight through the rocky walls of the side to reveal the full extent of the COMRA research vessel's find, laid out in glowing red; after that, it pulled back to show its massive scale compared with the rest of the world's known gas fields.

"What we have found here determines not just our nation's future but the arc of the world economy and, thus, our ultimate security and stability," said Wang. "What we have located, in a place where nobody else thought it possible and that we alone can reach, gives us a new way to think about the future, a future where we chart our own course."

A hologram of Xi Jinping, the old Communist Party leader, appeared behind him, accompanied by a recording of a speech he'd given to the old party congress in 2013: "However deep the water may be, we will wade into the water. This is because we have no alternative."

The image of the long-dead president elicited a nervous murmur in the room.

"Many of you are familiar with this speech, what Xi called the 'Chinese Dream.' The old party leaders were wrong in many things, but in this they were right. America's rise came first with its ensuring control of its home waters and then extending its global economic presence. And then the country had no choice but to assume its new responsibilities, including protecting the system from the powers of the past that would threaten it. I mentioned their thinker Mahan. Soon after he laid out the new demands upon the United States, war with Spain followed, as you remember, and the Americans reached across the Pacific, thousands of miles beyond their home waters, extending to the Philippines, patrolling not just our ports but even our very rivers. Just as Mahan told them, we similarly have no choice but to meet these demands."

Wang took in the room, searching for signs of understanding but also dissent.

A civilian on the far side of the room took the pause as an invitation. Chen Shi was the chairman of Bel-Con, China's top producer of consumer electronics, which had been formed by the merging of dozens of firms during the most recent crisis. His role on the Directorate's Presidium, though, was an extension of his reputation as a strategist and visionary in business, something that perfectly fit the Directorate's hybrid of military authority and market-inspired efficiency.

"Admiral, you began with a quote from the *Art of War,* so I will match you: 'Those who know when to fight and when not to fight are victorious.'" He paused. "I do not see your logic here. We always have choices. Does your old vision of power actually matter anymore in a world where we can choose to buy anything, anywhere? These notions you describe risk all that we have accomplished."

Admiral Wang nodded. "Then this failing is mine, and mine alone, if I have not made the case properly." He turned to the map, pausing to collect his thoughts. Along the wall, the naval commandos stood unnervingly still and held their weapons at the ready. Wang smiled at them and continued.

"All of us here who first formed the Directorate acted to pull order back from chaos. We chose to act. But we acted because there was no other choice in the end," he said. "In turn, who can argue that this is not the purpose of the Directorate? Thousands of years have brought us to this point. We protected China from the party leaders who held the country back, and we should not grow meek on the brink of the next great step."

A young woman's voice cut through the room. "Desire and ability are not the same thing, Admiral," said Muyi Ling. Muyi was not yet thirty, but thanks to her father's wealth, she now ran Weibot, the largest manufacturing consortium. "Didn't General Sun also say, 'Avoid overconfidence, as it will lead to disaster'?"

Damn those viz glasses. While the old man might have known Sun-Tzu by heart, Wang doubted she did. He noticed the Directorate commando closest to him shift his weight slightly. Maybe they were not naval commandos at all, despite the uniforms. Could they be from the 788th Regiment, which protected the Presidium? Were they letting him hang himself, word by word, for threatening the status quo that so many in the Presidium had profited from?

"That is always a concern. But as Sun also said, 'Make no assumptions about all the dangers of using military force. Then you won't make assumptions about the benefits of using arms either.'"

She smiled, but he saw her eyes scanning her glasses rather than looking directly at him. She was likely researching a retort. He realized that he had to move the discussion beyond the level of trading quotations. Wang turned to the wider group.

"Of course, we are all aware of the reasons given for why it will never be our time. Our population demographics are not optimal, they say. Our trade routes are too vulnerable, they say. Our need for outside energy is too great, they say. These statements are all true. And they will always be true if we turn our backs on our duty to make our destiny manifest. The worst thing we can do is fear our own potential."

His smart-ring finger clicked one last time, and around them played the famous scene of the tank in People's Square crushing the old Communist Party's riot-control truck, the crowd of protesters' initial looks of surprise and then their celebration as they realized that the military was on their side. He saw a few instinctively nodding their approval, reliving the moment when they had remade China into their vision.

"I have abused your time, so I will end my presentation with three questions. First, just as we acted then to meet the people's true expectations of their nation's leaders, we must ask, What would the people expect of us now? Second, what do you expect the Americans to do once they learn of our energy discovery? Third, and most important, is a simple question of the arc of history: If now is not the time, then when?

"You know the answers to these questions, and thus you know that you, the truly powerful, actually have no choice."

Admiral Lin appeared at Wang's shoulder and placed a hand on his back. Wang noticed that the commandos now surrounded them. Perhaps he had gone too far.

"Admiral, the Presidium thanks you for your views," said Lin. "These men will see you out."

As Wang walked down the hallway, wedged between the commandos, he replayed the presentation in his mind. He could find faults with his performance, but he was at peace.

At the elevator door, the commandos stood in silence. Wang wondered where they would take him next. Then he noticed that they were tensing up as the elevator lights numbered ever closer to their floor. The door opened and another armed phalanx emerged; these bodyguards were Caucasian in ethnicity and wearing civilian suits, but they were clearly military. While the two groups eyed each other warily, Wang watched how the elderly man in the middle didn't bother even to look up from the outdated computer tablet he tapped away on. Red diamonds and purple hearts reflected in his traditional eyeglasses. He was surprisingly fit for his age, but supposedly the old Russian spy was addicted to memory-improving games, an effort to stave off what Directorate intelligence suspected was dementia. A strong body still, but not the mind.

So, Wang realized, this had not been a strategy session but an audition. The Presidium had already made its choice.

PART 2

Attack your enemy where he is unprepared,
appear where you are not expected.

— SUN-TZU, *THE ART OF WAR*

Joint Base Anacostia-Bolling, Washington, DC

Armando Chavez exhaled when he made the initial slice. As his mentor Dr. Jimenez had explained so long ago, the key to precision was to move slow but steady, advancing the blade at a consistent pace. The cut complete, Armando reached down, picked up the withered rose branch, and placed it into the faded canvas bag slung over his shoulder.

Landscaping was a step down for someone with an MD from Universidad Central de Venezuela. But it was the only kind of work Armando had been able to get since he'd arrived as a refugee from the chaos in his homeland seven years ago. He could get angry or he could focus on achieving the little perfections that made life satisfying.

As he trimmed the flowers at the base of the sign, he glanced at the etching in the black marble: DEFENSE INTELLIGENCE AGENCY. He wasn't sure what the DIA did. Hadid, his supervisor, said it was something like the CIA, but for the U.S. military. It didn't matter. The landscaping crew was almost done here. After the break, Hadid said they would head over to trim the hedges behind the base's elder-care center.

Because of security, the landscapers were not allowed inside the building. When break time came, the others gathered in the shade, but Armando walked over to sit by the small decorative pond beside the entrance doors.

He flipped open the tablet he kept in his pocket to see if he had any messages. The screen projected a 3-D packet from his cousin back in Caracas. More pictures of his granddaughter. Such lovely eyes.

Armando's smile went unnoticed by Allison Swigg as she cut across the grassy field by the pond in her rush from the parking lot. The imagery analyst had gotten stuck in the traffic on I-295 on her way back from a networking lunch out at Tysons Corner. And now she was late for the staff meeting.

Neither of them noticed the other, but as she passed the landscaper, his tablet recognized the RFID chips embedded in Allison's security badge. A localized wireless network formed for exactly 0.03 seconds. In that instant, the malware hidden in the video packet from Caracas made its jump.

As Armando finished the iced tea his wife had made for him the previous night, Swigg approached the security desk manned by a guard in a black bullet-resistant nylon jumpsuit. A compact HK G48 assault rifle hung from the glossy gray ceramic vest that protected his chest. The only insignia on his uniform was the eagle-silhouette logo of the security company that guarded the DIA headquarters. *No Personal Devices Allowed* read the sign suspended above a row of silver turnstiles.

"Hey, Steve," said Allison. "How's the little one?"

"Pretty good," the guard replied with a smile. "She slept through the night."

She placed her iTab bracelet in a metallic lock box and pulled out the key. But Allison's badge stayed with her. As she walked toward the gate, the software in her badge automatically communicated her security clearance to the machine via a radio signal. And at the same moment of network linkage, the malware packet jumped again in less time than it would take to read the engraving on the entrance wall: *Committed to Excellence in Defense of the Nation.*

The idea of using covert radio signals to ride malware into a network unconnected to the wider Internet had actually been pioneered by the NSA, one of the DIA's sister agencies. But like all virtual weapons, once it was deployed in the open cyberworld, it offered inspiration for anyone, including one's enemies.

The turnstile gate lifted. Swigg rushed down the hall, too far behind schedule to make her ritual stop at the Dunkin' Donuts stand just inside the spy agency's entrance. By the time she had passed the old Soviet SS-20 ballistic missile that stood mounted in the lobby like a Cold War totem pole, the malware packet had jumped from the gate onto another security guard's viz glasses. When the guard walked his rounds, the packet jumped into the environmental controls that cooled a closet full of network servers supporting aerial surveillance operations over Pakistan. After that, it went to an unmanned-aircraft research and development team's systems. And bit by bit, the malware worked its way into the various subnetworks that linked via the Defense Department's SIPRNet classified network.

The initial penetrations didn't raise any alarms among the automated computer network defenses, always on the lookout for anomalies. At each stop, all the packet did was link with what appeared to the defenses as nonexecutables, harmless inert files, which they were, until the malware rearranged them into something new. Each of the systems had been air-gapped, isolated from the Internet to prevent hackers from infiltrating them. The problem with high walls, though, was that someone could use an unsuspecting gardener to tunnel underneath them.

Shanghai Jiao Tong University

A thin teenage girl stood behind a workstation, faintly glowing metallic smart-rings on her fingers, one worn above each joint. Her expression was blank, her eyes hidden behind a matte-black visor. Rows of similar workstations lined the converted lecture hall. Behind each stood a young engineering student, every one a member of the 234th Information Brigade — Jiao Tong, a subunit of the Third Army Cyber-Militia.

On the arena floor, two Directorate officers watched the workers. From their vantage point, the darkened arena seemed to be lit by thousands of fireflies as the students' hands wove faint neon-green tracks through the air.

Jiao Tong University had been formed in 1896 by Sheng Xuanhuai, an official working for the Guangxu emperor. The school was one of the original pillars of the Self-Strengthening Movement, which advocated using Western technology to save the country from destitution. Over the following decades, the school grew to become China's most prestigious engineering university, nicknamed the Eastern MIT.

Hu Fang hated that moniker, which made it seem as if her school were only a weak copy of an American original. Today, her generation would show that times had changed.

The first university cyber-militias had been formed after the 2001 Hainan Island incident. A Chinese fighter pilot had veered too close to an American navy surveillance plane, and the two planes crashed in midair. The smaller Chinese plane spun to the earth and its hot-dogging pilot was killed, while the American plane had to make an emergency landing at a Chinese airfield on Hainan. As each side angrily accused the other of causing the collision, the Communist Party encouraged computer-savvy Chinese citizens to deface American websites to show their collective displeasure. Young Chinese teens were organized online by the thousands and gleefully joined in the cyber-vandalism campaign, targeting the homepage of everything from the White House to a public library in Minnesota. After the crisis, the hacker militias became crucial hubs of espionage, stealing online secrets that ranged from jet-fighter designs to soft-drink companies' negotiating strategies.

That had all taken place before Hu Fang was born. She'd grown up sick from the smog; a hacking cough kept her from playing outside with the other kids. What Hu thought was a curse became a blessing: her father, a professor of computer science in Beijing, had started her out writing code at age three, mostly as a way to keep her busy inside their cramped apartment. Hu had been inducted into the 234th after she'd won a software-writing competition at the age of eleven.

Officially, militia service fulfilled the Directorate's universal military service requirement, but Hu would have volunteered anyway. She got to play with the latest technology, and the missions the officers gave her were usually fun. One day it might be hacking into a dissident's smartphone, and another day it might entail tangling with the IT security at a Korean car designer. The Americans, though, were the best to toy with — so confident of their defenses. If you pwned them — the word taken from the Americans' own lingo for seizing digital control — the officers of the 234th noticed you. She'd done well enough that the apartment she and her father lived in now was much bigger than any of her father's colleagues'.

But it was not the reward that mattered to Hu; rather, it was escaping the physical limitations that had once defined her life. When linked in, Hu felt like she was literally flying. Indeed, her gear worked on the same principles as the fly-by-wire controls on China's J-20 fighter. The powerful computers she drew on created a three-dimensional world that represented the global communications networks that were her battlegrounds. She was among the few people who could boast that they had truly "seen" the Internet.

Hu had made her mark by hacking phones belonging to civilian employees in the Pentagon. Despite the restrictions on employees bringing devices into the building, a few did so every day. Her technique involved co-opting a phone's camera and other onboard sensors to remotely re-create the owner's physical and electronic environment. This mosaic of pictures, sounds, and electromagnetic signals helped the Directorate produce an almost perfect 3-D virtual rendition of the Pentagon's interior and its networks.

She noticed with pleasure her pump kicking in. Access to the latest in medical technologies was another perk of the unit. The tiny pump, implanted beneath the skin near her navel, dumped a cocktail of methylphenidate and other stimulants into her circulatory system.

Originally designed for children with attention deficit disorder, the mix produced a combination of focus and euphoria. For well over a decade, kids in America had popped "prep" pills to tackle tests and homework, which Hu thought was laughable. It was another sign of America's weakness, kids using this kind of power just to make it through schoolwork. Hu's pump enabled her to do something truly important.

When she'd been told a week ago to prepare for a larger operation than they'd ever tried, she hacked the pump's operating system. It was a risk, but it paid off. She raised the dose level by 200 percent. No more steady-state awareness. Now it was like falling off a skyscraper and discovering you could fly right before you hit the ground.

Hu moved her hands like a conductor, gently arcing her arms in elliptical gestures, almost swanlike. The movement of each joint of every finger communicated a command via the gyroscopes inside the smartring; one typed out code on an invisible keyboard while another acted as a computer mouse, clicking open network connections. Multiple different points, clicks, and typing actions, all at once. To the officers watching below, it looked like an intricate ballet crossed with a tickling match.

The young hacker focused on her attack, navigating the malware packet through the DIA networks while fighting back the desire to brush a bead of sweat off her nose with her gloved hands. The

Pentagon's autonomous network defenses, sensing the slight anomalies of her network streams, tried to identify and contain her attack. But this was where the integration of woman and machine triumphed above mere "big data." Hu was already two steps ahead, building system components and then tearing them down before the data could be integrated enough for the DIA computers to see them as threats. Her left arm coiled and sprung, her fingers outstretched. Then the right did the same, this time a misdirect, steering the defense code to shut down further external access, essentially tricking the programs into focusing on locking the doors of a burning house, but leaving a small ember on the outside for them to stamp on, so they'd think the fire was out.

Having gained access, she set about accomplishing the heart of her mission. Hu's hands punched high, then her fingers flicked. She began inserting code that would randomize signals from the Americans' Global Positioning System satellite constellation. Some GPS signals would be off by just two meters. Others would be off by two hundred kilometers.

Of course, shutting it all down would be easy. But she could swing that hammer later; today was all about sowing doubt and spreading confusion.

332 Kilometers Above the Earth's Surface

If it weren't so frustrating, it would be funny.

Less than a millimeter's worth of extra metal on just one bolt was about to derail an operation that involved literally billions of moving pieces of software and hardware.

"Are you done yet?" asked Lieutenant Colonel Huan Zhou, an unmistakable edge in his voice.

The wrench that Major Chang Lu held in his gloved hand was a perfect copy of a HEXPANDO, just like the one that Colonel Farmer was banging at the ISS hatch with half an Earth orbit away. This wrench, though, had been produced from a design pirated by a patriotic hacker unit based in Shenzhen and manufactured at the Manned Space Engineering Office in Beijing. The problem was that, unlike the wrench, the bolt that Chang was trying to pry free was not a perfect copy and had become stuck. He pushed harder and harder, but it still wouldn't budge.

"Nearly," said Chang.

He saw the three other taikonauts reentering the Tiangong-3 space station. Lucky bastards.

The Tiangong ("Heavenly Palace") space station program had been planned ever since China launched its first manned crew into space, in 2003. Western commentators had mocked those early Shenzhou vessels as poor copies of the United States' 1960s-era Gemini spacecraft. But the program rapidly advanced, aided by a healthy amount of NASA computer design files that found their way into Chinese engineers' hands. After the Shenzhous came the first Tiangong space station, a ten-meter-long, eight-thousand-kilogram single-module test bed that launched in 2011. It was the equivalent of NASA's 1970s-era Skylab. That was followed in 2015 by the multimodule Tiangong-2, which was fifteen meters long and weighed twenty thousand kilograms, comparable to NASA's 1990s design of the first ISS. Soon after, the program accelerated fast enough to finally match its competitors. Western commentators no longer mocked but instead marveled that in a decade and a half, China had achieved what it had taken NASA sixty years to accomplish.

The twenty-five-meter-long, sixty-thousand-kilogram Tiangong-3 space station was the pride of the nation, its launch celebrated with an official state holiday. It had seven modules laid out in a T, including a core crew module that could support six taikonauts; four solar panels that extended out thirty-seven meters; and a docking port that could accommodate four ships. At the two upper ends of the T were parallel laboratory modules designed to conduct various experiments in microgravity.

At least, that was what the rest of the world thought. The portside module actually had a different purpose. And now, its cover just wouldn't shake free, all because of a single faulty titanium bolt.

Chang realized that to get enough torque to pry the bolt loose, he'd have to untether, which was against protocol.

"Repositioning," said Chang.

"Negative," said Huan. "Return and I will send someone to finish your work."

"There's no time," said Chang. "I'm now off tether."

Chang heaved on the long wrench, and the bolt loosened. He easily removed the hatch cover and found himself staring into the mirrored surface of a laser's lens. He studied the Earth's reflection in it, and his own form superimposed above the peaceful blue beneath.

"Done," said Chang.

"I didn't think you had it in you, Chang. Good work," said Huan, the edge in his voice gone.

Chang resecured himself to the space station and made his way to the main hatch while Huan brought Tiangong-3's weapons online. The station crew had realized they were moving to war footing twelve hours ago when Huan switched off the live viz feed of their activities. But it still felt slightly unreal.

Once the taikonauts were all inside the station, Huan powered up the weapons module. The chemical oxygen iodine laser, or COIL, design had originally been developed by the U.S. Air Force in the late 1970s. It had even been flown on a converted 747 jumbo jet so the laser's ability to shoot down missiles in midair could be tested. But the Americans had ultimately decided that using chemicals in enclosed spaces to power lasers was too dangerous. The Directorate saw it differently. Two modules away from the crew, a toxic mix of hydrogen peroxide and potassium hydroxide was being blended with gaseous chlorine and molecular iodine.

This was really it, thought Chang as he watched the power indicators turn red. There was no turning back once the chemicals had been mixed and the excited oxygen began to transfer its energy to the weapon. They would have forty-five minutes to act and then the power would be spent.

The firing protocol for mankind's first wartime shots in space was well rehearsed. The targets marked in the firing solution had been identified, prioritized, and tracked for well over a year in increasingly rigorous drills the crew eventually realized were not just to support war games down on Earth. The long hours spent in the lab would finally pay off.

"Ready to commence firing sequence," said Huan. "Confirm?"

One by one, the other taikonauts checked in from their weapons stations. Chang touched the photo taped to the wall in front of him. His fingers lingered on the image of his beaming wife and their grinning eight-year-old son. The smiling Ming, missing his two front teeth, wore his father's blue air force officer's hat.

What the photo did not show was how upset his wife had been when he'd given Ming that hat the night before. She thought it made her son look like a prop in a Directorate propaganda piece.

He moved his hand away from the photo and began his part of the operation, monitoring the targeting sequence. He startled even Huan when he cried out, "Ready!"

For years, military planners had fretted about antisatellite threats from ground-launched missiles, because that was how both the Americans and the Soviets had intended to take down each other's satellite networks during the Cold War. More recently, the Directorate had fed this fear by developing its own antisatellite missiles and then alternating between missile tests and arms-control negotiations that went nowhere, keeping the focus on the weapons based below. The Americans should have looked up.

Chang snuck another look at the photo and caught Huan pausing, his trigger finger lingering above the red firing button. He appeared to be savoring the moment. Then Huan pressed the button.

A quiet hum pervaded the module. No crash of cannon or screams of death. Only the steady purr of a pump signified that the station was now at war.

The first target was WGS-4, a U.S. Air Force wideband gapfiller satellite. Shaped like a box with two solar wings, the 3,400-kilogram satellite had entered space in 2012 on top of a Delta 4 rocket launched from Cape Canaveral.

Costing over three hundred million dollars, the satellite offered the U.S. military and its allies 4.875 GHz of instantaneous switchable bandwidth, allowing it to move massive amounts of data. Through it ran the communications for everything from U.S. Air Force satellites to U.S. Navy submarines. It was also a primary node for the U.S. Space Command. The Pentagon had planned to put up a whole constellation of these satellites to make the network less vulnerable to attack, but contractor cost overruns had kept the number down to just six.

The space station's chemical-powered laser fired a burst of energy that, if it were visible light instead of infrared, would have been a hundred thousand times brighter than the sun. Five hundred and twenty kilometers away, the first burst hit the satellite with a power roughly equivalent to a welding torch's. It melted a hole in WGS-4's external atmospheric shielding and then burned into its electronic guts.

Chang watched as Huan clicked open a red pen and made a line on the wall next to him, much like a World War I ace decorating his biplane to mark a kill. The scripted moment had been ordered from below, a key scene for the documentary that would be made of the operation, a triumph that would be watched by billions.

"And there's the one," said Huan. "Chang, it is good for us all that you did not miss," he said as he clicked the pen shut with a flourish.

"Indeed," Chang said, and then, smiling, he ad-libbed, "I would save you the trouble and walk myself out the airlock. Resetting for target number two."

Originally known as the X-37, USA-226 was the U.S. military's unmanned space plane. About an eighth the size of the old space shuttle, the tiny plane was used by the American government in much the same way the shuttle had been, to carry out various chores and repair jobs in space. It could rendezvous with satellites and refuel them, replace failed solar arrays using a robotic arm, and perform many other satellite-upkeep tasks.

But the Tiangong's crew, and the rest of the world's militaries, knew the U.S. military also used USA-226 as a space-going spy plane. It repeatedly flew over the same spots at the same altitude, notably the height typically used by military surveillance satellites: Pakistan for several weeks at a time, then Yemen and Kenya, and, more recently, the Siberian border.

With its primary control communications link via the WGS-4 satellite now lost, the tiny American space plane shifted into autonomous mode, its computers searching in vain for other guidance signals. In this interim period, USA-226's protocol was to cease acceleration and execute a standard orbit to avoid collisions. In effect, the robotic space plane stopped for its own safety, making it an easy target.

The taikonauts moved on down the list: the U.S. Geosynchronous Space Situational Awareness system was next. These were satellites that watched other satellites. The Americans' communications were now down, but once these satellites were taken out, the United States would be blind in space even if it proved able to bring its networks back online. After that was the mere five satellites that made up the U.S. military's Mobile User Objective System, akin to a global cellular phone provider for the military. Five pulses took out the narrowband communications network that linked all the American military's aerial and maritime platforms, ground vehicles, and dismounted soldiers. Then came the U.S. Navy's Ultra High Frequency Follow-On (UFO) system, which linked all of its ships. It was almost anticlimactic, the onboard targeting system moving the taikonauts through the attack's algorithm step by step, slowing down only when a cluster of satellites sharing a common altitude needed to be dispatched one by one.

The last to be "serviced," as Huan dryly put it, was a charged-particle detector satellite. The joint NASA and Energy Department system had been launched a few years after the Fukushima nuclear plant disaster as a way to detect radiation emissions. A volley of laser fire from Tiangong-3 exploded its fuel source.

When Huan finally put the pen back in his suit pocket, there were forty-seven marks on the wall.

They had been told that the ISS would be taken care of "by other means." On the other side of the Earth, discarded booster rockets were coming to life after months of dormancy. The boosters turned kamikazes advanced on collision courses with nearby American government and commercial communications and imaging satellites. The American ground controllers helplessly watched the chaos overhead, unable to maneuver their precious assets out of the way.

"I will run diagnostics and flush the laser power systems," said Chang. He kept moving in order to avoid thinking about what was happening on the Earth's surface below.

"Good," said Huan. "Then see if you can pull up the imagery from the attack; I want to watch it again later." *Of course you do*, thought Chang.

USS *Coronado*, Joint Base Pearl Harbor–Hickam, Hawaii

The coffee was just like that first cup his father had allowed him to sip from, back when he was seven. No sugar. No cream. It had tasted acrid, awful, not like the vanilla-flavored lattes his mom had loved.

"When you're in the Navy, you don't have time onboard to add in all that junk," his father had explained, typical of the kind of advice he gave his kids.

The boatswain's mate in charge of brewing up the coffee on the USS *Coronado* was no barista either, and so the bridge crew all sipped his awful coffee, watching the harbor wake up around them. Stim tabs and the other pharm provided by the corpsmen worked better, but the Navy clung to its traditions. The bitter coffee was as much a part of the morning watch as the sunrise.

Simmons set down his mug and eyed the sunlight illuminating the *Coronado*'s deck. The LCS had just celebrated its tenth birthday, but Jamie still thought the sharp, triple-hulled trimaran design gave it the look of a futuristic starship, like out of a Star Wars movie. His dad loved that old stuff, so much so that he had taken Jamie and his sister, Mackenzie, to one of the reboot movies when they were way too young to understand it. Their mother had gotten so mad when she'd found out. It was still a good memory, though, Mackenzie coming home with the empty paper popcorn bucket, cherishing it in the way that little kids make souvenirs of the most mundane objects. That was one of the few happy memories from before his father left, before Mackenzie died.

Simmons walked over to a spot near one of the port windows to inspect a blemish no bigger than a quarter. He ran his finger over the epoxy patch. On the last anti-piracy patrol, a burst of machine-gun fire had gone right through the window and two spots below in the ship's aluminum superstructure, now also repaired. No one had been hurt, fortunately, but it reminded the crew that the LCS had been designed for speed, not for heavy combat. Some of the crew had later wrapped Captain Riley's chair in aluminum foil as "ballistic protection," a joke that went over poorly with the captain.

As Simmons watched the morning sun paint the other warships in the crowded harbor orange, he savored the moment, knowing this was one of the last times he would command the bridge. He'd let Riley know what he'd decided when they arrived in San Diego.

Petty Officer Third Class Randall Jefferson, a young sailor on the bridge, approached, looking almost sheepish when he saw the XO lost in thought.

"Sir, I am sorry to disturb you, but you asked me to notify you if anything came up," said Jefferson. "The sonar grid picked up movement. It just flashes in and out, right up near the ship. It's probably some fish or a dolphin . . ."

"Don't apologize for not letting your guard down in port. Deploy REMUS and let's take a look."

He gave the orders to lower what looked like a neon-yellow torpedo into the water. REMUS, the remote environmental monitoring units, had actually started out in the commercial sector, much like its mother ship's original design as a high-speed ferry. The unmanned underwater system, essentially a robotic miniature submarine, had been developed at the Woods Hole Oceanographic Institution in Massachusetts, mainly for civilian applications like port facility inspection, pollution monitoring, and underwater surveying. It was a mainstay of Discovery and Travel Channel sims. But what worked to capture Shark Week footage also worked for underwater guard duty.

Simmons entered the bridge and stood behind Jefferson, who was now operating the mini-sub with a first-generation Sony PlayStation–type controller. The handheld video-game-style controller was supposed to be intuitive for the sailors, but it felt more like a relic to a generation who now gamed in 3-D immersion. The vid from REMUS played out alongside a live overhead satellite feed of the ship's position, a pattern analysis of surface and air traffic around their position, and a multicolor spherical chart that showed status reports of the crew and ship systems.

"Not picking anything up on thermal, sir," said Jefferson. "Let's see what visual has."

"Give me the full screen," said Simmons.

The camera pivoted and showed a gray mass of shadows on the screen. Simmons squinted, as if willing the murky water to reveal its secrets.

"Hello there," said Jefferson. He zoomed the camera in on a dark form slowly circling under the ship's stern. The camera began to focus.

There. No mistaking it. Against the dark blue background was the faint silhouette of a diver.

"Some damn fool local out messing around where he shouldn't," said Jefferson.

But then the diver stopped and raised his arms above his head as if praying beneath the LCS's hull.

"He's got something in his hands," said Jefferson. The diver held what looked like a trash-can lid. He lazily kicked his feet and inched closer to the *Coronado*'s hull.

Simmons fought down the coffee climbing back up into his throat.

"Sound Force Protection alert! Possible terror attack, FP Condition Delta!" shouted Simmons. "And wake the captain. Tell him we have a diver placing what looks like a limpet mine on the hull."

He picked up a headset and steadied his voice, knowing any fear in it would resonate throughout the ship.

"This is the XO. Force Protection security team to the port side. Cycle rudders and energize sonars. Set Material Condition Zebra," Simmons said. "FP team, we have a diver attempting to place an explosive device on the hull. I want him off. Batteries release. Fire at will."

Chaos broke out as sailors ran to the port side and tried to see where the diver was. Through the bridge's open hatch, Simmons heard the shouts getting increasingly desperate.

"There he is."

"No, he's over there!"

"Get the hell out of my way!" yelled Petty Officer Anton Horowitz. He had been standing guard duty by the gangway on the starboard side, and he pushed his way through the scrum to the port side.

Horowitz leaned as far over the railing as he could and fired his M4 carbine methodically into the water, making a looping pattern of splashes from bow to stern. It was a strange thought to have in the middle of a terror attack, Horowitz knew, but this was actually fun. He had reenlisted only two months ago for just this kind of work, with a promise from the skipper that he'd be allowed to try out for the SEALs. He'd already submitted the required DNA and blood samples for SEAL selection and had been maxing his hypertrophy workouts.

Back on the bridge, Jefferson saw the ripples that Horowitz's bullets made as tiny white lines on his screen that stopped after a few feet. When he switched to thermal view, they looked like a series of yellow needles jabbing into the water that quickly disappeared as their heat dissipated. Many were perilously close to the REMUS, but few were near the diver.

"Sir, they're not getting him," said Jefferson.

"Swing REMUS around and maneuver two hundred meters away. Then I want you to bring it back full speed at us," said Simmons.

"Sir?" asked Jefferson.

250 Meters Above Tokyo, Japan

They had said Tokyo was big, but up close it seemed to go on forever.

Captain Third Rank Alexei Denisov's MiG-35K fighter-bomber was doing 875 kilometers per hour, just beneath the sound barrier, to avoid leaving a telltale sonic boom. And yet the dense buildings below seemed like they would never end. The plan seemed to be working, though. The threat-detection icon on the luminous screen at his right did not register anything urgent. He kept his finger on the toggle switch for the plane's multifunction self-protection jammer, but so far the fighter had been unchallenged.

The reason was simple. The U.S.-Japanese combined air-defense network was designed for a threat from China, to the west. And east was where Denisov and his twenty-two other fighter-bombers had launched from the *Admiral Kuznetsov*. The Russian aircraft carrier was believed to be on exercises in the North Pacific, out of range of Chinese airstrikes. In fact, it had waited for a gap in satellite coverage and darted south at thirty knots for eight hours, moving just within the strike package's range. The MiGs flew in fast and low, and, once they were over Japan, they popped up to mimic the flight paths that commuter jets took from Narita Airport.

Denisov's MiG's radar-warning receiver rumbled as signals from an early-warning radar near Narita washed over it, this time close enough to overcome the plane's stealth features. Denisov's radio picked up the frantic calls of the air traffic controller. He hit the button and a digital recording began to play. It sounded like gibberish to him, but the FSB officer back on the *Kuznetsov* had been clear about the need to play it at just this moment.

To the air traffic controller on the ground, it sounded like the pilot of one of Sony's executive jets was having a heart attack.

As the MiGs passed Miyazaki and turned again toward the

Ryukyu Islands, it was clear that the defenses were finally onto them. Denisov's radar scope showed four Japan Air Self-Defense Force F-15s were vectoring as fast as they could, but they wouldn't get there in time. The ruse had bought Denisov only a few minutes, but it should be enough.

After scanning the sky above him for any incoming fighters, Denisov said a quick prayer for his men and his country. For himself, there was no need. A commander could operate only with certainty, not fear. He expected losses today, but also success. His latest imagery of one of his targets showed just eleven U.S. aircraft parked inside their hardened hangars. Dozens remained out in the open, as usual.

The MiGs dove to low altitude and pushed forward to their full sea-level velocity of nearly fifteen hundred kilometers per hour, well over the speed of sound. The new MiG-35Ks were called fourth-generation-plus fighters by the Americans. They weren't fully stealthy, but they had a significantly reduced radar signature. Each second counted now. When the jets neared Okinawa, Denisov's radar-warning receiver lit with a pulsing red icon. The Patriot IV missile batteries that the Japanese had acquired from the Americans were tracking his low-flying fighter. They had him in their sights and could knock him down at will.

This was a crucial component of the plan. He took a deep breath and waited, telling himself that the missiles were threats only if someone pushed the launch button. Japan's Air Self-Defense Forces, however, were not authorized to fire on targets without permission from that country's civilian leadership. The gamble was that permission wouldn't come in time. Two decades of near-daily airspace incursions by Chinese aircraft would have desensitized the Japanese, plus their communications networks were supposed to have been knocked offline by cyber-attacks. At least, that was the plan.

All the more reason not to miss on this first free run, Major Denisov had told his men during their preflight briefing. "You are about to fire the most important shots of your lives, and they may be your last. Make them count."

There was no rallying call to glory over the flight's communications. The only sounds on the radio this time were digital recordings of the voices of American F-22 Raptor pilots copied by a surveillance ship that had monitored the RIMPAC war games held each year off Hawaii. Anything to create uncertainty and delay the Japanese and American response by just a few more seconds.

The silent progress of an icon in his jet's heads-up display told him he had arrived: Kadena Air Base. His war started here.

A flash of movement caught Denisov's eye as four dark gray darts raced ahead of his squadron. It was a volley of Sokols (Falcons) fired by his second flight. A sort of miniaturized cruise missile, the electromagnetic weapon used pulses of directed energy to knock out air-defense and communications systems. Following a preprogrammed course, the flight of Falcon missiles separated, each leaving a swath of electronic dead zone behind it.

If his flight's opening shots were silent, the next wave of destruction would be deafening. Denisov released four RBK-500 cluster bombs over the unprotected U.S. Air Force planes parked near the base's three-and-a-half-kilometer-long runway. As he banked his MiG, he caught a glimpse of an F-35A Lightning II being towed out of its hangar in a rush to confront him. His MiG was designed to be a match for the F-35, and the pilots of both had always wondered how the planes would actually stack up against each other. It would have to wait for some other time. The RBK canisters opened up behind Denisov's plane, releasing hundreds of cluster bomblets, each the size of a beer can. Tiny parachutes deployed and the cans drifted toward the ground.

When proximity fuses detected that they were ten meters from the ground, the cans exploded, one after another. Hundreds of explosions ripped across the air base, blowing open scores of the U.S. Air Force's most advanced fighters.

Denisov's wingman made the next run and dropped three penetrating anti-runway bombs. The hardened tips of the massive bombs buried themselves almost five meters into the runway's concrete and then detonated with more than fifteen hundred kilograms' worth of explosives. While the limited number of American jets protected in hardened hangars might survive Denisov's bombs, none would be taking off from the biggest U.S. air base in the Pacific for days, if not weeks.

Six kilometers away, the flight's two trailing MiG-35Ks split past each other and then banked back hard as they raced toward the center of an imaginary *X*. That *X* was located in the middle of the largest U.S. Marine Corps base in Japan. The nine thousand Marines living there were supposed to have been moved to Guam five years earlier. But political wrangling between Congress and the Japanese government over just who would pay the $8.6 billion tab to relocate the Marines had delayed the transfer of forces. Time had run out.

The two planes passed each other at less than a hundred meters. At the imaginary point of their crossing lines, the MiGs dropped four KAB-1500S thermobaric bombs, each weighing just over thirteen hundred kilograms. The bombs opened to release a massive cloud of explosive vapor, which was then ignited by a separate charge. It was the largest explosion Japan had experienced since Nagasaki, and it left a similar mushroom cloud of smoke and dust hanging over the base as the jets flew away.

Denisov finally turned off the spoof audio recording and ordered his flight to report in. The strikes on the air bases, the ground bases, and even the U.S. Navy aircraft carrier harbored offshore had been a success. He'd lost only five jets to the late-reacting air defenses. Amazing.

He wasn't sure the Americans would appreciate the irony of the Russians following the same plan of attack the Americans had used on the Japanese some eighty years earlier, but Plan Doolittle had worked. Trying to conceal the relief in his voice, he ordered the remaining fighters to bank toward the Chinese coast.

That was the other part they'd copied from the raid the Americans had pulled back in the early months of their previous war in the Pacific: by coming in from an unexpected approach and making it a one-direction flight, they could strike at twice the range the enemy believed possible. The Russian navy had held up its end; now it had to trust that the Chinese aerial refueling tankers would be there as promised.

The raid wasn't Denisov's idea, but neither had the original raid back in World War II been Jimmy Doolittle's idea. Maybe, he thought, history would call this one after its commander as well; Denisov's Raid had a nice ring to it.

USS *Coronado*, Joint Base Pearl Harbor–Hickam, Hawaii

From the deck of the *Coronado*, Horowitz saw a sudden ripple in the water where the REMUS had turned, almost like what a fly-fisherman would take for a fish rising. It made him pause, then he focused on firing at the threat. The shell casings bounced off the deck and into the water, sizzling as they floated for a brief moment and then sinking beneath the surface.

"REMUS is coming back around, sir," said Jefferson on the bridge. "What now?"

"I want you to ram it up that diver's ass," said Simmons.

"Aye, aye, sir!"

Jefferson gently nudged the joystick to the right and then the left, centering the diver on the screen. Then he throttled it to full speed.

On deck, Horowitz's M4 clicked; his magazine was empty. Without looking, he reached into the pouch attached to his belt for another magazine and tried to slam it into the rifle, but his last mag slipped from his hands into the water. Thirty rounds that could have made the difference were lost.

Horowitz cursed at the water as only a sailor could but stopped when he saw a fast-moving shape coming toward the ship. Great; not just terrorists but torpedoes now!

The underwater view was projected onto the REMUS control station. The diver was in the midst of attaching the mine to the hull when some sixth sense warned him what was coming. He turned his head to look over his shoulder. The last picture on Jefferson's video screen was the diver's surprised expression behind the goggles, just before the REMUS smashed into his left jaw and then plowed into the ship's hull behind him.

On deck, Horowitz felt the crunch of the REMUS impact and then saw a roaring wall of white water flash up. And then silence.

Ruby Empress, Gatún Lake, Panama Canal

Arnel Reyes picked at a flake of black paint from the rail of the *Ruby Empress*, a Cyprus-flagged oil tanker.

"I like blue, you know, like the sky in the afternoon, and as a little boy, he will love it," said his wife. Arnel wanted to say that neither a newborn baby nor a full-grown man could care less about wall colors. But it was best to humor her with all the love he could scrape up, especially given that he was standing on the deck of a ship in the Panama Canal and she was back home in Manila.

"Blue it is, my love. I'll be back in two weeks and we can paint for him then," he said. "We've got plenty of time, you know."

"There's not enough time with you gone. There's just so much to do. And we haven't even talked about his name," Anna-Maria said over the phone. "Baby, I know your mother thought —"

Then the call dropped.

He worried Anna-Maria would think he'd hung up on her, but when he tried to reconnect, the call wouldn't go through. He put his phone back in his pocket and leaned away from the hot deck rail. It didn't help his mood that the transit through the Panama Canal was the slowest part of the trip, since ships had to wait in line to make their way through the canal locks.

As Reyes climbed back up the series of ladders, he heard the commotion on the *Ruby*'s bridge. Everything was squared away aboard the ship, but the radios were alive with traffic. Two ships ahead, the *Xianghumen*, a Chinese-flagged freighter, had turned on its engines. This was craziness. What was *Xianghumen*'s captain thinking, speeding up inside the transit zone? The canal master was screaming over the radio for the *Xianghumen* to acknowledge and stop. But there was no reply.

Reyes ran topside to see. It was like watching a slow-motion train wreck. The *Xianghumen* was moving at a mere four knots, slower than a jog. But with a hundred and twenty thousand tons of force behind it, the ship slowly ground its way into the canal locks, crushing the doors inward.

Reyes wasn't sure how long it would take the Chinese companies that ran the Panama Canal Zone to fix this mess, but their investment had clearly gone down the tubes.

"Well, it's not my hundred and eighty billion dollars," said Reyes to one of the crew, who chuckled in reply.

In any case, the highway between the oceans was likely going to be closed for a while. He reached into his pocket. He'd better try to call his wife again.

USS *Coronado*, Joint Base Pearl Harbor–Hickam, Hawaii

When Horowitz came to, he was floating on his back in the water. A broken shard of yellow metal drifted a few feet away, and just beyond that was the diver's body, floating face-down.

He looked up at the *Coronado*, trying to remember how he'd gotten here. His ears rang and his head ached worse than any shore-leave hangover. He saw the XO looking down at him from the bridge. He saluted the officer from the water, and the XO smiled and saluted back.

A launch pulled Horowitz and the black-clad body out of the water. The sailors hauled him aboard with smiles, but they handled the body with fear.

The launch stopped beside the *Coronado* and the diver was carried up to the helicopter deck at the stern. Horowitz scrambled up after it and joined the small crowd that had quickly gathered around the body. They all spoke quietly around the dead diver, as if worried their voices might revive him.

"Don't shove me," said a sailor. "I gotta viz this."

"You can't do that," whispered another. "He's dead. You know the rules."

"XO's coming," a voice hissed, and the crowd tensed and drew back into order, parting to allow Simmons through.

"Nothing like a morning swim, Horowitz," Simmons observed with a smile. "You solid?"

"Aye, sir," Horowitz replied. "Can't say the same for my swim buddy here."

A sailor pulled off the diver's mask to reveal bulging eyes. Horowitz felt his stomach turn. The left side of the man's jaw was bloody and caved in, but the rest of the dead man's features were still intact. With his cropped blond hair, he looked almost like a sleeping Viking.

"We get the right guy?" asked one of the sailors. "He don't look like any jihadi I've seen before."

Someone handed Simmons the broken dive mask. He turned it over in his hands, careful not to cut himself on the shards of plastic, and then knelt down to look closer at the body. A delicate scar on the chin and a nose that looked as though it had been broken as regularly as a boxer's.

"Roll him over," said Simmons.

As they turned the man, Horowitz noticed that the diver's suit wasn't neoprene; it was made of something thicker. Then he saw the man wasn't wearing conventional scuba gear.

"Sir, that's a closed rebreather unit," said Horowitz. "SEALs use them to swim without the bubbles. The wetsuit's got some thermal masking going on too."

Simmons nodded and studied the gear being stripped off the body. The dive computers strapped to the dead man's wrists looked sleek, clearly mil-grade. They also had Chinese markings on a protective cover.

The men looked confused as the XO sprinted back to the bridge without a word.

It wasn't a big ship, and Simmons was at the bridge within twenty-five seconds. Riley was there now, still in his skivvies but wearing his blue USS *Coronado* baseball cap with the CO's scrambled-eggs insignia sewn in gold thread above the brim. Jefferson was playing the REMUS video back for him. Riley turned to see Simmons burst into the room. Simmons didn't walk around the projected screen but went right through it, rippling the picture.

"Got him?" said Riley.

Simmons seemed to ignore him and looked right at the communications officer.

"Get PACOM on the horn, now! Prep an OPREP-Three Pinnacle message." Any message with PINNACLE in the identification line was automatically flagged of interest not just to the entire Navy chain of command but also to the National Military Command Center, which monitored events for the Joint Chiefs and the president.

"That's a little extreme for one diver, XO. Let's notify the duty sonar ship first and see if they have any further info," said Riley.

"Too slow. We need to send a Pinnacle out now, sir," said Simmons.

The communications tech looked from Simmons to Riley. "Sirs, nothing's working here. I can't even get my own phone to hook on to the network. It's like the whole spectrum is down."

On the main deck below, Horowitz rubbed the ache at the base of his neck. He angrily slammed another magazine he'd cadged from a fellow sailor into his M4. They'd found his weapon still lying on the deck. He absent-mindedly ran his tongue across his lips, realizing he was thirsty despite being soaking wet. He'd read that this was what happened when you went into shock, but he wasn't going to say anything about it now. Falling off the ship and then bitching about being scared seemed like a good way to blow his shot at becoming a SEAL.

Horowitz looked around the harbor at the wall of U.S. Navy steel assembled there. He couldn't wait to get to sea and wreak some revenge on whoever had done it.

Then the USS *Abraham Lincoln*, a nuclear-powered aircraft carrier tied up just across the harbor, seemed to lift a few feet from the water, as if the hundred-thousand-ton ship were being conjured skyward. The shove of the blast wave pushed him back to the bulkhead.

As he scrambled to his feet, Horowitz stared, agape, as the *Nimitz*-class carrier settled back into the water with orange flames and black smoke pouring from its deck. He watched as the carrier's hull began to break apart about two-thirds of the way down from the bow.

"Oh, shit. The reactors," muttered Horowitz.

Pier 29, Port of Honolulu, Hawaii

What the hell? They weren't supposed to be offloading for another day.

When he'd first seen the ramp come down, Jakob Sanders had pulled out his tablet to recheck the manifest. The *Golden Wave*, 720 feet, flagged out of Liberia. A RO/RO carrying cars from Shanghai. It had been pre-cleared on the manifest but it was twenty-four hours early. And now it was screwing up his day.

Even standing in the guard shack in the neighboring parking lot, he could feel the impact of the doublewide metal ramp slamming down onto the pier. Sanders had always thought the big roll-on, roll-off ship had the aesthetic appeal of a Costco plunked down on top of a boat. But that was the idea. It could carry 550 vehicles, and those vehicles could drive right off the ship and into his lot. Then they would sit, waiting to be driven to various dealerships around the island.

Sanders tried to raise his boss on the radio but all he got was static. He shook his head and looked down to check the time and date on his Casio G-Lide watch. Yep, he had it right. They were offloading too soon. More important, the web-enabled watch's last update showed that the offshore buoy readings looked promising for some head-high swells. Just five more hours in the lot and then he'd be free of his guard shack and back in the water at Kewalos. If the surf was as good as his watch promised, it would be one of those days when it just didn't matter where you'd gone to school or that you wore a black polyester uniform on land.

A series of distant booms snapped his attention from his watch. He hit the deck and covered his head with his arms as the shack's flimsy metal walls shook. After a few seconds, he got to his knees and peered through the open door at the fuel-tank farm next to pier 29. No fire. Blue skies didn't indicate thunder. Then the pier began to vibrate again from another low rumble, like an earthquake. Damn, he didn't want to be caught here by the water if it led to a tsunami.

More distant booms echoed off the hills, but the noise was washed out by hundreds of motors starting up inside the *Golden Wave*. What were they doing? Didn't they feel the quake? There could be more aftershocks.

Sanders remembered the public-service announcements he'd watched as a kid said you should stand in a doorway during an earthquake, but he looked at the flimsy shack walls and then crawled outside. He felt more booms reverberate and saw some smoke rising behind the *Golden Wave,* but the bulk of the huge ship blocked whatever was happening across the harbor.

Then one of those new Geely SUVs rolled down the ramp. Maybe they were trying to get the cars off before another quake? But where were they going to park them? They'd be better off keeping them on the ship and riding it out.

Sanders watched as another and then another of the SUVs moved down the ramp and parked. He'd always thought the Geely looked like a ripped-off Range Rover Defilade. But they were so cheap that he could almost afford one. The paint sure sucked, though. The first dozen were a decent silver or blue. But the rest were a faded matte green.

Then he heard a piercing squeal, like something gouging the steel deck of the ship. Behind the last SUV, what looked like a telephone pole on its end gradually emerged and pointed down the ramp. Behind that pole was a massive green bulk that slowly nosed its way out to the top of the ramp and then tilted downward.

Shit, that was a tank! Then another tank moved down the ramp, followed by an eight-wheeled vehicle that looked like a tank's little brother.

Sanders saw the red stars on the tanks. What were Chinese tanks doing coming off the ship? The manifest said nothing about that. And who the hell would be buying those? Maybe they were for training exercises out at Camp Schofield?

Jakob looked around and realized he was alone.

His next move was to bring out his phone and start shooting video. It would be worth a couple beers; maybe he could even sell it on the viz-net.

Then what looked like six beer kegs flew up into the air and raced toward downtown. "Drones?" Sanders said in a whisper.

Each squat Pigeon surveillance drone was indeed about the size of a fourteen-gallon beer keg, and each had a small rotor bay at its bottom. They all took off to seek out the highest points in Honolulu, where they would land. From these perches, the unarmed Pigeons would suck in electromagnetic and digital signals and then throw out an island-wide wave of electronic disturbance.

Just then Jakob heard another bang on the pier. It was the ramp coming down off the *Hildy Manor*, another RO/RO tied up beyond the *Golden Wave*. None of this shit was authorized. They didn't have the paperwork, and the lot was already going to be jammed. There was no way he'd be able to fit the cars from not one but two ships into the waiting lot, let alone a bunch of tanks.

He held the phone at arm's length, cursing his stupid job again, this time because he couldn't afford some viz glasses.

"Jakob Sanders at Pier Twenty-Nine in Honolulu," he said, staring into the pinhole camera. "Got an unauthorized delivery here as you can see," Sanders said. "Some trucks, Geelys, and check this out, tanks!

Chinese tanks. Not sure what the drill is today, but we're about to go find out. Bet you never saw anything like this in real life. Me either. Stay tuned."

Sanders set his phone on the windowsill in his shack so that it was recording the scene and then marched with a bold step toward the *Golden Wave*. Dumb-ass sailors. They'd just have to stay on the pier until it all got sorted out.

By the time Sanders had made his way to the ramp that connected the pier to the parking lot, he could literally feel the power of the tanks' engines in his chest. The tanks slowly moved forward, a few feet at a time, testing the ramp.

A flash of movement and an earsplitting clang made him whip his head around. Big metal panels were being tossed over the side of the *Evening Resolve* — a 480-foot cargo container ship registered in Dalian — and landing on the pier. Then a miniature air force began to assemble in formation above the *Evening Resolve*. To Sanders, the quadcopters looked like those spy drones the paparazzi used to buzz any Hollywood star dumb enough to still have an outdoor wedding. The Directorate's electric V1000 drone actually shared a heritage with the commercial systems, but its agility and stealth had made it the platform of choice for covert Chinese "risk-elimination" strikes in Africa and the former Republic of Indonesia.

The tanks throttled their engines again and regained Sanders's attention. He raised his right hand in the universal sign to stop.

"Halt! You are entering private property. I need you to stop that vehicle immediately."

The lead tank slowed and then stopped at the bottom of the ramp, just ten feet away. Sanders looked down and raised his voice, more confident now that he had established who was in charge.

"Good. Now, I don't know what's going on but you need to turn that vehicle around and get back on the ship . . . immediately."

The engine belched smoke, and the tank suddenly bounded forward.

Seen on the screen of his phone, it looked like a symbolic act of bravery. In actuality, all Jakob could think about was running, running as fast as he could, to get out of the sixty-ton beast's path. But his feet just wouldn't move.

Marine Corps Base, Kaneohe Bay, Hawaii

Captain Charles Carlisle was losing patience with his crew chief. In other words, it was just another day in paradise with a jet more finicky than his fiancée.

The 25 mm gun pod on his F-35B Lightning II fighter kept jamming after each helicopter-like vertical landing he performed. This was the fourth time this week, but no one could figure out why. The plane's autonomic maintenance computers were supposed to point fingers at any gremlins, but adding more to the twenty-four million lines of software code already in there just proved Murphy's Law beat Moore's Law every time.

"I don't know what to tell you, Worm," said Miller, the civilian crew chief, using the call sign Carlisle had earned after losing his rations and living off worms during the survival-and-evasion phase of his pilot training. "I didn't design these planes; I just fix 'em."

Worm shook his head. He'd never understood why the Marine Corps put the world's best pilots in the cockpits of the world's most expensive weapons system only to turn maintenance over to the lowest bidder.

Worm was about to offer another round of profane observations about what $1.5 trillion ought to buy — like, for instance, a working gun — but then he held his breath and listened. Weird. A series of bass-like thumps. Then he heard the buzzing of rotors. It came from the direction of Pearl and moved toward the air station located on the Mokapu Peninsula. The blood drained from the aviator's face when he saw the incoming flight of choppers and tiny quadcopter drones.

"Get the fuel hose off, now!" Worm shouted.

The crew chief was about to argue when he tracked the pilot's gaze and saw the formation. Miller looked old, but he was down on the ground before the first wave of rockets hit the hangar complex on the other side of the 7,800-foot runway.

"Miller, up! Get up!" shouted Worm.

Lying prone, Miller watched four of the quadcopters dive and attack a communications tower at the end of the runway. Just before the V1000s launched a volley of micro-rockets, they flared back into formation, which made them look like Xs on a fiery tic-tac-toe board.

"I'm on it!" said Miller. You could question his competence, but you couldn't fault the man's bravery, thought Worm.

As the two men worked to pull the fuel line from the F-35, Miller spoke between panting breaths.

"Chinese?" he said.

"Does it matter?" said Worm. "Get me up there, and I'll send a few down here for you to pick through and find out."

They could see the drone helicopters methodically working their way across the base's hangar buildings, hitting one aircraft after the other. That they remained in an X formation the whole time made the attack seem all the more menacing. A few Marines shot rifles at them, only to be taken out by rocket fire from above. Fortunately, Worm's F-35B, like its predecessor the Harrier jump jet, didn't need to approach the killing field of the runway. The aircraft had a shaft-driven fan in the middle of its fuselage that could lift the jet into the air like a helicopter, once the main jet engine pushed it forward with over forty thousand pounds of thrust.

The tradeoff of packing a second engine in the middle of the plane was that the Marine version of the F-35 couldn't carry as much payload, but Worm's jet would be flying with a light load anyway. The good news was that the training exercise they had been prepping for was a live-fire drill. The bad news was it was for close air support, so he was loaded with only dummy air-to-air missiles and a gun pod he couldn't trust.

Worm clambered into the cockpit and looked down at Miller, the top half of his head encased in a heads-up-display visor-and-helmet combination that looked like a bug's carapace. He shouted and pointed at the jet's fuselage: "The gun? The gun?"

Miller scrambled up the ladder to the cockpit and leaned in close enough to Worm that he could smell the sharp stink of sweat mixed with jet fuel. "Maybe a hundred rounds before it jams," he shouted. Shit. At the machine cannon's rate of fire, that was possibly three seconds' worth of shooting.

Worm gave a quick look at the plane's cockpit screens to make sure the aircraft was running the preflight checks. At least something was working as it should.

For a second, maybe two, Worm allowed himself to think of his fiancée. She'd be out surfing about now, working off some of the dark energy her dreams often left her with. They were supposed to meet at the Moana Surfrider hotel that night for a drink. She hadn't told him which of the bars she'd be in, though; she never did. He would have to find her, and then they would sip mai tais and fantasize about what it would be like to get married there. He had promised her a fairy-tale ending to her story.

The image was dashed as the canopy closed down. Worm flashed a thumbs-up to the crew chief below and mouthed a word.

Payback.

USS *Coronado,* Joint Base Pearl Harbor–Hickam, Hawaii

An antitank rocket fired from a nearby freighter hit the USS *Gabrielle Giffords,* moored nearby. It was unnecessary; the *Giffords* was already taking on water from an explosion below the water line, as were most of the U.S. Navy warships in the harbor.

"Is ATHENA online yet?" shouted Captain Riley. The Automated Threat Enhanced Network Awareness program was like the ship's nervous system, tying together sensors and network nodes with software that was as close to artificial intelligence as the Navy would permit aboard a warship. The ship's autonomous battle-management system allowed a short-handed ship like the *Coronado* to track targets and coordinate with other forces faster than a human crew could manage.

"Almost ready," said one of the crew. "It's still booting up."

"Wake the bitch up! I want targets. And I want this ship protected," said Captain Riley.

"Sir, even when it's online, ATHENA's going to have trouble in port," said Simmons.

"We're already in trouble," said Captain Riley.

"The data flow might overwhelm it. If ATHENA crashes, it'll drag down the rest of the ship's systems, or we might get some blue-on-blue, given the range we're dealing with," said Simmons. "Let the crew fight the ship. Trust them."

Captain Riley squinted the way he did when he knew someone else was right. "Good call, XO," he said. "When ATHENA comes up, keep it in watch mode."

This gave Captain Riley, still in his skivvies, the chance to deliver the order he'd yearned to give all his life. "Main gun, batteries release! Engage enemy ship, the fucker that fired at us," he shouted.

The *Coronado*'s 57 mm main gun came to life; the turret pivoted, pointed an accusing finger off the port side, and then fired across the harbor at the Directorate freighter from which the rocket's smoke trail still extended.

After seven rounds, the main gun's firing paused. And then the realization sank in among the bridge crew. The tiny cannon's five-pound shells were far too small to do any real damage to a hundred-thousand-ton freighter twice the size of a World War II battleship. The LCS had a main gun fit for chasing away pirates, but not much more.

Tracer rounds began to flash toward the *Coronado*, yellow lines reaching out from the freighter and two other ships in the harbor. Their fire hadn't had much of an effect, but it had gotten the other side's attention. Heavy machine-gun rounds clanged into the *Coronado*'s superstructure. A sailor struggling to untie the ship's forward lines from the pier's cleats disappeared in a puff of red.

Simmons peeked his binoculars through the open bridge hatch and panned them quickly around the harbor. He frowned. He could see small boats being launched from the freighters. There were at least nine Navy ships sinking and four others being swarmed by what looked like boarding teams. A fast-moving black dart, a helicopter of some sort, sent a volley of rockets into the bridge of the USS *Pinckney*. In the distance, green tracked vehicles moved down the road closest to the shoreline. He suspected they were not friendly. He put the binoculars down when he heard Captain Riley shout into his headset, "Just someone cut the damn mooring lines!"

The *Coronado*'s foredeck was empty. Bloodstains on the deck marked where two more sailors who'd tried to free the ship had been cut down. Simmons winced, knowing that they would need every sailor they had to get the ship out of this kill zone.

Nearing the *Coronado*'s bow, Horowitz looked up at the bridge. He'd run out of 5.56 mm rounds for his M4 and had been ferrying ammunition to a sailor firing an M249 machine gun at the nearby freighter.

"On it!" Horowitz shouted. He raced inside the nearby passageway and pulled out the fire ax. He ran toward the rope but slipped on a pool of blood and cut his palm on the blade of the ax. He couldn't help himself and laughed. The absurdity of slicing yourself with an ax in the middle of a gunfight.

Horowitz belly-crawled out to the mooring line, staying low to avoid the fire. When he reached it, he jumped up, held the ax high over his head, and then smashed it down on the thick braided-Kevlar line tying the *Coronado* to the pier.

It made little impression; the ax parted only a few strands. He lifted it again, and again. Soon his chest heaved and his arms burned, and he couldn't hear anything but the buzzing in his ears. At some point, a bullet struck the ax head, but Horowitz held it fast despite the ache in his hands.

One of the ship's caterpillar-like SAFFiRs (Shipboard Autonomous Firefighting Robots) crawled onto the deck nearby and was immediately hit. The child-size robot sprayed a cloud of chemical retardant all over the deck before rolling into the water. "One last time," Horowitz said to himself with a grunt, "and then we are out of here."

He didn't see the Directorate PGZ-07 antiaircraft vehicle that rounded the corner on the rise above the pier. Without any targets in the sky, the PGZ trained its twin-barreled 35 mm cannon on the U.S. ships in the harbor, the closest being the *Coronado*.

"Shit," said Simmons as he watched Horowitz's shredded body cartwheel into the water.

"Target, starboard side. Hit that bastard! He's the one who just lit us up," shouted Captain Riley.

The ship's 57 mm Mk 110 cannon rotated away from the freighter and toward the Directorate vehicle as fast as the gunner could pull the targeting joystick. While the main gun couldn't make much of an impact on a hundred-thousand-ton ship, the rounds chewed apart the lightly armored twenty-two-ton vehicle, and it exploded, sending flaming shrapnel through the building behind it.

Simmons was in command mode, listening to his crew on his headset as much as directing them. He heard shouting one moment, then dispassionate descriptions of overheating or damaged equipment. The crew was proving to be good under pressure, which was exactly why he had driven them so hard.

"We've got to go now, Captain. Line's all but cut through," said Simmons.

"You heard him, get us out of here," said Captain Riley.

Simmons recognized the false confidence in his captain's voice. They both knew the *Coronado* would have to battle its way out of the flaming harbor.

A sudden buzzing noise made everyone on the bridge duck. A quadcopter appeared right in front of the bridge's windows, nervously hovering, like a wasp looking for a way inside.

The Mk 110 main gun spun to engage the V1000, but the quadcopter hovered inside the gun's arc of fire, feinting and dodging with the turret's jerky moves as the gunner tried to slew the joystick fast enough to get a shot at it.

The bridge crew froze, expecting a volley of armor-piercing fléchette micro-rockets. The V1000 flared back, flashing a backlit view of its empty rocket pods, and then raced straight up and out of sight.

The crew members looked at one another as if they'd just missed being hit by lightning. Then the quadcopter reappeared a football field's length away and dove between a pair of long warehouses. It popped back up into the air and vectored toward the KITV Channel 4 news chopper that had arrived to collect video of what had been reported as a gas explosion down at the harbor. The V1000 fired a TY-90 air-to-air missile that struck the helicopter well before the weapon reached its Mach 2 maximum speed.

The drop-down bow thruster pushed the *Coronado* slowly away from the pier, and then Stapleton, the main propulsion assistant, gently moved the joystick forward. The *Coronado* roared, its engines moving from idle into action, and the water jets roiled the harbor water. The last Kevlar mooring line started to unravel and then parted with a snap. As the ship began to gather speed, another antitank missile arced from the freighter and exploded inside the helicopter hangar. It felt to the crew like someone had driven a garbage truck into the side of the superstructure, but the ship kept moving.

Simmons looked over at the communications station as heavy machine-cannon fire ripped through the ship's aluminum hull and shattered the sailor sitting there. Sparks and blood mingled together in an instant. More gunfire peppered the bridge, blowing out windows that were strong enough to handle the angry ocean but no match for armor-piercing rounds. He fell to the deck and covered his head as shrapnel fell around him.

When Simmons opened his eyes, he saw Captain Riley next to him on the floor, but sitting upright, his back against the mauled captain's chair. Blood soaked his shirt and pooled on the deck around him.

Another burst of fire slapped into the captain's chair. Frantically, Simmons looked around to see who was driving the ship. Nobody. Stapleton lay in a heap next to his chair, and the ship slowly drifted toward the opposite side of the harbor. Only one of the 3-D battle displays was working; the ATHENA system projected fragmented visuals of the chaos across the room.

"Helm! Somebody drive the goddamn ship," shouted Simmons.

Jefferson ran to the helm and pushed the joystick forward. In one of the many exercises the sailors hated, Simmons had made sure that everyone on the bridge crew was trained to take over the other stations, just in case.

Riley tried to force himself up by his elbows but slid back. Simmons knelt by him and ripped open the captain's shirt, but after that he didn't know where to start or what to do; Riley's entire chest was a bloody mess, his heart pumping more of his life onto the gray deck with each beat. Riley coughed up blood.

"Get back to conning your ship . . . Captain Simmons," Riley said with a slight smile.

Dylan Cote, the ship's corpsman, entered the bridge at a run but slipped on the blood underfoot. On his hands and knees, he crawled to the captain and pushed Simmons aside.

As Cote tried to stanch the blood flow, Simmons carefully rose and stood behind Jefferson at the helm. The captain's chair had jagged holes punched in it, and he wasn't ready to sit in it just yet.

Marine Corps Base, Kaneohe Bay, Hawaii

Worm banked the F-35B hard to the left immediately after takeoff. The jet shifted smoothly into forward-flight mode, and he tried to gain some kind of situational awareness, just like they'd taught him in flight school.

The AN/AAQ-37 electro-optical distributed aperture system fed his helmet with data from visual and IR sensors located around the plane, allowing him to "see" through the plane below. And what he saw was chaos. He'd once flown through a forest fire during a training mission in California's Sierra Nevada mountains; this was worse. All the smoke and debris in the air had created a swirl of darkness with patches of bright sun. Chinese drones darted in and out of the smoke at low levels, and on the deck, along with fragments of Marine Corps helicopters, his squadron's fighters lay scattered about like puzzle pieces. He scanned up and around the sky and confirmed what he'd feared: his was the only U.S. jet in the air.

He started to check on the jet's other systems. No sound came over his radios. The fighter's GPS-coupled inertial navigation system was wrong, showing him as flying over Maui when he knew damn well this was Oahu. Electronically generated false targets flickered on the horizontal situation display and then disappeared. The plane, with its novel software systems and millions of lines of code, was designed to be its own copilot, capable of automation and interpretation never before possible in battle. But at this moment, Worm thought, the fighter was having trouble getting out of its own way, electronically speaking.

Marine aviators had flown for generations with just guns and guts, Worm told himself. He could do the same.

At the near corner of the airfield, he saw one of the tiny Chinese quadcopters firing, its autocannon peppering a parked Osprey tiltrotor aircraft. First, the starboard wing buckled, and then the MV-22's massive engine dropped to the ground, tipping over the ungainly aircraft.

With one hand, Worm slowed the jet's approach, and with the other, he targeted the quadcopter on the touchscreens before him. Then he saw her.

The defiance was unmistakable even at this distance. He magnified the image through his helmet optics, effectively creating a picture inside a picture on the screen superimposed in his cockpit. The Marine fired her pistol at the drone that had rocketed the Osprey. She stood with her feet braced and leaned over the still-smoking engine to steady her aim. She fired a full magazine, then ducked down to reload.

As she drew the magazine from a pouch on her flight suit, the quad-copter dropped to within a few inches of the ground and circled back around her position. She spun around too; Worm saw her chambering the next round as she raised her weapon. He willed his jet's cannon-arming protocol to speed up.

She fired and then darted to the other side of the wreckage, racing to keep it between her and the quadcopter, like a lethal game of musical chairs. Then she slipped in a pool of oil seeping out of the gutted Osprey, twisted her left leg, and fell down in a heap. The pistol skittered a few feet away.

"Shit!" shouted Worm.

The gun-pod light turned red. Active.

The jet shifted position slightly as Worm tried to line up the F-35's cannon. But then the quadcopter drone rose abruptly. It had caught on to the game and was moving to gain an overhead shot on the fallen Marine.

Worm nudged the jet up using its thrust-vectoring nozzles, in effect dancing in the air. As he maneuvered to line up his gun pod, his helmet display showed the Marine crawling toward her pistol. It was lodged beneath a smoldering wing from a nearby wrecked F-35. Jesus, what balls she had, thought Worm.

His finger was already over the trigger, and he pressed down lightly; the jet buffeted as the rounds fired off. The drone opened fire at the same time as Worm's jet loosed a line of training rounds that walked their way up the runway to the quadcopter. The image on the helmet display dissolved into an explosion of smoke and flame, and the drone spun down into the burning Osprey wreck.

Where was she?

His headset suddenly growled at him, and a flash of color danced across one of his displays. The warning from the jet's radar-threat-detection system was unmistakable: an air-defense system was tracking him.

The readout showed that the radar that had washed over his jet wasn't a U.S. system but an H-250 phased array, the updated Directorate mobile-SAM type.

"Oh, shit," said Worm. "That can't be."

It wasn't the threat of being shot down that chilled him despite the sweat in his flight suit. What this meant was much worse than that: they somehow already had major forces on the ground.

The Directorate armored column from the *Golden Wave* and *Hildy Manor* had bulldozed through the parked cars in the lot and left pier 29 behind; after that, the column had split, and the two lines headed off in different directions. One column of Type 99 tanks and their supporting vehicles raced off to link up with Directorate airborne troops disembarking from a trio of Harmony Airways Airbus A380s that had just landed at Honolulu International Airport. The other armored column went down the North Nimitz Highway out of town.

Worm knew where they were heading.

For all the historic value of taking Pearl Harbor, Camp H. M. Smith was the real prize. The headquarters of Pacific Command was designed to house the military's peacetime bureaucracy, not fight off an invasion force. The Marines there would fight to the last round, Worm was certain. But there was no way they could stop a column of tanks. And then the command and control hub of the entire Pacific would be in . . . what? Was the right term *enemy hands*? It was incomprehensible.

Worm rechecked his weapon's state: seventy-one rounds.

He took the plane back down for the deck and raced low across the runway. As he passed, he saw the Osprey's wreckage, and then he saw a figure pop out from behind it. And she waved. What a warrior.

"That Marine needs to get the hell out of there," said Worm, finding himself in conversation with his jet again, as happened when he needed to lock down his fear.

The jet's horizontal situation display revealed a Chinese-made Z-10 attack helicopter moving in toward the runway. It wouldn't take long for the Z-10 to discover the woman's position, and she was clearly fool enough to start taking potshots at it. A fellow Marine needed him and he'd been taught since training that you never, ever left a Marine behind.

But there was the force headed for Camp Smith. He didn't have enough rounds left to take the tanks out completely, but a few low passes might stall them. Maybe he could hit a command vehicle or disable the lead tank.

He eased the jet skyward and gained another five hundred feet, seeking an answer and more knots for the next strafing run.

His options were clear. His choice was not.

U.S. Navy P-8, Pacific Ocean

"Too much jamming, turn off the feed," said Commander Bill "Sweetie" Darling. "Let's focus on Foxglove Two, not the whole war."

Darling couldn't believe he'd just said *war* so casually. That's what it was. America was at war in the Pacific, and he assumed elsewhere in the world. And a few minutes into the war, he could already tell that a major problem would be filtering out useful data from the flow that gushed over them as if from a fire hose.

"Understood," said Hammer, the naval flight officer who handled the plane's communications. "I'll bring it back up if the jamming stops."

Ninety miles from the formation of U.S. ships, Darling's P-8 was on the hunt. A Type 93A submarine that had been tagged Foxglove 2 lurked somewhere nearby. The attack on Pearl Harbor was under way, but for Darling and his crew, the task was the same as it always was on patrol: find and prosecute. This particular submarine had been tailing the USS *George H. W. Bush* for a couple of days. Yesterday, it was just a nuisance that had added some edge to their flight ops. Today, it was an immediate threat that they had to shut down in the next few minutes or face a lifetime of knowing they had failed to protect a big-deck carrier with over four thousand sailors onboard.

Fortunately, Darling's crew had help hunting the Directorate submarine. The USS *John Warner*, a *Virginia*-class nuclear attack submarine, was herding the submarine away from the carrier strike group into the P-8's picket line of sonobuoys. Pinned in, Foxglove 2 would die.

The main battle-network communications feed blared into their headsets, garbled from the jamming.

"Damn it, Hammer, turn that —" said Darling.

Another voice cut him off. "Hydrophone effects. Sonobuoys just located Foxglove Two," said Hyde, one of the two crew members who handled the acoustic sensor systems. "It's heading on a course away from the strike group, twelve knots."

Darling nosed the P-8 over hard to get closer to the sea, pushing the throttles forward and banking the jet toward the intercept point projected on the screen in front of him. The plane's speed edged up to almost five hundred knots as the crew counted down the seconds until they could fire on the submarine.

"At five hundred feet, releasing Mark Fifty-Four —" said his copilot, Fang Treehorn.

"Incoming, incoming. Stonefish inbound on the *Bush*," interrupted Jekyll, the plane's other sensor operator. "Goddamn NSA hackers were supposed to be able to keep those things from even getting off the ground."

Near the horizon, faint white stalks grew skyward from the area around the *Bush*. The fleet's defense systems began firing dozens of RIM-161 SM-3 missiles, designed to intercept incoming Stonefish ballistic missiles as they entered the atmosphere.

"*Bush*'s ATHENA shows it as twenty-six inbound. Our SAMs are countering," Jekyll reported, giving a play-by-play of the air battle.

"Mark Fifty-Four away," said Fang. The plane lifted slightly as the Mark 54 was released, and the torpedo splashed into the water below, its propeller already rotating toward the submarine.

The air-defense communications feed coming through the headphones suddenly became intelligible, then quickly reverted back to garbled noise. Fang had a pair of binoculars up, trying to track the dozens of air-defense missiles that raced up into the sky to meet the warheads arcing down toward the carrier and its escort ships.

"Where'd they come from?" said Fang.

"China," said Darling.

"Yeah, asshole, I know," said Fang. "Surprise attacks don't have just one surprise. Think they're nukes?"

"Nope. If it was a nuke, they'd only send one," said Darling.

"Stonefish inbound in fifteen seconds," said Jekyll, her drawl an attempt to hide the stress she was feeling.

"Mark Fifty-Four impact; Foxglove Two destroyed," said Hyde.

"Ten seconds," said Jekyll.

"Keep working the sonobuoys, Hyde," said Darling. He felt no satisfaction from taking out the sub; the Type 93 hadn't been the main threat after all. He felt worse than unsatisfied — he felt useless. His plane and crew were of no help at this moment.

"Wait, I got one — damn, it's pretty close to us," said Fang, watching through his binoculars. "And here it goes . . . splashdown."

"Shit, ninety miles off target. That's quite a miss," said Darling. "Maybe the Stonefish isn't the bogeyman after all."

Fang kept staring through his binoculars.

"Fang?"

A flash on the horizon gave Darling his answer.

"Impact . . . impact, impact," said Jekyll.

Darling thanked God that they were so far away from the blast, and then a wave of guilt washed over him.

"Get *John Warner* on the net," said Darling, "and see how they want to help with recovery. We need to set up a sonobuoy perimeter around the task force."

"Update from the *Stockdale*'s ATHENA," Jekyll said, naming one of the escort ships. "Confirms what we saw. At least three Stonefish hit the *Bush*. The ship's, um, offline now."

"Can't raise the *John Warner*," said Hammer. "GPS is offline again."

"Same up front. Checking *Warner*'s last location," said Darling. He tried not to look at Fang, who was fiddling with his helmet and surreptitiously wiping tears away.

The P-8 was banked in a turn when Darling saw something in the water below. He squinted, willing the jet lower so he could see. Fang brought his binoculars back up even as the display screens showed the debris in detail.

"That's too far from the task force to be from the *Bush* or any of the escort ships," said Darling. "What is that? Our Directorate sub?"

"No, Foxglove Two's last position is on the grid way over there," said Fang, jabbing a finger at a cockpit screen.

"Shit," said Jekyll, nervously tapping her hand on her knee. "This is the impact point for that Stonefish we saw. It didn't miss. That's what's left of the *John Warner*."

Marine Corps Base, Kaneohe Bay, Hawaii

The F-35 rotated its nose up and then looped over in a corkscrew twist, giving Worm one last view of the sky through the bottom of his plane.

Seventy-one rounds. Worm designated the target, feeling the jet adjust slightly.

As he arced back down toward the Osprey's wreckage, he saw the defiant Marine pop up and begin running.

Just seventy-one rounds.

Worm found the Z-10 strafing a smoking hangar 100 yards away from her. One of the quadcopters saw her and raced toward her position, then hovered to beckon the helicopter over. Worm dipped the nose of the jet and eased the throttle forward. With a gentle adjustment, he rolled out and centered the helmet-mounted pipper on the Z-10. He relaxed his g slightly to stay on the target and then squeezed the trigger.

The opening burst from the F-35's cannon went high, passed over the Z-10, and ripped apart the runway just beyond.

Forty-seven rounds.

She ran faster, not looking back even at the ripping sound in the sky behind her.

Worm fired a longer burst and the whole jet vibrated like a tuning fork. The Z-10 jerked sideways, then broke in half, spewing flame and debris in a near-perfect circle. The fuselage groaned in protest as Worm pulled back on the stick to arrest his descent.

The runner was nowhere to be seen. She had made it; he'd done his first duty: he hadn't left a Marine behind.

Worm jammed the throttle forward to its stops and unloaded to accelerate toward Camp H. M. Smith as fast as possible. Having some American airpower overhead might give the armored Directorate column second thoughts, maybe even force it to divert to another target. He had nothing else to offer. The cannon was empty. Landing to rearm was out of the question. He'd harass the Directorate column as long as he could and then punch out somewhere up north near one of the parks.

As the F-35 accelerated away, the robotic quadcopter turned and loosed an air-to-air missile. It then blithely went back to its original task of raking the row of Ospreys on the runway.

Even before Worm heard the alarm buzz, the plane's AN/ASQ-239 Barracuda system had automatically activated. The system's ten tiny antennas embedded in the F-35's wing edges began to track the enemy missile's radar. Worm's visor projected that it was a TY-90, a fire-and-forget missile, so even with its robot master focused elsewhere, it was still a threat. With the missile homing in on him, he pulled the F-35 hard right toward the Ulupau Crater at the end of the base. With just a little bit of luck, he thought, he'd disappear in the clutter around the old dormant volcano. He'd be damned if he was going to be the first Marine pilot to get shot down by a drone.

Worm's fate, though, had been decided several months earlier. A section of microchips had been replaced during maintenance. This was nothing unusual for a plane packed with thousands of chips that ran everything from avionics to the gun camera.

The first microchips that had powered everything from the early computers to the jet planes of the 1960s had all their components visible to the naked eye. By the turn of the twenty-first century, however, microchips packed millions of transistors into an area measured in square millimeters. And every chip was further divided into multiple subunits, called blocks, each of which carried out different functions. Much like the chips inside a smartphone, the processor in Worm's F-35 gun camera, for example, had blocks that did everything from store frames of video to convert files.

When the microchip industry took off, it grew from just a handful of companies to more than two thousand, most of them in China, each creating five thousand new chip designs every year. These designs involved thousands of people at multiple locations, each team working on a different block, sometimes building it from scratch, sometimes contracting it out, and other times buying it from a third-party specialist. And each of those block designs was integrated into millions of chips, and those chips went into everything from toasters to Tomahawk missiles.

The result was a dangerous combination: The chips became so complex that no single engineer or team of engineers could understand how all their parts actually worked; the design process was so distributed that no one could vet all the people involved; and the chips were manufactured and bought in such great numbers that not even a tiny percentage could be tested, which almost no buyers, including the big American defense firms, even tried to do. Efficiency always beat security.

For a long time, defense analysts had worried about the notion of a kill switch — a chip that would shut down an entire computer system on command. But on Worm's plane, the opposite happened. In each of just twelve microchips, a tiny piece of technology inside a single block woke up.

The F-35B was protected by its shape and stealth materials that shrank its radar signature to a size smaller than a metal fist. But as the Directorate missile's radar washed over the plane, it activated a tiny antenna hidden in the ninth block of each of twelve microchips that linked Worm's helmet-display system to the plane's flight-control system. Even if the helmet's manufacturers had performed a security scan when they'd bought the microchips, they still would have missed it. Each antenna was microscopic, hidden inside a one-millimeter square and activated only by a specific frequency of an incoming missile. While each antenna had just a tiny amount of energy on its own, the combination of them sent enough power to broadcast what was, in effect, a homing signal.

As Worm accelerated away, the missile picked up the signal and pursued the fighter.

Worm dove toward the palms of the Ulupau Crater in a bid to mask his plane from the missile's radar. He grunted as the g-forces pushed him down into his seat, then he jinked hard. He should have been able to shake it. But whatever he did made no difference today; the missile followed his every move.

In his last moments, Worm glanced down at the watch his fiancée had given him for his thirty-first birthday, a Breitling Aggressor digital chronograph. It was as much to think of her one last time as it was to, like a physician, mark the time of death.

The missile rode the giveaway signal like a rail and slammed into the side of the F-35, splitting the jet into two pieces that tumbled into the Pacific.

USS *Coronado,* Joint Base Pearl Harbor–Hickam, Hawaii

Simmons knew the outcome of the next few moments would be a binary choice: Win or lose. Live or die.

As the *Coronado* pushed back from the pier, fresh air began flowing through blown-out windows and holes shot through the aluminum superstructure. Only Directorate helicopters and drones circled in the sky. One of the helicopters had just dive-bombed into the open side of the hangar deck of the USS *Boxer.* The amphibious assault ship, used by the Fifteenth Marine Expeditionary Unit, burst into flames, setting fire to the ship moored behind it, some kind of transport Simmons couldn't identify.

A chainsaw-like noise and then a line of yellow tracers arcing out from the ship snapped Simmons back into focus. The *Coronado*'s Mk 110 gun engaged one of the smaller surveillance drones that swooped inside its line of fire.

Simmons couldn't see any other U.S. ships moving from their moorings; that made the *Coronado* an even more conspicuous target.

"All ahead full. Take it to twenty-five knots," said Simmons. "When we pass the *Arizona* memorial, make it forty, and then once we're clear in the channel, flank speed. No matter what, fast as the ship can make."

"Aye, Captain," said Jefferson without hesitation. Good man. Normally, running a 418-foot ship at that reckless speed inside a harbor was a quick way to a brutal collision or grounding, not to mention a court-martial. But now all that mattered was escaping the harbor's kill box.

The *Coronado* jerked forward, and it felt for a moment as if the trimaran's hull was moving at a different speed than the superstructure above. Simmons hoped the ship wouldn't come apart. Between the rocket hits and the earlier impact of the REMUS, there was no telling how much damage had been done. The squat effect of the engines' powering lifted the bow higher than the stern, like a kid doing a wheelie on a bike, but the ship evened out as it accelerated onto a plane past the smoldering hulks of the Pacific Fleet and then the old *Arizona* and *Missouri* memorials. The first ship had already been sunk, while the second didn't seem to have a scratch on it. The *Coronado* had a clear shot at one of the Directorate freighters but Simmons didn't bother. The LCS was fast, but another wrinkle of her design was that the main gun wobbled so badly at high speeds that it wasn't even worth the shot.

The *Coronado* was accelerating around the turn in the bay when the burning USS *Lake Erie,* a *Ticonderoga*-class Aegis cruiser, detonated its entire magazine. The shock wave pitched the *Coronado,* almost swamping the ship before the ride-control system automatically righted it. The water jets were picking up speed, though, and the ship exited the harbor at forty-eight knots, racing away as a final Directorate rocket-propelled grenade landed a hundred feet short.

"ATHENA, damage? Crew status," Simmons barked into his command headset.

"Sys-fig ship tor ween loss," the computer replied. "Par rew tactical ment offline ties."

"What the hell? Cortez, damage and crew status," Simmons said, cupping his hands around his mouth against the wind rushing through the bridge.

Lieutenant Horatio Cortez, the tactical action officer who was now the XO by default, looked over and nodded. Then the former Naval Academy water polo player seemed to stare right through his superior officer. It wasn't fear or disrespect; he was focusing on the projections inside his Oakley tactical viz glasses. A bloody thumbprint smeared the left lens, but from the inside, he could see visuals of the ship's data stream.

"ATHENA's still monitoring the ship, but something in its comms hardware has been damaged. Superstructure — well, you can see that, sir. One of the diesels is leaking coolant, so we're going to need to bring our speed down soon. Bow section has a foot of water, but it's under control. Main gun down to fifteen rounds, and fire control is iffy. Communications are still out," said Cortez.

"Casualties?" said Simmons, looking at the captain's chair. The *Coronado* was already undercrewed by design; for the sake of efficiency, went the thinking. In peacetime, losing anyone out of the tight duty rotation was a headache. During war, it could be deadly to the ship and the entire crew.

"ATHENA shows twelve KIA," said Cortez. "Eleven wounded."

"Goddamn it," muttered Simmons, then, realizing he'd left the headset microphone on transmit, he fumbled to shut it off.

"Where to now, sir?" asked Jefferson. Simmons could see a dark wet spot on the top of Jefferson's head, but he wasn't sure if it was Jefferson's blood or someone else's.

"Sir?" someone else quietly asked.

What now? His father had said this was what command was like, a constant stream of questions. He wheeled sharply. It was the corpsman, Cote. Shit, how could he have forgotten about the captain? Then he saw Cote's face and realized it didn't matter anymore.

"A moment, sir," said Cote. "Take off your shirt."

Simmons looked at Cote with a mix of anger and incomprehension. "Not now," said Simmons.

"Sir, let me do my job," said Cote.

Simmons quickly pulled off his uniform top and felt a sharp sting behind his right shoulder blade, some kind of cut he hadn't even realized was there.

Cote removed a small silver aerosol bottle from a waist pack and sprayed it on the wound. In an instant, the pain was gone, and Simmons could feel his shoulder relax.

"Okay, Cortez, when Cote is done, help him get Captain Riley's body below. He doesn't deserve this," said Simmons. "Jefferson, let's dip the towed-array sonar to see what's out there. I'll try to link with PACOM to find out what the hell they want us to do. Keep everyone at stations."

While Simmons was tucking his shirt in, Cote studied his new captain. Without a word, the corpsman detached a hard plastic case from his belt and examined the dozens of color-coded pills inside, reverently holding the case as if it were a small Bible.

"Here, sir," said Cote. "There's a —"

"Just give them to me," Simmons said, and he downed three tabs. He knew what they were by the colors: a green modafinil for endurance and focus, an orange beta-blocker to steady his nerves, and a yellow desmopressin to boost his memory and keep him from having to leave the bridge to pee.

Cote and Cortez were carrying the body toward the hatch when an alarm from the tactical display made them both stop. They left Riley's body at the sill of the hatch and raced back to their stations.

"Ah, shit, hydrophone effects," said Jefferson as the sonar readings started to come in. "Torpedo in the water, sir. Bearing oh-four-five. It's close, three thousand yards."

At that moment, Simmons realized that his first ship command would not be a long one. Of course the Directorate would leave nothing to chance. Some Type 93 sub was probably lurking at the entrance to sink any survivors who managed to make it out of Pearl Harbor. All he'd accomplished was to take the *Coronado* from one trap right into another.

Simmons tried to stay calm. "Bring us back up to flank speed. If they want to get us, they're going to have to race for it."

PART 3

All warfare is based on deception.

— SUN-TZU, *THE ART OF WAR*

Duke's Bar, Waikiki Beach, Hawaii Special Administrative Zone

She was a goddess.

Xiao Zheng knew he would never have had a chance with a girl like this back home in Wuhan. When he was in elementary school, he'd thought being surrounded by so many boys and so few girls was a good thing. But at eighteen, Xiao realized that all it meant was that even the ugliest ducklings had their pick of the boys. And he was not the kind of boy they picked. He wore thick black bamboo-framed glasses because he was the only one in his unit whose eyes hadn't responded well to the mandatory vision-enhancement surgery.

The goddess wore a flowing blue skirt and a tight white tank top; she had a leather backpack-style purse slung across her shoulder.

As she entered Duke's, she adjusted her white-framed sunglasses on the bridge of her nose and let down her ebony hair. Xiao had to tell himself to start breathing again. He'd been deployed in Honolulu for three months now and he still had trouble working up the courage to speak to the female marines in his unit.

As she crossed the room, a group of sailors shouted at her in broken English to come drink with them. She ignored them, and Xiao's heart soared.

The vision made her way through the crowded bar, smiling at the other girls scattered among the tables drinking vodka shots or white wine with the various Directorate soldiers. These were prostitutes, most of them flown in from back home. But this one was clearly something different. Xiao Zheng knew he was staring, but the young Directorate marine couldn't help himself. She stopped at the bar and pushed her sunglasses up on the top of her head. The way she held herself made it clear she could not be bought. She had to be earned.

For the next hour, he watched her. With someone so beautiful, sometimes watching was enough.

"Another round!" shouted Bo Dai from the barstool next to Xiao Zheng, elbowing Xiao in the ribs. A microphone on Bo's digital dog tags around his neck transmitted the command to a small translator he wore on his belt. The card-deck-size device scratchily conveyed his bellowed command in tinny English a moment later. Bo was the senior enlisted marine in Xiao's squad, and he usually looked out for him.

Nine brimming shot glasses arrived quickly, as if the bartender had anticipated the order.

"Drink, you pussy," Bo shouted at the top of his lungs before putting Xiao in a gentle headlock. The translator device started to convey the bawdy order before Bo silenced it with a drunken slap.

Xiao cringed and downed the shot. It was warm tequila, and he gagged as Bo whooped.

"Okay, no more of this mooning over some local whore. I need to know my best assistant machine gunner is not afraid of girls, because if he is, then what's he going to do when the Americans from California come for us with both barrels?" Bo mimed an enormous pair of breasts.

The big sergeant dragged Xiao over to the goddess and set him down on the barstool next to her like an offering. Xiao stood back up. His knees trembled. He had to get out of there. Go anywhere but where he really wanted to be.

Xiao's legs were unsteady; he turned to go but knocked over the stool. A lithe and deeply tanned arm reached out to catch him by the shoulder before he fell too. "Easy there, sailor," she said.

She touched me! Xiao wanted to shout.

What to say? What was the Hawaiian phrase for "hello" they had learned? O-la-ha? No — he wanted her to hear his own words, even if he didn't know what they should be.

But before he could say anything to the goddess, her sunglasses fell to the floor, and she slipped off her stool and bent down to pick them up, giving Xiao an unforgettable view.

"I need to go wash these off. Then you can buy me a drink?" she asked.

Xiao nodded silently and she smiled before disappearing into the back of the crowded bar. He fished in his pocket for some bills to pay the bartender for another wine for her so it would be waiting when she returned.

"Shit!" he cursed out loud. He stumbled and rushed back to the table where he had been sitting earlier. His wallet had to be there.

His squad mates registered the intense look on Xiao's face as he dropped to all fours in front of everyone in the restaurant and began crawling under the table, looking for his wallet. There. Under a wrapper of soy chips lay his wallet, damp with beer. He stuffed it into his back pocket and stood up.

The other marines were laughing at him. Some barked like small dogs.

"Little friend, if you need a condom, I've got plenty," Bo said.

Xiao turned away from Bo's crude hand gestures and pushed through the crowd to the back of the bar, stumbling over toes and slipping on a slime of spilled liquor and beer. He made it without falling and stood in the darkened entrance to the bathroom. Was this the right place to wait? It was quieter. He cast a look over his shoulder to make sure none of his squad were going to humiliate him again.

All clear. When he turned around, there she was, standing close enough for him to kiss, if he had had the courage.

"Did you forget my drink?" she said.

Xiao flushed and looked down at his feet, again catching another eyeful of her breasts. She put a hand on his belt buckle and tugged slightly. He leaned back, and she tugged just a little bit harder.

"That's okay, we don't need it. Come with me," she said and led him away from the bathrooms. "Where it's quieter."

"Yes, better," he muttered, but not loud enough for the translator to pick up. He followed her down the humid stairway that led from the bar's main room to a pitch-black storage area.

As they reached the bottom of the stairs, he realized that she was taller than him. But as she drew his face into her breasts, he decided he was just the right size.

Lavender and talc. It felt like all the blood that had rushed to his cheeks was now flowing to his groin. He felt a new courage rising up inside him. *Bo was right! I should have gotten a condom when I had the chance.*

She sighed and held him closer, drawing the moment out.

His body stiffened and then spasmed as the sharpened stem of the white sunglasses drove in just behind his jawbone, severing his internal carotid artery.

University of Wisconsin, Madison

When she saw the two men in matching gray suits enter the back of the lecture hall, Vernalise Li realized she should have listened to her mother's warnings.

But instead she'd told her mom that she needed to stop reading *Wikipedia*, that what had happened to the Japanese Americans in the 1940s wouldn't happen in the twenty-first century. People were better than that now. Or so she'd thought.

She continued lecturing, unconsciously adopting a more Southern Californian accent with each word.

"From here, you can see that a rack-mount power system has its limitations. What are they? Space, for sure," she said.

So what if she'd been born in Beijing? She had grown up in Santa Monica.

"But the advantage? Density. By using a fluid-based energy-storage system that, with a conformable design, we can address industrial pulse-power applications where the current rack designs fall short."

She had played beach volleyball in high school. Varsity!

"The switch today operates for four milliseconds, and we are working to increase power density. That goes back to the question of how to store the energy. It always comes back to density, and fluid is the answer."

She watched the two men take seats. The suits were evidently cheap, likely Dockers, but it didn't matter. If they wanted to blend in, wearing suits and ties on campus any day but graduation wasn't the way to go. Then she noticed they weren't wearing viz glasses, so they weren't even recording the lecture. Were they just checking in to make sure students were actually in class? It wouldn't be surprising; the whole campus knew conscription was coming.

"The other element is addressing contamination in the switches, which always, always, always leads to shorter minority carrier lifespan.

Plus, we're maximizing peak power again, which makes contamination a major cause of degradation in these light-activated switch designs."

So what was their deal? No one attended a lecture on the mathematical dynamics of pulsed-power systems for fun.

"Okay," she said, wrapping up. "You know where to find me on the course sim later if you have any questions."

"I'd like to ask one, with your students' permission, of course," said Professor Leonowsky, who'd stopped by earlier and was sitting in the front row. He perched his viz glasses atop his bald head and smiled with the ease of someone for whom the pressure of the tenure clock was a distant memory.

"Everyone, we're not done yet. Have we all got a few more minutes? Of course we do," said Leonowsky, as ever answering his own question.

"Certainly," said Vern, hiding her trembling hands behind her back. Why did believing you were about to be accused of an unnamed crime make you feel guilty, even when you knew you were innocent? She could barely speak Mandarin, at least not without a horrible American accent, as her mother never failed to remind her.

"Let's get to the practicalities. What can anyone really do with a fluid-based battery the size of a house with only short-term storage capabilities?" Leonowsky asked. "There's no market for that as far as I can see. Can you?"

He was on the tenure committee and would often drop in on junior professors' lectures and ask pointed questions, just so no one would forget his role as a gatekeeper to their future careers.

"We don't know. Yet," Vern said, fighting the stammer welling up inside her. "What I'm saying is, no one can anticipate what future needs might be. Maybe it's bigger sims, or . . ."

The men in the back of the room stared intently at her. They did not even blink.

"I'm just not sure. But that we don't know the applications now doesn't mean we won't find a use later. Back when computers were first developed, the CEO of IBM thought the world market would be only five computers in total. We know how that worked out," said Vern.

"Indeed, but obviously, not every invention is comparable to the computer," said Professor Leonowsky.

Tenure be damned, Vern just wanted out of the room, away from those men. She looked down at her sandals and back up at her future.

"My answer is that I will have to get you a better answer," said Vern.

"I think that would be for the best," said Leonowsky.

Students were bolting out of the room. Vern was embarrassed by her performance but relieved to see that at least the two men were gone now.

Professor Leonowsky was occupied with a pair of first-year graduate students. If she moved quickly, she could get out without having to talk to anyone. Right now she needed something to eat and a half-hour dive somewhere tropical to chill out. Maybe the Turks and Caicos sim.

She was bent over her bag, struggling with the buckle, when the letters *FBI* appeared a few inches in front of her face.

She looked up. One of the suits stood before her. He held a worn black leather wallet that revealed a badge and ID. The other man was back at the door, blocking the room's only exit.

"Miss Vernalise Li? We need you to come with us."

That's Dr. *Li,* she thought to herself. But she didn't bother to correct him.

"No handcuffs?" she asked bitterly. "You're not even going to frisk me? You'll at least get a good write-up in the campus paper: 'Chinese Spy Busted in Our Midst!'"

The agent shook his head and put his hand on her shoulder. He spoke in a whisper, with the awkward gentleness of somebody not used to caring what other people thought of what he said.

"Miss Li, it's not like that. Not at all. We're here for your protection. Everything you said today matters more than you can imagine."

Fort Mason, San Francisco

Captain Jamie Simmons wiped the sweat from his forehead. Having to take a bus and then walk uphill from the stop was not the way he imagined a Navy officer would return home after nine months at sea. But at least he was home.

Home now meant an officer's quarters in Fort Mason, in San Francisco's Marina District. Overlooking the Bay, it was priceless real estate even in wartime. The Navy might have been pushed around at sea, but it was clearly having its way on land. Marines guarded checkpoints and blocked civilian traffic from entering Bay Street. A pair of tan air-defense Humvees, bristling with missiles, were parked at the corner of Laguna and Bay. Each pointed four AIM-120 SLAMRAAMs (Surface-Launched Advanced Medium-Range Air-to-Air Missiles) accusingly to the west. Across the water, high up on Hawk Hill in Marin, were more missile batteries and a radar installation under construction. The Directorate had made no moves to push beyond the edge of its so-called Eastern Pacific Stability Zone, so the only action the National Guardsmen manning the mobile batteries had seen so far were after-noon games of soccer with the neighborhood kids.

On the sidewalk in front of Jamie's house, a small crowd had gath-ered. For the most part, they were people he did not know. Squaring his shoulders, he forced a smile and walked up to them. They took in his captain's insignia and then paused at the scar just above his right eye. They shook his hand. Some even hugged him. He was the hero who'd commanded the only ship that had fought its way out of Pearl. Everyone needs some hope, and people seemed to get it just from touching Jamie. They chose to ignore that everything since that day had gone from bad to worse, both for Jamie and America.

The front door opened and his kids rushed out, crashed into his legs, and hung on with their lovingly desperate grip.

"Claire, Martin, I missed you sooooo much," said Jamie. "You're all grown up!"

He lifted a child in each arm, swaying slightly as if he were back at sea. The crowd on the sidewalk backed off, giving him space. They knew how it was.

Martin leaned in to Jamie's ear. "Daddy, I made you a sign inside. Did you bring me anything?"

Jamie smiled sadly. "Sorry, not tonight," he said. "Show me the sign."

"I made it first," said Claire, trying to win back his attention.

Jamie set the kids down as Lindsey approached.

Her dark brown hair was shorter than he remembered. She stood on her tiptoes and he kissed her, savoring the feel of her hair as it brushed across his cheek. That moment was something no sim could capture.

She also looked thinner than he remembered, likely from the worry he'd put her through. She was even thinner than when he'd first seen her, running the Burke-Gilman trail near the University of Washington on a rainy spring morning. A smile was all it took for him to notice her. Though he had already been exhausted from crew practice, he'd kept running just for a chance to ask her name when she finally stopped, four miles later at a water fountain.

"Over here," said Claire, pulling on his hand. "Come see the sign we made."

Martin studied his father's uniform intently. "I like your ribbons. Do you want some cereal?" he said.

"Later we can have some," said Jamie. "Right now, I want to see this sign."

Martin and Claire led their father into the sparsely furnished living room, no rug, only a couch and a single chair.

"Not much here," said Lindsey. "The rest is still in San Diego."

"Lots of room for parties, at least," said Jamie, looking around the room as the guests began to file in. Navy dress uniforms, spouses in suits or cocktail dresses, and a lot of kids. Before the war, you wouldn't have seen so many kids at a party like this, Jamie thought. Now, everyone wanted to keep them close.

"They've all been waiting for this moment. I've been waiting. All part of Navy life, right, Captain?" said Lindsey, stretching out his new rank.

Jamie took in her smile and brought her close. Wives were usually there for promotion ceremonies, but it had all been done on the fly as they prepped for the shitstorm that the Guam relief mission had turned into.

"Daddy, over here!" shouted Martin. "No kissing!"

Jamie navigated through a series of hugs and handshakes to get to where a three-foot-by-five-foot *Welcome Home Dady!* sign hung. Purple and green crayon, the kids' respective favorite colors, covered the entire sign, which meant no one else had been allowed to contribute.

"Wow, this is amazing," said Jamie.

He knelt down and hugged both kids hard, fighting back tears.

Then he detected a faint, acrid smell. It was the pungent musk of a life pledged to steel ships, to wooden piers coated in tarry creosote, and to a losing battle against rust and rot. Still kneeling, Jamie slowly looked over and saw the black leather work boots. The boots were old, worn, nicked, and creased. But they still shone, the bulbs of the steel toes giving off an eight ball's luster. The boots were turned out slightly, maybe ten degrees at the left, fifteen degrees at the right. It was a ready stance, as if the world might pitch or heave at any moment. Jamie's body recognized it all first and sent an icy blast of adrenaline into his veins before his brain could process the presence of his father.

"Chief?" said Jamie as he slowly stood. "What are you doing here?"

Lindsey jumped in before an answer could come. "Your father's been here every weekend since we arrived, doing everything from machining a new pedal for Martin's bike to playing games with the kids so I could take a shower," said Lindsey. "He's been really helpful."

Mike just held out his right hand. It was meant to be a welcoming gesture, yet the sheer size of the hand hinted at malice or injury. The back of the hand was scrubbed red, but creosote, rust, and grease still seemed to ooze from the pores. The missing tip of the pinkie was more evidence that these hands were tools first.

"Hello, James," said Mike. He stared at Jamie, daring his son to say what he really thought.

"He's made a real difference here," said Lindsey, still trying to smooth over the moment.

"I wish I could take credit for the sign, but I have been able to help with the house. With all the Directorate cyber-attacks, the fridge won't talk to the phone, and the toilet doesn't know whether to flush or clean itself without instructions from its Beijing masters. I can't fix the digital stuff, but I can at least clean up and rig some workarounds," said Mike.

Jamie released his two kids and shook the hand, suddenly without the confident grip he had expected to use.

"Okay, kids, go show your friends the sandbox Grandpa built," said Lindsey.

For the next hour, Lindsey stayed close to Jamie. She had always been good at this sort of thing, the chitchat, the empty *How are you*s, and all he could think about was his father walking the perimeter of his yard, keeping an eye on his kids, nursing a can of Coke.

Soon, the party began to break up, the guests having put in their appearances but knowing they weren't supposed to linger.

When Lindsey went inside to clean up, there was no longer a way for Jamie to avoid talking to his father. The two men took their drinks and stood on the back patio, their silhouettes indistinguishable from each other. They looked down at the Fort Mason Green, toward the piers that had once hosted jazz concerts and winetastings. A pair of pockmarked Littoral Combat Ships and four Mark VI patrol boats nuzzled the piers. Their tiny silhouettes made the absence of the larger warships that should have been there all the more obvious.

"Helluva nice house, Captain," said Mike. "Can't say I've ever had any admirals for neighbors. Must go with the promotion."

"What's going on here?" said Jamie, ignoring his father's attempt at small talk.

"I figured Lindsey could use the help," said Mike.

"You did? You don't even know her, or the kids. You didn't even come to our wedding," said Jamie.

"War changes things for all of us," said Mike.

"I'll say." Jamie looked at the walnut-size knuckles he knew were as hard as stones. "I don't think I ever saw you drink a soda in my entire life."

Each man took a sip of his drink and waited for the other to speak. The silence was occasionally broken by the laughing and howling of kids.

"The Navy Cross is a helluva thing, James," said Mike, changing tack.

"It's because I got the *Coronado* out," said Jamie. "Riley died right in front of me at Pearl."

"Still don't know how you did it with an LCS," said Mike. He growled out each letter with disdain. "Better ships didn't."

"Easy, Chief, *Coronado* is still my ship," said Jamie. "At least, what's left of it."

"Well, she made you captain; you're always gonna owe her that," said Mike. "Any idea what they're going to do with her?"

"Maybe make a museum or memorial out of it, when the war's over," said Jamie. "Or maybe turn it into dog tags. All that metal we need has to come from somewhere . . . We could patch up the hits we took at Pearl, but the missile hit we took in the Guam relief op wrecked the whole engine room for good."

"You don't belong here with her. You belong at sea."

"Of all the people to say that," muttered Jamie.

"So now we're starting again?" said Mike. "Okay, I deserved that. I wasn't as good at the home stuff as I was at the job."

"You could have been," said Jamie. "If you'd just tried half as hard at your more important job of taking care of your kids. Both of them."

"Goddamn it, don't you lay that blame on me," said Mike. "Even if I'd been home, I couldn't have saved her."

"It's *Mackenzie*. Say her name," growled Jamie.

The two stared at each other in silence as Martin and Claire played tag in the yard beyond them.

"So, how is it really for the fleet?" said Mike, trying again to steer the discussion to easier ground.

"There's a word for doing the same thing over and over and thinking it will have different results," said Jamie. "I'm sure you heard, they sunk the *Ford* and the *Vinson*. The exact minute we crossed their Eastern Pacific Stability Zone line, just like they had warned. Both the carriers and even the subs. We still pushed on after that, and things got worse."

"What the hell is going on? Too much power in those ships for 'em to be just torn apart like that."

"Air Force's toy planes are all hacked and can't get off the ground while the Directorate owns the heavens — satellites, space stations, everything. They can see every move we make and target at will. We knew they'd eventually be able to do that to the surface ships, but now even the subs can't hide. And if they can't hide —"

"They go from sharks to chum," said Mike.

"Only the boomers were left untargeted," said Jamie, referring to the ballistic missile submarines that made up the strategic nuclear force.

"They wouldn't hit them, not unless they wanted us to cut their population by half," said Mike. "We should have done that when the Chinese first showed up at Pearl. After what the airstrikes did to the Twenty-Fifth ID base in Hawaii and all those Marines on Oahu? Fucking butchers. They were asking for us to nuke them. We still should."

"I really hope it doesn't come to that," said Jamie.

"It will, mark my words," said Mike. "I'm telling you, we should have nuked 'em the minute things started to go south. At least the chairman of Joint Chiefs had the honor to resign when the so-called commander in chief pussied out."

"That's just the spin he put on it after he got fired," said Jamie. "By the time the national command authority figured out what was happening, it had already happened. After that, strategic calculus changed; going nuclear would just be revenge to the point of suicide. Hell, given how deep the Chinese penetrated our comms net, no one could even have known if the nuke orders would go through. We might just have been giving them a pretext to strike us first."

"We should still just do it, and do it now. Just nuke Beijing, Shanghai, and make sure you get Hainan too," said Mike. "No diplomacy, no more of that 'reimagining-our-world' bullshit from those eunuchs on TV. We should make their cities glow."

"What about Moscow?" said Jamie. "Should we nuke that too? How about Paris, Rome, and Berlin, for not stepping up to join a fight an ocean away from them that was already over? And Tokyo, for kindly helping us clean up our bases and then asking us to leave? If we went with your plan, the whole world would be glowing, including here." He nodded over to where the kids were still chasing each other.

Mike tipped his Coke can to the unlit Golden Gate Bridge and the black void separating San Francisco and Marin.

"The greedy bastards could have just bought the Golden Gate," said Mike.

"I thought they already did, four years back," said Jamie.

"No, that was the Carquinez Bridge, some toll-road crap," said Mike.

"Well, this isn't over. Hawaii's not giving up either. Resistance is heating up there. A lot of the troops who made it out fought in Iraq and Afghanistan. They saw insurgency up close, and I hear they're trying it themselves now," said Jamie.

"Payback is a bitch," said Mike.

Both men paused to listen to the chorus of kids' laughter as they ran by in the dark.

"Lindsey's been really good through all this," said Mike. "Some people, they literally forgot how to drive, so they've been paralyzed since the Chinese knocked out our GPS. No more auto-drives, and they're just stuck without anyone at the wheel. Like America. Not your wife, though; I wish there were more like her in this country," said Mike.

Jamie paused mid-sip and gazed silently at his dad. How was it possible that he was here? How was it possible that he knew better than Jamie how his own wife was doing?

"Just look at this party," Mike continued. "You'd never think her husband's ship had been shot to pieces and assumed lost just a little while ago. You will not find a stronger or better woman. You know how I know that?"

"How?" said Jamie.

"She let me in the front door," said Mike.

"That's because she doesn't know you," said Jamie.

"James, I made the effort. It's been fourteen years since you saw me. I'm different now, because of your mom, because of your sister's death, because of a lot of things," said Mike.

"And here you are. Like I should just forget it all," Jamie said.

The two men stared at each other in silence.

"All right, then, have it your way. I tried. I should get going anyway," said Mike. "I've got an early day tomorrow."

"Aren't they all now?" said Jamie. "Mentor Crew job, eh?"

The initial wave of losses had whittled down not just the frontline fleet but also its human capital. The Mentor program was started as a way to tap into the expertise that still remained among those too old to be drafted back into service. The old, retired noncommissioned officers had been spread out among the fleet, the idea being that they would help guide the transition for all the new crews that had to be trained up.

"I damn well wasn't going to fight this war as a contractor," said Mike.

"So, where do they have you working?"

"I can't get into it right now," said Mike. "Not even with you."

"Some things don't change," said Jamie, with a bitter edge in his voice.

"You'll see. They really do," said Mike, turning and walking down to say goodbye to the kids.

Directorate Command, Honolulu, Hawaii Special Administrative Zone

I live in lonely desolation,
And wonder when my end will come.

Pushkin should have joined military intelligence, thought Colonel Vladimir Andreyevich Markov. The Russian Spetsnaz officer poured himself another glass of hot tea and continued to read, the world of poetry his one escape from the stack of memos from General Yu Xi-lai's office. The collection of Pushkin poetry was well traveled, having accompanied him to Chechnya, Georgia, Ukraine, Tajikistan, Sudan, and Venezuela. And now another war zone's humidity and grime was working its way into the book's spine, softening it, loosening its grip on the pages one by one.

His office door slammed open, shaking the flimsy desk and making tea spill all over. He used his sleeve to sop up the liquid before it soaked more of the book.

"What!" he shouted in English, the one language they shared.

His aide, Lieutenant Jian Qintong, stood at attention in front of him.

"A Directorate marine is dead, sir," said Jian. "A young private from the Hundred and Sixty-Fourth Brigade."

"It's a war; you should expect people to die," said Markov.

It had been three weeks since he'd arrived at this former vacation paradise. The assignment was part of the alliance deal: he was to liaise with the Directorate to provide a Russian presence and, supposedly, to pass on his hard-won expertise in counterinsurgency. But so far, no one other than Jian was listening to him, and Jian listened only because he'd been tasked to spy on him, Markov was sure.

At his first briefing for General Yu, Markov had led with the overriding lesson that defeating an insurgency was accomplished not by crushing one's foes but by understanding them.

Maybe it was a translation error, or maybe the general was just too thickheaded to get it, but Yu had taken his recommendation for empathy as a sign of weakness, and the meeting had gone south from there. Yu clearly resented the idea of an adviser being sent into his command, as it required one to admit the possibility that one was in error. At the end of the meeting, General Yu was polite in his thanks but said he had more than enough experience in "population-supervision techniques" from his time stamping out the last rebellion in Tibet. Markov then wondered aloud how long it would take the general to realize they were dealing with something different than holdout adherents of the last Dalai Lama.

After that exchange, the Russian had been kept busy, sent off base on various missions, but he was never again part of the actual command sessions. And for every trip outside the wire, Jian would be by his side, his around-the-clock shadow, not so much to keep him out of trouble but to make sure he didn't cause any.

"The local commander reports it as an assassination by insurgents," said Jian now.

Markov raised his eyebrows. "Assassinating an enlisted man? The only thing less effective would be assassinating staff lieutenants." Markov had turned the burden Yu had placed on him into a gift; teasing Jian was one of the rare joys he had during this deployment.

"Some marines likely got rid of a weak link," said Markov. "There's a runt in every litter, and they don't tend to fare well on tough deployments like this."

"His unit claims it is not the case, and the screenings back them up," said Jian.

"Hooking some sergeant up to a brain scan isn't going to tell you what actually happened. Sergeants spend their whole careers learning how to lie to officers," said Markov. "Let's go."

The aide blustered that there was no reason for them to leave unless ordered. Markov brushed Jian aside as he stormed out of the room.

They were onsite at Duke's Bar in less than five minutes, driving there in one of the Wolf armored fighting vehicles that General Yu insisted his senior officers use every time they ventured into Honolulu. If Yu had bothered to listen, Markov would have told him that this was a classic mistake, choosing force protection over situational awareness.

Markov strode past the Directorate sentries and walked through the empty bar, Jian following a few paces behind. He closed his eyes once he got to the stairwell and let his other senses absorb all they could. It was dank and humid, the salty-sweet smell of almost-dry blood mixing with that of old beer. He opened his eyes and took in the scene. The body sat against the wall, almost as if taking a drunk's rest. A river of dark red caked the young marine's neck, his face now forever locked in an expression of shock.

Markov smiled at the thought of what Jian would make of this and slowly and intently examined the body. No penetration points other than the neck, no obvious struggle. No sign of sexual trauma.

"So, Lieutenant," he asked his shadow, "how many people in a war zone would bother to kill a lowly enlisted Directorate marine by gouging a hole in his neck?"

He did not wait for the rote response that anything that did not go according to plan was the fault of the insurgents. Perhaps the lieutenant had been right for once; if it had been the marine's mates who'd done this, they would have beat him unconscious and held him under the surf. He'd seen that one already.

Yet this was an oddly personal way for an insurgent to kill. A killing of intense proximity.

Markov stared hard at the sticky floor. Who but someone this runt knew could get close enough to kill him without leaving bruises or any sign of struggle? It was a savage killing, but with a delicate weapon. A paring knife, perhaps? It had to be somebody the marine wanted to be very close to in a dark stairway at the back of a collaborator bar. A woman? One of the locals? Or perhaps a man? Maybe one of his squad mates, who had killed him to make sure their secret went no further?

War rarely offered answers, only questions. That was why Markov enjoyed it so much.

Blue Line Metro Stop, Pentagon

At the Pentagon, everyone waits. You wait at the Metro station to get to the escalator. You wait at the security line to get your badge. You wait at the screening gates. And once inside, you wait at security checkpoints to move between the five-sided building's ring-like corridors. Later you wait to enter the food courts and the bathrooms.

It depressed Daniel Aboye. This place of waiting was for sour-faced people preparing to explain why they were losing.

He handed over his freshly printed and still warm ID badge to a submachine-gun-wielding hired guard.

"Thank you," the guard said. "Just need a little patience, and you'll be fine."

Aboye snapped his head up and stared into the guard's eyes. How many years had it been since he'd heard the Dinka dialect of South Sudan? Aboye answered with a smile and responded in the tongue he hadn't used for years.

"Thank you, brother. Long way from home?"

"Home? Home is here now," replied the guard in the same language. "For you too, I see."

Aboye nodded, grateful for the connection. Maybe it was a good omen. He moved past the checkpoint and joined the next line. Such serendipity no longer shocked him. After his parents had been killed by the *janjaweed* gunmen, he'd walked for weeks and weeks on an empty belly and bloodied feet. Oprah had called his group of wartime orphans "the Lost Boys." The name did not fit. Daniel did not think of himself as lost. That he could build a life of incomprehensible good fortune atop such sadness seemed so improbable that it could only be part of something unexplainable, something much bigger than himself. That was why he'd easily fallen into engineering at Stanford. It was predictable, the opposite of what his life had been to that point. And so it was Daniel's ability to distinguish between what was predictable and what required serendipity that had powered his rise through Silicon Valley's venture-capital investment firms; he knew which tech startups to back and which to avoid.

After he finally made it through the security line's sequential body scanners and DNA tagging, a petite young redheaded woman in a light gray pantsuit stepped forward, her rubber-soled pumps squeaking as she halted before him.

"Mr. Aboye, I am Catherine Hines, special assistant to the principal deputy undersecretary of defense for Acquisitions, Technology, and Logistics," she said, rattling her title off like an auctioneer with a rare treasure. "We can talk in my office," she said, not waiting for him to reply. "Please follow me."

They walked 317 steps — Aboye counted — and he did not see one window.

Once in her cubicle, they sat, and she looked at him as if expecting him to explain himself.

"Are we still on schedule to meet with Secretary Claiburne? The security line was quite long and I hope I have not inconvenienced her," he said.

"I'm afraid there has been some sort of misunderstanding, Mr. Aboye. Your meeting is with me," she said. "The SecDef isn't even in the building today."

He stood up immediately, rising to his full six foot five inches, and looked up at dusty fiberboard and crop-like rows of LED lights. He paused, and then glared down at her.

"If I'm not meeting Secretary Claiburne, why am I here?" he said.

"Secretary Claiburne was pleased to receive the senator's note about finding you a role, but he should not have promised that," she said. "The way things go in Silicon Valley does not always carry over to here. There's a war on."

"Please do not speak to me as if I do not know war," he said.

"I am sorry, I didn't mean any offense," she said. "What I meant is that we are appreciative that you want to contribute to the war effort, but there are procedures we all have to follow, whether we like them or not. I would urge you to speak with either of the Big Two firms here in the Beltway, perhaps to explore their interest in some sort of partnership. They'll also have the best means to navigate any projects through the various offices in the building and, of course, the relevant congressional committees. I have to warn you, though, the profit margins are not going to be what you are used to."

"This is not about contracts or making money!" Daniel said, his voice rising. "I came here to see how I could give back to the country that has done so much for me."

"Ah, if that's what is motivating you, our model for citizen involvement is the National Guard. I would urge you to explore that. Or perhaps speak with the senator about joining a special study commission?"

She took a quick but obvious look at her watch and then widened her eyes and tilted her head, the universal signal among bureaucrats that a meeting was over.

"I see. Thank you for your time and explanation," said Aboye. And he walked away.

Kakaako, Honolulu, Hawaii Special Administrative Zone

She pressed the blade lightly across the flesh, focusing on the oblivion it offered. The warm blood dripped faster and faster and she knew that she had arrived again at that perfect moment of power, where all she had to do was put her full weight behind the blade and drive it in deep. To feel so in control again was electrifying; she could lose herself in this moment.

With a gasp, Carrie Shin forced herself to open her eyes. She looked down at her arm and pressed her fingers over the cut.

Her arm ached, but it was a familiar pain, terrible but comforting. She felt centered for the first time in months. As she fumbled with a towel to stanch the bleeding, she knew she could handle all of it now.

It had been his hairbrush that did it.

The black plastic brush was a throwaway. Their condo was filled with any number of reminders of him: his photos, his surfboard, his bike. But then she had seen a few of his hairs on the brush. Irreplaceable pieces of him.

Before this, she hadn't cut herself since he'd caught her doing it three years back. She'd been embarrassed, scared what he would think, but he'd just held her. Told her she didn't need to hurt alone anymore. He was there to protect her. Who better to keep her safe than a man in uniform? He'd bought her an expensive Swiss nanoderm cream that wiped away the scars, and he'd never spoken of it again.

Well, where was he now?

Time to dispose of the clothing. Some blood had gotten on the white tank top, but fortunately not enough for anyone to notice in the dark. She started to cut the garments into playing-card-size pieces and then stopped.

Her fiancé's face popped back into her mind again. Then the face of her father, whom she hated as much as she had loved her husband-to-be for reasons both similar and appallingly different.

She stuffed the pieces into a plastic bag, arm trembling, barely able to hold the five-gallon jug in her right hand and keep the bag open with her left.

She stopped again.

She removed a scrap of fabric and wiped the cut on her arm with it. Back into the bag. Then the sunglasses. Last into the bag went the wallet.

She'd already thrown up once after the rush of adrenaline faded, the moment her key unlocked her front door. She'd staggered to the toilet on weak legs, heaved and vomited for ten minutes, then lay down on the floor and passed out.

When she woke, she knew what she had to do. That was nine hours ago.

Now the stench of the chlorine-bleach jug made her gag; she felt vulnerable for an instant. She thought of her fiancé. What had he thought of just before he'd died? She steadied herself and prepared to pour the bleach into the bag. After that, she'd take it to the building's incinerator with all the other trash.

A black hair on a scrap of the white tank top stopped her. She immediately knew whose it was. She reached into the bag and placed it on the hairbrush.

My pain, your pain, their pain, all mixed together.

USS *Zumwalt,* Mare Island Naval Shipyard

Mike winced every time he saw Brooks's Mohawk haircut. Where did this kid think he was, the Army? Let the Special Forces wear pajamas and play dress-up all they wanted; the Navy's uniform was meant to be just that: uniform.

But the Navy needed this boy with the Mohawk. So instead of screaming at Mo, Mike's nickname for the kid, who was maybe twenty, Mike unloaded on Davidson. The seventy-year-old was an easy target, since the two knew each other so well. They both had the same old but still fit build; in low light, they might have been mistaken for twins. Davidson had served with Mike at the start of Gulf War I. Each measured the passing of the years since then in how the other's skin grew leathery and his stubble turned gray, neither one seeing the age in himself until it registered that the other man was his near mirror.

"You need to strip the paint down all the way—your goddamn grandkids could tell you how to do it," said Mike. Of course Davidson knew that, but it had to be said. This was not anger, it was a performance for Mo.

"Then, when you've got a bare surface, smooth as a freshly shaved . . . shit, now I went and got distracted. Then you apply the epoxy, just like I showed you two hundred years ago. Then Mo here is going to attach the antenna and zap it with the UV gun, and you can seal it up with more epoxy."

Davidson and Brooks had been installing a new set of synthetic aperture radar antennas that looked like giant bumper stickers. They were only halfway through.

Davidson protested. "The thing is, Mike, you scrape it down, it's not steel, like my pecker. Superstructure is made out of—"

"Davidson, I don't care if the ship's built out of Girl Scout cookies. You scrape off the goddamn frosting until it's ready for the epoxy. You know what that should look like and you don't need me to tell you this shit, so just do your job!"

"Thing is, the composite has so—" said Davidson.

"Damn it, you know what, Davidson? You're starting to sound like one of them. Maybe you ought to ask Mo for fashion tips too," said Mike.

Brooks had pulled down his respirator and was picking at a fresh tattoo on his cheek, a tiny pictogram of his initials in that new computer text. He gave a high-pitched snicker. "Might help you old farts get some tail," Mo said.

Mike leaned in to the young sailor's face. Brooks recoiled at the rank coffee breath.

"Are you laughing, Mo? Is my Navy a joke to you? If this was thirty-five years ago, I would haul you below decks, take off my stripes, and kick your ass. The Mentor Crew isn't here for your amusement. Listen to what this man has to say," said Mike. "This 'old fart,' as you put it, was working on ships when you weren't even a cum stain on your father's *Playboy*."

The young sailor looked confused and asked, "What's *Playboy*?"

Davidson laughed, and Mike turned on him and began speaking in a calm, deliberate voice.

"Davidson, shut the hell up. He may have a haircut that looks like a bird shat on his head, but Mo is smarter, faster, and better than you," he said. He turned back to the young sailor. "But Mo, when we were your age, between the two of us we got more tail than you will get in your lifetime — including, most likely, your mom, six ways to Sunday."

Mike raised his voice again to the volume he used when on the ship's deck. "This conversation is now over. The new captain arrives in twenty, so get your asses cleaned up and topside. God help the old man with a ship like this and a crew like you."

Mike walked to the ship's stern and took a deep breath, trying to slow his racing heart. He didn't have it in him anymore to drive a crew this hard without making his own blood pressure rise. And that was something he had to watch carefully now.

He looked out at Mare Island Naval Shipyard. Just past Suisun Bay, where the Ghost Fleet had been moored, it had opened in 1854 under Commander David Farragut. Farragut had gone on to gain fame during the Battle of Mobile Bay in the Civil War by giving the order, "Damn the torpedoes, full speed ahead!" This kind of connection made real the bond Mike felt across the generations of sailors. Men at these same piers had repaired the clipper ships after their long hauls carrying the Forty-Niner gold miners around the cape, and had built some of the Navy's first submarines at the turn of the last century; some fifty thousand workers had been employed here during World War II. Closed down after the Cold War ended, the Mare Island docks were buzzing again now that America needed them once more. Mike felt responsible for kids like Mo and for what the historians would one day write about the Navy.

Davidson walked up with a pack of cigarettes in hand. "Smoke?"

"I thought you'd quit," said Mike.

"Yeah, but I know a guy in Vallejo who still sells," said Davidson. "Figured I'd make it an interesting race between a Stonefish missile and lung cancer."

Mike accepted a cigarette as well as a light off Davidson's butane lighter.

"These kids are shit workers," said Mike.

"You're right, but you don't need to ride them so hard," said Davidson. "They know the stakes."

"That's just it — do they? They can do things I'll die not knowing how to do," said Mike. "But do they understand what losing this war will mean?"

The two watched one of the older men on the Mentor Crew carry a cardboard box unsteadily along the starboard rail. Then a kid with short, spiky dreadlocks pitched in to help guide him inside the ship.

"They're just like we were at that age. Full of confidence and full of shit," Davidson said.

Mike took a deep drag on his cigarette and then flicked it into the water off the stern.

"If the Directorate wins but lets them keep all their viz and group sims, will they even know the difference?" said Mike. "I mean, when those goggles are on, they could be anywhere in the world."

"You've never done it, have you?" asked Davidson.

"I like the real world well enough," said Mike.

"Once you try it, everything looks different," said Davidson, scratching at a flabby, sunburned biceps. "Or at least it looks like it could be. If I had my viz on right now, I could fly right up to the top of the hangar and look down at us. Well, I could have before the war started. The viz doesn't work quite the same anymore. I bet a lot of kids want to win this damn thing just to get their glasses working right again."

"Atten-huht on deck! . . . Dress-right-dress!"

Captain Jamie Simmons walked up the gangway, his footsteps quiet for such a big man. He saluted as he stopped to take in the menacing look of the USS *Zumwalt.*

The ship was massive: 610 feet long. If the Washington Monument were laid down beside it, the ship would be a full 55 feet longer. Its superstructure above the water had no right angles, a design meant to make it fifty times less visible to radar than any ship before it, while below decks it had the sonar signature of a stealthy submarine. But that was not what made its exterior appear so formidable; it was, ironically, the lack of any apparent weaponry. The *Zumwalt* had a stripped-down exterior that seemed to conceal countless weapons of destruction.

But Simmons knew the ship was not as fierce as it looked.

Once envisioned as the vanguard of the twenty-first-century U.S. fleet, it had instead turned out to be an orphan that no one wanted. The DD(X)-class was conceived in the early 1990s. The design, meant to revolutionize naval warfare, included all sorts of innovations, from the signature box-cutter-blade wave-piercing tumblehome hull to an integrated power system that used a permanent magnetic motor to produce ten times the electric power of normal engines. Highly automated, a DD(X) was to be crewed by half as many sailors as a warship of similar size had needed a generation earlier. This game-changing new design would allow the ship to carry an arsenal of equally game-changing new weapons, most notably an electromagnetic rail gun that would shoot farther than any other gun in history. The U.S. Navy hoped the *Zumwalt,* the first of what was later renamed the DDG 1000 class, would be a historic vessel, like the USS *Monitor,* the first ironclad ship of the Civil War, or the HMS *Dreadnought,* the first true battleship. It was meant to break all the old rules of shipbuilding and so bring in a new era of war at sea.

That was the plan. By the time Jamie had gotten his master's degree at the Naval War College, the story of the Z was taught as a case study in how not to build a ship. The design had had too many risky innovations bundled into one project, plus cutting-edge shipbuilding expertise had shifted from the United States to Asia by the end of the twentieth century, and a defense budget focused on fighting land wars in the Middle East couldn't cover battleships that cost more than seven billion dollars each. The Navy had planned to buy thirty-two copies of the Z. By 2008, it didn't want any. Only the *Zumwalt* and two more ships were eventually approved, and then only due to the intercession of a powerful senator on the Appropriations Committee who threatened to filibuster all other Navy contracts unless the project was completed. It wasn't about saving the ship itself; mainly, she was trying to keep a shipyard in her district from going out of business.

The actual ship that came out of the yard was revolutionary, to be sure, but it suffered from all the kinks that come with anything that is the first of its kind. It was unsteady at sea; the systems were faulty; the propulsion system was prone to random stoppages and didn't deliver enough juice. The hull design leaked water at poorly fitting seams. And because so few of the new ships of the line were actually built, the revolutionary new weapons that were to arm the Z were never put onboard.

When the defense budget was slashed in the fiscal crisis after Dhahran, the admirals were delighted to send the Z to early retirement in the Ghost Fleet. One of the two sister ships that were still under construction was gutted and turned into a floating engineering site for a technical college in Newport News, Virginia; the other was used to test a new generation of shipboard firefighting robots.

"Sir, crew, USS *Zumwalt*, all present and accounted for."

Simmons made his way slowly down the lines of sailors and civilian technicians assembled for his inspection. He offered each sailor a confident greeting, a reassuring smile. Behind him trailed his executive officer, Horatio Cortez, who followed with careful steps, still occasionally catching his new prosthetic left leg and left arm on the hatch edges.

"XO, how we doing?" asked Simmons as they walked.

"We're making progress on the systems rip-out and rewiring, but doing it at the same time as we're trying to install new uncorrupted and untested hardware just gets harder and harder," said Cortez. Now belatedly obsessed with hardware attacks, the Navy had ordered the *Zumwalt* to have any suspect prewar systems removed and destroyed. That the *Z* and the other ships in the Ghost Fleet had not received the past few years of upgrades had suddenly become one of their strengths. "It's all about making the old and new gear blend together."

Then Simmons stopped abruptly and turned sharply to stand face to face with a man his own height. All along the formation, sailors leaned slightly forward to see what the holdup was.

"Cortez?" said Simmons, turning back to his XO and trying to mask his evident anger.

"Sir?" said Cortez.

"Didn't you look at the crew roster?" asked Simmons.

"Yes, sir. They used a NAVSEA selection algorithm based on a mix of qualifications and experience," said Cortez. He looked from the captain to the old sailor in front of him. The viz glasses flickered with a glimmer of pink and blue. Through his glasses, Cortez could access the Navy records system with a secure version of Google's PeopleView software. It meant never forgetting a name, but he didn't need the program when he looked from one face to the other. Cortez started to smile and then hid the grin behind his artificial hand as he feigned clearing his throat. The Navy's algorithm had seen fit to assign Chief Petty Officer Michael Simmons to the ship his son commanded.

Haleiwa, Oahu, Hawaii Special Administrative Zone

With a dirty hand, the woman opened the plastic sandwich bag. The blue and green dinosaurs that decorated it gave her a shiver of discomfort. Her fingers muddied the small garage clicker she pulled out. She tried to wipe it off on her black T-shirt, but the fabric was so grimy with sweat and earth that she only smeared the mud around.

Stop. It doesn't matter if it's clean, she told herself. The batteries were good to go. That was what mattered.

She nodded at the prone man beside her, the signal to start filming with the GoPro camera he'd mounted on his rifle.

She held her breath and moved her thumb over the Open button.

Exhale.

"May all our enemies die screaming," she said. It was a line taken from a show she used to watch, and it seemed apt today.

Send.

A hundred yards away, four IEDs detonated in sequence, starting at the front of the convoy and moving toward the rear. The Wolf armored personnel vehicle in the lead tipped over in flames. The next three trucks in the convoy disappeared in a phosphorous bloom. The fourth truck was untouched, its driver ducking down below the dashboard.

Major Carolyne "Conan" Doyle of the U.S. Marine Corps put the garage-door opener back in the plastic sandwich bag and shoved it into the cargo pocket on her pants. Nothing could go to waste in this kind of war.

It was all so different from any of the combat she had seen in Yemen from the pilot's seat of an MV-22K Osprey gunship. Here everything itched, everything rusted, and everything had to be scavenged. There was no just-in-time delivery of whatever ammunition or spare part you needed. And instead of government-issue combat footwear, they fought in sandals and running shoes, the group being made up of a few escapees from the captured bases and those who'd been lucky enough to be on leave the day of the attack.

Between the dirty civilian clothes and the tactical playbook they were cribbing from, the insurgents quickly realized they were becoming the very bastards they'd spent most their professional military careers fighting. That's where their name had come from, the North

Shore Mujahideen, or NSM, as they spray-painted it when they were in a rush. It was the darkest of jokes, born not out of admiration or even respect — they'd lost too many friends in the Sandbox for anything like that — but because the goal was the same: to become what the other side loathed, the danger that waited around every corner, the nightmare that just wouldn't go away, the opponent who wouldn't play by the rules.

Doyle raised her left arm and waved the trucks forward. Two quick shots came from Conan's right. Finn, a retired Navy comms specialist who'd spent his time in a forward operation base in Marjah Province, Afghanistan, on an individual-augmentee deployment, shot at the passenger-side window in the undamaged truck's cab with his M4 carbine. The thick bulletproof glass held but cracked and spider-webbed from the bullets' impact.

Nicks, an army military police staff sergeant with the Twenty-Fifth ID who had made her bones on detainee operations in Iraq and Syria, sprinted up to the truck, jumped on the running board, and repeatedly smashed at the cracked glass with the butt of her rifle, finally punching a small hole. She pressed a flash-bang grenade into the cab and jumped back down. It detonated with a flash of light equivalent to a million candles and a deafening 180-decibel bang. They'd lifted a box of the grenades, used by SWAT teams for storming rooms, from an abandoned police station. The flash-bangs were technically considered nonlethal weapons since they stunned and dazed targets but didn't actually hurt them. That is, unless they were used in an enclosed space the size of a truck cab.

Nicks jumped back up, stuck her rifle barrel through the hole in the window, prodded one of the bodies, and then fired a single round.

"Clear!" Nicks yelled, louder than she thought because she still had the earplugs in.

"Anything?" Finn whispered to Conan, now rummaging around in the back of the truck.

"Not yet; still looking," said Conan.

Finn checked his watch. They had maybe two minutes until the drones arrived. This was a new route for an ambush, so they might get a little extra time. Given the way the convoy ran unprotected, it seemed like the Directorate forces had not expected to get hit. Or it was a trap to lure them in and they were wasting valuable seconds before the counter-ambush force arrived.

"I'll get the bikes," said Nicks, disappearing into the forest. "We need to go."

Conan appeared from the back of the truck holding up two shoe-box-size metal containers.

"All blues?" said Finn.

"I think so," said Conan. "Might be some greens and reds too."

"At this point, I'll take anything," said Finn.

Nicks emerged from the woods wheeling a pair of mountain bikes draped in thick wool blankets mottled with stains. Sweat dripped off her nose.

"What are we waiting for?" asked Nicks.

"Nothing; let's move," said Conan. "Anything in the other trucks?"

"Got a few dozen mags, some nanoplex bricks, some protein bars," said Finn.

"It'll do. This was really about the footage," said Conan. The NSM moved constantly, by bike when they could and on foot when they had to. There was no time for a full night of rest or a solid meal. But all that they really needed was in the metal boxes from the back of the truck.

"Playtime's over, children!" shouted Conan. "Back to school!"

Fourth Floor, B Ring, Pentagon

As an aviator, Commander Bill "Sweetie" Darling had spent his career chasing the horizon. But it wasn't until his assignment to the Navy staff offices at the Pentagon that he realized he'd been taking the sky for granted. It had been two weeks since he had seen the sun.

In truth, he had almost seen it once. A week back, a construction detour had forced him to walk across the Pentagon's inner courtyard. It was daytime, and he knew the sun was somewhere up there, hidden behind the finely woven anti-exploitation netting that covered the whole building now, making it look like it was wrapped in a silk cocoon. Christo City was the nickname going around, a play on the name of the nearby military-industrial complex of office buildings known as

Crystal City and the renowned artists who used to wrap monuments in fabric.

But even if Darling's work was unrelenting, he still had to eat. Maybe it was the pilot in him, but he was damned if he was going to let some drone get him his food. *You have to draw the line somewhere,* he thought as a train of iRobot Majordomos purred by carrying their honeycomb-like storage containers filled with wraps and sandwiches.

He found Jimmie Links waiting next to a vending machine in front of the entrance to the new Naval Intelligence office. The two men had known each other since the Naval Academy, but their careers had taken very different turns. Though neither of them enjoyed being assigned to the Pentagon, they could commiserate within a few minutes' walk of each other.

"Darling, you shouldn't have waited," said Links, trying to sound like a housewife in an old commercial.

"Original," said Darling.

"Tough crowd today," said Links. "Let's get going. I'm about sixty seconds from humping the vending machine."

Darling peered through the finger-smudged glass of the machine and sighed.

"Maybe that Snickers bar and two of those mango squeezes, then you might have the ingredients for a pretty good time," said Darling.

"I knew you flyboys liked it kinky," said Links.

They set off, but Links stopped after only a few paces. "Shit, I forgot my wallet."

"Go get it, I'm not buying," said Darling.

"Come with me, you can check out the new DIA analyst, the one I was telling you about," said Links.

"You didn't invite her?" said Darling.

"I have to work with her, so better to watch you crash and burn," said Links.

He led them into his office, first going through a retina scan, then swiping his access card, and finally punching in a number code. After they entered the secure cell, the door locked behind them with a magnetic click.

They passed through an inner door of frosted glass with the words

Non-Acoustic Anti-Submarine Warfare stenciled across it. Fresh dry-wall dust covered the door handle.

Links led Darling into his cubicle, a drab, sterile space. The only decorations were a 3-D topographical map of Oahu and, hanging from a thumbtack, a lipstick-smudged Chinese air-pollution-filter mask.

"So this is where the magic happens?" Darling asked dryly.

"There's damn little magic happening here, I'm afraid," said Links soberly. "We still don't have much of a clue how they're tagging our subs." The opening missile strikes that had hit the Pacific carriers had been a shock to the fleet, but the way the enemy had found and destroyed the Navy's submarines was a more disturbing mystery. The U.S. intelligence community had known the Chinese were catching up in surface-ship construction, but they believed that, under the sea, the U.S. had an asymmetric advantage. Ever since the Cold War, if an American sub didn't want to be found, you couldn't find it. But somehow the other side had figured out how to make the ocean transparent and thus deadly to the sub fleet that was supposed to give the U.S. its overwhelming edge.

Darling sat down and, picking up on Links's sober mood, said quietly, "Tell me more."

"I don't even know where to begin," said Links. "I keep thinking of what this lecturer once told us, back in training. He was old-guard CIA, had done Afghanistan both times, during the Cold War and then again after 9/11. He compared the intelligence task to solving a jigsaw puzzle, except that you didn't get the box cover, so you didn't know what the final picture was. And you got only a few pieces at a time, not all of them. And even worse, you always got a bunch of pieces from some other puzzle thrown in."

"Start with the detection, and then the targeting," Darling suggested.

"We spend all our time looking backward, trying to understand how," said Links. "One argument is that the Directorate is using its own subs to shadow ours. And we just keep failing to detect them somehow."

Darling stiffened in his chair as he recalled losing the *John Warner* to a Chinese ballistic missile.

"No way," he said. "The Directorate sub we were following was too far away from the *Warner* to be able to get any kind of pinpoint tracking. And there were no transmission traces. If their sub had communicated the *Warner's* position back to Hainan, we would have caught it. Besides, that sub was too busy running from us to do anything. About the time the Stonefish were firing, it was sinking. We got it, that's one thing I am certain of."

"Could they have used your comms to track the *Warner,* maybe even gotten into ATHENA?" asked Links. "Did you pick up anything like that?"

"Nope, nothing. Have you thought about big-data collection from environmental sensors, like how those fishermen kept detecting our Trident missile subs off Bangor a few years back? Or what about space-based underwater detection? Tracking the IR or even something like the Bernoulli effect, from the water distortion?" said Darling. "Maybe a Ouija board?"

"We've run them all down. The environmental sensor one is out, as you have to seed the area beforehand. There's no trace of that, plus the Chinese are picking up our sub traffic everywhere, no matter where we go. The *Oregon* paid the price for us testing that theory off the Aleutians. Space-based detection is the working theory, but no one knows how the Chinese could manage that either. NAASW is looking at synthetic aperture radar as an option for undersea detection," said Links. "During the Cold War, there were some attempts to make that work in tracking Soviet boomers, but nothing stuck. More important, they can't cover an ocean area without broadcasting enough energy down from space that we'd pick it up."

"How about the other way around?" Darling suggested. "How about magnetic detection of the sub's hulls? That's the working theory at the analysis section we have set up down at the B-ring urinal."

"No, that's another Cold War tech that was tried and failed," said Links. "It just doesn't work from space. There's too much backscatter to pull out anything metallic at that range. They'd be plinking pretty much every piece of metal on the sea floor with Stonefish warheads. Plus, you also have the mystery of how they were able to track the subs and the carriers but couldn't pinpoint the escort ships," said Links.

"Maybe the escorts weren't worth the trouble? Maybe the Chinese didn't have enough missiles?" said Darling.

"No way. You think they'd try to save a few bucks if they could take out all of our Aegis ships too?" said Links.

"So if that's the case, it's something that's letting them track the nukes," said Darling.

"Yep, which puts us back at, as we call it in the intelligence community, square one," said Links.

"So the real question is, what's so special about a nuclear reactor?" said Darling. "If you want to find one from really far away, you have to be able to collect whatever it emits. But, shit, at range it's never going to emit anything more than low-level Cherenkov rays."

"What did you say?" Links asked with a catch in his voice.

"Cherenkov rays," said Darling. "Did you sleep through the nuclear physics class at the Naval Academy? It's what gives nuclear reactors their blue glow, something about charged particles passing through the medium that surrounds the nuclear reaction at different speeds than light. Some Russian named Cherenkov discovered them like a hundred years ago. He won the Nobel Prize for it."

"*Star Trek*. You bastard," whispered Links to himself. He tossed his wallet onto the desk with a shaking hand. "Lunch is on me. I've got to run, got an idea."

"Whatever, man. Your DIA analyst better be worth it." Darling picked up the wallet and was just beginning to stand when he heard the security door shut with a heavy thud.

Moana Surfrider Hotel, Waikiki Beach, Hawaii Special Administrative Zone

"Ms. Shin, please, over here," said the voice box, translating the guard's Chinese into English. The guard was male, but the device had been set to speak in a digitized voice that matched the gender of the person being spoken to. Carrie wasn't sure if it was a joke or if some Directorate scientist had concluded that if a woman heard a female voice coming out of a burly, armed male Directorate marine, she would somehow find it more reassuring than a male's voice.

"Okay, okay," Carrie said. She put her arms out and threw her head back, cruciform-style, her long hair reaching to her waist.

"We have selected you for extra assurance measures," the marine said. He stood at about her height but had around twice her mass in muscle. The telltale acne and thick neck showed how he had gotten so big. So many of their marines had that look.

"Do you understand?" said the voice box.

"Yep," said Carrie.

"The Directorate appreciates your compliance," said the device. That was the latest phrase the voice boxes were spitting out. She couldn't tell if it was what the guard had actually said or if it was just a stock phrase from an automated setting.

The chem swabs tickled when they ran down her arms and legs. It felt like a spider exploring her.

"I am complete," said the voice box.

She opened her eyes. The swab had not turned red, as it would have if it had detected explosives. Instead, it was a light brown. The guard looked quizzically at the swab, unsure of what the earthy substance was.

"It's okay," said Carrie. "It's makeup, from my arm. I cut myself cooking." She ran her fingers across her cheeks as if putting on foundation and flashed a smile.

The voice box translated for the marine, who nodded, paused, and then muttered a phrase she could barely hear.

"Thank you for your compliance," the box said. By this time the marine was looking to the next person in line.

She walked away slowly, calming herself, unconsciously rubbing the thin scabs on her arm. At least this check hadn't been as bad as the checkpoint at the bus station; there, the guard made her bend over and speak directly into the voice box on his belt. She caught a glimpse of Waikiki Beach across the street and for a moment she found herself thinking of her fiancé, the sunset walk on his birthday. The wind had been up that night.

The grind of rubber wheels on asphalt behind her snapped her out of the memory, and she leaped to the right, onto the sidewalk. The hybrid-electric Wolf armored personnel carrier glided quietly by as the Directorate marine manning the machine gun on the roof offered a timid wave.

Adrenaline pumping, she strode purposefully through the four columns of the hotel's grand entrance and shivered despite the heat and humidity.

Before the war, she'd had to use the staff entrance. The gleaming white hotel had been built just three years after the American annexation in 1898 on land originally owned by the Hawaiian royal family, so having both the guests and the staff use the main entrance was part of some Directorate propaganda about how the Chinese forces were there for similar reasons, to ensure security, but they, unlike the Americans, would show respect for the "true" citizens of Hawaii. The Directorate was real big on who had been on what island first. But whether you were native, *hapa* (of mixed ethnicity), or from the mainland, you still had to go through the screening checkpoint out on the street.

Inside the hardwood-floored lobby, Chinese soldiers, sailors, and marines, along with a few civilians, lounged about, drinking and chatting. Just as it was back in World War II, the old hotel had been converted into a hub for shore leave. She passed through the lobby and went out to the back porch. From her perch at the sports-equipment-rental desk, she couldn't see the ocean, but she could hear it. That counted for a lot.

"That was amazing," a man's voice said, taking her out of her thoughts. He spoke English without one of the translator devices. "What a beautiful sport it must be for those who are truly skilled."

He set a still-wet longboard against the wall. There was a brief pause as he stepped back to make sure it would not topple over.

"It's a lot to expect for anyone to pick up in just an hour," said Carrie. "I bet you did great."

"I spent most of my time swimming next to the board, not riding it," said the officer. He was clearly fit, washboard abs, but not bulked out by chems like so many of them. His hair was cropped short, but in a stylish manner. She guessed it had been done professionally rather than in the military assembly line.

"The sport of kings is not for everyone," she said, offering a wink. "I know we're not supposed to ask questions of the guests, but where'd you pick up English? Yours is excellent."

"UCLA, where else?" he said, raising two fingers in the sign that went along with the UCLA alma mater song.

"Go Bruins," she said, smiling slightly.

"Listen, I could really use a lesson," the officer said. "Sorry, I should introduce myself. My name is Feng Wu. My friends in LA called me Frank."

Carrie looked down at her tablet.

"I can set you up with one of the hotel instructors, no problem. They're great. Several of them were pros before all this," said Carrie.

Frank leaned closer, dripping seawater on the counter. He smiled, showing perfect white teeth.

"You're a great teacher, I bet," he said.

"Well, I'm not that good . . ." she countered.

"I can pay you, or give you an extra ration card if you want, or whatever else."

Carrie pressed lightly on the scab on her arm.

"There's no need for that. Helping out is part of our job, actually," she said. "Any of us can offer the guests our services. I just thought you would want someone more experienced."

"When should we meet?" he said.

"Monday night is when the outgoing tide's supposed to be best," Carrie said. She tilted her head slightly, giving him a glimpse of her neck.

"That's a long time to wait! How about tomorrow night?" he said.

She smiled back, looking him in the eye.

It wasn't just her beauty that made her gaze so striking; it was that she was the first local to look at him directly since he'd arrived in Hawaii. All the others tried to avoid eye contact, some mix of shame and fear. She didn't have that; instead, she was just — what, normal? More like the American girls he remembered fondly from before all this.

"If you are going to be my student, you have to learn to trust me. We'll meet next Monday. The moon will be full, and so amazing," she said. "I know just the place; it's quiet and there's not a better break on this side of the island."

"It is a date, then," said Frank.

USS *Zumwalt*, Mare Island Naval Shipyard

From the water right now, Jamie Simmons thought the *Zumwalt* looked less like floating death and more like one of those ramshackle floating tidal towns off what used to be Indonesia, people weaving sheets of metal, plastic, and wood into improbable geometries to create homes.

What Vice Admiral Evangeline Murray thought of the Z, Simmons could not tell. She'd hardly spoken to him during her waterside tour of the ship. But her eyes didn't stop moving. She was coming to understand the ship, Simmons felt, in a way he'd never bothered to. At one point, she had the launch brought up alongside the hull, and she put her hands on the ship like a healer and closed her eyes. What she heard or saw, he did not know. What he did know was that she had a status within the Navy that was unmatched. She'd been the first woman to command an aircraft carrier strike group before the war. More important, she'd been fortunate enough to be serving as president of the Naval War College when the shooting started, meaning she'd escaped both the Stonefish missiles and the congressional inquiries that had decimated the senior ranks.

She signaled for the launch to return to the pier.

"Captain, before we go aboard, I want to say that it is an honor to meet you," she said. "We don't have a lot of heroes in this country right now to inspire us. Your leadership and experience are invaluable and I just want you to know that if this ship does not work out, I will personally ensure that your talent is not wasted."

"Thank you, Admiral," said Simmons.

"In fact, they tell me we could use someone like you right now in Washington, perhaps more than out here," said Admiral Murray. "You survived when nobody else did; that has a huge value to the war effort."

Simmons did not blink; he kept his eyes locked on hers. Was she evaluating him too, not just the ship? This was one of those moments with a black-or-white outcome: Lindsey or the sea. Safety or duty.

"You're right, ma'am. I don't belong here," said Simmons.

She nodded and furrowed her brow.

Simmons pointed toward the Golden Gate Bridge. "Admiral, this ship, or any ship we have, has to be out there at sea, where the fight is," he said. "That's where we belong."

He said it instinctively, then paused to question whether he was voicing his father's opinions or his own.

An elfin smile revealed the admiral's yellowed teeth; unusual, because most people had had theirs whitened or replaced by her age. "That is for damn sure," said Admiral Murray. "Now why don't you introduce me to the crew."

They didn't pipe the admiral aboard, as she preferred not to disturb the work at hand.

"One thing that impresses me is all the camouflage here," said Admiral Murray as they walked the deck.

"It might look like camouflage, but the reality is that all the scaffolding and tarps are really necessary. We ended up having to do a top-to-bottom overhaul here," said Simmons.

As they approached a knot of crewmen — some in their teens, others decades older — clambering over a scaffold, the admiral said, "Tell me about the crew. How is the new mix going?"

"The mix of generations has its strengths and weaknesses. We have the remnants of the pre–Zero Day fleet. I was given my choice of the best of my old crew, which I understand I have you to thank for. Then there are the draftees, some of whom have never seen the real ocean, let alone been out on it," said Simmons. "But what they do know are computers; they've been with viz in one form or another since birth. They see problems differently than regular sailors, even sailors who were in the Navy when the war started."

Simmons pointed to a pair of teenagers with facial tattoos that were partially obscured by their brushed-titanium Apple glasses. The kids were having a conversation with one of the Mentor Crew.

"And then, Admiral, there are our most experienced sailors, the Mentors, many of whom joined the Navy before the First Gulf War," said Simmons. "With the sense of history the younger sailors have, they might as well have been on Noah's crew for all that means to them."

"This is going to take some adjusting for all of us," Admiral Murray observed, "and I don't mean just those in the Navy. It's the same everywhere now. People who wouldn't have had a thing to do with each other a few months ago now have no choice but to join together, whether they're growing food in a condo's victory garden or working in the same shipyard. Bottom line, are the Mentors working out? We've had some conflicting reports from the other ships."

"On the *Zumwalt,* they prefer to be called the Old Farts. I had my doubts, ma'am, but the older guys drive everyone hard. More important, they know the old tech and its secrets better than anyone else."

Simmons led her farther astern.

"You can't separate the people and the technology, really. But it's not just about the old gear. What we've done in upgrading the ship's wireless nets will help us run the ATHENA replacement but also give us some more protection against network attack."

"Local networking is going to be essential; focus on that," she said.

"These are the vertical launch cells for the cruise missiles," said Simmons, continuing the tour.

"Magazine capacity?" asked Admiral Murray.

"We're at eighty now," said Simmons. "But we have to reevaluate what that means while the Office of Naval Research is figuring out a new targeting system. Without GPS, they aren't going to pack the punch we need. To have any kind of effect, we'd have to give up the magazine-allotment space for the air-defense missiles."

Admiral Murray leaned forward. "We've been working on a GPS replacement for years, but it's the same story — it just isn't panning out," she said. "It's now or never, but if it's not ready in time, then you've got the right approach. Make up for lost accuracy with volume of fire. Use the space for anything that has a strike capability. We need to bring as much fire as we can."

They ducked beneath a tarp and stood before a slate-gray box with a honeycombed face. Known as the Metal Storm, it was a kind of electronic machine gun. But instead of dropping bullets in individual rounds to be fired out of a single barrel, one after another, here, bullets were stacked nose to tail inside the multiple barrels that honeycombed the device. Sparked by an electronic ignition, the rounds would fire off all at once, like a Roman candle.

"For close-in defense, we've rigged the Metal Storm as well as the pair of laser turrets just above the bridge," said Simmons. "Directed energy should do for single targets, while the Metal Storm can throw up a literal wall of bullets, thirty-six thousand rounds fired in a single burst." He patted the box softly. "Some of the kids have also been playing with the software to speed up reaction times."

"Make sure you get that code to the fleet — we need to keep pushing the development," she said.

"The question is how effective it will be, and then how much of the air-defense missiles we can unload," Simmons said. "The simulation models give us a pretty wide mix of possible outcomes."

"Perhaps I wasn't clear," said Admiral Murray. "I understand why you want to have both options when it comes to balancing this ship's strike capability with its defense systems. But it's a zero-sum game for what I need. I need *Zumwalt* to think of itself as a battleship if we're going to use it."

"Admiral, this is not a battleship, at least not in the old way people thought of them," said Simmons, consciously steadying his voice. She was testing him again. "A battleship counted on the sheer throw weight of what it could fire, but also on its own weight. Sixteen-inch guns, but also sixteen-inch armor plating. Big enough to hit hard, but also to be hit hard. We're not that. Yes, the Z is the biggest surface combatant in the fleet, but it can't take those kinds of hits. We have to punch first, and kill at a distance."

"Exactly," she replied. Test passed. "Then show me how you're going to do that."

They walked forward to where the ship's original 155 mm gun turrets had been. In their place, workers were welding the fittings on what looked more like an angled tractor-trailer than the usual sleek gun mounting of a warship. Painted on the side was the program's official motto: *Speed Kills*.

"This is the old prototype from the Dahlgren facility?" asked Admiral Murray.

"The very same. Some of the bits and pieces got lost after they shut down the program when the Z class got retired early, but it's most of the original. Shipped over by rail from Virginia."

"This is why you're here, Captain. A working electromagnetic rail gun will be a game-changer for the fleet; maybe for the entire war," she said.

The rail gun represented a break point, a shift away from over eight hundred years of ballistic science. Instead of using the chemistry of gunpowder to shoot a metal object out of a long barrel, the rail gun used energy that came from electromagnetic forces. A powerful current ran through two oppositely charged rails on either side of the barrel. When a conductive projectile was inserted between the rails (at the end connected to the power supply), it completed the circuit. Just as the gases expelled by exploding gunpowder propelled a bullet out of a conventional gun, the magnetic field inside the loop created a burst of incredible power, called a Lorentz force, that slung projectiles out of the open end of the gun barrel. There were no fuses to light, but the rail gun did require a massive and reliable supply of electrical current. Without electricity, a ship with a rail gun would be like a nineteenth-century ship of the line with a waterlogged powder magazine.

"We sure could've used it at Pearl," he said, thinking of the popgun they'd had on the *Coronado*.

"I can imagine. But I don't plan on anyone ever being stuck in a kill box like that again. What do you anticipate the rail gun's effect will be on fleet action?" Another test. Still the college president at heart.

"It gives us speed and range, ma'am. It slings out a shell with a velocity of more than eighty-two hundred feet per second, allowing us to strike targets out to a hundred and eighty miles. It's a double gain. Faster than any missile and impossible to jam or shoot down."

She nodded, but she seemed to be waiting for more.

"But more important will be their effect. The shells are small, but with that kind of speed they'll hit with a force equaled only by the old *Iowa*-class battleships' cannon shells, and those were the size of cars. It also solves the capacity and targeting problem we have with the long-range strike missiles. Even without a precise GPS location, we can lay down a pattern of fire that saturates a target set. That's where the similarity with the old battleships holds best."

"The Hand of God is what they called it during development," said Admiral Murray. "I was a junior officer working on the Navy staff in the Pentagon back then, N-9 Warfare Systems. I remember the rail-gun program; officers had it all over their PowerPoint briefs when they came in. It was a cool name, but it didn't stop us from slashing their budget when the cuts came. How are you dealing with the thermal and power management issues that bugged it then? You can't exactly replace a melted barrel in the middle of an engagement."

"There's two ways to deal with the heat. This is actually not the original barrel they had problems with back then. It uses a nanostructure that dissipates the heat. Of course, we still have to be careful, but we can fire in what we call a surge strike. The power management is more complicated, and, frankly, Admiral, that's my concern. The rail gun requires the power equivalent of a small city. This ship was supposed to be designed with that in mind, but you know how they overpromised and underdelivered."

No other surface ship besides the *Zumwalt* had a power system that could generate and, more important, store the tremendous amounts of electricity required for the electromagnetic push that was the essence of the rail gun's design. This was why the Navy had lost its original excitement over the rail-gun program once the *Zumwalt* class had ended. Even with a design tailored for the new weapon, the Navy's models projected that each firing of the rail gun would require stealing energy from other systems onboard, including the ship's propulsion.

"We are all too aware of that problem with the old defense-industrial complex," she said. "So what are you doing about it?"

"We're approaching it through both tactics and reengineering," said Simmons, trying to shift his tone so that she wouldn't think he was making excuses. "Tactically, the plan is to use the power drain to our advantage, so to speak, by building drift into the anti-detection protocols. The key is not to get boxed in again, as you put it, but to disappear in the expanse of the ocean. On the reengineering side, we're getting good results from the new energy-dense liquid-based battery being built for the ship. It's giving us added power beyond what the original design in the nineties envisioned. We've been assigned a specialist in liquid-based batteries, a woman from the University of Wisconsin. Frankly, there's a lot riding on her expertise."

He paused to look directly at her.

"But the answer, Admiral, is that the rail gun is power hungry. My concern is that if things do not go according to plan, we will be stuck with only bad options."

"Captain," she said, stressing his rank. "That's the thing you learn as you move from an executive-officer role to that of command. It's never about choosing the best option; it's about choosing the least bad of the bad options."

She paused to let her lesson sink in. Simmons thought about that day at Pearl Harbor and how she hadn't needed to pass on that particular nugget of wisdom.

"Captain, I believe in you. And I believe in what this bastard child of a ship might accomplish. Risks that were once unacceptable to us are now the price of doing business." Her eyes grew dark, and Simmons saw the warrior side come out of the old war-college president. "I need you to get this ship ready, because I need you to kill things out there, as many as you can, as fast as you can. I need the Directorate to feel something new: fear. You will make them feel that fear, Captain. Understood?"

Subbasement Level, G Ring, Pentagon

The door to the small conference room shut with a soft sigh and everyone in the room felt the pressure change. The naval officers there pinched their noses and exhaled to clear their ears, while the civilian scientists kept trying to swallow.

This secure space was a new design, built to defeat Directorate's eavesdropping and network attack. The original Tank, the Joint Chiefs' situation room, had been thought completely secure right up until the moment it was discovered that it had been compromised by hardware bought by a U.S. defense contractor on the cheap from a Florida subcontractor that turned out to be a shell company run by two college kids who were just reselling chips from a Chinese vendor. Everyone called these new chambers the Box, though the design was actually a box within a box. Between the two nanoparticle-infused sets of walls was a fluid that circulated at high speed in order to diffuse any signals or transmissions going in or out. Rumor had it the fluid was radioactive.

"Okay, then, let's dispense with the formalities; none of us want to sit in the Box any longer than we have to," said Admiral Raj Putnam, head of Naval Intelligence.

Links, sitting next to Darling, took his cue. "It starts in Beijing, sir. I was finishing up my assignment to the embassy — I was actually at my going-away party on my last night there. There was a Russian officer, a lifer in Beijing, whom I'd gotten to know, and he was helpful to me from time to time."

"You mean you got shitfaced with him a few times and he was running you?" said Admiral Putnam.

"No, sir, I know the game," said Links. "I'm not chipped, but you can check my viz and other records. That ties back to the party. As you know, everyone is either chipped or recording with derm mikes or viz or what have you. So I assumed there was no way he would say anything interesting."

"Yes, I've reviewed the viz from the party myself," said Admiral Putnam. "He didn't."

Links shot a look of disbelief at Darling. In the moment of silence, the womblike sound of the fluid pumping around the room seemed to intensify. Then Links cleared his throat and continued.

"It's the context that makes our conversation interesting. As you saw, we were talking about Star Trek, the old television and film series. I'd talked about a lot of things with Sechin, but never science fiction. Usually he just gave me gossip on the Directorate's internal politics or upcoming promotions, that kind of thing. So this stuck in my mind," said Links. "Sechin explained how proud he was that one of the characters, Chekov, was named after this Russian scientist, Pavel Cherenkov. Honestly, Admiral, I figured he was just drunk. Then yesterday, after hearing about what happened to the USS *John Warner*, it clicked."

Links wondered how old the admiral was. He wore his gray hair shaved to the skull, like most of the population of the Pentagon, some kind of show of commitment to the war effort. The admiral had smooth, unblemished skin but a nose like a moon rock. He might be old enough to have watched the first wave of Star Trek movies.

"So how does his sci-fi drinking tales square with what you saw?" said Admiral Putnam to Darling.

"I believe it relates to how they targeted our undersea assets," said Darling. "There were no Directorate submarines or surface ships in our area of operations other than the target we engaged. Nor were there any aircraft. We owned that box. Or so we thought."

Darling chewed his bottom lip in evident frustration. "To answer your question, though, we need to give some context, which Dr. Shaw from NASA is best situated to provide."

He turned to the man seated at his left. Shaw did not look the part of a scientist, being tall and wiry with a swimmer's broad shoulders. He also wore an expensive suit, flashy, in the 1930s-style now back in fashion. And to cap it, he had his slender, rose-tinted viz glasses perched on his head, almost like a tiara. The intended effect, whatever it was, was lost on the admiral.

Shaw stood and began to speak as a video projection appeared behind him. The content failed to match the vibe he gave off.

"When a photon exits a vacuum and enters a dielectric medium at a speed greater than the phase velocity of light, a wonderful result occurs, which proved to be key to science's understanding of everything from the nature of black holes to the stars. Let us begin with the mathematical foundations."

As Shaw scribbled out an equation that was projected on the wall of the Box, Admiral Putnam turned to the two officers and said, "Gentlemen, I don't have time for a dissertation defense; we have a war to win. How does this link to Cherenkov and the subs?"

"He's coming to it, sir," Links responded. "Dr. Shaw, perhaps the metaphor you used to explain this to us might be more helpful now than the math."

"Ah yes," said Dr. Shaw. "You are familiar with what happens when an aircraft breaks the sound barrier by traveling faster than the speed of sound: A sonic boom trails behind it. Cherenkov radiation is that, in a sense, playing out at the electron level. What we know as light speed is possible only in a vacuum. When light travels through different mediums, such as water, it is slowed down by the matter in those mediums. Thus, it is possible for charged particles to travel faster than light through those surroundings. These particles, however, are still interacting with the same medium, exciting the molecules in it to release photons that pile up behind. Thus, the boom is a sort of cone traveling behind the subatomic particles. In nuclear reactors, which I understand you are interested in, the particles move away at higher speeds than light does, giving the wonderful blue glow you might be familiar with. That is Cherenkov radiation."

Links jumped back in, knowing he was going to lose his audience if he didn't intervene. "And, sir, that may be connected to another mystery. In the antisubmarine group, we've been focusing on the Directorate offensive at Pearl Harbor and then out at sea. But the attack, of course, began in space. And when you speak with our DIA colleagues about that, they'll tell you that one target didn't make sense, a particular NASA research satellite. We'd assumed that the Directorate had gotten their intel wrong and thought it was a clandestine spy satellite.

That's why Dr. Shaw is here. Doctor, could you tell the admiral what your project at NASA focused on?"

"It was originally designed to collect Cherenkov radiation for research into the origin of black holes. But because NASA wanted to show Congress 'tangible results'" — Shaw put that phrase in air quotes, as if to show his disdain for applied research — "it was also used to study nuclear power plants and the real and potential dispersion of radiation after events like the Fukushima and Maine Yankee incidents."

Darling cut in. "So, sir, I ran down the old Pentagon budget funding for R and D programs and found that back in the twentieth century, the Office of Naval Research did some studies that showed that tracking a reactor via the Cherenkov radiation it emitted was theoretically possible. But the subject was never really explored. It wasn't just that the project had a low likelihood of success; it was that even if it worked, there wouldn't be much of a payoff for us. Our entire sub fleet was nuclear, while the Russian and Chinese subs that were the most problematic for us were the quiet, diesel-driven ones. There were no incentives for investing in that kind of research. ONR assumed that no one other than us was advanced enough to do it, and strategists worried that if we made the effort, well, the research might get out, and we would just be doing the other side a favor."

Links jumped back in. "We have to conclude that they made a breakthrough and discovered how to track the Cherenkov radiation, which allowed them to de-stealth and target our submarines, as well as anything else powered by a nuclear reactor. And that solves both mysteries, the attacks at sea and the targeting of Dr. Shaw's satellite. Because if you and the other side both had that ability, you would want to make sure the other guys lost it. You'd take it away from them, even if they hadn't known they'd had it in the first place."

The admiral didn't respond for a full ten seconds. But his jaw clenched and a single bead of sweat formed at his temple. Then his words poured out in the quick cadence of someone who cannot quite believe what he is saying and so wants to get it out as fast as possible.

"This theory sounds like an improbable mix of drunken gossip and answers looking for questions. Which means it's probably correct. And if it is, we have a very, very serious problem."

Ka'ena Point State Park Beach, North Shore, Hawaii Special Administrative Zone

Major Conan Doyle aimed for the break in the reef, navigating the standup paddleboard out through the mellow swell. The Boeing D-TAC microcomputer strapped to her forearm vibrated, indicating she was close to the rendezvous point. She'd been wearing the standard-issue black plastic device the morning of the invasion, part of the emergency kit used to communicate securely with downed pilots. Three days after the convoy raid, it had suddenly pulsed with an incoming message.

A quick scan of the stars overhead, the shore behind her, and the jet-black ocean farther out showed nothing.

Had she incorrectly decoded the message? She dropped to her stomach and used the paddle to hold the board against the current, feeling a sharp hunger pang as she lay prone. She should have taken a blue before she left, but she wanted to conserve them.

The microcomputer had directed her to this location. Earlier, Nicks had revealed that the group had it at four-to-one odds that it was a trap.

"That's why God gave us grenades," Conan replied.

And so here she was, exposed. "The real reason you want to go," Nicks had said, "is so you can wash your clothes." That was true. She'd paddled out barefoot but kept on the pants that she'd worn for two months straight.

A twitch beneath the surface caught her attention. Something had moved. Something big.

The innate animal sense of being near something bigger and more powerful chilled her immediately and blocked out her hunger pangs. It was like pounding a handful of stims. Doing that wasn't her style, though. Everybody was different. Some people needed stims when they entered the breach. Others needed focus. Beta-blockers worked best for her, as she was naturally keyed up enough.

She held herself steady on the board, fighting to keep her legs from shaking. Another dark glimmer beneath the surface. A faint eddy whirled in front of her.

Even if she'd had a gun, she couldn't have shot it. Directorate sensor balloons would vector a patrol to the area, and she'd be on the rack within an hour as Chinese and Russian interrogators cut her open and pumped her full of drugs. Combat medics had their golden hour to save a life. The Directorate interrogators had their golden hour to exploit it. Or so she'd heard. It would be better to die here, alone in the jaws of a giant, than be rent into pieces, physically and mentally, by the opposition.

The water stirred maybe twenty feet from the board's nose as the dark form closed in. This was it, then.

Doyle got to her knees and changed her grip on the paddle; now she wielded it like a sword. The irony, she thought, that Conan had no real blade when she needed it most.

A dark fin sliced the water's surface. She raised the paddle over her head. At least, she thought, her last act as a Marine would be a violent one.

She brought the paddle down with all her might just as the wave glider's tubelike hull broke the surface of the water. The paddle bounced off the hard black plastic, and Doyle fell off her board and into the sea. She found herself swimming alongside the manta-ray-shaped drone, running her hands over it to convince herself it was not a shark. These nearly undetectable vehicles used almost no electricity. They relied on the ocean waves' energy, rather than traditional engines, to drive them forward. Doyle's D-TAC buzzed again to indicate that the wave glider had established a network connection with the microcomputer. A faint green message reported it had downloaded a series of files, and then another message told her what to do.

To open the cargo hatch, she first had to pull off a collection of trash hung on the vessel's foils. The drone must have transited through the Great Pacific Garbage Patch. Inside the vessel's hold were two waterproof duffle bags. The way their camouflage pattern shifted to match the rippling ocean surface and then the paddleboard's deck made it clear something important must be inside.

Presidium Boardroom, Directorate Headquarters, Shanghai

When Vice Admiral Wang Xiaoqian stepped through the holographic globe onto the raised podium in the center of the room, all conversation stopped.

There was no longer a need for his old classmate to introduce him. Most of the audience he had never met in person, but they all knew Admiral Wang's face from the viz updates. The newscasters called him "the new Sun-Tzu," the architect of the new victory who had been inspired by the wisdom of old. He knew it was not a true assessment of his place in history, merely a creation of the Information Ministry's algorithms and driven by what tested best with the public. It was pleasing, all the same, and more important, it created a new responsibility to be seen and heard. That was the reason for holding the briefing in Shanghai, rather than Hainan: to ensure the civilian leaders felt involved.

The room was sleeker, more stylish than the military's command center. It also held a much larger group. Assembled today were dozens more than usual; the core Presidium membership had brought their aides and cronies. This was a triumphant moment, after all, one to be shared widely.

As Wang took his position at the front of the room, a large holographic banner fluttered behind him — the United Kingdom's new red-and-white flag flapping in a nonexistent wind, the blue of Scotland having disappeared after the second independence referendum in the wake of the attack.

"Just one! In Europe, only one ally stands with the Americans: the no-longer-great Great Britain," said Admiral Wang. NATO's dissolution had been a long time coming, but the alliance's sudden unraveling by a simple diplomatic vote was almost as big a shock to Washington as the Directorate's surprise attack had been.

"And they have what to offer their Yankee allies? The very same F-35 fighter jets whose electronics we know well, and a carrier jointly owned with the French that Paris refuses to allow to go beyond the Atlantic."

The flag receded into the corner of another flag.

"In the Pacific, who stands with the United States?" asked Admiral Wang. "Again, just one. Australia." Wang eyed the audience. Most seemed attentive, a sign of their respect, and it was almost time for them to put on their viz glasses.

"How recently did they believe that our need for their minerals was a vise clamped around our balls? What good are they now? You are more skilled in business than I," he said, knowing it was important to show deference to this audience. "But even a mere sailor like myself can understand that their entire economy is based on something that they can no longer sell without our consent. The blockade remains unbroken, and our mineral reserves are more than adequate. Soon enough, they will beg us to take what they once threatened to withhold." Wang added, paraphrasing Sun-Tzu, "To subdue an enemy without fighting is the acme of skill."

The last flag appeared: the American flag. He stepped forward, and the flag shrunk behind him, the symbolism not lost on the audience.

"Please put on your glasses," said Admiral Wang. He donned a matte-black carbon-and-titanium mesh pair of Prada viz glasses, a Shanghai-only limited-edition model that his mistress had bought for him soon after the invasion of Hawaii. They were too flashy for his taste, but he knew they would go over well with this crowd.

The viz feed took them through the flag and into a sweeping tour of images collected from both intelligence sources and open-source feed. A line of F-35 fighter jets sat abandoned at Kadena airfield, the base now back under Japanese control as part of the neutrality deal. Then a line of American families waiting at a food-relief center in Indianapolis, all of them eyeing the neon-orange boxes on the other side of a taped blue line. The next image was the floor of the U.S. House of Representatives, where lawmakers from the Second Congressional District of West Virginia and the Sixth Congressional District of Washington flailed at each other with liver-spotted fists. That was followed by a bed of wilting roses laid around the hooves of the famous bull sculpture on Wall Street, a gloomy reminder of the rash of trader suicides that had followed the stock market's collapse.

"These images show the new reality the Americans are learning to live with. In time, they will see the advantage of their fate."

The audience was then flung high into orbit alongside the Tiangong-3 space station. A collective gasp of awe followed, predictably. They gazed down at the Pacific, and then there was another wave of gasps as they began to free-fall through the atmosphere, dropping all the way down to Pearl Harbor. Slowly, the audience took in a panoramic view of the harbor from the perspective of the second deck of a Chinese warship moored there, which allowed them both to catch their breath and see the at-ease sailors, who looked like they belonged there as much as at any home port in China. The Presidium members and their guests burst into applause at the journey and where it had ended, in evident victory.

"But the beginning of wisdom is to call things what they truly are. That was a magnificent tour of our achievement to date. Yet we must understand this: We are at a stasis point, not a completion point. We are no longer fighting battles, but the war is hardly over," Wang said. "America's conventional forces cannot reach Hawaii, let alone attack us here. But those facts don't stop the Americans from harboring such ambitions."

The scenes then flashed quickly: A company of American Marines in desert camouflage, a mix of shame and anger on their faces as they trudged down the stairway of one of the civilian passenger jets the United States had been forced to lease from Brazil in order to extricate its troops stranded in the Middle East. Next was a warship in San Francisco Bay covered with a ramshackle assortment of tarps and scaffolding, clearly undergoing some kind of refit. Then a time-lapse satellite image of a Connecticut shipyard making painfully slow progress constructing a single submarine. Then the sad face of a little girl as her father helped her place her pink tablet computer, decorated with ribbon, inside a handmade victory box at her school. The tablet would be taken apart for its microchips, which were no longer available from China.

"The combination of our opening strikes and your actions on the economic side since have been devastating," said Admiral Wang. "But we must remain alert. I told you months back that we had no choice, and now they have no choice. Their dignity drives them to believe they must try once more. And this strike they prepare is one we should welcome, not fear. Only after it fails will they accept the new turn in history, theirs and ours.

"My reverence for Sun-Tzu is well known and so I will close with a quote that shows the journey yet to come. 'To secure ourselves against defeat lies in our own hands, but the opportunity of defeating the enemy is provided by the enemy himself.'"

The viz feed ended, and Admiral Wang removed his glasses. He felt a hand patting his shoulder in congratulations and turned to see

Wu Han, the economics minister, who would be making the next presentation.

"Sterling" Wu had built his fortune through Macau's gaming industry. During the transition, he had been a crucial source of intelligence and thus leverage against the old Communist Party bosses and their cronies, many of whom had been indebted to Wu in some financial or personal way.

Wu's presentation lacked dancing girls but little else when it came to showmanship. The music built steadily as he discussed how the Directorate was beginning to gain more favorable trading concessions from countries in Latin America and Europe. It reached a crescendo as he announced that preparations to extract natural gas from the Mariana Trench site were ahead of schedule, while Mexican and Venezuelan oil imports were already increasing.

The economics minister largely steered clear of Admiral Wang's purview until he reached the topic of the Panama Canal. It still remained a sore point between the two sides of the Directorate. Shutting down the Americans' ability to swing forces easily between the oceans had been a necessary part of the attack plan, drawn from analyses Wang had commissioned about mistakes Japan had made during the previous world war. The Americans' only other route through Cape Horn was thousands of miles beyond their air cover and being dealt with through a mix of submarine picket lines and a debt swap for basing deal with Argentina. But to the business side of the Presidium, the elegant military solution was viewed as an investment lost. The compromise the two sides had worked out was that the canal-repair costs would be included in the reparation demands that the Brazilians would pass on to the Americans.

Wang nodded as if in empathy with Wu's lament but then switched from watching the presentation to catching up on his real job: running a war. A short viz report his aide had sent him showed the christening of a new *Luyang IV*–type guided-missile destroyer but also noted a decrease in crew preparedness.

Next up was the information minister, a young technocrat who had made his fortune in the software industry. He kept his blue-tinted viz glasses on the entire time and looked timidly at the floor while he spoke.

"Our Weibo micro-blog analysis reveals positive feedback from the public is seven percent greater than the most optimistic models predicted," he said. "We have the kind of support that will allow us to continue without worrying about any unexpected expressions of disharmony."

Admiral Wang's face showed intent interest, but his focus remained on his work as he scanned on the viz through the latest intelligence reports on American ship movements.

"Optimism about the economic future is high, again reinforcing the stability and harmony necessary for enduring growth," the information minister concluded. Still staring at the floor, he mumbled his verdict: "The people are with us because we are winning."

"No, they are with us because they feel that the war is over," General Wei, commander of China's land forces, interjected. "And it is. The Americans are . . ."

He paused, looked over at Wang, and said, "Defeated."

It was a veiled attack on Wang, all the more notable for taking place in front of the Presidium's civilian members. The prior meeting of its military members at Hainan Island had been contentious as the officers argued over whether to consolidate their gains or follow Wang's proposal and press their advantage against the Americans in order to provoke one last action before they were truly ready. The question was whether the general's retort in front of the civilians was personal, due to jealousy over the plaudits that Admiral Wang had received, or institutional, part of the army's ongoing play for power. Wang quickly made eye contact with his aide to alert him that what he was about to say might cause trouble for them both.

"Of course, I agree with General Wei that we are all swimming in success." A gentle reminder that the victory had been determined at sea, not by Wei's land forces. "But I must disagree with his word choice. *Defeated* implies that this war is over. One cannot make a foe accept defeat even when they have lost everything all at once. Remember that," said Admiral Wang. "Our ultimate victory is built upon their acceptance of defeat. They are not there yet and that understanding is not likely to be reached through a peaceful process."

"What can they do to fight us?" asked Wu, the economics minister. "Their economy, and its military-industrial complex, is so dependent on manufacturers elsewhere for spare parts that it cannot help but grind to a halt."

"Projections show the next three to six months should see its complete collapse. That is defeat in my eyes," added General Wei.

"We can hope so," Wang countered. "But history shows that great powers have trouble accepting their own decline. They tend to go down in a very messy manner."

"They wouldn't dare to mount an offensive at this point," said General Wei. "Will they christen ships just to see them sink? Fly aircraft only to see them shot down? They now know that we control the heavens and can track their every move."

"Let them try," said the information minister, still addressing his shoes. "New battle footage would be most helpful for our approval ratings as well as the combined harmony index. Quite a bump."

"Do you not see they are now in a situation we were once in, facing a foe who operates with unfettered access to the air, space, and sea, who could watch and deny their every move?" said Admiral Wang. "But that does not mean they are a defeated nation. Our next steps will require guiding them to this realization."

He explained his proposed strategy to block the United States' maritime trade. This included targeting the Atlantic routes of supply, where the Directorate had not yet deployed its Stonefish missiles for fear of triggering a conflict with Europe.

"Our goal should not be more fighting for fighting's sake, but fighting to provoke the right response, a final sortie by the remnants of the American fleet that will allow the war to be ended on our terms. And yet, then, we must give the Americans a means to save face when defeat is to be accepted. As Master Sun advised, 'We must build our foes a golden bridge to escape across.'"

The economics minister responded. "Admiral, the question of what to do with the Hawaii zone is as simple as it would be on any card table. You do not just return to your foes what they have lost. They must give you a proper exchange for it. Both our energy security needs and the honor of the nation deserve that. And, indeed, even if you are right, and the Americans do make another attempt before they accept they have lost, this is for the best. You do not want someone to flee the table; you want him to remain and play the game, hand after hand, until his wallet is empty and his will is gone."

The meeting continued in circles like this. At eighty minutes in, Wang's aide came over to him as planned. The admiral rose without a word, feigning disappointment that duty was now taking him away from the others' company. His aide remained in his place, recording with his viz glasses and ready to reach Admiral Wang if needed.

In the bright, sunlit hallway packed with assistants and aides, Admiral Wang heard someone call him.

It was the Russian liaison officer to the Directorate's military planning group. Admiral Wang struggled to remember his name, wishing he were still wearing his glasses.

"Admiral, my congratulations," said the officer in fluent Mandarin. His dress uniform was well worn, but immaculate. "I know you are a busy man. I only wanted to say, as one warrior to another, that how you conducted yourself in there was impressive. I'm not sure I could have been as restrained."

Wang weighed the remark. He judged the faded blue eyes, set wide apart beneath a forehead bisected by a faint scar. The tone of his voice was conspiratorial, in the manner of one professional addressing another.

"I don't envy you, having to engage with civilians like that while you also have a war to win," the Russian officer continued, clearly enjoying his own voice. "It is, though, of course, the price of the compromise your Directorate has made, to be led by both those in uniforms and those in business suits. In Russia, it is much simpler: Whatever our dear leader says goes."

"Indeed. Your leader still has the killer instinct," said Admiral Wang.

"So do you, Admiral, so do you." Wang nodded his thanks, but the officer continued on. "More important, you told them an essential truth I must agree with you on. The Americans cannot be counted out. Ever." Major General Sergei Sechin smiled.

Sandy Beach Park, Hawaii Special Administrative Zone

Lieutenant Feng "Frank" Wu stopped in the warm, waist-deep water and froze.

He'd lost her.

Then she reappeared. Ten meters ahead.

A minute ago, she was wearing a black bikini top. Now she was topless, beckoning him farther out.

It was all the motivation he needed, despite this being only his second time on a surfboard. He had enjoyed many privileges as a son of a member of the Directorate's Presidium, but surfing was not one of them. Though he had gotten his degree at UCLA before the war, he had not wanted to have reports reach his father that instead of studying mechanical engineering, he was spending his time as a beach bum. No, he had always done his duty, even now in this show of shared patriotism, where all the Presidium's second sons had joined the military. Not the heirs, of course; his older brother stayed safely back in Macau.

But no one said duty didn't have to come with deserved rewards. There were better things to do than pore over casino ledgers. And learning to surf with a beautiful, topless girl was one of them.

Frank paddled eagerly, arms crashing down into the water, which kept making the board shoot out in front of him. Strength did not matter in the water. He was sure he heard a giggle over the rush of the surf, and then he caught a glimpse of flesh as she dove again.

The surf breaking on the reef was getting louder. Yet the water was shallow here; he could stand up if he needed to. Besides, Directorate sailors weren't supposed to be afraid of the ocean, or beautiful girls.

I'm one of the good guys, he'd wanted to explain to her.

She emerged just beyond his reach, her naked chest gleaming in the moonlight. Then she dove again, the flash of white revealing she was no longer wearing her bikini bottom either.

He nearly fell off the board when Carrie reappeared at his side, treading water and flashing an enormous smile. It must be deeper here, just outside where the waves were breaking. At least it was calm.

She climbed up on the board and sat behind him, her body so close he could feel her nipples press into his back.

"We're nearly at the break," she said. "You have to feel it. It's magic."

She explained how she wanted him to paddle into the wave. If a wave was about to break on him, she explained, he should just duck under the water and wait for it to pass. You just had to be patient.

"Be brave," she said. "That shouldn't be so hard for a soldier like you."

He was a sailor, but before he could correct her, she dove under again. He pressed his body into the board, arched his back, and paddled smoothly now. As he paddled, he realized the waves were much bigger than they had looked from shore.

In an instant, a wave lifted the board upward and toward the beach, then dumped him into the surf. He tried to get up by kicking off the bottom with his feet. But he couldn't reach the bottom here.

He surfaced, blinked salt water from his eyes, and reached out for the board, but another wave washed over him.

Where was she?

He closed his eyes as another wave started to break over him. With a big breath of air, he ducked under the water, just like she had said to do.

Then he felt a soft touch on his cheek: the board's leash flickering about underwater. He brushed it aside, but then it became taut, pulling around his neck. He grabbed the cord, but the hand trying to push it away was gradually drawn closer to his throat. His other hand reached out, but the current kept turning him around. He kicked, trying to reach the water's surface, trying to breathe, swim, and fight all at the same time.

The harder he fought, the tighter the leash squeezed as wave after wave broke over him.

JFK-Citigroup Airport, Queens, New York City

"You want a letter of what?"

Admiral Beyer didn't like having to leave the Pentagon in the middle of a war. And he definitely did not like having to sit inside a 787-9 executive jet that had been done up like the Studio 54 nightclub from the 1970s.

"A letter of marque, Admiral. My lawyers tell me I need one," said Aeric Cavendish. He added, sotto voce, "I would have assumed a sailor would understand this from his naval history, but I guess not."

Admiral Beyer dug his fingernails into the seat's brown velour. Sitting beside him, the president's deputy chief of staff, Susan Ford, watched the admiral, ready to intervene if he took the bait. Fortunately, Beyer didn't react. He'd read the intelligence profile and was prepared for a great deal of nonsense.

Sir Aeric K. Cavendish had been born Archis Kumar to a middle-class family in the suburbs of Melbourne. Trained as a geneticist, he had made his first billion from several key patents in cell regeneration and cholesterol blockers. But Kumar soon figured out his talents lay in organizing other scientists to make money, and he'd ridden the biotech boom to the ranking of seventh-richest man in the world, notably the only billionaire among the world's top twenty-five who did not live in China, Russia, or the Middle East. And when the world economy tanked, he scooped up everything from the business holdings to the private islands of the overextended billionaires farther down the list.

Whether it was changing his name to something more royal or buying Manchester United and forcing the team's manager to put its new owner in as goalkeeper in a match against Leeds, the billionaire seemed to follow whatever whim he woke up with in the morning. And apparently, Beyer thought, his latest whim was to waste an admiral's time.

"Let me put it in your American terms, then, since trying to meet on common naval ground was apparently unwise on my part. I want a hunting license," said Cavendish. He made a pistol with his right hand and pointed it upward, miming shooting at the lime-green shag-carpeted ceiling. "For up there."

Beyer sat back heavily in his seat and began softly tapping his fingers. If Cavendish had known Morse code, he would have recoiled at the insults the admiral was hurling at him.

"Sir Aeric, please tell us exactly what you have in mind," Ford said.

Cavendish closed his eyes, as if collecting his thoughts. In fact, he had collected them carefully over the past several days. The idea might have started as a whim, but Sir Aeric had thoroughly investigated and vetted it. He knew that it was feasible, though it would seem outlandish.

"The United States military's predicament is evident," Cavendish said. "Your airpower projection is limited, especially given that you no longer trust your own warplanes. The land forces are now mostly in the retail and border-security business. Guarding stores from looting and the border from people who no longer want to cross it is, I suppose, the best way to keep the country on its feet," said Cavendish. "Your navy's primary mission, given that it cannot sail past what the Chinese have aptly labeled a demilitarized zone — demilitarized for you, not them, of course — is corrosion avoidance. That is also a battle you will lose, I am sorry to say."

Beyer looked at Ford and began to stand. "I don't have time for this bullshit. I need to get back to the building," said Beyer. Ford responded by putting her hand on Beyer's.

"Sir Aeric, you are testing the admiral's patience, and now mine. And when you waste my time, you waste the time of the president of the United States," she said.

"Please, I apologize," said Sir Aeric. "I grew too . . . excited. Allow me to pause the conversation a moment and reset."

A traditionally dressed English butler came in and wordlessly offered each a flute of champagne. There was no way Beyer was going to drink with this man, but he couldn't find anywhere to set the glass down other than the shag carpet, where it would tip over.

Cavendish's flute was half empty when Beyer looked back up. Good. Maybe the arrogant bastard was nervous after all.

"Admiral, please, you must try it, I bought it just for you," said Cavendish. "It is one of the last 1907 'Shipwrecked' Heidsiecks. This bottle was on a freighter that was sunk by a U-boat in the First World War and sat on the bottom of the Baltic for the next century, perfectly preserved in the icy waters."

"You were saying . . ." Ford prompted as Beyer looked at the world's most expensive champagne with new respect. He had to admit, he was charmed by the twit's nautical touch.

"This predicament is intolerable to you, but also to me. To fully enjoy my assets, I need the world back the way it was," said Sir Aeric. "I have identified some impediments to this goal. Chief among them is the Tiangong station orbiting above the Pacific and what it does to limit your ability to act in the manner that I need you to act. It allows the Directorate to effectively command the heights of any battle. And, as best as I have been able to determine from my extensive contacts, you have failed in all your attempts to attack it. This, you worry, ultimately leaves you only the option of a nuclear response, which you are not certain would succeed and which, more pertinently, would escalate this conflict in a manner that would truly make all our lives intolerable."

"I cannot confirm or deny any of that, but for the purposes of our conversation, let's assume you are correct," said Beyer. He felt the champagne flute warming. From 1907? It would be a shame to waste it.

"From the heavens come . . . oh, forget all that," said Cavendish, his cultivated accent slipping back into his native Australian one. "Look, mate, if you want to win back your waters, and I do believe they are providentially yours, you are going to have to do something about that damned space station. But without provoking a nuclear fuss. Righto?"

Beyer nodded. It was now or never with the champagne. He drank it down in one gulp.

"Well done!" Cavendish, his British accent returning. "In exchange for a letter of marque, *sicut aliter scitur* my hunting license, I will eliminate this impediment to your operations at a time of your government's choosing."

"How might this work?" said Ford.

"First the contract part. My lawyers advise me that, as allowed under article one, section eight of that fantastic old document, the United States Constitution, I will require a letter of marque in order to be registered as an official privateer," said Cavendish. "You know, perhaps I might be able to acquire one of the original copies of the Constitution. What would that run, Ms. Ford? Safekeeping and all that."

Beyer interrupted. The champagne had been pretty decent, but the little twit was back to wasting his time.

"Look, I don't care what the lawyers think. Not my job. What I care about is winning this war," said Beyer. "Because I'm not here just to help you cross an item off your bucket list."

"No, Admiral, I am here to help you," said Cavendish.

"How?" said Beyer. "All I see is a guy with a funny name who's sitting in a plane rigged out like a porno set and drinking a glass of old champagne in a country that's trying to explain to kindergartners how rationing works. So what are you going to give us in exchange for this letter you want?"

"A secret weapon, the likes of which the Directorate has never faced before," whispered Cavendish, softly touching his empty flute against his temple. "My imagination."

USS *Zumwalt*, Mare Island Naval Shipyard

Vern Li wiped the sweat from her brow and looked again. There. She took off her viz glasses and the graffiti was gone. She dabbed the sweat from her nose and put the glasses back on. There it was again.

She wobbled as if the ship were pitching at sea. The fresh red paint looked like blood.

We are watching you, Chink.

"Vern, you okay?" asked Teri, a thirty-five-year-old software engineer from Caltech who was working with her in the confines of the engine room.

"Uh, no. I mean, I think so," said Vern.

"Sit down here," Teri gently commanded. "Do you want a stim? We've been at this for, like, twenty hours."

"Do you see anything odd here? At all?" said Vern.

"Yeah, everything I see on this ship is odd," said Teri.

"No, I mean, do you see anything around us, like writing on the wall over there?" said Vern.

"Writing? No. You want me to get the corpsman?" asked Teri. "This is not good. How much did you take?"

"It's not the stims," said Vern.

"I heard there was a bad batch going around. Might have been Directorate tampering; at least that's what the gov feed said. But the smart money says someone's cutting it with laundry soap to make a few extra bucks."

Chink. What century was this? How dare they doubt her!

"Here, sit down," said Teri, more firmly this time. "What's the matter?"

Vern opened her mouth to explain what she was seeing and then clenched her jaw shut. If the power systems failed in combat, the ship and likely whoever wrote that would die. And the power systems depended on this *Chink's* graduate-school science project. It was that simple.

She flung her viz glasses at the spot on the wall. They hit where the graffiti would have been if someone had had the courage to write it in actual blood-red paint.

"Vern?" said Teri. "Take it easy. I'm going to go get somebody; you just rest."

Vern crawled on hands and knees to pick up her glasses. They weren't even scratched. How she wished they were broken. She pushed the reset button at the temple and waited for them to reacquire the *Zumwalt's* network. She closed her eyes when she put them on. When she opened her eyes, the graffiti was still there.

The sound of heavy footsteps made her get up.

"Vern, this is Chief Simmons," said Teri.

"Dr. Li, I hear you're not feeling well," said Simmons.

"I'm just tired of this shit," said Vern.

"From what I understand, you may be the most important person on this ship," said Simmons. "So you're part of the equipment, then, and that makes you my responsibility. Let's get you topside, give you some air, feed you, and get you back to work."

Vern laughed at the notion of her being literally a part of the ship. This world seemed so absurd because it was true.

"More important than the captain?" said Vern.

"Well, that's a complicated answer for me, Dr. Li." Mike laughed. "I'll just say definitively you're more important to the ship."

Vern laughed again. Teri gave them both a nervous grin.

Vern studied the old sailor. It seemed he'd never had a day of doubt in his life.

"Teri, I need to have a word alone with the chief," said Vern.

"Uh," said Teri. "All right. I'll go grab some water and then meet you by the stern."

Mike stepped aside to let Teri squeeze past. Despite his heavy footsteps, he had a surprising ease about him on the deck, at least for an old guy.

"So, Dr. Li, tell me what's really going on," said Mike.

Vern took off her viz glasses and held them out.

"You have to see for yourself," said Vern.

"Why don't you just show me," said Mike.

"I am," said Vern.

"No, I mean *actually* show me," said Mike.

"I can't. You need to wear my viz," said Vern.

Simmons held the glasses out in front of him with a mix of disdain and, Vern sensed, fear.

"These won't fit," said Mike. "How about you tell me . . ."

Vern saw that uncertainty was a rare feeling for him, and that made him even more uncomfortable.

"You've never used viz before, have you?" she asked.

Mike looked down at the scuffed toes of his boots.

"No. I haven't," said Mike. "I never saw the point."

"I know you're an old fart, but you're not that old," said Vern. Her face reddened with embarrassment, and anger flashed across Mike's features. "I'm sorry. That's what they said we were to call you guys. Please. It's important," she said. "It's about the ship."

Before he could move, she placed the glasses carefully on his face. She noticed that his right ear was slightly lower than the left and that his nose had been broken at least once. He stiffened and then relaxed once she backed away.

He lost his balance, and she lunged forward to steady him with an awkward hug.

"Sweet Jesus," said Mike. It was so real. He'd heard it was something about the way they projected a data stream onto your retinas that made it so different from the first-generation Google Glass. With these, you weren't so much looking through the glass at the world; it was more like the world was being brought inside your brain. It gave you the sense of not just seeing, but feeling. And it felt damn weird.

Vern led him by the hand to the graffiti. He saw the sticky red that part of his brain said was real, even down to its smell, and that drowned out the other part of his brain whispering that it wasn't real, that it hadn't been there just a few seconds ago.

"What *the hell* is that?" asked Mike. "Blood?"

"Yes. At least, it's supposed to look like blood," said Vern.

"Who did this, goddamn it?" said Mike. He squinted and slid the glasses down on his nose and then back up. Down, then up again.

"That's the sickest, most cowardly thing I've ever seen," said Mike. "Anyone else see this?" She noticed his breathing had gotten deeper and the veins were bulging at his neck.

"I don't think so. Just my viz feed," said Vern, starting to collect herself. "Don't worry about it. This bullshit too will pass."

Mike stepped back and looked her over.

"No, Dr. Li. I have to do something about it. This bullshit doesn't happen on my ship," said Mike. "The captain has to be informed. The XO too."

"Shit," said Vern. "What if they think I'm some kind of a risk and make me leave? I had to get the FBI to watch my mom's house because of all the threats she got after I disappeared to come work here. People assumed I'd left for China."

Mike scuffed his boot along the deck and shook his head.

"Actually, Dr. Li, as I understand it, you'd be the last person to leave the *Z*, no matter what the graffiti on those glasses says. Whether you like it or not, you are now part of this ship. And let me be clear: I take care of my ship."

Directorate Command, Honolulu, Hawaii Special Administrative Zone

The pistol's barrel was pointed right at Colonel Markov.

This is the fourth time I've had to endure this performance, he thought.

General Yu Xilai shook the weapon slightly, as if he could not understand why Markov had not grasped the gun in thanks. "Did you know I found it with an empty magazine?" said the general. "He fired his very last round right at me."

"But how did you survive unscathed?" said Markov, taking the pistol, playing his role.

The general sat on the edge of his desk and ran a hand over his freshly shaved scalp. He shifted his body before he began the story, the wooden desk groaning under his bulk. Yu looked the role of a warrior, an image that, like too many generals, he'd traded on for much of his career. He was built like an Olympic heavyweight wrestler: a shaved skull, deep-set eyes beneath a thick brow that presided over prominent cheekbones and a large, sharp nose. But long ago, Markov had learned not to confuse the look of a warrior with actual military ability.

"Like all battle, a mix of skill and luck. This American Marine general was a warrior. Straight from the viz. He knew he could not be taken alive. After all, he was in charge of their Pacific Commands most important base. When I entered the room, there was so much smoke. But I was ready," said General Yu. "My pistol was drawn. 'Grenades?' they shouted behind me. 'No!' I shouted back. 'No!'"

"And why not?" said Markov.

"Honor," said General Yu. "He was a fellow warrior who deserved to die fighting. It was so smoky, sparks and a little fire over in the corner where one of those phosphorus grenades had already gone off. Theirs or ours, I don't know. It smelled of burning plastic. The incense of battle, right, Colonel? I could barely see. But I could sense the danger. He fired and I fired back."

"How many times?" asked Markov, on cue.

"Just once," said General Yu. "One shot was all I needed." He put his index finger between his eyes as if to make clear he did not miss.

"General, I am impressed," said Colonel Markov. He'd had his doubts after the first telling, but the story was actually true; Markov had checked with one of the commandos who'd been with General Yu that day. The weapon had indeed been pried from the dead hands of the Marine base commander killed by the Directorate general himself. But that didn't earn him Markov's respect as a leader.

He passed the SIG Sauer P226 pistol back to the general, who might have been good at leading a small unit of men in the heat of a gunfight but who was out of his element in a war that no longer followed his rules. Markov had always thought Americans would make fierce insurgents, so strongly did they believe their national narrative. After the first suicide bomber, at the King's Village shopping plaza in Waikiki, Markov knew he was right. That's why Yu kept telling the damn stories about the opening assault on Honolulu over and over. It was the one day of this war that made sense to him.

"Now to business. We have to deal with the problem at hand decisively," said General Yu.

"Just like the general you shot," said Markov.

Yu's fingers twitched and clutched the SIG pistol.

"Exactly. At least he fought with honor. I've lost enough of my men. Every night I record a message for each one's parents, or wife, or maybe a brother. Whoever is left. They deserve to know their loved ones died doing something important. To hear it from me." The general paused. Markov eyed the massive man, who seemed to grow just a little bit weak at the thought of his nightly ritual. He'd seen it before. Yu was taking the losses from the insurgency personally, a mistake too many tactical leaders made, missing their greater responsibilities.

The huge officer gathered himself and slammed the pistol back on the shelf. "It's time to put a stop to it! To be relentless in our patrols, to follow them where they hide and exact a price for every man of mine they kill."

"General, my value to you is in my candor," said Markov quietly. "So let me say that this is all wrong. The people here control our fate; you do not control theirs. It is a lesson I learned the hard way from our own experiences with insurgency. Indeed, even the Americans learned it during their own last few wars."

"Their lessons of failure are the least we should learn," said Yu. "We don't need to make friends with them. We need them to acquiesce, and that may require us to show more resolve."

"And ever more bodies?" said Markov.

"Shanghai is concerned about the optics of these attacks in the run-up to the trade conference with the ASEAN nations. They're sending a high-level delegation to visit the planned locations," said General Yu.

"Locations? You mean here? A Presidium delegation is coming to Hawaii?" asked Markov.

"Yes, and the son of one of them has just chosen to go missing," said General Yu. "The idiot's a navy lieutenant, his father's the economics minister . . ."

"All the more reason not to take the insurgents' bait," said Markov. "You don't need another car bomb or an arson spree right now, not with the delegation coming. Don't provoke the insurgents."

"*Provoke?*" said General Yu. "You fail to grasp the new reality, just as the population fails to see theirs. Let me deal with these criminals my way. Colonel, your job now is to find this lieutenant, nothing more, nothing less."

"Very well, sir," said Markov. As he left, he cast a look around the office, taking in the other vulgar trophies from the invasion. A scorched F-35 pilot's helmet sat on a shelf. The American flag that had flown at Camp H. M. Smith was folded in the glass case that also housed the pistol. A cracked gray Honolulu Police SWAT team ceramic vest was affixed to the wall next to a live tactical situation map of Directorate military patrols in the city.

The general had gathered all the totems of his opening-day victory, thought Markov, while failing to see he was on his way to losing a different kind of war.

Pineapple Express Pizza, Honolulu, Hawaii Special Administrative Zone

The first thing Major Conan Doyle noticed was the smell. Warm mozzarella, the sweet tang of tomato sauce, and the pungent funk of fresh Hawaiian marijuana. Her mouth watered, and she clenched her stomach muscles to check the pain in her gut.

They entered through the alley off Ala Moana Boulevard and made their way down to the basement. By the time they reached the bottom step, the food aromas were gone.

"Smells like shit in here," said Nicks.

"That the dope?" asked Finn.

"Nope," said Conan. "More likely us."

The restaurant's owner, Skip, came down a few minutes later with a boar-sausage-and-pineapple pizza. "Can't persuade you to have a broccoli with signature sauce?"

"The last thing my team needs is to get stoned," said Conan. There were literally a hundred ways to mix marijuana into a pizza. Skip's specialty was infusing it into butter and olive oil, which kept the pungent taste from ruining the tart flavor of a fresh tomato sauce.

"You uniforms are all alike, always stressed out, pills only. But you come back for the house special when the devils are gone," said Skip. "Got any new footage?"

"Already left it at the dead drop," she said. "You'll have to wait till you get back Stateside to see it."

"If that day ever comes."

"It will," she assured him and herself.

He handed her a blister pack of red-and-black polka-dot pills. "Ladybugs. For dessert."

"Thanks, brother," said Conan.

"I have to head back; I left Sharon up there," said Skip, and he waved a quick goodbye.

As Skip went back upstairs, Conan nodded at Nicks and Finn. "You know what to do. I'll stand guard at the door."

She drew a stubby matte-black Mossberg riot shotgun, Honolulu Police issue, cracked open the storeroom door, and poked it through. With her other hand, she picked up a slice of pizza.

Nicks and Finn moved aside some drums of flour and pulled up the grate on the basement floor that covered the sewage feed. They wrestled with the pipe's fitting and then dropped a yellow-striped tube ringed with tracks into the pipe. The Versatrax 300 had once been used by the Honolulu sanitation department for sewer-pipe inspections, but the block of nanoplex explosive duct-taped to it now gave the sewer-bot another capability. In military parlance, it was a VBIED, a vehicle-borne improvised explosive device.

Voices were raised upstairs. Quiet footsteps followed, and Conan pulled back into the room.

"Is it in?" whispered Conan. "Someone else is here. Quit dicking around."

"Bot's in, and inbound toward target," said Nicks. She sat cross-legged and could have been meditating but for the viz glasses and control gloves she wore to guide the Versatrax through the sewer system.

A girl's loud voice upstairs made them all wince. Skip's daughter, yelling at some customer.

"Just got red light from the command detonator," said Nicks. "Timer is set."

"I don't like it," said Finn. "We should just hit 'em now. Take out a sector commander, at least."

"No, they've got dignitaries coming in from Shanghai, Seoul, and Tokyo, remember? Hit the targets from off-island and we make sure the outside world knows we are still in the fight," said Nicks.

"Whatever," said Finn, pulling another slice of pizza from the plate. "Just get the little bot there first."

"Roger that," said Nicks, her hands still guiding the bot from afar, waving in the air as if she were playing patty-cake with an invisible child. "But first I need you to feed me a slice."

"What am I, your parent? Feed yourself," said Finn.

"I can't. I take my hands off the controls and our little surprise goes up someone's toilet," said Nicks. "And I know I can't trust an animal like you not to eat it all before we get done."

They quieted at a girl's scream. Skip's daughter, but clearly scared this time. They looked to see what Conan's orders were.

"Shit," said Finn. "She's gone upstairs."

USS *Zumwalt*, Mare Island Naval Shipyard

Laughter echoed through the corridor. It had not been a good day aboard the *Zumwalt*, so Mike saw no reason for this kind of screwing around.

One of the fire-suppression bots had detonated its retardant payload in the wardroom during the 0200 meal. "It looks like a herd of elephants had an orgy in there," a sailor had said, brushing past him.

Then there was the bigger problem this morning. The ship was supposed to be testing out the Navy's new ODIS-E (Objective Data Integration System — Enhanced) program, a replacement for the prewar ATHENA. But from what he could see, all the system had done was blow out a power coupling.

The devastated look on his son's face had said it all. If the ship's captain couldn't contain his disappointment, then this setback meant something ominous. What were they thinking, naming a ship's control system after a story about a Greek guy lost at sea for ten years? Nobody knew their history anymore, and apparently nobody knew network engineering either. Mike's bigger concern was the coupling. Spare parts were in short supply, and they couldn't just order another one from the Chinese manufacturer.

In the corridor, Mike stepped out of sight and listened. He heard deep laughter, the kind that's amplified by a thick gut. A woman's voice, angry, followed:

"You should be apologizing for much more than that," the woman shouted. "If you don't attach this shielding here and here, then I'm going to be the least of your headaches."

It was Dr. Li.

"You need to understand that nothing you know about gunpowder or cannonballs or whatever you did a long time ago is relevant now," she said. "If you don't shield the power cables, the energy they release, which is mostly—"

"Stop right there, lady," said one of the crew. "We get it. That's why we put some shielding there already. If you want it changed, you put it in the work-order system and we'll get to it. Your job ain't the only one that matters. Besides, who's going to verify your, uh, work?"

"Verify my work? What's that supposed to mean?" she asked.

"Yeah, well, to make sure it's done right. That it can be trusted, you know. Or maybe you already got it checked out with Beijing?" More laughter. "This might not be good enough for you, but it's the goddamn best America can do right now. Next rail shipment isn't coming into Oakland until, oh, next week? So as of now, it's good enough."

Mike couldn't place the voice. Whoever it was talked with a faint slur, as if he used a jawbone-implanted hearing device. Time to see who.

Mike stepped around the corner and cleared his throat.

"I'm hearing a lot of laughter today. Something funny?" he said. "Share it with me. Not much makes me laugh lately."

"No worries, Chief," said Parker, a petty officer second class in his thirties. "We got this handled; we're just fixing some of the shielding on the ray gun."

"Rail gun," said Vern.

"Whatever you wanna call this Star Wars shit, lady," said Parker.

Mike eyed the sailor. Parker was clearly taking advantage of the Navy's free hormone-enhancement therapy. His skin was drawn and dry, but his neck and biceps were frighteningly thick, like a bodybuilder who was five months pregnant. Mike shook his head in disappointment. The Mentor Crew was supposed to guide the new generation of wartime sailors but also to remediate new noncommissioned officers like Parker. The Stonefish strikes had cut down the ranks of the Navy's enlisted leaders, and the wave of promotions to fill the gaps had elevated far too many men and women who were not up to snuff. Mike could see why Parker had topped out just below Mike's own old rank. Becoming a chief petty officer required more than just time in service; you also had to be able to make it past a selection board of your peers.

"Her name is Dr. Li," said Mike to Parker. "You will address your betters by their titles." He turned to Vern.

"You getting what you need, Dr. Li?" Mike said, drawing out the *Doctor*.

"We need more shielding on the power cables before we can run the live-fire test," said Vern.

Mike looked at her and then turned to Parker. He stepped up so he was chest to chest with the sailor, unfazed by the younger man's bulk. As big as Parker was, he lacked Mike's ability to intimidate.

"Well, Parker here, he's concerned about America and her fleet," said Mike, speaking to Vern but looking the sailor directly in the eye, daring him to disagree. "So seeing that you are a fellow American — hell, a civilian working her ass off to help arm said fleet — Parker just volunteered to weld it in for you, since working with metal seems to be something he's got a passion for," said Mike, a backhanded compliment for a sailor who spent too much time in the weight room.

Vern pinched the bridge of her nose with obvious exasperation. "You can't use metal welding. It is an electromagnetic gun. Needs to be welded with plastic, otherwise the electromagnetic energy will . . . You want to be the guy who blew up the ship because he didn't understand the future? Let's leave it at that."

"All right, all right," said Mike. "Parker, you have one job now: Find me more shielding and install it like she wants it. Just make sure you understand what she's talking about. If you have to strip apart your beloved weight room to get it, you will. If you have to use all the plastic chow trays in the shipyard, you will. Understood? If you need to bribe, screw, or steal to get what Dr. Li needs, you will."

He turned to the others. "I know I don't have to tell Parker here, but if anybody questions one of his fellow crew members' patriotism again, I'll grind you up and feed you to the seagulls myself. Now get back to it."

Pineapple Express Pizza, Honolulu, Hawaii Special Administrative Zone

The Directorate marine was twice the size of the pizza-shop owner and he was not holding back. A desperate gasp followed each blow as Skip's lungs emptied of air.

The translator on the marine's belt was oblivious to the violence, stating the order in a digital monotone.

"Your daughter will come with us to a fancy party," said the device.

Another marine held Sharon. He pinned her arms behind her back, forcing her to stick her chest out. Her head hung down, so her black hair veiled her face.

"She's just fifteen," said Skip, gasping for breath. "She stays here—"

Two more quick blows. The crack of Skip's ribs made Sharon scream again.

"Shut it!" said the marine in English, tugging hard on her arms.

Conan ducked back into the stairwell.

A roundhouse kick from the giant marine sent Skip sliding through a cloud of flour and down behind the counter. With his brow covered in white powder, he looked up at Conan peeking through the stairway door.

Help, Skip mouthed. It looked like he couldn't even get enough air in his lungs to speak.

Conan squeezed the riot gun's pistol grip and ducked back out of sight.

A burst of Chinese among the marines followed.

Conan closed her eyes. There were four Directorate marines. She had eight rounds of ten-gauge street shot loaded. She could blow apart the restaurant in a matter of seconds.

Skip got up from his knees and charged the marines. The wet sound of his head hitting the hard yellow tile made Conan's stomach turn.

Enough.

She raised the riot gun and flicked the safety off. She would have to get in close to make sure she didn't cut down everyone in the restaurant with the gun's wide arc of fire. She counted down.

Three. Two. One.

Exhale. Go.

And then she froze. This was not the mission. She clicked the safety back on.

Skip tried to get up from the floor but made it only to his hands and knees. He spat out a sticky crimson stream that mixed with the blood pooling from his split scalp. Then another kick landed with a thump on his temple.

Sharon wailed, "Don't touch me!" Then muffled screams.

Conan dashed back down the stairs silently on bare feet.

"What the hell was going on up there?" asked Finn.

"You're fine. I had you covered," said Conan. "Just some customers getting rowdy. We gotta go out the back way, though."

Finn put his hand on Conan's arm. "What the hell is going on up there?" he asked again.

"I said let's go. That's an order," snapped Conan.

Finn, Nicks, and Conan filed out the back of the restaurant into the alley and slunk out in the darkness, slowly working their way toward their extraction point, an eight-by-six-foot steel recycling bin a few blocks away. They climbed in and covered themselves in the wet and moldy cardboard and aluminum cans that would break up their bodies' thermal signatures.

"Ten seconds to detonation," whispered Finn, and he began to count it down.

"And contact," he said.

Nothing.

"Well, at least the pizza was —" said Nicks.

An explosion detonated in the distance, the blast wave shaking the recycling bin a bit.

They waited the next hours for the morning pickup in silence broken only by the occasional siren going by. It was just reaching early morning when Finn finally decided to bring it up again.

"Conan, I'm serious," Finn whispered. "What was all the noise upstairs about? Are Skip and Sharon okay?"

"Yeah, they're fine," Conan said quietly. "Let's stay focused on the mission."

Wal-Mart Headquarters, Bentonville, Arkansas

"The act is so questionable in law as to make it positively un-American."

Jake Colby's talking points had been produced by analytic software and then checked by Legal and Public Relations. Both had advised Colby, the chief executive officer of Wal-Mart, that the most effective approach was to flip the script and paint the White House's proposal to use the old Defense Production Act from 1950 as something out of the Directorate playbook.

The act, passed at the start of the Korean War, gave the U.S. president the power to require any American company to sign any contract or fill any order deemed necessary for national defense. The CEO was now explaining to the shareholders that Wal-Mart was joining a coalition of leading multinational firms that, using both the courts and congressional lobbying, would attempt to block the act's resurrection.

"Losing is un-American!" a seventy-year-old woman in a denim pantsuit shouted back at him. He knew not to ignore her. Lee-Ann Tilden was a multibillionaire who owned 4 percent of his outstanding shares, and yet she still worked as a greeter at the Tulsa store.

The CEO tried to repeat the talking points' core premise, that a corporation's status as a legally defined individual meant that the government couldn't tell it what to do, even in a time of war.

"Legally defined individual?" Tilden retorted. "Mr. Colby, you know that's bunk and you know that Sam would want to help the country any way he could."

Before he could reply, another voice broke in. A Swiss-German accent. One of the institutional investors, in this case representing a sovereign wealth fund from Qatar that had bought a 17 percent position when the share price collapsed after America lost Hawaii. "Madame, I appreciate this company's quaint practice of letting anyone speak at these forums, but you simply fail to understand the multinational nature of this enterprise now. The global shareholder base must come first. This concern is not in the business of any one nation's war. No matter where it is based, it is a global retail chain, definitively neutral in its activities and intent," he said. "The desires of Uncle Sam, or whatever your outdated idea of a patriotic patriarch in a funny hat is, are now beside the point."

Hearing the crowd growl, Colby winced at the fund manager's gaffe. So typical. The internationals loved the company's returns but didn't bother to understand its story. *She meant Sam Walton, you moron.* Hell, the company founder's desk was on display in the museum just down the road, the papers he'd been working on the day he died still on it, as if he had just stepped out for a coffee break.

"Ladies and gentlemen, let's try to keep focused," the CEO interceded. "This is not just about the U.S. government overstepping its powers, however limited those now may be. We're on the razor's edge. The Directorate has rigged our corporate network with enough tripwires and viruses that we might lose control of the company if they don't like the way I part my hair."

"Then what do we have to lose?" said Lee-Ann. "I'm calling a vote."

There was no loss of life at Lee-Ann's Revolt, as it would become known nationwide once the viz of the meeting leaked out, but it was nonetheless momentous. The voting bloc of sovereign wealth funds proved unable to stop the small investor pool once it was mobilized. And by the end of the meeting, shareholders were no longer voting about whether to resist U.S. government rationing schemes. Instead, Wal-Mart declared war on the Directorate.

The color drained from Colby's face as he stared out at the thousands of cheering people in the company auditorium. Two thoughts crossed his mind as the tunnel vision took over. The first was that he'd have a hard time finding another job after this debacle. And the second was that America now had a new kind of logistical backbone the likes of which had never before been seen in war.

USS *Zumwalt*, Mare Island Naval Shipyard

Mike found Vern hunched over, running her hands along the thick fiber cabling that ran behind the bulkhead. The smell of ozone hung heavy in the air, a reminder of her insistence that they cut open the ship's bulkhead so she could get access to this very point. What exactly she was doing was beyond him, Mike knew. But he liked the change it brought on in her. She might have had a PhD, but it was clear to Mike that in her heart, she was a maker, a doer, like himself.

She abruptly ordered the rest of the engineers out of the area to let her work on her own. "Mike, you teach her to talk like that?" said one of them on his way topside.

She spent more time aboard than at the shore-side network data center, and, to the best of his knowledge, she had not left the shipyard in a week. She no longer talked about her life pre-Z. He knew the feeling, and how all-encompassing it could be.

He set a bottle of cold water down next to her. She continued to look at the tablet on her lap without acknowledging his presence. He stood back and studied her as she craned her neck to look behind the bulkhead. He pulled out an LED light and knelt down next to her, his knees cracking.

"Let me help," he said. "A little light."

She smiled and kept working as he held the light, shining it where she told him to in her clipped diction. He had to lean in close enough that she could appreciate how long it had been since he had had a free moment to shower. She did not recoil, however.

After about five minutes, Mike got ready to leave.

"Keep the light," he said. "I need to get back topside. They're pulling the rail-gun turret and it's a damn foggy night. If you need anything, just holler."

Vern didn't say anything; she just kept poring over her tablet computer and peering into the dark behind the bulkhead.

He stood up unsteadily and walked away with careful steps.

Just as he ducked through a hatch, he could have sworn he heard her say, "Thank you."

He stopped and turned around.

The eleven paces back to her hunched-over form seemed a long way for Mike. He needed to know something, and now was the time to ask it.

"Dr. Li, a minute with you?" said Mike.

"Now?" asked Vern.

"Yes, please," said Mike.

"Well?" said Vern.

"What I have to say, or ask, really, isn't easy but it's something I've been meaning to bring up for a little bit now," said Mike.

She stood up and pushed her viz glasses up onto her forehead, brushing a bead of sweat off the tip of her nose.

"This is hard to say, so I'll just outright say it," said Mike. "The rail-gun power system, something's wrong with it. Am I right? That's why you're pushing both the crew and the geeks so hard. You know something they don't."

He expected her to dismiss him. Instead, she smiled.

"You're right, it's not going to pass the test," said Vern.

"Shit," said Mike. "This is going to kill the captain."

"And maybe all of us," said Vern. "We'll have to see."

"I need to tell him," said Mike.

"You care for him," said Vern.

"If the ship can't fight, well, he can't," said Mike.

"He's your son; why wouldn't you want it all to work out for him?" said Vern.

"I'll get going, then, Dr. Li," said Mike.

"There's something else you forgot to ask me, isn't there?" said Vern.

"Uh, what would that be, Dr. Li?" said Mike.

"The big question," said Vern. "The most important one."

Mike looked at her quizzically.

"Will it *ever* work?" said Vern.

He smiled. "Well, I guess that will depend on you."

"Give it time," said Vern. "An old guy like you should know how to be patient."

Fort Mason, San Francisco

Jamie Simmons slipped into bed, but he was too wired to fall right asleep. He thought of all the cobbled-together Ghost Fleet ships in the Bay. His own ship, the one that the country needed most, was turning out to be the weak link. He lay back, studying the fog bank, now at the deck level of the Golden Gate Bridge. Its rise was almost imperceptible until it obscured something big from view. There was nothing you could do to drive it away. It did not have the tide's regularity, and for that reason it was all the more spectacular when it robbed you of the sight of something you took for granted, like the bridge.

A loud gurgle of the pipes woke Lindsey, who groggily turned over. "You're here. I didn't hear you come in," she said.

"Yeah," he whispered, "I didn't want to wake you. What's all that with the pipes?" he asked.

"Toilet," she said, starting to wake up. "Broken again."

"Damn it," he said. "I'll take a look in the morning."

"When? You're always out so early," she said.

"Then when I get home," he said.

"And when will that be, Jamie? You can get a warship fixed up, but the toilet is too much to handle?" she said. "I'm sure that makes sense to somebody, just not me anymore."

There was an old Navy saying that ships were like mistresses: beautiful, alluring, mysterious, requiring lots of attention, and, ultimately, marriage killers.

"I'll look at it right now," he said. The edge in his voice caused her to prop herself up on one elbow and study him.

"You can say it, Jamie," she said. "Whatever you want, just say it."

He kissed her on the forehead, not trusting anything that might come out of his mouth. His heavy footsteps said enough. The same frustration he felt at work was now part of his home.

After a half hour of struggling in vain with the toilet, he gave up and went back to the bedroom to find the kids asleep in bed with Lindsey. He must have woken them with all the rummaging around with the tools his father had left wedged behind the sink. He sat down in the old leather recliner in the corner of the room and watched them in the near darkness, trying to let the sounds of the trio's breathing drain away his stress and frustration. What he wanted to fix most, he feared he could not.

When he woke, it was just past five in the morning. Shit. He had overslept by an hour.

"Did you fix the potty, Daddy?" asked Martin groggily from the bed.

"No, sweetie, it's still broken," he said.

"Call Grandpa! He can fix it," said Claire.

"You should call him," said Lindsey, eyeing him warily.

He shook his head as the room's sensors picked up their movement and began to gradually brighten the overhead lights. "I said I'm gonna fix it and I will."

"We want Grandpa!" Claire and Martin shouted.

"It's not time to get up yet, kids," said Lindsey, shooing them out of the bed. "Back to your rooms."

"We're not calling him," said Jamie in a whisper as she walked past, leading the kids down the hall.

He went to the bathroom and showered. Under the unrelenting spray of the cold water he cursed himself. There were too few days before he went out to sea for them to have a night like this. He turned off the shower and shivered. Was this how his dad had felt when he helplessly watched his connection with the family fray? Or had he just been unwilling to try to fix it? That was the difference; his dad hadn't wanted to try. It had to be the difference. Jamie was not willing to give up.

I'm a better man than my dad, Jamie told himself as he blinked away the fatigue and cold water. *Even on my worst days.*

Honolulu, Hawaii Special Administrative Zone

Carrie wiped her hands on the front of the old black Hurley pullover that she'd worn to the beach. Then she took her backpack into the bathroom and shut the door.

She pulled her still-wet bathing-suit bottom out of the bag, tossed it into the shower, and rinsed out the sand in the hot water. Then, as the bathroom filled with steam, she undressed, looking at herself in the fogged mirror. The naked body she saw, its beauty obscured by the moisture on the glass, could have been anybody's. She was anonymous.

After she got out of the shower, she pulled a small makeup compact from the backpack. She tapped it twice on the counter and the cover popped up. She licked her index finger on her right hand and rubbed it around the rim of the compact. There.

She held up her hand to the light and saw the hair. She pulled her fiancé's black plastic brush from the jewelry box on the counter. She blew gently on her finger, and the hair fell onto the brush. Carefully, she put the brush back in the box.

Carrie sat down on the toilet and closed her eyes. Now she saw them again. Then she saw her fiancé, and, finally, she saw her father.

The inch-long cuts she made on her left thigh wiped the images of the men away. Eyes still shut, she didn't see the blood dripping onto the blue tile at her feet. The clatter of the scissors on the floor jarred her back from the moment. She stifled a cry of pain and began to wipe the blood away with her palms. She moved to the sink for a towel and then stopped. The fog on the mirror receded just enough for Carrie to look herself in the eyes.

I am not anonymous, she told herself. *I am death.*

Wal-Mart Printing Facility, Ogden, Utah

In many ways it was like watching an old Xerox copy machine in action. A thin layer of graphene chips was sprayed down by a roller that moved from one side of the table to the other. Essentially carbon atoms laid out in the same hexagonal structure of chicken wire, graphene was light and strong, and it was a great conductor. But more important, it was made from the same carbon atoms that formed everything from graphite to charcoal, so it could be sourced easily. Indeed, the graphene in this run of the machine had been pulled from the smoke of a coal-fired power plant.

There was a burning smell as a laser fired, igniting a tiny flame where the light beam came into contact with the graphene dust, melting and fusing the particles together. Then the roller swept back in the other direction, laying down another thin layer, the laser firing again, back and forth, back and forth.

In each microscopic layer, the laser carved out new shapes in the powder. Slowly, a form began to rise, akin to pieces of paper stacking up. As the laser fused it all together, the form grew into an intricate latticework, almost like a honeycomb. The roller paused as a robotic hand reached over, turned the object thirty degrees, and inserted a feed of electrical wire, and then the layering began again. In ten minutes, the form was complete. The robotic hand reached back in and lifted it up, and a spray of air blew off the remaining dust that clung to the object. The arm then moved the object outside the machine and put it in a cardboard box. After sixty forms had been placed in the box, an alarm rang.

A human worker scurried over, quickly closed the box, and ran a line of packing tape over it, sealing it shut. He slapped a barcode sticker on it, and another worker loaded the box onto a robotic pallet mover that drove itself down the aisles. Where once garden gnomes and children's bicycles had been stacked and stored, ready for distribution across the retail network, there now stood boxes of reverse-engineered spare parts, from machine-gun belts to wheel brackets to, in this case, a power coupling needed at Mare Island. Outside the warehouse, an eighteen-wheeler truck waited with a manifest for the various items that would be distributed and delivered by the next day.

Back inside, the direct-digital manufacturing machine, also known as a 3-D printer, continued its work. A new software package had been downloaded, and now the device began to build an entirely different object. The process had the efficiency of an assembly line but the flexibility to shift on demand and build any design that could be modeled with computer software.

And, even better, it could reproduce itself. The protocol, as voted on by Lee-Ann's shareholders, dictated that every tenth run would produce parts for additional 3-D printers. These would then be sold at a discount to the firms that had originally been in Wal-Mart's supply chain. The seeds of both a manufacturing revolution and a new kind of defense-industrial complex were being sown within the world's largest retail chain.

Lotus Flower Club, Former French Concession, Shanghai

Ritual could be deadly. But ritual also offered its own protection. If you followed the same patterns day after day after day, those watching knew that you had nothing to hide.

So Russian air force major general Sergei Sechin had been going to the Lotus Flower Club now for three years. The same girl. He never asked her name. He knew her only by her number: Twenty-Three.

Twenty-Three wore her jet-black hair short, cropped in a spiky mess that looked sultry, not sloppy. She might have been from Tibet; he wasn't sure. He never asked, never bothered her with fake conversation. Maybe that was why her dark eyes seemed to light up just a slight bit whenever she saw Sechin, which was once every two weeks. That was enough. He was no longer a young man.

She was chipped, of course. His Chinese counterparts could have all the biofeedback they wanted of an old man's best effort at screwing his way toward a fleeting moment of escape from age and decay. But at the Lotus Flower Club, that also meant she was wired into the room's screens on all four walls and the ceiling. The screens pulsed colors depending on her level of arousal. Whatever pills she took worked, because the explosions of light that finished off each session were unlike anything Sechin had ever seen. It was like an aurora borealis in the bedroom.

The concierge guided Sechin to his usual room and left him. Sechin knocked once, then entered.

But she was not the usual Twenty-Three.

The girl under the purple sheets had blue hair and sharp Nordic features.

Shit. Moscow must have sent her. If this was an attempt to kill him, it was not the way he'd thought it would happen. He turned to leave. *Let them shoot me in the back, the cowards.*

"Be' 'IH mej 'Iv?" she said.

He froze.

Klingon. She had just spoken Klingon.

"What did you say?" he asked.

"Be' 'IH mej 'Iv?" she repeated.

Now he was intrigued. This was too artful for the Directorate or his own intelligence service.

"Who leaves a beautiful woman" indeed?

He sat on the bed and placed one hand on her leg.

"So, we have a language in common — what shall we talk about?" he replied in Klingon.

"Come here," she said. "I'm cold. I need you to warm me."

"If you're not careful, such clumsy talk may make an old man lose his will," he said.

"Perhaps I can help." Then she lowered the sheet, revealing her breasts. "I can make them bigger if you like," she said. "Or smaller. Whatever you wish." She put a device the size of a matchbox on the nightstand.

Biomorphic breast augmentation was increasingly common, and inexpensive, in China. In Russia, it was taboo and therefore a rarity. Whoever had performed the surgery was very talented.

"There's no need," said Sechin under his breath. "They're perfect as they are. Really."

He undressed quickly, leaving his clothes in a pile at the foot of the bed.

"Your socks," she said with a giggle.

"What about them?" he said as he climbed in.

"You can take them off," she said.

"Never. So I can make a quick getaway," he said with a wink.

"Not too quick, please," she said. She pulled the sheets over them. Then she pulled another blanket made of thin metallic fabric over the sheets.

She put a hand over his mouth, and her eyes turned cold and serious, and Sechin realized he was probably not going to get laid. Nor was he going to die. The good with the bad. *Such is the intelligence business,* he thought.

She stuck her hand out from under the bed's blanket, and he heard a faint click. What he heard next stunned him. The sounds of Sechin and the previous Twenty-Three making love echoed through the room. *Do I really sound like that? Like a boar with a spear stuck in its side,* he thought.

"Our mutual friend from the Federation sends his best," she whispered in his ear.

So the American had heard him after all.

"Then tell me this: Why did he not listen to me when it mattered?" said Sechin. "I risked everything just by using the word *Cherenkov.* He could have done something."

"He is doing something now, and you can too," she said.

"Wait, are you chipped?" he asked.

"Yes, but not by Lotus Flower. I'm still a new girl," she said. "They're going to wait to see if I work out before they invest in me. Now tell me about Cherenkov, and none of the Star Trek shit."

The air under the blanket was heating up quickly and Sechin felt his face flushing from the warmth and his proximity to her. He watched a rivulet of sweat carve an arc between her breasts and move toward an enormous tattoo wreathing her waist.

"It was developed about three years ago at the Russian Foundation for Advanced Research Projects outside Moscow, our equivalent to your DARPA," he said. "It's nuclear-reactor detection from space."

"How does it work?" she asked.

"There is not enough time now. I will get you something to take to them next time," he said. "I suppose your superiors will also need to know why I am doing this?"

"Why you're in bed with me, you mean?" she said.

"They would understand that, I hope. Americans are not that prudish," he said.

"Okay, then, why?" she asked.

"Our dear leader so badly wants to matter in his old age that he fails to see that one day this will all go bad for Russia. America and Russia had our row in the last century, and it is done. I've been here long enough to know that the Directorate is the real threat, and this war only makes them stronger. Russia is merely the junior partner, and it just happens to have fifteen million Chinese residing inside its borders. It does not take an old spy to see that one day very soon the Chinese will assert their 'right to protect' their compatriots in Siberia, just as we once did to the weak states on our borders. So that is why I tried to warn your officer, for all the good it did."

"It's usually more personal. What do *you* want from this?" she said.

Sechin sighed and ran a finger between her breasts.

"My dear," he said. "Don't we all want the same thing? Money? Sex? A bit of power. Any of the three are fine with me. I'm not particular anymore."

She rolled her eyes. At that moment, the recording of one of his sessions with Twenty-Three ended with an animal abruptness. She reached out to start the recording over.

"Don't worry, it's been modified so it will sound like we're beginning again," she whispered in his ear, then she pulled back and looked him in the eye as the grunts started once more. "I don't believe you. We've seen your profile. You're too much of a romantic for the usual banal causes."

"'Too much of a romantic,' says the whore I am in bed with."

"Okay, have it your way," she said. Her voice went from a purr to command mode. "Put your hand here."

She took his hand and placed it at her waist, stopping at the tattoo. "Do you know what that is?"

He didn't feel a thing, but he knew enough to make a guess. "It's one of the new e-tattoos."

She looked surprised for a second.

"I am not as old as you might think," he said.

The ink of the tattoo was actually a derivative of the electronic ink used in the old tablet-computer readers. This modified version allowed the liquid injected into the skin to act as a sort of pillow above and below tiny embedded silicon chips wired together in an origami-like pattern. The liquid and microscopic serpentine wires formed a miniature network woven into her skin. He closed his eyes and traced its outlines while he hummed the middle section of Dmitri Shostakovich's Fifth Symphony.

"I'm going to need you to do something for me, and I can't lie, it's going to hurt," she finally said. "But we think it's the best way to securely get us the information you offer."

"I was afraid you might ask that," he said.

She kissed him gently on the chin.

"How can you know pleasure without understanding pain?" she responded as she kissed him again.

North Fork of the Kaukonahua Stream, Oahu, Hawaii Special Administrative Zone

"Push the pace," Conan hissed, walking in the knee-deep river water. "Or we're going to miss our window to get inside the perimeter."

Finn didn't reply; the only noise was his sandals' soft sucking in the mud.

The stream was low, hedged in on either side by thick emerald vegetation and slashes of brown. The two walked with hunched backs, their wool blankets drooping heavily on aching shoulders. They were the tail end of the patrol, four more Muj strung out ahead. Charlie had point. He wasn't military like the rest, but it was time to break him in. He'd been a golf pro at the Turtle Bay Resort, once a star player for Wake Forest University but never making it past the Nike tour level. Finn had served with Charlie's older brother Aaron, the three of them going out drinking whenever Aaron visited on leave. The Muj had used Charlie's apartment as a hide site two months back, and he had demanded to go with them. Charlie had said that his big brother had kicked his ass bad enough when they were little, and he wouldn't survive what happened after the war if Aaron found out he hadn't been in the fight.

The cuts and scrapes on their legs attested to the night's hike almost to the top of a nearby peak. They had pulled up a hundred and fifty yards short of the summit to avoid highlighting their position along the ridgeline, and Conan had disappeared for an hour while the rest set a security detail below. Conan would not tell Finn or any of the others why they'd had to go there. They knew she kept it from them for operational security, but it still made the whole trek a sullen expedition.

Now, after a long hike back down, it was raining. Finn splashed into the swollen stream behind Conan and trudged on through the water. Going that way, they left no tracks and erased their movement signature in case they were being monitored from above, but really, he'd have chosen to go the stream route anyway. He had an infected cut on his heel that felt better in the water.

They arrived at a small pedestrian bridge they had hidden the bicycles under. It was a motley mix they'd picked up along the way, just like their array of weapons. Finn had scored the best, a 27.5-inch wheeled carbon downhill mountain bike with motorcycle-like suspension they'd stolen from a vacation villa whose owners were unlikely to come back until the war was over. Conan rode a three-speed faded green beater with a narrow white racing seat that they'd found unlocked by the side of the road. Their guess was that it had been a drunk-cycle, a bike used to pedal from bar to bar, before it was pressed into wartime duty.

They left in ones and twos, going out through Hidden Valley Estates to California Avenue. Movement in the open like this had to be carefully choreographed because of the Directorate's tracking algorithms, which pored through aerial and satellite-sensor footage. Over time, any unusual patterns would become distinct and therefore targetable. The trick was to find patterns that were part of the standard ebb and flow but also had slightly random components that could explain away any anomalies. Patterns like the daily rhythms of kids biking to and from their elementary school.

As the flow of children heading into Iliahi Elementary School, a few on their own, others dropped off by their parents, started to slow, Conan nodded at Finn. Like on patrol, they staggered their arrivals. They'd go in with the latecomers and then swing toward the back, where there was an outbuilding used for storing athletic equipment. For the past four months, Coach Moaki, the gym teacher, had allowed the Muj to stash a few boxes of grenades, stims, and ammunition there. The insurgents also slept there from time to time. It was one of many caches they used in the area. They knew a few of the other teachers were likely aware of what they were doing, but not a single one ever made eye contact with them.

"You know, before all this I used to do triathlons," Finn said to Conan as they waited in the vegetation by the road. "Get up at oh-five-hundred for a trail run and then go twenty miles on the bike. Oh, and camping. For fun. That's pretty much what we're doing now, right? Well, screw that. When this is all over, I'm going to move to New York City and never go outside again."

They had just mounted their bikes when a shot rang out.

"Pistol," said Conan. "At the school."

Moana Surfrider Hotel, Waikiki Beach, Hawaii Special Administrative Zone

He had been to the old hotel many times before. Never to sleep; the place felt too much like a target for a truck bomb. He came every so often just to swim and drink fresh pineapple and guava juice. The beach was perfection, perhaps worth the invasion for just this stretch, Markov thought. If they had let him, he would have slept on the beach; he would have preferred it to the cheap motel by the airport that the Chinese had turned into barracks.

At the moment, he was in the wrong company for a day on the sand. Jian, as ever, dutifully followed behind.

Markov wore his Russian army fatigues, which were getting more and more faded with each day in the Pacific sun. He would rather have worn local clothes, but the few times he had done that, it had only brought him grief with General Yu.

The two men crossed the lobby, slowing their pace to take advantage of the air conditioning. As they weaved through groups of Directorate sailors, soldiers, and marines, Markov noticed that Jian had taken to walking five meters behind him. The bastard was trying to act like he was simply going in the same direction, embarrassed at his peers' seeing him with the Russian.

As they passed one of the bars, Markov almost stopped, stricken by a sudden thirst. Then he pushed past the temptation and moved on to the intended destination.

"Hi, boys," said the woman behind the surf desk. "I'm sorry, but your teammates took them all. No boards left."

He was struck by the banal tone of her voice. In his whole time in Hawaii, he had never heard a local speak without some fleck of anger. But this woman sounded as if she were talking to a sunburned family of four from Chicago. Either she was on quite a cocktail of drugs or she was an utter idiot.

"It's too bad, you know," she continued, "because today there's a perfect swell for beginners."

Markov walked closer to the desk and locked eyes with her.

"Regrettably, this is work," he said. "We're looking for information about a Directorate officer whose body was found on the beach."

"I heard," she said. "It's so sad."

The nameplate on the desk identified her as Carrie Shin. Markov walked his eyes down Carrie's body, passing over her breasts but looking closely at her arms, searching for signs of needle tracks that might explain her demeanor. Maybe a little makeup on her forearm, but he couldn't be sure without looking at the skin up close.

"It is sad. How did he get possession of one of the hotel's boards?" said Markov.

"We think he took it after hours. We didn't think we had to lock them up anymore," said Shin. Her voice lowered and her shoulders sagged, as if even the possibility of theft saddened her.

"When did he last rent a board here?" he asked.

"I saw him once," she said. "Maybe two weeks ago? I think that was his first time surfing. He was really excited. He asked about a lesson but I couldn't do it then. I wish I had. Sandy Beach Park is one of the most dangerous places on the islands to surf—not a good place for a beginner."

Markov studied the way her tanned skin seemed to give back some of the sun's warmth. He leaned in closer for his next question, wondering just how dark the circles under her eyes were when the makeup was washed away.

"Are there any other employees whom I should talk to?" he said.

She smiled and leaned away, arching her back in a subtle stretch. "This hotel is the safest place in town, for everyone. That's the point, isn't it?" she said. "Why would anyone do anything to upset that?"

"Yes, certainly."

"The one thing I never heard was how he died." She chattered on, slaking her curiosity in a way other locals never would have dared. "What did happen to him?"

"The board's leash got caught around his neck," said Markov. "But it is not yet clear whether it was an accident or not."

"Oh my God. That's horrible," she said. "Wasn't there any video of the beach? Maybe a wave-cam?"

"Nothing," he said. "Nothing at all." He paused. "But as part of the revised security measures, we will be collecting something better from all the staff here."

"Better than pictures?" she said.

"Much better. DNA," he said. "That way we can track our friends throughout the island," he said.

"Friends like me?" she said.

"Exactly," he said.

Iliahi Elementary School, Wahiawa, Hawaii Special Administrative Zone

The body lay sprawled face-down on the ground. The mesh bag of soccer balls that the Chinese marine had brought for the students to play with had opened and the balls had spilled out; bright pink and yellow spheres rolled around the courtyard, leaving trails of blood behind them.

Nicks's grip on her SIG Sauer P220 loosened for a moment, then she squeezed the pistol tighter. Her hearing returned and her field of vision widened, allowing her to take in the chaos. Parents and children screamed over the ringing in her ears.

This was what the coach had been trying to warn them about when Nicks and the three other insurgents turned left off California Avenue. The coach had smiled a welcome but had waved his hands off to the side. Nicks cursed herself for missing the cue, caught up momentarily in the flash of normalcy brought on by the giddy kids around them.

"Contact!" shouted Charlie.

"A bit late for that," said Nicks. "You hit?"

"No, I don't think so," said Charlie. "There's got to be more; where are they?"

A Chinese marine burst around the gym corner, his assault rifle spraying wildly. A shot took Charlie in the neck. Nicks, with her pistol already up, instinctively fired two .45-caliber rounds at a distance of ten feet. The marine spun and collapsed over a blue hippo sculpture in the school's courtyard.

More fearful shouts in Chinese came from where the marine had been.

Nicks and the two other insurgents rounded the corner and found a lone Chinese civilian, evidently a member of one of the new community development units they'd been sending around to split the population from the insurgents, crying into a radio. She had a pistol but made no motion to use it; her two escorts were now dead.

They dragged her past Charlie's still body and over to the entrance of the building, and they took cover by the doors. After a moment, the woman stopped crying, and the unsettling calm that followed close combat came over Nicks. Her ears rang, her hands tingled, and she felt like her feet were so firmly planted in the ground, she couldn't take another step if her life depended on it. The feeling would pass, as it always did after the adrenaline waned, but in the moment, it took everything she had to stay focused and think about what was supposed to happen next.

"She was on the radio," Nicks shouted to her squad mates, too loud because her ears were still ringing. "I don't know if she got someone on the other end. But we gotta tell Conan this place is blown and get clear."

She looked up and saw three kids peering down at her from be-hind the blue-painted railings on the school's second-floor balcony. They looked blankly at the dead bodies and then at the NSM members. Then, one by one, they began to look skyward, until they were all squinting at the sky to the south.

That was when Nicks's ears cleared and she heard it too, the thumping of helicopter rotors coming closer.

Hidden Valley Estates, Wahiawa, Hawaii Special Administrative Zone

Conan and Finn cut through the empty parking lot of the Mormon church adjacent to the school, jumping off their bikes as they entered a stand of trees separating the church from the houses nearby. They kept beneath a long canopy of thick green foliage that ran through the clusters of one-story and two-story homes in the Hidden Valley Estates housing complex. Seeing a quadcopter drone zoom down the road toward the school, they ducked down and hid among the trees.

"Hold here," said Conan.

"Screw that, let's go," said Finn. "We can get to the cache, arm up, and then get them out."

Conan shook her head. "No, we can't," she said.

Neighbors had begun to spill out of their homes into the street, pointing and screaming. Some of them, probably parents, were rushing toward the school, racing against the arrival of the Directorate forces.

Finn turned to look at her, trying to puzzle it out. "Conan, our guys are one thing, but the kids. There are kids there."

"Exactly," said Conan quietly.

"What? What do you think is going to happen?" said Finn.

She didn't answer, just stared back at him. Finn tried to get up, but she wrestled him down. He had just shrugged off her grip when a pair of Directorate Z-8K assault helicopters roared overhead and then spun to flare just above the playing field next to the school. One after another, black-suited Directorate commandos jumped out. They fanned out around the landing point, the equipment shed with the weapons cache now inside their perimeter.

Finn ducked back under the brush and looked at her angrily. "Conan. You know our guys — they are going to fight. And those kids and teachers are going to be stuck in the middle of a shitstorm."

"It was always a risk that something bad would go down at the school," said Conan in a whisper. "Why do you think I chose it?"

Fort Mason, San Francisco

"I love you."

Jamie knew what Lindsey would say when he walked through the door. She said it every night, even when he knew it was a struggle for her to get the words out.

Nights like tonight when he returned home late, exhausted and drained. The adrenaline had ebbed months ago; what propelled him now was a cocktail of caffeine, stims, and anger.

The boat hit the dock's edge gently, perfectly done, and he sharply saluted the shipyard launch that dropped him off at pier 2 in the dark. It was a perk of command that spared him the long autobus ride home and kept him on the water that much longer. Plus, it was only a quick walk up to his house in Fort Mason and he could be home in a few minutes once he set foot on land.

Like every night, though, he first stopped and sat down on a bench, a vestige of a time when this was an area for festivals and tourists. From his seat he looked west through the Golden Gate Bridge. The bridge was illuminated tonight, the LEDs woven into the cable wires showing a winking flag displayed, fifty stars bright. It was something the governor had decided to do, against the advice of the Defense Department. The bridge was a symbol of what they were fighting for, he argued, and should not be lost in the fog of war and the Bay. That speech had gone over well; no doubt one of his public affairs team's own social-engineering algorithms had come up with it.

Jamie took a last sip of coffee and slowly dumped the rest out, watching it spatter the ground at his feet. It was oddly soothing and had become a ritual as he tried to slow his mind down from the past sixteen hours at work.

"Halt!" said a voice in the dark.

Simmons looked up and saw no one. He was tired, but tired enough to hear things?

"Identification," said a sentry. It was one of the California National Guard troops who patrolled the waterfront around the clock.

"Proceed," said Simmons. "Captain James Simmons. Navy. I live at the fort, house forty-nine."

The sentry scanned the barcode next to the left epaulet on Simmons's uniform.

"Thank you, sir," said the sentry. "Quiet night."

"No trouble?" said Simmons.

"No, there never is," said the sentry, suddenly sounding old and tired. "What's that smell?" He clutched his M4 closer to his chest and inhaled deeply. "Damn, is that real coffee?"

"Yes, from onboard," said Simmons.

"I knew I signed up for the wrong service. When you work as a barista at Starbucks and then the country runs out of coffee, well, you just can't drink the fake stuff, on principle," said the sentry. "That's when I joined up. Spent the first few weeks of basic with the worst headaches, though. I'd charge the beach myself if they could promise me a fresh cup of Kona reserve on the other side."

"We'll get you that Hawaiian coffee soon enough," said Simmons.

"Thank you, sir. You have a good night," said the sentry.

"You too," said Simmons, and he started up the hill for home.

Jamie opened the front door quietly and slipped inside. At eleven o'clock, he'd missed the kids and dinner, but he could still spend an hour with Lindsey. Squeaking floorboards announced his arrival.

The dining room was empty. He looked in the living room to see if she had fallen asleep on the couch reading.

"Hey? Linds, still up?" he whispered.

He looked around the floor of the living room. Where were the toys? Oddly, there was nothing underfoot. He remembered the frenetic cleanups his father had imposed on him when he was the same age as his kids now. The sight of toys out of place, any sign, really, that children lived in his house, would set his father off.

"Linds?" he called again.

He gingerly walked upstairs. A faint glow emanated from their bedroom.

When he walked in, his heart soared and his stomach ached. Lindsey stood before him holding out a glass of sparkling wine, wearing only a red silk robe. Candles from their disaster kit lit the room. From a big pink beach bucket filled with ice, the neck of a champagne bottle stood at attention.

"Happy anniversary," she said.

He took the flute and kissed her. How could he have forgotten?

"Fifteen years," he said.

"I found you, lost you, and got you back again," she said.

"Happy anniversary," he said. "Sorry I'm late for it."

"The kids are asleep, and the house is ours. For the next little while."

"I have to be in early tomorrow," he said.

"I know," she said. "You're going to be tired."

"Very," he said, removing the robe. They made love with the patient pleasure that comes from focusing on each other completely.

Afterward, they lay back and looked out at the bridge in the dark, fog beginning to devour its pillars.

"One day you're going back out there," she said.

"I know. And I know what I promised before all this. But I have to be out there now. You know that, right?"

"I'm not going to tell you not to go," she said. "But all I think about is that we haven't had enough time together. Fifteen years is not enough."

"No, it's not," he said. "What I do each day, I do to make sure I will be back. That's it, in its simplest sense."

"I know," she said.

"My dad left my mom after fifteen years, did you know that?" he said.

"Is that why you forgot tonight?" she said.

This wasn't one of those binary choices. He could go in so many different directions. Anger. Denial. Submission. Regret.

"I am so sorry, Lindsey," he said. "For tonight. For everything. For staying in the Navy when I told you I was done. I'm sorry. It's all I can say."

"Just don't do it again," she said, and kissed him deeply.

Hangar One, Moffett Field, Mountain View, California

The thing that always jarred Daniel Aboye was the smell. The space was cavernous, 1,140 feet by 308 feet, to be exact, the size of three Superdomes. But the smell filled even that void. To someone from outside the valley, it was the tangy funk of old pizza and people who'd gone too long without a shower. But to anyone local, it smelled like money. Fame. Power. Success. So much had changed in Silicon Valley's startup scene during the past few decades, but there was one constant. This smell.

And the fact that it now filled Hangar One made it all the more appropriate.

In 1931, the city fathers of Sunnyvale, California, had come up with a unique plan for economic development. They'd raised $480,000 to buy nearly a thousand acres of farmland and then sold off the land to the U.S. government for one dollar. What was to make it such a good investment was the topography of the farmland: it was the only part of San Francisco Bay not regularly shrouded in fog. The deal was that Sunnyvale would then become the home for a new planned Navy fleet of "flying aircraft carriers," massive helium-filled airships that would serve as bases in the air for propeller biplanes.

The plan didn't work out as anticipated, not for Sunnyvale or the blimps. In 1933, the USS *Akron*, the Navy's test airborne aircraft carrier, crashed. The plan was shelved, its only legacy that the airfield was renamed after Admiral William Moffett, the head of the Navy's Aeronautics Bureau, who had been killed in the crash. But, fortunately for the town, World War II interceded a few years later, and Moffett Field became a base for patrol airplanes and then the home of the U.S. Air Force Satellite Test Center. By the 1950s, several big aerospace firms clustered around the base and the test center. The thousands of scientists and engineers who moved into the sunny valley built close ties with local universities, and the old farmland became the hub of a different industry. The city fathers' plan of economic growth through blimp basing instead spawned what became known as Silicon Valley.

In the defense drawdown of the 1990s, most of Moffett was abandoned and the facility was handed over to NASA's Ames Research

Center. Little remained of the military presence except for its signature building, the largest hangar in the world.

Bits and pieces of the base were sold off to private industry over the ensuing years, starting when Google acquired Hangar One and turned it into a site for executive jets. When he had first arrived in Silicon Valley and seen all that ambition and vision, let alone cash flow, Aboye felt outgunned. Now, he just had to make a phone call and the massive hangar was at his disposal. Larry and Sergey had not asked what would happen inside; they knew only that he needed a massive space away from prying eyes.

Now Hangar One was the team's new home, though they had taken to calling it Aboye's Ark. Taj Lamott, chief technology officer of Uni, had come up with that, a joke about either the size of the place or the crazy vision of the man who'd brought them all together. Daniel had been an early investor in Uni, which was now one of the leading video-game studios in Palo Alto, and in a few of the firms he had quietly reached out to. At other firms, though he wasn't an investor, his reputation had been enough. That, and the simple lure of the offer. It was the opportunity, he had said, to be part of Silicon Valley's most important startup ever.

The rule for selection had been simple. The CTO of each firm Aboye talked to would designate his or her three best programmers. The limited numbers were ostensibly to keep the project in stealth mode, as the investors called it. The goal was to hide their business not only from Directorate spies, but also from the National Security Agency. Even if the NSA's networks weren't pwned by the Directorate, which most people suspected they still were, anger over the sneak backdoors of the old Snowden-era scandals lingered. The NSA had cost Silicon Valley hundreds of billions of dollars, and its citizens weren't in a forgiving mood, even years later.

But the limited numbers were also about the value of an idea, its yield as well as its transformative power. Aboye and his group couldn't throw hundreds of thousands of programmers at the problem, as the Directorate had done before the war with its so-called human-flesh-search-machine censorship that had morphed into the massive hacker attack that opened the assault. Nor did they want to. They all knew that a great programmer was literally orders of magnitude better than a good one. And they also all knew from experience that the best way to accomplish something considered undoable was merely to bring the right minds together.

Some of the CTOs had sent their top executives, including a few billionaire founders who relished the chance to get their hands dirty again. Others sent the smelly, misanthropic coding beasts they usually hid away in the basement. The sum total, though, made Hangar One the greatest gathering of geniuses since the Manhattan Project.

The only other contribution each firm was asked to make was a single corporate jet. That was a key part of the cover. The volunteers would show up at Hangar One as if they were heading out of town, and then the jets would fly off to various business conferences and corporate offsite meetings. However, each jet would fly out just a few people short. It had been a perfect cover story, until the matter of pizza had come up. Daniel had solved that by creating another startup company located in an office complex just across the street. Although the business was supposedly an app maker for the health-care industry, its sole purpose was to serve as a destination for the pizza deliveries.

It had all worked so far. As Aboye waited for the test, he pinched the skin at the inside of his wrist, just as he had done as a boy when the hunger got so bad he would see double. How long had it been since he'd had to worry about his next meal? Thirty years? Forty? Now, the familiar pain soothed his anxiety.

He had a lot to worry about at this moment. The bank of monitors along the wall in the southwest corner of the control room flashed and winked with a rainbow's array of colors, each a hue hinting at failure.

"Here it goes," he said to the engineers assembled in a circle at the center of the room. Together they stood, staring hard into the shifting light form in the middle of their grouping, moving their gloved hands in syncopated rhythms. They had depicted the Directorate data networks as a library. There were three levels to the holographic building, and a white-painted atrium let in an amber sunset that illuminated the central hall. The hologram rendered six of Aboye's team in the middle of the atrium, each as a featureless black form that looked to be made of turbid smoke. The wraithlike bodies had no identifying features.

Aboye watched Taj maestroing his part, his fingers in the gloves dancing away like a conductor's as he stood uneasily on a swiveling chair mounted on casters. It was something that he swore helped him focus, even if the risk of falling, and failure, was higher now than it ever had been. A few billion richer, he was still the same Taj that Aboye had met nine years ago during a job interview at which Aboye had told Taj he was so talented that he could not in good conscience hire him. They had been friends ever since, and Aboye now wondered if this was what he had actually wanted Taj to do all along.

"This is the jumping-off point," said Arran Smythe, nominated by the group to be the program's chief engineer, largely because of her comparatively calm demeanor. Outside the hangar, she worked on network design for Amazon. She was a tall, thin woman who moved with precise, choppy gestures whether or not she was working in a sim. Like the rest of the engineers and programmers, she wore the same kind of formfitting one-piece gray utility coveralls used by astronauts. That had been the Tesla team's idea. At first it seemed to Aboye like they were playing dress-up, but over time he saw how they stood taller when they put on the suits.

"Wyc, you're first." Smythe's voice almost bubbled with excitement. Aboye knew why she and the rest of them were happy. They were re-experiencing the joy of a startup, discovering what their unbound minds could accomplish.

In the holographic projection, one of the dark forms dashed from the library atrium into the shadows of the stacks. Then another.

"Taj, next," said Smythe.

The casters on Taj's chair began to creak and he twisted slightly back and forth as he manipulated the control rings on his fingers. What he saw on his goggles was only for him, but the jerky gestures attested to a problem.

On the holographic screen, the black forms ran in and out of the atrium, dropping off books in what was now a burning pyre in the middle of the room.

"Fudge!" shouted Taj, still the innocent little boy at heart. "Gosh-darn mother-fudging network!"

The library's glass ceiling crashed in and water began to come through, the simulated network's automated defenses now reacting. First came a heavy rain, which the wraiths tried to shoot fire back at, the visualization of their counterprograms, but then came a vast, unending deluge, as if a river had been diverted and was pouring into the atrium.

Taj's chair toppled over and he tried to catch himself but landed hard on his tailbone. He rolled over onto his side, clutching his wrist.

The hologram's library pyre was now extinguished and the black forms found themselves underwater. They flickered out one by one as the water rose quickly from floor to floor. Smythe turned off the hologram and looked at Aboye with something like shame. The automated defenses had detected and defeated them. The cone of light around them brightened slightly, indicating the test was over.

Aboye moved to help Taj up but then checked himself. Angrily, he thought that perhaps Taj needed to learn a lesson from the pain, and maybe grow up a bit. He turned his back on the group and made for the darkness across the hangar, walking past row after row of murmuring servers, the waves of warmth washing over him.

He reached the exit. He faintly heard Smythe issuing commands to the room, but the rushing of blood in his ears prevented him from understanding them.

As soon as he was outside, he sat down, closed his eyes, and covered his head with his arms. He sighed. What else could he do? This was not working out like it was supposed to.

He felt a hand on his shoulder. He sprang up and saw Taj, a white cryo-pack on his wrist.

"Is it all right?" asked Aboye.

"My wrist or the project?" said Taj. "Thanks for making sure I was okay."

"My apologies. I didn't handle that well," said Aboye. "You know how I can be, and, well, this didn't go as planned."

"Look, there's no sugarcoating it. We're in trouble. Running out of time and money too," said Taj.

"I will spend every last dollar I have," Aboye said. "I started with nothing, so that is not my fear. I fear failure, and what it would mean for this country. We need to succeed because of the importance of our mission, yes. That is crucial. But there is something bigger on the line. Do you know what it is?"

"I've been going full tilt for three days. Stop with the riddles," said Taj.

"We need to become again the country that breaks the hard problems, that sees the virtue in innovation and the reward in risk," he said. "If we do not succeed, then I worry that all truly is lost."

"Daniel, stop trying to put the weight of the world on our shoulders. We'll never crack it if we think that way. We all joined for that stuff, but also for the challenge. That's the fun part."

Aboye could muster no reply. Instead he turned from Taj and walked slowly down the runway, gazing up at the starry sky.

As he walked along the deserted tarmac, the massive hangar building slowly shrank behind him and clouds gradually hid the stars above him. A gust of wet wind left a fine mist on his face, and he stopped in the middle of the runway. He felt truly lost, and he did the only thing he knew to do when he felt that way. He sank to his knees and began to pray.

USS *Zumwalt,* Mare Island Naval Shipyard

"Smells like victory!" somebody said. Laughter followed.

Vern Li peeked out between the fist-size gap in the curtain on her bunk. Flashes of flesh. Gray underwear. She wrinkled her nose as the stink of digested rations worked its way into her bunk. It mixed with the smell of her coveralls: her sweat and the remnants of epoxy from some of the structural reinforcements she had been trying to work around a few hours before. She smiled and stifled a laugh. It was so awful, all of it, that you just had to give in to it. It had been three days since she'd showered.

Closing her eyes, she tried to wedge herself into the corner. But what had started out as laughter flipped over to tears as quickly as powering on a pair of glasses.

She felt silly, knowing the mix of laughter and tears was just from being so tired and loopy. Before the war, she had planned to redefine how to power machines. Energy, the magic of the battery, was the essence of their utility. It was what gave machines life and gave humans their life force: an electrical spirit. Or so she'd thought when she was smoking weed in high school. Now she was just a machine herself. No different than any other device on the ship. She felt drained, empty.

Vern wiped her tears away and slipped on her glasses to check the time: 0443.

She batted the curtain aside, trying to ignore the yellow pulsing *14.3* in the corner of her vision that indicated the number of hours of REM sleep she needed in order to return to average performance. She hoped the rainbow glow of the code she reviewed as she made her way to the galley would help obscure her red eyes. Somehow, she would get through another day.

Out in the hallway, or passageway, as the crew kept correcting her, she followed the line headed toward the galley.

"Good morning, Dr. Li," said a voice behind her.

Mike stood in the middle of the passageway, a massive ceramic coffee cup held loosely in his left hand. He wore his usual orange utility vest over the navy blue overalls, a color combination that made him look like one of those prisoners from the Syrian intervention. But the old guy still had that something, she had to admit. He'd aged well, sort of like that old movie star the *People* zine kept putting in their annual list, decades after his first time on the cover.

"Can I ask you to come with me to the rail-gun magazine? Need you to take a look at something I'm working on," he said.

She looked at him blankly, still trying to wake up fully.

"If you want, you can grab some chow. The work can hold for a few minutes," he said.

"Maybe for you, old man. But all a modern girl needs is a little will-power and a lot of pill power." She stepped into the galley and grabbed a bright red can of Coke Prime and an inch-long foil packet of energy and sustenance pills.

Vern's stomach was growling, but she didn't want to show weakness. She smiled to herself. It was all the same, whether you were on the high school volleyball team, in grad school, or at war: never let 'em see you sweat.

"All right, then," he said with a slight tone of admiration. "Breakfast of champions it is, Dr. Li."

But as Vern followed Mike down the passageway, she held the cold metal of the can to her forehead, trying to keep back the headache until the pills hit.

They came to a hatch, what the Navy guys called a door, and Mike moved aside to let her pass through first. She thought he'd smell like old man or engine grease, but instead she smelled citrus.

"Don't want you getting scurvy. We had to worry about that back in my day," he said as he held out a freshly peeled orange to her.

She took the orange with a smile.

The rail-gun magazine extended below the turret, deeper into the ship, and that was where Vern sat, on an upturned plastic crate. She watched Mike welding and slowly ate the orange slices, savoring the tartness. This space was cramped, and she sat within arm's reach of Mike. Looking through her goggles, she saw the flare of the welding torch create an eclipse-like profile of the old chief. Streaks of sweat tracked down his neck. Then the torch abruptly snapped off. He lifted his welding mask, eyes blinking at the smoke, and moved so that she could see the rack that held the armatures for the rail-gun rounds.

"You see how it's done, Dr. Li?" said Mike.

She slowly chewed her last orange slice, unsure what he meant.

"The welds? I want you to see how it's done," he said. "Up there, in the turret, we can do it your way, but you're missing the technique, the art of it . . . If you just melt the surface of the wire or fitting and let it stick to the surface, it might be good enough for some lab, but it wouldn't hold under the kind of pressures we could get in action. It's about doing it smoothly, to ensure a proper mixing of the materials. Let me show you. Put my mask on and pass me your goggles."

He motioned her over to the square of blue-foam padding he'd been kneeling on and handed her a pair of welding gloves.

"Those gloves should fit. I had to guess the size, but I think I got it. So this is structural, what we're doing. Nobody's going to see it, but everybody's going to depend on it," he said. "We'll do a first pass then we'll see how it goes."

She knelt and he sat on the box behind her, reaching around to her left side to help her keep a steady hand as the torch flared. Back and forth they went until Mike let her use the torch without his help.

"There you go. Make a puddle, keep track of that as it builds," he said, guiding her hand slowly across the seam where the armature rack connected to the deck. "We'll need to make a few passes and then let it cool. Then again. Good technique comes with practice."

"Why aren't you using a laser welder?" asked Vern.

"Because there's no reason to get fancy," said Mike. "The old MIG welder works, so why change? No need to teach an old dog new tricks if the old ones still get the job done. You'll learn that one eventually."

Lotus Flower Club, Former French Concession, Shanghai

He knew not to ask her name, so for now, she was just the new Twenty-Three.

Sechin opened the door and found her waiting under the sheets. Her eyes were wide open, unblinking, and tracked him with the kind of focus that came from a pill. To Sechin, she looked harder and, while still beautiful, slightly less inviting. The downsides of a professional's existence. Once again, purpose trod upon pleasure, thought Sechin.

With the old Twenty-Three, everything was about what he wanted. With the new Twenty-Three, it was about what she wanted, first details on the Cherenkov program and now information on Directorate defenses in the northern Pacific.

Once he'd undressed and folded his clothes, he slipped under the sheets. They were orange this time. The delight of being under the covers with her warm, naked body was undeniable. It was that moment he savored, that first moment of contact with her skin as she quickly pulled the sheets over him.

She put a finger to her lips and he nodded. She lay back and closed her eyes. He watched her chest rise and fall with her steady breathing. He studied the tattoo at her waist. It was an intricate wreath of roses and snakes. He made out a cobra and a coral snake. There were two others that he could not identify. The roses were beautiful.

Then she turned on the recording of Sechin and the previous Twenty-Three's lovemaking and began to arrange the thin blanket that would shield their conversation. He felt his cheeks flush with embarrassment.

"I think it is everything you are looking for," said Sechin. "But I can't guarantee that I was able to get it out clean. I tried but there is an urgency to all of this that —"

"Are you compromised?" she demanded, leaning on one elbow. She ran a finger down his chest and stopped at a fresh scar just below his navel. It was about an inch wide and was covered with the clear surgical glue used to seal the incision. Sechin had made the cut himself using the surgi-pen he found in the CIA dead drop behind an eel vendor's stall at Shanghai's Tangjiawan Lu wet market.

"Entirely," he said with a dramatic sigh that released a warm cloud of stale tobacco and vodka under the covers. Twenty-Three wrinkled her nose with disappointment.

"This is not the time to make jokes," she said. "So tell me, are you compromised?"

"I'm fine," he said. "Like I said, I moved quickly because I had to. But I was careful. I always am."

"Then let's proceed," she said. "And you can relax."

"Happily," he said. "Do you want to be on top?"

She shook her head and shifted her weight under him. Her hand probed around the area of his incision. He winced at the pain, and she apologized.

"Okay, I feel the chip," she said. "Move a little to the left. Your left. There."

The epidermal electronic reader hidden in the tattoo's ink vibrated faintly as it downloaded Sechin's file with a tickling sensation. He tried to kiss her and she pulled back.

"Stop!" she hissed. "Hold very, very still."

The vibration continued for almost a minute and then both of them looked at each other as the sensation abruptly ceased.

"That wasn't so bad," he said. "Is it enough to end a war? Certainly wars have been started for less."

"I need to go," she said, trying to roll him off her. "This cannot wait."

"Of course it can," he said. "Besides, if I leave too quickly, won't they think you're not up to the job?"

With a resigned look, she nestled next to him. "You're going to just hold me," she said. This time, it seemed her command was not about the job. He grasped her shoulder and felt her tremble for a moment.

"If you were not scared, you would not be doing it right," he said gently.

He'd begun to tell himself that they were making a connection when the recording stopped and she abruptly threw the sheet off them.

"Our time is up," she said as she turned her back on him and began to get dressed.

"Of course it is," he said.

USS *Zumwalt*, West of Alcatraz Island, San Francisco Bay

"Remember, just don't hit the bridge," said executive officer Horatio Cortez as the *Zumwalt* passed Angel Island to starboard.

Two cups of coffee ago, the ship had cast off from the pier at Mare Island for the first time since its overhaul. It was an anxious moment. Had it not been for the Mentor Crew's ease in handling the ship's lines, Simmons was pretty sure the ship would still be in port; the kids who'd helped refit the ship's systems had no idea how to get a warship under way. The *Zumwalt* had carefully processed from the shipyard at Mare Island down to Alcatraz Island, where it maneuvered to a very specific patch of the Bay, just off eBay Park's pier.

The highly anticipated visit was timed to coincide with a San Francisco Giants game against the Washington Nationals. The Directorate well knew the Americans were refurbishing the ship by watching from above; they just didn't know any details. So the public rollout at the baseball game on a night when military personnel were given free tickets was billed as a morale booster. Secretary of Defense Marylyn Claiburne was even coming in to throw the first pitch.

After her debut on the pitcher's mound, however, she was not going to the owner's private box, as most visiting dignitaries would do. Her next stop would be the *Zumwalt*'s bridge, where they could use the night game at the park as a cover to test out the ship's new power systems.

Pier 1, Honolulu, Hawaii Special Administrative Zone

She actually had to fight for this one.

At Local, a nightclub off Ala Moana Boulevard near pier 1, Carrie nearly caused a brawl trying to get this marine to dance with her. The

Russian prostitute he was with looked like a junkie, and all it took was a discreet and well-placed foot to send her sprawling on the dance floor. Local's security, off-duty Directorate forces, whisked the prostitute out before she even had a chance to get back to her feet. It was her pimp that was the problem. He took Carrie for competition and grabbed her by the back of the neck to pull her off the dance floor. A roundhouse kick from her dance partner sent the pimp into a group of Directorate sailors stuffing money and pills into a naked table dancer's scuffed white boots.

After another close dance, she asked him to take her somewhere they could be alone. That turned out to be an eight-wheeled armored assault vehicle that looked exactly like one of the vehicles she used to see around her fiancé's air base. Cocooned inside the welded steel hull, the two sat facing each other in the compartment that was big enough to carry up to seven soldiers. A monitor's faint red light shone down from the opening of the wedge-shaped 105 mm cannon turret above them. With the stench of sweat and stale food inside, the Directorate marine must have felt like he was trying to get laid in a dumpster, but apparently he didn't care.

He turned his back to her and reached forward to the music player rigged between the front seats. She could see the muscles in his shoulders ripple and looked at the four rainbow-hued tiger tattoos that covered his back and upper arms. His shaved head revealed a Morse code of scars, a lot for someone who couldn't be more than twenty-five.

"I have jazz," he said. "Chinese. Okay?"

Carrie laughed. "Sure."

Through the open rear hatch, she could hear the faint lapping of the water just beneath the pier where the vehicle was parked.

"Your English is good," she said.

"My parents made me learn since I was two," said the marine. "For business."

Carrie raised a shot glass of the *baijiu* he'd poured for her. It tasted like shitty vodka.

"To your parents," she said. "But this is not business. A thank-you for your rescuing me . . . I think you should shut the door now."

"The hatch," he said and squeezed past her to shut them inside the vehicle. The heavy steel and the layer of reactive armor affixed to the exterior suddenly made the soundproof space they shared feel very small.

She climbed forward on all fours with a feline fluidity and straddled him. She still wore the black silk cocktail dress, but her high heels hung from a gear rack. He wore only the sheer black pants that seemed to be the Directorate off-duty uniform for nightclubs and bars.

The piano playing on the speakers was barely acceptable; it sounded kind of like Art Hodes, if he were a half-drunk robot and had a stim pump running on overdrive. Carrie's father had come from Gary, Indiana, in Chicago's shadow, and had taught her about the beauty of jazz and the horror of men.

She kissed him, tasting only alcohol, then she arched her upper body away from him.

"Do you have any restraints?" she said.

"I'll do anything." He grinned.

"Of course you will," she said. "I mean like a rope."

"Can I record it for my feed?"

"This is for us, nobody else. No viz, okay?"

She leaned forward and kissed the nape of his neck and then his ear, careful to let her nipples move their way toward his face.

"Over there, in the bag," he said. "There should be something for prisoners. Careful."

She pulled out a roll of fluorescent-yellow nanopore tape used to bind wrists. It leached its bright color into the skin, creating a visual trace that announced you'd been nabbed; the substance was also rumored to be traceable by Directorate sensors.

In the red light, the tape glowed bright, and it unrolled silently as she began to bind his left wrist to the honeycombed aluminum base of one of the jump seats running along the interior of the carrier.

"Whoa, I thought we were going to tie you up," he said.

"Are you scared?" she asked. "A big guy like you?"

She stepped back, tape still in hand, and slid out of the dress, now fully naked. "Frisk me if you want, there's no weapons on this insurgent."

"Okay, but only my left hand," he said. "Leave the other free. You may be beautiful, but you're still an American."

She responded by stepping forward, kneeling before him, and placing a kiss on his navel. Seeing him nod in pleasure, she continued to tie his left wrist to the seat post. She kissed him again and then abruptly stopped. A look of pity came over her face, followed by her gleaming smile washed in the red light.

She reached back into the bag where she'd found the nanopore tape and pulled out a folding knife with a five-inch blade.

His right hand started to reach out fast, but before he could grab her wrist, she placed the knife in his open palm, the blade still locked shut.

"See, nothing to fear," she said.

She kissed him, starting with his ears, then his chin, and then his neck, drawing out her progress until she stopped at his belt buckle. She reached up and held his free hand, still holding the closed knife. The metallic snap of the blade flashing open was easily heard above the rhythmic piano.

"What are you doing?" he said. The knife was open in his right hand, and her fingers wrapped around his, closing his fingers around the handle.

Their two clasped hands together, she raised the knife to right in front of her eyes, admiring the sharp edge from up close, its black anodized blade reflecting none of the red light.

Then she drove their clasped hands down, directing the blade's tip toward her chest.

She stopped the blade's descent when there was just the faintest pressure on the skin right above her heart. A light prick drew a single drop of blood. It happened so quick, he was too surprised to scream, and he sucked in air that should have come out in a howl but could not. She closed her eyes and breathed deep, seeming to savor the moment.

"See, it's okay," she purred. "You can trust me."

"I don't think so . . ." he said.

"Don't be scared, you'll always have the knife to do whatever you want. I just need my hands free now for something else, a little more fun. See, I'll even make sure you don't lose your long knife in all the . . . excitement."

He nodded. And she began to wrap the tape around the hand that held the knife, the blade emerging out along the pinkie finger. Then she took that hand and pointed the knife at her neck, poised just above her jugular vein.

"See, just like your army, you'll be in total control," she whispered.

The blade in his hand then followed her down the same path she'd taken before, always an inch from her neck, until she stopped at his belt buckle. She looked up at him and smiled.

With a movement so fast it was hard to see, her hands brought the knife in toward him, and the blade slashed through the leather of his belt; his pants fell to the APC's floor.

"You're going to have to explain this one to your commanding officer," she said.

He laughed. "Let's stop the games. Come here."

She slid forward and up again onto his naked body. Leaning with all her weight, she pressed her body onto his, his arm with the blade now wrapped behind her, pulling her in close. Her hands caressed his face, and he started to say something.

"Shhh, now the fun really starts," she said.

In an instant, Carrie slapped a strip of the nanopore tape over his mouth and nose.

Instinct took over and he didn't even try to cut her as she slithered quickly down to the floor and then just out of reach. Instead, he began frantically trying to cut the tape binding his hand to the chair. The tape held. He grunted, sucking the tape over his mouth as he tried to breathe, and he looked at her, his eyes angry and then almost begging.

Carrie tilted her head slightly and studied him, watching silently as he awkwardly turned the taped hand with the blade back at himself, the angle just off, almost like a toddler trying to feed himself but holding the utensil the wrong way.

He poked the blade at first, tentatively trying to create a hole in the bright yellow tape that covered his mouth. But when he couldn't cut the tape and instead just pushed it inward against the bubble of air trapped beneath, he quickly grew more desperate.

He looked at her and gave a piteous whimper as he saw her expressionless study of him. He stabbed harder, and the sharp blade finally sliced through the tape and into his lower lip and tongue.

He grunted with pain, unable to fully scream. A spray of blood marked with the yellow leaching color shot outward from the slit in the tape. He tried to suck in air through the half-inch-long slit, but the blood welled inside his mouth, choking him, and another burst of yellow bubbles and red blood spouted from the gash in the tape. He tried to use the blade to widen the opening in the tape over his mouth, gasping through the thin slit. In his frenzy, he didn't even notice the weight of Carrie's hand, now back again on the knife.

USS *Zumwalt*, Rail-Gun Turret

Two hundred years ago, a wind like this would have played on a sailing ship's rigging with a wonderful harmony, thought Mike. On the *Zumwalt*, the twenty-five-knot wind merely sounded like someone had turned up the air conditioning. Just another reason to hate this ship.

He snatched another glance at Vern, worming her way inside the rail-gun turret to double-check the wiring harnesses that kept shaking loose. She had not spoken once during the past hour. Somewhere above them, Secretary of Defense Claiburne was glad-handing the crew, speaking in the easy, confident drawl that to Mike always sounded like she had just finished a modest glass of neat bourbon.

The tension Vern carried in her shoulders made her look like she was bracing for a crash.

Mike shook his head and eased his way into the turret. Wordlessly he opened the turret hatch and let the rush of salt air fill the small area. For a moment, the space smelled of somewhere far away in his imagination he rarely visited, the scent of a woman and the sea. Then the acrid smell of hot plastic and ozone returned.

"Three minutes, Dr. Li. You best wrap things up."

Ship Mission Center, USS *Zumwalt*, eBay Park, San Francisco

The bridge had been the command center of ships going back to the time of Noah, but like so much else in the *Zumwalt* class, the Navy designers had decided to make something new, different, and big. The ship mission center stood two stories high, the bottom level filled with four rows of sailors seated at computer workstations, and a second level with a balcony for the officers to watch down, almost like an interior bridge of the ship. On the walls were massive liquid-crystal screens that displayed the ship's location and systems' status and, at the moment, the third inning of the Giants game. It was that particular screen that held Secretary Claiburne's attention, a pitcher's-cap-cam focusing in on the squinting eyes behind the catcher's faceplate. The pitcher then pivoted and threw out the runner on first, ending the inning.

"All right, let's light it up," she said.

The secretary of defense, who'd been an aerospace executive before she was brought into the administration, casually held a cigar in her right hand. It was part of her shtick, that she was more of an old boy than anyone in the old boys' network she'd knocked down on her way to the top of the business. Simmons noticed the cigar was the real thing, not the e-cigar his former mentor smoked indoors. Admiral Murray seemed unfazed by the purple smoke starting to cloud up the room, but this was the first time anybody had smoked inside the *Z* during his command. He had no idea where she would put it out. There was no ashtray aboard the ship.

The test was designed to see how quickly the *Zumwalt* could deliver a peak power load and how long it could sustain it. This had been a problem during the refurbishment, because they couldn't utilize such power over an extended time without the Directorate noticing the surge, which would potentially give away the ship's new capabilities.

Simmons nodded at Cortez, who began barking out orders to shift power from the ship systems to the cables linking to shore.

"You know, Captain Simmons," said Secretary Claiburne, "President Conley is watching tonight back in the situation room. Not just for you, of course; he's a big Nationals fan. He had their closer, T. D. Singh, over at the White House a month ago." One of her military aides, an Army major who scowled at Simmons from behind a pair of thick black assaulter viz glasses, appeared at her side with an empty coffee cup. Claiburne dropped an inch of ash into it.

"Thank you, Secretary Claiburne. We're the lucky ones tonight, getting paid to watch the game," said Simmons, smiling at her through the smoke.

"Something like that, Captain," said Secretary Claiburne. "Take this." She handed him a San Francisco Giants jersey signed by the team. She shot a look over at her aide and motioned for a pen. He was there in an instant, hovering over her as she took back the jersey, added her own signature to it, and then returned it to Simmons.

"Wear it in good health," she said.

Simmons thanked her with a bemused smile, handed the shirt over to Cortez when she turned away, and then turned to watch the screens showing the ship's power production. On deck, the crew stood near the cables that snaked off the ship and ran under the Bay's waters to the pier near the park.

"At ninety-nine percent power capacity," said Cortez. "ATHENA is online, it's green for go." After the failures they'd had with the ODIS-E software, the decision had been made to keep using the old ATHENA management system. It would have to be isolated, not networked with any other ships for security reasons, but at least they knew it worked.

"Execute the transfer," Simmons ordered.

The lights flickered out on the bridge, causing Admiral Murray to wince. Onshore, a microsecond later, the stadium lights flickered and then returned to normal, the ship's systems now feeding their demand as well as the surrounding neighborhoods'. The Z's crew could hear cheering from the park. They knew it wasn't for them; the forty-four thousand people inside were celebrating a leaping catch that had robbed the Nationals of a home run. But the crew felt like it was for them all the same.

A tense silence took over the room. Claiburne mostly tracked the game — the Giants were now at bat and ready to add to their 5–3 lead. Simmons and his officers monitored the screens playing beneath them on the lower deck, windows onto the ship's systems status. None of the crew frantically chasing software glitches or figuring out ways to dump heat buildup were visible, yet their grueling work was revealed by the soothing reds, blues, and greens of the monitors. The Z was feeding the shifting demands of the park, but at a cost. Self-defense systems went on- and offline; secondary systems collapsed; and ATHENA itself started to act up.

Cortez caught Simmons's attention and tapped his own ear.

Mike's voice boomed into his headset.

"Captain, we can't keep this going more than a minute more," said Mike. "We've got thermal-management problems with the battery. Fans are running full speed, but they're just heating it up more."

"Anything Dr. Li can do with the software? Any tweaks?" said Simmons.

"Nothing yet," said Mike.

"Let me talk to her," said Simmons.

"She's fighting with one of the machines right now," said Mike. "Don't think she can stop."

"Stand by," said Simmons into his headset.

He put his trigger finger over the microphone near his mouth and, using his command voice, addressed the room.

"Nice work, everybody. Nobody has ruined the president's game so far. We've got one more play to make. Admiral Murray and I spoke beforehand and it's time we threw a curve ball." They wouldn't get more tests like this, so it was important to understand the ship's limits.

"XO, take ATHENA offline," said Simmons. "Then bring power output up to a hundred and ten percent."

Mike started to shout, but Simmons just dropped the channel, and the profanity-laced protest disappeared from his ear.

A faint smell of burning plastic began to seep into the room, competing with Secretary Claiburne's fragrant cigar.

"Max the fans," said Cortez.

His father's voice boomed again in Simmons's ear. He winced out of instinct, an all-too-familiar feeling.

"Captain, we're losing it. Ambient temp in the control room is at a hundred and fifteen degrees. Two of the boxes are cooked. You could put a burger on them. Dr. Li here says that—" said Mike.

"I understand, Chief. Task a team to replace them," Simmons said, trying to keep his side of the conversation calm in front of the SecDef.

"I'd do it if I had anyone to send. This goddamn ship doesn't have enough crew on it."

"Understood, Chief. Keep the power coming," said Simmons, again for the crowd.

A flicker on the monitor that was showing the game caught his attention. The stadium lights had gone out for a second and then returned.

"Give me Dr. Li," Simmons ordered. "Now."

"Yes, Captain?" said Vern in his earpiece. He could hear her inhale and exhale loudly, as if she were coming off a run. "We need to tail off the power now. We weren't expecting to go above the test thresholds.

Otherwise I'm not sure what we can do to keep the ship from burning itself out."

The game's lights flickered again.

"Dr. Li, you have one chance to understand me," said Simmons, his voice rising in volume now, a bit of anger for the audience in the bridge. "I don't care about the equipment. The Z is the means, not the end. Now, get me results or get off my ship!"

He looked over at Admiral Murray. Her face was a mask, leaving him uncertain if he'd just blown it in front of her. Secretary Claiburne looked impressed by his performance; that is, until her aide handed her a phone and whispered, "President Conley."

Moyock, North Carolina

"Not our usual sort of acquisition, is it?"

Sir Aeric Cavendish wore a baggy white dress shirt over a brand-new pair of formfitting technical pants. He looked out the window of the Cadillac Cascade SUV and took in the sprawling camp. As they drove, he felt the vibration of an explosion in the distance resonate through the vehicle's polished aluminum body.

"Well, sir, there's nothing about this location that's usual," said Ali Hernandez, a retired command master chief from DevGru, the U.S. Navy's Naval Special Warfare Development Group, more famously known by its original name, SEAL Team 6. "Not for a long time."

As the lead of Cavendish's personal security team, Hernandez spent a lot of time answering questions. The Sir didn't see the world the same way others did, which was why he was so damn rich. But his curiosity could be overwhelming. A day with the Sir meant more questions than Ali had been asked in his thirty years in special operations. At times it was like traveling with a toddler.

"Why does everyone still insist on calling it Blackwater?" said Cavendish, starting up again.

Make that a toddler who could buy anything he wanted, be it the company of a supermodel or a company of private military troops.

"Sir, the waters surrounding the site are murky, and that's what the first business here was named. So even with all the changes, it's the name the locals still use," said Hernandez. "But the way I look at it is, while the lawyers get paid to come up with new names, it's like a call sign: the good ones stick."

"I should have a call sign," said Cavendish. "What was yours?"

"Mine, sir? It's Brick," said Hernandez.

"I suspect that has a story behind it that I will need to ask you about later. But first, let's focus on the important thing. What might mine be?" said Cavendish. "I assume I cannot pick it for myself."

"Correct, sir. Let me do some thinking, as it's a serious matter," said Hernandez.

"Very well. I read the due-diligence report on this transaction, did you?" said Cavendish.

"Yes, sir. Eight different owners for the facility," said Hernandez. "You would be the ninth."

"That's a lot of lawyers," said Cavendish.

"It is, sir," said Hernandez.

"And how do you rate our new name for it?" said Cavendish.

The SUV bucked as Hernandez drove straight over a speed bump at forty miles an hour.

"Exquisite Entertainment?" said Hernandez.

"I told people I bought it to turn it into a viz studio. All in the name of cloak-and-dagger. But what if we renamed it Blackwater?" asked Cavendish. "I mean, is it a good name?"

They drove by a roofless three-story apartment building with blackened window frames and a half dozen black-clad men rappelling down its face.

"How do you mean, sir?" said Hernandez. "It's a name my community knows well. Still pisses a lot of civs off. So it's good by me."

"Very well," said Cavendish. "We have to keep cover, you know. How about Blackwater Entertainment?"

Hernandez laughed and punched the Cascade's accelerator as soon as it was on the compound's airfield. The electric SUV's speed silently rose to 130 miles an hour.

"Perfectly quiet and exceedingly fast," said Cavendish, his eyes closed in thought. "Just like space."

Ali braked the Cascade hard and then turned inside an airplane hangar. The doors shut behind it. It was almost pitch-black inside; only a soft blue glow lit the corners of the hangar.

"Here we are, sir," said Hernandez.

They stepped out and Cavendish ordered into the air, "Lights!," confident that someone somewhere would follow his command. The lights came on, and thousands of beams of bright rays reflected back at them. A mischievous smile lit up Cavendish's face, while Hernandez just stared with a squint.

"Well, what do you think of it?" said Cavendish. It was a question that Hernandez couldn't even begin to answer.

USS *Zumwalt*, Mare Island Naval Shipyard

He was too damned old, and now he knew it.

Mike could feel the fatigue in his chest. For the first few days it had felt like a bug, and he'd just worked through it, finding that shouting orders had eased the fatigue's grip. But this morning, it had been like waking up bound to the bed. He would never say it aloud, but Mike was sure he had never been this tired before. It was pure old-man exhaustion crossed with the profound fatigue that only those in the military and a few other professions know, the type of weariness you feel when your responsibility for other people's lives far exceeds your physical and mental reserves. This was the kind of tired that no amount of stims or coffee would help.

He swayed and steadied himself near the entrance to the bridge.

"Chief, you okay?" said Horatio Cortez, the XO. "You look like shit. You take the younger generation out barhopping last night? Teach 'em how you did it back in the day?"

"Wishful thinking, sir," said Mike. "They couldn't even begin to keep up with us."

Cortez wasn't fooled by Mike's banter. He could see the fatigue in the old chief's Tabasco-red eyes and he quickly excused himself and went back to the bridge.

Mike knew he could find one of the better nooks to sleep in aboard the ship down near the magazine for the rail gun. A sailor taking a power nap in a cool, dark spot was an honored Navy tradition, but it could also be a warning that something was not right with that sailor. As Mike lay back against the cool bulkhead, he wondered which it was in his case, wondered if he had what it took anymore. Then he drifted off.

It was the smell that woke him.

Fresh soap and violets.

Dr. Li.

He opened his eyes and saw her curled up on the other side of the bulkhead. Their legs crossed each other's in the middle; her feet looked so tiny compared to his. *Jesus, if anybody saw this,* Mike thought. He expected to wake up with the ship under attack more than he expected to wake up and see her next to him. How she'd found him, he did not know.

She stirred and arched her back like a cat, then sat up. She spoke as if she knew what he'd been thinking.

"I finally had time to grab a shower and then I saw you head down here to your hiding spot" — she smiled — "and I thought, *He knows what he's doing, he's just taking care of the equipment, as he so kindly calls the crew.* So I decided to follow the old man's lead."

"Who are you calling an old man? You look just as tired as me, Dr. Li."

"You got me there. I've got nothing left," she said, rubbing her eyes. "And it's Vern. If we're going to sleep together, you can start using my first name."

Mike felt the *Zumwalt* lurch and lifted his head slightly, like a hunting dog. They must be drilling the engine restart again, he thought.

"Listen, I'm sorry about the captain last night. He knows this ship is no damned good," he said.

"It's okay," Vern responded. "He was right, and he had the right to let go like that. Captain's prerogative that they keep talking about."

"No, he doesn't have the right to take his anger out on someone else. It took me too long to learn that lesson, so I couldn't pass it on to him," said Mike.

He avoided her eyes and stared at the bulkhead.

"You know, nobody ever told me what I'm supposed to do if things start burning again," she said, consciously changing the subject to one that might put him back in his comfort zone.

"The damage-control drills? You don't remember any of that?" he asked.

"If the ship's fate hangs on my ability to play firefighter," she said, "then we're all doomed."

Mike noticed that although she'd sat up, she'd done it in a way that kept her legs intertwined with his.

"You'll figure it out. Just follow an old man's lead, as you say."

She smiled again.

"Well, we'd better get back to work," he said. "I'm pretty sure the Z will be leaving port soon, most likely for Australia."

"What makes you say that?" she asked.

"I'm guessing from what Brooks, that tech with the stupid Mohawk, told me about some of the software mods to ATHENA. Weapons load-out is full, which we wouldn't be doing for another test."

"Australia's dangerous?" said Vern.

"It's the Navy — what isn't?" said Mike. "But it means we'll be escorting reinforcement ships. You're less likely to be shot at when you're looking for the easiest way to get to friendly territory than when you're out looking for trouble. There are no guarantees, though."

The *Zumwalt* shuddered again and Mike sat up. Then he reached out his hand to help Vern to her feet. She noticed the rough feel of the skin.

"Don't worry," he said. "I'll be at your side when it counts."

USS *Zumwalt*, Mare Island Naval Shipyard

"Status report!" said Captain Jamie Simmons into the intercom. "What's going on up there?"

The system was dead; there was not even static in reply. From his stateroom, he peered out into the dark beyond the hatch. Nothing. No klaxon. No shouting.

It was almost pitch-black dark, the only light the yellow emergency reflective tape along the corridor floor. Shaking the sleep from his head, he started to make his way along the passageway toward the bridge. He knew the route well enough.

A sharp jab at his forehead made him curse in pain. He ducked, too late, and dropped to one knee until the specks of pain-driven light faded. He reached for the bulkhead to carefully stand back up and felt something warm. Soft. Hair.

"Who's there?" he asked.

"Seaman Oster Couch . . . sir," said a timid voice. The fear evident in the hesitant pronunciation of the word *sir* made Simmons's head ache anew. He felt his cheeks get hot and his stomach knot in rage.

"This is Captain Simmons, what are you doing here?" he said, fighting to hold back his anger.

"I was coming back from the head and heard a big bang, and then the lights went out," said Couch. "So I waited. But they didn't come back on."

"You belong at your station, Seaman Couch. Up!"

"I don't know where it is, sir," said Couch. "In the dark, sir."

"Find it if you have to crawl on your hands and knees," said Jamie. "I'm heading to the bridge and if I find you here again in the dark, you'll learn there are far scarier places the Navy can send you."

"On my way, sir," said Couch.

Simmons had almost gotten to the bridge when the *Zumwalt* shuddered and all the lights came back on.

"Cortez! What is going on with this ship?" said Simmons.

"Power surge, sir," said Cortez. "It's rail-gun related, and we're trying to figure out why it took the entire ship offline."

"Everything? ATHENA too?" said Simmons.

"Yes, sir, everything," said Cortez. "But there're no fires, and Dr. Li is down working on it now. We'll be okay."

"XO, when you have the bridge, this ship is yours," said Simmons. The anger at Seaman Couch welled over, and he spat his words out at Cortez. "Treat it that way. There is nothing okay about this. You know what's going to happen when we get a surge like this out there?" He pointed west, toward the ocean. "Do you? We're nothing more than a target for the Directorate. First we blow the last part of the test with the admiral and SecDef onboard, and now we can't even get the goddamn gun turned on without it killing us? What kind of a ship do we have here? This is on you, Cortez. Get Dr. Li and fix it!"

The captain spun around to see his father entering the bridge. The old chief had that look of only slightly veiled disappointment he knew too well. He brushed past his father without acknowledging him.

"I'm going to be in my stateroom," said Jamie. He started to leave, then stopped. "Belay that. I'm going down to speak to Dr. Li about her fix. Cortez, you have the bridge."

He heard footsteps behind him as he stormed down the ladder wells.

"Captain, I'll accompany you," said Mike.

Jamie kept walking, mindful of any new overhanging fixtures and cabling that might strike his already aching head. He put two fingers to the spot he'd hit, certain it was bleeding. It was. What a sight that must have been on the bridge.

"A word, if I may, Captain," said Mike.

"As we walk," said Jamie.

"Sir, you need to get some rest," said Mike. "I'll say it because nobody else will."

"How can I? I'd say this port time is making us dull, but we're so far from sharp that it's not even worth bringing up," said Jamie.

"Still have to rest, Captain," said Mike. "The job demands it even if you don't think so."

"This job?" said Jamie, stopping abruptly and standing close to his father. "You don't understand this job. I'm the senior officer and it's my ship. You can't understand that."

"I can't?" said Mike. His face began to redden and that all too familiar angry blood vessel that snaked down his forehead began to pulse. "I can't?"

"No. I'm an officer," said Jamie, no longer afraid of that pulsing. "I have actual responsibility."

Mike leaned forward with the intent look that signaled to anyone, even an officer, that he or she was a single step away from receiving a heavy blow from one of his massive hands.

"The hell with you, Jamie," said Mike. "I don't care if you embarrass yourself in front of me, but you ought to think twice before you embarrass yourself in front of the crew again."

Mike turned around and stomped off, each angry footfall muffled by the non-skid rubber in the passageway.

Nautilus Restaurant, Palo Alto, California

Daniel Aboye couldn't help but stare. Before the war, this had been a regular haunt of his investors, the types who had net worths so big they'd stopped counting their money. He'd come here tonight with a new sense of awe, mostly at how wrong the place felt on so many levels.

He watched a tuna as long as his motorcycle swim steadily around the restaurant's tank in the ceiling. The readout on his glasses showed how many other diners had bid on it. Seven. He decided he would be the eighth and end the auction. The other bidders would likely interpret it as his showing off the depth of his wallet, but it was more an indication of the depth of his annoyance that they were all still carrying on this way in the midst of a war.

When he looked down, there she was.

"When you asked to meet for dinner," said Aboye, "this was certainly not the place I expected you would choose."

"I like the fresh fish," said Cory Silkins with mock innocence. "It's at least something that isn't rotting around here."

Aboye took in the woman across from him. She was always smiling, but ironically. Back at Stanford, they'd been first-year hall mates. It had taken him a while to get used to her sarcasm, but he quickly came to appreciate the fact that she didn't put him on a pedestal like the other students did once they knew his backstory. Instead, she treated him like she treated everyone else: as a target.

They'd even become friends of a sort after Cory realized his gentle nature truly was genuine, and he realized that her acidity meant that she couldn't help but tug and trick. She soon found bigger and better targets than the gangly but confident Aboye. Besides writing code, Cory's main passion on campus had been pranking assholes. Faculty or student, it didn't matter; she'd outed the members of a secret fraternity after they tried to cover up a date rape that occurred at their initiation ceremony, and she'd posed as a former U.S. president, using his hacked e-mail account to carry on a three-month-long online conversation with the old provost.

Of course, Cory had grown up and "sold out like the rest of them," as she joked at the sale of her software-encryption company, a deal brokered by Aboye. When he asked what she was going to do next, she told him that she was off on a quest for a glass of the most remarkable red wine in the world. He'd thought it was another joke, but she'd spent the past year chronicling it all in real-time for her online followers. Before this, he hadn't heard from her since the post about a Malbec in Argentina.

"So what brings you back?" asked Aboye now.

"I heard you went to Washington," Cory said. "I thought they might have drafted you, so I had to come back and rescue you."

"They wanted nothing to do with me," he said. "That, I must say, hurt deeply."

"Morons . . . You know, I've gotten a few quiet offers to leave. Finland. Brazil. Argentina," she said. "I wish France, but I think I am still on some blacklist there."

He'd heard the same from several of his other friends. From a business perspective, it made sense to him: America's wealthy were distressed assets themselves right now. The right luminaries, along with their intellectual capital and their bank accounts, could be had cheap.

"Are you considering it?" he asked.

"No, I prefer the life of an itinerant bacchanal," she said.

"That's for the best; you are indeed a national treasure," he said. "Okay, what is really up, Cory, why did you ask me here?"

A waiter wordlessly brought them their wine. Neither needed to be told what it was because the Firestone Petite Syrah's label was already displayed on their viz glasses. She pulled her wineglass over and held the stem between her long fingers, which were adorned with a dozen slim brushed-platinum-and-diamond rings. The rings gleamed with flecks of light from the fish tank's blue glow overhead and the red wine before them.

"Daniel, do you know why I love wine? It's not the taste. It's the history. And not just the history of the grape or the terroir that defines it. I mean the history of wine itself. Wine was the very first drink of equality," said Silkins. "The ancient Greeks would pour it into a bowl in the middle of a room and guests would gather around. They'd share it, the same bowl, and just talk. Philosophy. Rights. Democracy. Hell, maybe even sports. Anyone and everyone could take part in the conversation, from Socrates to his youngest student."

She laughed to herself. "Of course, it was all men, and then the

Romans ruined it by conquering Greece and turning wine into a prestige item so assholes like me could run around chasing a perfect glass of it."

He looked at her and took a sip. Clearly Cory was building up to something.

She swirled her glass. "That sense of equality is what made the Internet so great. Anyone and everyone could gather and participate. And that too is at risk of being ruined by assholes."

"And?" he said.

She looked down at her glass and then directly up at Aboye. "I know what you're up to."

Aboye distractedly glanced up at one of the divers gently herding a fish into a net. "What could I possibly be up to?" he asked.

"Daniel, you're not a good liar, so let's not screw around," she said. "I know what you and your buddies are doing in Hangar One, and I know that it's not going well, what with all the water damage to your library."

Aboye pinched the bridge of his nose, pausing as if to think but mostly to cover his concern. If she knew, who else did? And was Cory going to cause problems just because she was pissed off that he hadn't asked her to join?

"Let's go," said Aboye in a whisper.

Aboye and Silkins walked out of the restaurant, Silkins paying with her iTab bracelet at the table as she got up. They stood outside in front of the motorbike stand.

"Okay, Cory, what is it you want? And I still don't get why you asked me here."

"You needed a visual reminder. Restaurants like this? They're for a certain kind of person, the kind you've been hanging out with. Nobody is angry. How far is San Francisco? The city is transforming itself into a Navy town again. Ugly, rusting gray ships being fixed all over the place. Sailors getting drunk and fighting, not out of malice but to release something, anger at not being out there or maybe just some newfound hate. Down here, it's business as usual. Where can I get my fresh fish . . . or my favorite pizza next?"

She climbed aboard his yellow electric BMW C1, as usual taking things without asking.

"You have great people in Hangar One, but they know only how to build. You also need people who know how to tear down," she said. "You need assholes like me . . . Get on, and I'll show you."

Aboye folded his body uncomfortably behind her under the C1's canopy and they glided off silently through downtown Palo Alto.

Light from restaurants and storefronts that were being used as sidewalk cafés after hours spilled out onto the road before them. Since the war, everyone wanted to spend more time outside, it seemed to Aboye. It made Palo Alto more festive than he had ever seen it, as if all of the town's residents were Stanford seniors and this was commencement week.

They soon were sitting on Silkins's thickly carpeted living-room floor. She booted up her connection into the virtual world. Daniel watched as she put on a bright pink helmet with a matte-black visor. He thought it made her look like a cross between a teenage skateboarder and a fighter pilot.

She wouldn't let him join her inside the 3-D environment. "Too much for you to handle, plus they scatter when any outsider comes within a mile. That's how we've kept it going," she said. Aboye watched Silkins navigate on a screen above her fireplace.

He saw Silkins's avatar, a bizarre yellow-and-blue cartoon fish that looked like Salvador Dalí had designed it, swimming alongside what looked to be an abstract, submerged rendition of Las Ramblas, in Barcelona. She darted and drifted among other resplendent but unnerving avatars, everything from Hello Kittys to nude supermodel bodies with robot heads. Then, trailing bubbles, each apparently an encrypted key that verified who she was, she stopped at the open door of a hat store. She flicked open her visor and looked at Daniel, jumping from the online world back to the real world.

"Let me make this clear. This is not about patriotism," she said. "Our reasons are not yours — you know that, right? We're about the net itself. Songs about flags, sending kids to die, mom and apple pie, all of those lies? We don't buy any of that crap the system sells. But in this case, our interests align. We'd like to help you."

"What do you mean, 'we'?" he said.

"You don't need to know that. My friends prefer to remain anonymous."

USS *Zumwalt,* Mare Island Naval Shipyard

Mike moved as fast as a man his age could move through a warship's cramped passageways and ladder wells. The shouting got louder, and he forced himself to move even faster. The clanging of metal on metal had him nearly running.

"She's one of them," said Petty Officer Parker. "Just look at her."

Mike took in the scene in less than a second: Parker. Wrench. Vern.

He swung a left-handed punch with his entire body weight behind it and hit Parker square in the stomach. A following jab from his right hand landed just above Parker's heart, knocking the sailor back into the bulkhead. Just like he'd taught Jamie to do in the garage so many years ago.

Vern was sprawled on her back on the deck. He reached down to give her a hand just as she looked behind him and screamed.

Mike ducked at the last moment, and the blow from the wrench glanced off his shoulder. He grunted with anger, more at himself than Parker. It had been over twenty years since he'd last gotten into a fight, but some things he should not have forgotten. As he had been told by a senior chief when he was starting out in the Navy, there were two rules to remember in a bar fight: punch second, and leave first — but only after you're 100 percent sure the other guy is completely out of the fight.

The arc of Parker's swing had left him off balance in the tight corridor, so Mike bent lower to duck the backswing. He turned, feinted with his right, then moved in close and punched with his left, a short, stiff uppercut, a liver shot; he felt his knuckles crack as they smashed into Parker's side at the ninth and tenth ribs. He'd taught Jamie that move, told him to use it only when the fight moved from boxing to brawling. A liver shot was shocking and debilitating, causing the other guy to lose his breath and sometimes even consciousness. It was also excruciatingly painful.

Parker's desperate suck of air energized Mike. He hit him again hard with a close-in combination. And then another. He couldn't hear the thuds that echoed inside the room; the adrenaline made his own ears ring. But he could feel the impact of the strikes resonating through Parker's flesh.

He caught his breath, and as Parker crumpled, he struck with one more combination. Though he knew Parker was in too much pain to hear anything, Mike shouted at him: "You coward! How's it feel?" This was a show for the others who had gathered and were now standing back in a mix of awe and fear of the old man.

And then he stopped hitting him. Parker, like Vern, was equipment. He was part of the ship, and Mike was responsible for him too. Through it all, none of Mike's blows had touched Parker's face. Stand him up at attention before the captain, and no one would ever know he'd just gotten his ass kicked by a man old enough to be his father. That was the way of his Navy.

He turned to the thick crowd of sailors.

"Who else agrees with him? Maybe you want to intern all the Chinese in San Francisco? Ship 'em out to Angel Island like in the last world war?" shouted Mike.

Parker, trying to get up, was now on his hands and knees, wheezing.

"Dr. Li is one of us," said Mike. "If we win, it'll be because of her. If we die, it's because of ass-hats like you."

He reached down and yanked Parker up by his arm. The man cast his gaze down to avoid making eye contact.

"Look at me. And this goes for the rest of you too. You don't like it? Then you have five minutes to get off my ship. If you stay and this happens again, I won't just play patty-cake like today. Test me. See if I am not one thousand percent serious. Dismissed!"

Parker shuffled out of sight along with the rest of the crowd.

"Vern, everything okay?" asked Mike, helping her up.

"We lost time just now that we can't afford to," said Vern. She glared at him, angry at Mike for rescuing her as if she were some lost little girl and livid at herself for feeling so damned vulnerable.

"I'm not asking about the ship, I'm asking about you," said Mike.

She didn't respond, but she leaned into him. He stood there, unsure of what he should do. She started shaking, and he wrapped his tattooed arms around her. He couldn't see her face, pressed into his chest, so he looked down at his left hand, pretty sure the ring finger was broken. He felt good, though.

Moyock, North Carolina

"Please don't tap the glass, sir," said Hernandez. "It makes the animals crazy."

Cavendish pressed his face right up to a porthole. The shipping container, which was connected to two more in a U-shaped form, had been made watertight and then filled with water. Each container was about the size of a large apartment, or one of the bedrooms in Cavendish's South Kensington, London, block-long flat.

"I don't see anything. Are they in there?" said Cavendish. He tapped on the Plexiglas porthole again.

"Yes, sir," Hernandez said. "Why don't you try the viz glasses they gave us?"

Cavendish put on the matte-black, special-made viz glasses that had been hanging around his neck; his fingers rubbed the firm's old bear-paw logo on the side.

"What a simple proposition this all was. How did the original owner so truly screw the business up?" said Cavendish. "I have my theories but —"

He instinctively ducked as soon as the glasses clicked on. A long knife lunged for him, and he virtually counterpunched using some kind of ancient-looking brass trench knife. He settled into the fight, watching through the viz, becoming a part of the sparring from the perspective of a mask-cam worn by one of the commandos.

The lighting inside the container varied; every few seconds, the lights brightened and then faded to almost pitch-black again. The men seemed to be wearing gray-and-black tiger-striped bodysuits that were accessorized with a variety of edged weapons. Swiss micro-rebreather units, the kind used by cave divers, were affixed to their upper backs. When the lights flashed on inside the tank at one point, Cavendish realized that those were not tiger-striped camouflage patterns on the gray bodysuits. They were slash marks.

He felt a tap on his shoulder.

"Sir, this is Aaron Best; he was at DevGru with me. Best is the one who provides the adult supervision for selection and training," said Hernandez. "I'll let him fill you in on where we are."

"Welcome, Sir Aeric, it is an honor to have you here. What you're watching is the refinement of our tactics, techniques, and procedures. This is a simulation of a partial power-plant failure. That is why the lighting goes in and out. We also simulate total power failure, which plays out the way you would expect: a knife fight in a closet in the dark. This is a ten-minute evolution. It involves a nine-minute air supply, and the man with the fewest slash marks on his suit wins. He gets to get out first. The loser has to wait until the ten-minute mark before he can exit the tank."

"Quite an incentive," said Cavendish.

"In a man-on-man scenario, it's tough but appropriate. Where it gets tricky for the guys is when you put three of them in there," said Best. "The last guy out has it pretty rough."

"What about those outfits they're wearing?" asked Cavendish.

"Standard long-range recon swim kit. Blast-proof. Thermal regulation, which we enhanced for the mission. We think it will be effective," he said.

Cavendish's attention wandered and he stared at a set of seven connected shipping-container halves.

"That's the training box," said Best. "Same idea as what you see here, but it's for them to practice team on team. Same protocol, ten minutes for the losers. It's a lot harder, actually, not just because of the teaming, but also because we put a bunch of metal junk in there to simulate the interior. Essentially, it's like you're fighting a group of rabid monkeys in an airplane bathroom."

An arched eyebrow was Cavendish's only response.

Hernandez passed Cavendish one of the weapons. It was a titanium-handled steel-bladed brass-knuckled trench knife about a foot long. The anodized black coating had worn off on the knuckles and blade edges, both of which Cavendish inspected closely with the authority of someone who'd spent a year of his youth cornering the market on Japanese fighting swords.

"More sword than knife," said Cavendish. "Can I keep this?"

Hernandez looked at Best with a nod.

"Yes, sir. Technically you already own it," said Best.

"Too kind," said Cavendish.

"We will make the final selection seventy-two hours before launch," said Best. "The top six out of twenty-four. Four will be in the boarding party, two will remain in reserve."

That explained the intensity of the underwater fight he'd just watched, thought Cavendish. "These men really want to go, don't they?" said Cavendish.

"Of course, Sir Aeric. The awards you've offered are more than generous, but really, they just want to get back in the game," said Best. Cavendish returned the viz glasses to Hernandez. "Do you have all the medical-performance investment you need?" said Cavendish.

Best looked at Hernandez, who nodded.

"When we make the selection of our final six, I would like to authorize further cognitive augmentation, and a couple other things that the JSOC meat department is now using with the One Hundred Sixtieth helo drivers and the Persistent Operations Group," said Best.

"That is, I believe, a permanent change?" said Cavendish.

"It's in their contract," said Best.

"Very well," said Cavendish. "Hernandez will see to it. One last question before we meet the team. Something's been bothering me," said Cavendish.

"I am sorry to hear that, Sir Aeric. What is it? We have time before launch to address it," said Best.

"What are we going to do about all the blood?" said Cavendish. "It can't exactly flow out the scuppers. We need to figure out how to clean up the mess afterward."

Fort Mason, San Francisco

Jamie Simmons chewed his pasta quietly and stared at the coffee mug that he'd set on the table.

As he chewed, he worked his way through the day's decisions on the Z, especially the regrets, the *should've* and *could've* moments that were all the more important now that they were running out of time. He went over the day from start to finish, but he kept fixating on the fact that he should've stopped at the pier-side bench before coming home. He'd let himself rush in to see Lindsey. But that five-minute decompression was one of the most important moments in his day, a time to pause and master his thoughts, to transition through the purgatory zone between duty and home. Between war and family. He knew he was on edge and shouldn't have rushed back, but it was the fact that he was missing them at home that had made him rush.

This led him to recall his life before the war, when he'd never thought twice about what he ate or threw away or whether some *should've, could've* decision of his would end up leaving his sailors among the many burned carcasses cast into the Pacific. He became angry at himself for not following through on that prewar longing to be with his family, for his failure to act before their separation could turn permanent.

Jamie looked up and saw Lindsey studying him as he ate. She knew something was not right. His tension was clearly feeding hers.

"You look tired," said Lindsey. "What's wrong?"

"Nothing," said Jamie. "Let's start over. I'm sorry, it's just been one of those days."

"Seems like you have those every day," she said, a slight edge in her voice.

"I do," said Jamie. "The closer we get to deploying, the harder it is. The crew is exhausted, and they know the ship is not where it needs to be."

"It's getting harder for all of us," said Lindsey. "You need to make time for the kids. They were asking . . ."

"Asking what?"

"When you're leaving again."

"What'd you tell them?"

"You'll have to go soon, but it won't be forever."

"It better not be."

"I need to ask you something. I let it go after Pearl Harbor, but I have to know, I just do. Did you ever tell Riley you were done?"

"Jesus, Lindsey. Does it matter? Does it really matter? He died, bled out in front of me as close as we're sitting here. You want to know what he thought of my career?"

"It does matter. To me. There's no —"

A banging and a crash from upstairs stopped her. They heard an old man cursing, and then Martin laughing. Jamie's eyes flicked over to the sound. Lindsey looked down.

"Why are the kids still up? And what's he doing here?" said Jamie. He put his fork down with a sharp clink and reached for his coffee mug. Staring hard at Lindsey, he took a pull of the cold, bitter coffee dregs that should've ended up at his feet an hour ago.

"He's fixing the toilet. It couldn't wait," she said. "He came by the other day and worked with Martin to print the part we needed with a three-D printer he cadged from one of his harbor buddies. They had a lot of fun. I know what you told me about him coming here, but I think he just wanted to be with his family before . . . What could I do?"

"You could actually do what I ask," snarled Jamie.

"I could say the same thing," Lindsey replied coldly. He didn't know whether she was referring to the broken toilet, time with the kids, or his promise to leave the Navy. He didn't care. In any case, he knew he was in the wrong. And he didn't like it.

"I don't have time for this. I need to prep for tomorrow."

He grabbed the weighty folder full of personnel-assignment reports and walked out of the room, leaving his plate of shrimp and pasta mostly uneaten, a testament to his disappointment.

He went down the hallway quietly, passing the open bathroom door. He'd disappointed enough people tonight and hoped he wouldn't run into his father, since that would only lead to the knockdown argument he'd just avoided by walking out on Lindsey. It was probably the wrong call, going to bed angry, especially with so little time left. Yet another bad decision to regret. He quickly rounded the corner and walked into his office.

Door shut, he sat at his desk. He reached to turn on the desk lamp but then paused in the dark. His eyes slowly adjusted to the room until he was almost able to make out the picture his son had drawn, tacked to the wall next to the window facing west. It was a magnificent green, yellow, and blue warship, taking up three pieces of paper taped together lengthwise.

Depending on what part of the vessel you looked at, it was either a triple-decker or a double-decker, armed with red turrets from which bird legs jutted out at all angles. Pink hearts covered the hull, and a small flag with a blue star flew from the stern with the words *Win, Daddy* on it. His wife called it the Love Boat, and the sight of it made Jamie's eyes well up with tears.

A soft click in the hallway meant the bathroom door was closed. The heavy tread of Mike's boots going down the stairs told Jamie he no longer had to worry about seeing his father tonight. He wiped his eyes, got up from his seat, and looked out the window at the top part of the Golden Gate Bridge. Every time he saw the bridge like this, in the fog, his stomach tightened. He knew the next time he passed under it, he would be with his father on what would likely be their last cruise.

Moana Surfrider Hotel, Waikiki Beach, Hawaii Special Administrative Zone

"Ten o'clock."

That was all he had said when he slid the room card across the rental counter to her. Nothing more, just a wink and a smile before he walked off, his hair still dripping seawater. A gold Rolex dive watch hung loosely on his left wrist, exposing a whisker of paler skin beneath the tan. He hadn't even given his name, assuming she had to know who he was. And he was right. Supposedly, his uncle ran Bel-Con, the electronics company in Chengdu. One of the maids Carrie occasionally drank coffee with had shared the gossip when he first arrived. "A creature of the night," she had added with a shiver.

The really rich were like that, Carrie had seen, no matter what country they were from. They always assumed you knew what they wanted and that you needed to be told only when and where to provide it.

In this case, he didn't have to tell her where. The hotel keycard said that for him. It was polished to look like platinum, but really it was cheap aluminum. As she waited in line for another security checkpoint to access the staff elevators to the hotel's VIP suites and rooms, she ran her finger across the outline of three palm trees cut out of the middle of the card, indicating it was the key to the Moana Surfrider's penthouse suite number 3.

The Chinese marine on duty was making everyone go through a portable body scanner, and the staff members waiting to be scanned one more time before they could get on with their jobs were getting annoyed. The most annoyed were the waiters, standing silently in their white pants and fitted black short-sleeved turtleneck shirts, who knew they'd be berated for being late.

Waiters, that was the right word for them all. Waiting for the checkpoint line to move, for the war to end, for death.

Carrie bided her time, putting the room key in her back pocket next to her ID and filing her nails with an emery board. The floors in the hallway area were scuffed, and only half the lights worked. It was the kind of neglect she had started to see all over the hotel. Knowing the stakes involved with this new clientele, the staff kept the exterior and guest hallways brighter and cleaner than they'd been even before the invasion. But behind the scenes, where the staff worked and lived out their days, the hallways were taking on the worn and tired feel of subway tunnels.

Carrie picked a piece of surfboard wax from under the nail of the ring finger of her left hand and subtly flicked it to the ground. After he'd dropped off the card, she'd stayed busy scraping the boards down, getting the sand-flecked wax off inch by inch.

"Next," said the Chinese marine. He did not use a translator device; his English was pretty decent. She flashed her hotel ID at him and returned it to her back pocket, then set the emery board down on the table and stepped through the scanner.

The scanner warbled like a tropical bird as she picked up her things.

"What's in the back pocket of your shorts?" he said.

"It's my ID, okay? The lanyard broke." She flashed him the ID again, the room key hidden behind it, holding the two cards up with a stiff arm like she was some kind of special agent. He ran another body scan and found nothing. Two of the waiters behind her stifled chuckles.

"And that, what's it for?" he said, motioning to the emery board. He picked it up and examined it closely.

"It's for my nails," she said, taking it from him and putting it in her pocket.

"You can go," the marine said, turning to the next person in line.

The elevator doors hissed open and she stepped inside. She pulled out the emery board and started to file again, this time more intently.

The elevator sighed, slowing down as it came to the top floor. As the door opened, Carrie brushed the edge of the metallic keycard lightly across the inside of her elbow. It was now sharp enough to draw blood.

Moana Surfrider Hotel, Waikiki Beach, Hawaii Special Administrative Zone

"Lieutenant, you're missing the view," said Markov. "It really is a great place to die."

Lieutenant Jian was too busy dry-heaving over the railing to take in the aquamarine panorama of the Pacific that lay before them.

The young officer finally looked up and angrily wiped his mouth with the back of his right hand. He scanned the horizon, squinting at the rooftops of the nearby buildings, with his hand resting on the pistol at his hip.

"You're right, Jian, there could be insurgent snipers here also admiring the view," said Markov. "Why don't you go back inside and tell them to turn the hot tub off? Come get me when our friend stops boiling and we can take a better look at the body. It'll be easier up close." He smiled.

Jian was stone-faced when he returned a few minutes later. The water in the tub was now calm, no longer bubbling, but still wine-dark red. The dead man lay with his head resting on the teakwood behind him, revealing a crimson gill-like slit across his neck.

"Lieutenant, is he naked?"

"Sir, I cannot see into the water," said Lieutenant Jian. "It's too, too, uh . . ."

"We need to know if he's wearing his shorts or not," said Markov. "Find out."

Jian looked toward the body in the room and then back at Markov.

"Come on," said Markov. "You don't get to earn your combat zone badge without seeing a little blood and some naked bodies. Roll up your sleeves and get to work."

Markov pretended not to watch as Jian tried to figure out what to do next. Finally he started toward the tub, rolling up his sleeves.

"Stop!" shouted Markov. "It is an expression the Americans use. You were actually going to reach down in there? Maybe you are braver than I thought."

Markov continued to chuckle to himself as he reached into a duffle bag full of equipment and turned on a black-light tube about the size of a D-battery flashlight. He found another one and tossed it to Lieutenant Jian. "Of course he's naked. From what we heard from the guard downstairs, he likely spent half his time in Hawaii naked."

He and the aide entered the room; Markov passed Jian a pair of goggles and put on a pair himself. The ultraviolet light swept the room for DNA traces, skin, blood, and any human fluids.

"Extraordinary," said Markov as white splotches filled his view of the room. "How did he even get up there?"

He realized Lieutenant Jian had gone back to the balcony again and shouted, "It seems your boy here was a very busy young man indeed. Start tracing them. But be sure you're wearing gloves . . . and I hope you've had all your shots."

Markov began to take swabs, and the DNA analytics started cross-checking databases for identities.

Throughout the hotel suite, tiny faces began to appear in the field of view provided by the sensor goggles. One popped up wherever there was a concentration of DNA from a particular person, and soon there were faces looking back at Markov from all over. A few were from Directorate security sweeps, some others were linked to prewar Hawaii driver licenses, but the vast majority were mug shots from the Hawaii Police Department files. The colorful, faintly shimmering profile pictures were mostly of young women.

He reached out, touched the closest virtual card that hung in the air, and flipped it over to see the file display. An arrest record for prostitution. He flipped another. Prostitution and drug charges. And then another. Prostitution and drunk and disorderly.

Markov then swept his hand across the room, virtually grabbed all the pictures, and began to sort them, putting those with criminal records in a stack on one side of the room and those with non-arrest records, a smaller stack hanging in the air on the other side.

Lieutenant Jian rejoined him and started pulling down the tabs of those with arrest records. "I am sure the general will want us to round them all up, and then we can process them on our own terms," said Jian.

"Think so? Your boy made his way through half the prostitutes in Hawaii. Arrest them all and you'll have an uprising on your hands, but not from the locals," said Markov, tabbing through the stack of those without arrest records, mostly hotel staff. "These poor maids, they deserved combat pay to come in here —"

Markov's index finger stopped and rested on the image of a young woman that hung in the air. A driver's license. He had seen her before. He flipped the picture over. Yes, the look in her eyes was different, but that was her, all right. What had the surf-shop girl been doing all the way up here?

Alto Café, Queen Street and Ward Avenue, Honolulu, Hawaii Special Administrative Zone

"Traitor," one of them snarled.

The glares of the locals waiting out the day in a thick cloud of marijuana smoke inside the old Quonset hut on Queen Street told her she was in enemy territory, even though she was among her own people. Their scowls and squints after they took in her outfit, a sea-blue tank top as tight as a bathing suit and iridescent white formfitting pants, gave the room a new menace.

"Whore," another said with a cough.

A subdued Colombian reggae band played in the background. It was one of the banned global peace movement songs. She had to speak up to be heard by the girl behind the bar when she asked where the bathroom was.

"Customers only," said a teenage girl with a crown-of-thorns tattoo wreathing her bald head.

"I just have to pee; please," said Carrie.

"Then buy a coffee or a smoke," said the girl.

"Just coffee," said Carrie, tossing a hundred-RMN note on the counter.

"Bathroom's back there. Lock's broken," said the girl with a look of disdain.

Carrie weaved her way through the low tables to the back of the restaurant. She kept her eyes on the floor, not out of embarrassment but out of fear that someone would trip her if she didn't watch her step.

A man in this fifties wearing a dirty white wool cap mottled with ash burns winked at her from behind a pair of taped-up viz glasses. Then he beckoned her over, curling a plump finger. The simple act of signaling her made his massive weight stress the wooden chair further. He brushed crumbs and ash from his clothing, a formless black T-shirt that went down to his ankles like a dress. She gave him a quick glance that he would replay again and again on his glasses later.

"Piss off," she said. "You can't afford it." Playing the act of someone past caring. Or was it an act anymore?

Then she moved carefully past him toward the bathroom.

She looked at her translucent G-Shock and saw she had three hours until the nine o'clock lockdown. The return of curfew had done more damage to Directorate troop morale than the local insurgents had.

She leaned in toward the mirror, reapplying lipstick. She was sure the two men following her had been Directorate. They'd had flip-flops, loose linen pants, and bright floral T-shirts, but the colors were too bright. The shirts had clearly been bought recently; they didn't have the weathered look that real locals' clothing had. Definitely Directorate, and she knew why they were after her.

She waited in the bathroom for fifteen minutes. Then she fixed her hair and washed her hands. Maybe they weren't following her anymore, which made it time for her to go back out there and face the hate, anger, and poison she saw in the expressions of her fellow Hawaiians every day.

Hand on the doorknob, she paused and breathed, preferring the stink of the dirty bathroom to the lazy funk of the coffee shop.

The door crashed in before she had a chance to open it. A pair of black-gloved hands threw her against the bathroom wall, knocking a faded photo of Waikiki Beach to the ground; its cheap wooden frame broke into pieces. Then she was hauled to her feet, dragged along the corridor, and thrown forward onto the café floor.

She looked up just as a knee drove into her back. Coffee dripped from one of the tables onto her head and down her face, and she blinked the stinging liquid from her eyes. The customers were gone. She didn't have to check to know the door was locked. Nobody who'd seen her walk in was going to call for help.

Carrie tried to push herself up, straining against the weight on her back, but a foot pressed down on her left arm. Then her right.

There were two of them, and they spoke in Chinese, short bursts that were getting angrier. She tried to see who was speaking, and a fist slammed her face into the wet floor. She strained again and was forced down by a forearm across the back of her neck.

Carrie opened her eyes wide, her breath escaping. She felt one of them pulling at her legs, tugging off her pants; one pant leg caught on her right ankle and was then yanked off. She could hear the man a few feet away arguing with the other one about something. Maybe chickening out, or maybe wanting to go first.

Carrie kicked free, scrambled to a corner, and then curled into a ball and started shaking, her half-naked body covered in spilled coffee and ash from the floor.

She closed her eyes. She thought of the visits at night, always after her mom had drunk herself to sleep. How she would lose herself, escaping to the moment after she would fall from her board, entering the churning froth beneath a powerful wave, inches from the razor-sharp beauty of a reef. In that chaos, there was a beckoning peace. In the churn, you could hear nothing at all, just a ringing in your ears. If you chose, you could lose yourself in that moment forever.

Then the wave would pass, and she would rise again to the surface with a gasp.

She reached back to the inside of her left upper arm and peeled away a rectangular Band-Aid three inches long. A searing pain and the red trickle of blood began to flow.

The closer commando grabbed Carrie, pulled her out of the corner, and roughly dragged her upright. She did not fight him; her arms hung limply by her sides, and the Band-Aid dropped to the ground. He wrapped his right hand around her throat, his thumb just under her jaw. He was strong enough to lift her entire body up so that her toes barely touched the ground. Growling, he pulled her in close, reached down with his free left hand, and undid the clasp of his belt. He began to unzip his pants, but then he looked into her eyes, and froze.

The stillness and tranquility of her eyes drew him in, confused him, just for a moment. He didn't even notice the flash in her right hand.

The blade itself was short, only one and a half inches and just a bit wider than a sheet of paper. Made of ceramic, the box-cutter blade she'd taken from her fiancé's toolbox was sharper than a razor and would never rust, not even when hidden in her pain.

He did not even feel the first slash arcing upward; so fine was the blade's edge that his body had difficulty registering the damage being done. Even before his opened carotid artery began to spray out, she had slashed downward, arcing across his stomach at an angle just above his bellybutton. He was pulling his left hand back to punch at her, his pants now falling to the floor, when he noticed his intestines were spilling out.

As he fell, grabbing at his stomach, Carrie charged at the other soldier. He struggled with his concealed holster while trying to wipe away the blood from his partner that had sprayed into his eyes. He'd just barely drawn his pistol when she slashed across his wrist; the gun clattered to the floor, and she sliced at the other hand. He countered with a karate chop, but weak, as if he'd already given up. The box-cutter blade met his hand in the air and sliced off his left pinkie and ring finger. And then, in a frenzy, she was upon him, slashing again and again.

She lost herself in the moment, hearing nothing at all, just the ringing in her ears and the beckoning peace.

And then she rose to the surface with a gasp.

Carrie looked down. The soldier's face was gone, just a patchwork of red lines. She couldn't remember what it had looked like. Her father's face was all she could recall.

Fort Mason, San Francisco

Captain Jamie Simmons kicked the soccer ball one last time down the rolling hill, marveling at how sure-footed his son was now. Jamie wore a Giants jersey over his uniform, as if he were trying to shield his kids from the morning's uncomfortable truth.

The sun soaked the grassy field behind their house in Fort Mason. It was great weather for playing with his kids, but a part of him that was always tethered to the *Zumwalt* couldn't help but wish for the concealment of a thick fog. In truth, the Directorate satellite that covered Northern California could see through any weather, but there was something comforting in feeling hidden.

He sprinted after Martin, whooping as he picked up speed running downhill toward the boy, past the Marines at the air-defense battery. By the time he caught up, Jamie found Martin sitting on the orange-and-yellow ball looking out at the Golden Gate Bridge.

"If you go out past the bridge, how can I see you?" asked Martin.

Before Jamie could respond, a pair of Marine Corps AH-1Z Viper attack helicopters thundered past the waterfront, raced out into the Bay, and then disappeared from view under the bridge.

"The whole ship is going with me," said Jamie. "It's my job. We have to go scare the bad guys away so they won't try any bad stuff here."

"Grandpa going too?" asked Martin.

Jamie paused.

"He's coming too," said Jamie. "He loves you, but he has to go."

"How come you're the captain, but he's older?" said Martin.

"He got to choose his job a long time ago," said Jamie. "Besides, there can be only one captain. Isn't it good that it's your daddy's job?"

"Make sure to be nice to him, then. Grandpa doesn't come over as much anymore," said Martin. "I miss him. Is he mad at me?"

"No, nothing like that," said Jamie. "He's just been really busy with work."

The knot in his stomach wound itself tighter as Jamie leaned over and kissed the stubble on Martin's shaved head.

"I thought he left already, and you didn't want to tell me. Who's going to take care of us if you're gone and he's gone?" said Martin.

Jamie felt as if he'd been punched in the chest. But he tried to show no change.

"How about you?" Jamie asked. "Can you take care of your mom and your sister for me?"

Martin picked at a piece of grass.

"Okay," said Martin. "I think I can do it. Because Mom needs somebody to help her out, you know. It's actually hard when you're gone."

"I know it is," said Jamie. "Let's go see Mom and Claire now."

Jamie put his son on his shoulders and walked back up to the house. Jamie noticed the other houses had people in the backyards, all of them engaging in the uncomfortable rituals of goodbye. The next few hours were going to be his last with his family before he left. He had to make them count.

Those few hours passed quickly amid a flurry of well-wishing visitors and their children, giving the day a rhythm of alternating moments of laughter and tears. Before Jamie knew it, he was standing on the porch with his wife, holding Martin in one arm and Claire in the other.

Lindsey reached out and wiped a tear from Jamie's eye.

"Kids, up in your rooms I left something for you," said Jamie. "Do you think you can wait until I get back to open it?"

They started squirming immediately, and he set them down.

"Okay, okay, go!" said Jamie.

From the front porch, he watched them scamper up the stairs.

He turned to Lindsey and pulled her close in a hug whose pressure built with each second. The only words that came to Jamie's mind were *I'm sorry.* Before he realized he had spoken them, Lindsey said, "I'm sorry too."

A hoot of joy upstairs punctuated their apologies.

"Not the best goodbye we've had," said Jamie.

"Not the best war we've had," said Lindsey, trying to smile. "Just make sure to see the end of it with me. Do everything you can out there to make sure this never happens again."

"I promise. There won't be a next time. I lost myself in the ship, and I know I had to, but it wasn't something I meant to do."

"Your dad never knew how to say goodbye, did he?" said Lindsey. "You do. Be safe."

"I'll send a letter as soon as I can," said Jamie.

A thunder of eager footsteps came down the stairs.

Martin wore a baseball cap with the *Zumwalt*'s silhouette on it and gold braid on its bill. On the back it read *Captain Martin Simmons.* Claire clutched a stuffed gray dolphin wearing a gold-and-blue U.S. Navy T-shirt.

A steady horn blew from down on the pier.

"Captain can't be late," said Lindsey. "Say goodbye to Daddy."

Jamie crushed his kids with one last hug, inhaling the smell of shampoo and grass. He stood and kissed Lindsey hard, then pressed his forehead against hers.

"I love you. Forever," he said.

"Forever," she said.

He turned and started to walk with unsteady steps across the front yard to the waiting launch.

"Wait!" said Lindsey.

She ran toward him and tugged on his shirt. He looked down. He was still wearing the baseball jersey. She pulled it off him as he held his arms up to the sky.

PART 4

Use the normal force to engage;
use the extraordinary to win.

— SUN-TZU, *THE ART OF WAR*

(Note: This is the motto of the PLA Command Academy in Nanjing,
displayed on its library wall.)

Forty Miles North of Thule, Republic of Kalaallit Nunaat

Admiral Agathe Abelsen didn't know what else to do, so she squared her broad shoulders and sharply saluted the first American she saw.

It was all disorienting. First the helicopter ride and then landing on an airfield that was as large as the town she'd grown up in. The airfield's control tower, which the Americans called an island, loomed above, taller than almost every building in her country. And the ship was too large to think of as an actual vessel; it didn't even seem to sway with the sea.

The American sailor Abelsen had just saluted gave her a quizzical look. The seaman second class tying down the helicopter's wheels was now just as confused as the admiral; he had no idea why the senior naval officer from the Republic of Kalaallit Nunaat, formerly known as Greenland, had just saluted him.

"Admiral Abelsen, welcome aboard," said Rear Admiral Norman Durant, striding forward to salvage the situation. "We're honored to host you onboard the USS *Nimitz* for the first joint operation between the United States and Kalaallit."

Instead of saluting him, the admiral squeezed Durant with a powerful bear hug.

Once she let him go, the carrier strike group commander stepped back and threw her a crisp salute, trying to ignore the rest of the deck crew staring in astonishment. The admiral stood at least six inches taller than Durant's five foot ten, and she must have outweighed him by a good fifty pounds. She had delicate features, thick eyebrows, and the kind of pale skin that made her green eyes seem luminescent. Her uniform coat was a sort of down parka, the standardized kind that fishing companies issued their crews, but with a patch sewn on the right shoulder. The patch displayed a flag, a rectangle with a half-red, half-white circle in the middle. Durant had read up on Kalaallit before the admiral arrived, so he knew that the white half of the circle in the flag, the lower part, signified something about icebergs and pack ice, and the red half above signified the sun setting in the ocean.

"I wish it were under better circumstances, Norman," she said, already on familiar terms with him, it seemed. "But don't you worry. We will get you through. You have let our dream come true, and now we will show you the way."

Starting in 1721, Greenland had been a colony of Denmark, its population originally living off subsistence fishing. Indeed, for most of the island's history, half its entire economic output had been shrimp exports. By the turn of the twentieth century, the citizens of Denmark saw this last legacy of their failed colonial ambitions as a burden (the Virgin Islands, their only other major holding, had been sold off to the United States in 1917). They resented having to send a yearly subsidy a thousand miles away to feed, house, school, and clothe a population of mostly non-Danish indigenous peoples, or Eskimos, as they were popularly known.

But in the twenty-first century, the relationship flipped. The frozen waters off the massive island opened up due to global climate change, and eight massive oil fields were discovered, totaling as much as eighty billion barrels. Greenland's citizens realized that if they could break that old colonial link, instead of sharing their island's wealth with six million Danes, they could keep it at home and divide it among just fifty-seven thousand Greenlanders. Greenland, or Kalaallit, in the Inuit tongue, could become the world's richest petro-state.

Greenlandic independence had really been just a dream, though, as NATO would never allow the territory of one of its own members to be torn asunder, especially with a key U.S. military base located in Thule. But then, three days after the current conflict began, NATO's North Atlantic Council, its political body, voted not to join a war already seemingly lost in the Pacific. Unfettered by the old politics, American strategic planners had soon after taken note of the fact that the potential new country had nine commercial icebreakers in its ports, while the U.S. Coast Guard had only one remaining icebreaker, and it was sixty years old and presently stuck in the wrong ocean at the port of Bremerton, Washington.

And so a deal was struck: The United States would recognize and protect the sovereignty of the nation of Kalaallit, instantly making it the thirteenth-largest country in the world by geographic size and the richest by per capita income. In exchange, Admiral Abelsen and the world's newest navy, made up exclusively of icebreakers, would escort America's Atlantic Fleet through a new path to the east.

Mount Ka'ala, Hawaii Special Administrative Zone

The approach to the mountain had taken Conan and the insurgents two days of slow movement. Hiking up the one gravel road would have taken them only a few hours, but they would have risked bumping into the twice daily patrol from the Directorate guard force at the foot of the mountain.

Judging from the ache deep in her left elbow, Conan guessed that the cut there was infected. All the crawling over the forest's slimy dirt and roots made it inevitable. But this was the best she'd felt in weeks. It felt good to be doing something other than running, which to her had started to feel like slow-motion defeat. Since the ambush at the school, the Muj had done nothing but escape and evade. But now they had a mission.

Maybe that helped too. The fact that someone else had finally made the call eased the weight of decision and the aching heaviness of responsibility. How long had it been since she had just followed orders? Until her D-TAC buzzed and that sea glider showed up, all she'd had was her instinct and Marine Corps training.

The physical toll of getting to the target site might kill them before the Directorate could, though. Mount Ka'ala was Oahu's highest point. At just over four thousand feet, she told herself, the mountain wasn't that high compared to the ones in the mountain-warfare courses she had done. Yet the sinister way the heavy mist wreathed the jagged range made it an angry reminder of how cruel the world could be. The constantly attacking mosquitoes would not let her forget it. Focus on the mission kept her and the rest of the NSM inching higher, minute by minute, under their sweltering woolen blankets, willing themselves to reach their position before nightfall.

As they trudged along, she couldn't help admiring how the

descending sun lit up the Directorate aerostat surveillance balloon. Its silver skin reflected the sunset in orange ripples.

"Like a big fat juicy peach there for the taking," said Finn, steadying a spotting scope. "Ready to go shopping, sir?" He was still making jokes, but there was a palpable tension between the two of them since the school shootings, an undertone of challenge even in the way he now called her *sir*.

"Seems right," said Conan, trying to ignore the tone. That was what she had been taught at Officer Candidate School: squelch it immediately or ignore it. She couldn't squelch it now; the NSM was too fragile to hold together under the force of discipline. Indeed, she'd already noticed the looks from the other team members they'd met up with and heard their disapproving whispers about the kids who'd died at the school and the comrades who'd been deserted there.

She signaled to the three other insurgents nearby to keep advancing. Shrouded in their blankets, which would help defeat thermal-imaging surveillance, the fighters took the formless shape of decomposing stumps.

"Pass me the suppressor," she said to Finn.

Conan wriggled out of her pack and set up the Chinese weapon, a QBU-88 rifle. The suppressor screwed on easily and within thirty seconds, the rifle's scope had established a network connection with a TrackingPoint spotter.

"I have the impact point," said Finn, getting back to business. The scope, which they had taken from a Dick's Sporting Goods, automatically adjusted for range, wind, and ballistics and was connected to a networked tracking engine. Wherever the target, a hit was guaranteed for even an amateur marksman, especially as an auto-lock wouldn't allow the gun to fire until it was pointed exactly at the mark the spotter had laser-designated.

"You know, my brother-in-law had one of these. Point, click, and shoot. Asshole would assassinate Bambis from a thousand meters away, all the while sipping his Pabst Blue Ribbon. And not ironically, mind you."

"How we looking?" Conan asked.

"Got nothing at IP Alpha," said Finn. "Pissing in the wind. Well, you know what I mean, right, sir?"

"Roger that," said Conan. "See the aim point?"

"Got it," said Finn. "Anyone else you want me to clip while I'm up here? Maybe one of us, sir?"

Conan ignored the bait and adjusted the rifle on her shoulder; the scope and spotting device recalculated the round's impact point.

"Did you leave the seat up again?" said Conan.

"Me? Never," said Finn.

"All right, then, you're safe for now. How's IP Bravo?" The pair worked out the firing solution so the three shots she fired would hit their targets in close sequence. That was essential to the opening phase of the mission.

The old radar dome building, a sphere atop a lattice-structure base, looked like a dirty golf ball fished out of a septic tank. The site had been built in 1942 as part of Hawaii's first radar defense network and had operated through most of the Cold War. Then budget cuts had left it mothballed for decades. But high ground would always remain valuable real estate. The silver aerostat, a faint smile of the sun's final light cast across its crown, hovered three hundred and fifty feet above the old dome, its sensors unobstructed out to the ocean in all directions.

"How are we for time?" said Conan.

"Three minutes," said Finn.

They covered themselves and their gear with their blankets and waited. Sweat pooled in the crook of Conan's arm and stung her infected elbow.

From under his blanket, Finn said: "Why don't we just shoot the radar up on the balloon? Be a lot easier."

"Everything worthwhile is hard," said Conan, her voice muffled by the blanket. "An old gunny said that once to us."

"You're still a Marine, then, sir?" said Finn. "Then why'd you break the credo of never leaving anyone behind?"

"This is more important. Mission above the man," said Conan. "Besides, we plink the radar, they'll just reel the bitch in and fix it."

"That's why they pay you the big bucks, then," said Finn.

"Don't know why they want it taken out now, but I think you can imagine," said Conan.

"I don't need the cavalry riding in; I'd be happy with a few dozen Tomahawks. Why do you think they haven't done that yet?" asked

Finn. "Just push a couple buttons; that shit's easy. Some days a tactical nuke would be okay by me. If Washington had just gotten off its ass when this first went down, we never would have had to fight like this. Should have just gotten it over with at once. Show your cards, motherfuckers. Instead, we draw them off the deck one by one every day. Is anybody back there afraid to die anymore?"

"You just answered your own question," said Conan. "Nobody wants to die as bad as we do."

It all sounded good, but she knew something Finn didn't. She knew she was already dead. After that day on the airfield, it had all been borrowed time. Hunkering behind the Osprey wreckage, she'd decided that if she was going to die, it was going to be with purpose. That the time she had left hadn't been the expected few seconds but had stretched into days and then months didn't matter.

Conan's stomach tightened and she took in a deep breath. She let it out slowly as she peeled back the woolen blanket.

"Sixty seconds," said Finn.

Finn swatted a fly, causing Conan to flinch. She exhaled deeply, steadying her nerves.

"Damn it, Finn, keep still," said Conan, feeling a mosquito bore into her forehead.

"Roger," said Finn. "Ready to launch the zipper?"

Conan nodded.

"Go."

Finn crouched and lightly tossed a Frisbee-size disc toward the aerostat. This was one of the other gifts they'd received in the duffle bag from the undersea ocean glider. As the disc took flight, a tiny lift fan whirred to life, and the device raced into the forest canopy, disappearing from sight almost immediately. The zipper could fly for only twenty minutes, but what it did during its brief electronic life was what mattered. The carbon-fiber zipper scanned for electronic signals — like from the surveillance systems surrounding the aerostat site — and then repeated those signals back until its batteries ran out. A small green light on a candy-bar-size stick beside the rifle indicated that it was functioning.

"Time to blow out the candles and make a wish?" said Finn.

A click of the rifle's safety and Conan adjusted the aim point on the scope, a final touch to make sure.

"May all our enemies die screaming," she whispered.

The rifle fired, the noise under the suppressor almost like a muffled sneeze. The first shot took out a camera mounted in a tower overlooking the site. The second round smashed into a mushroom-shaped antenna. A third shot shattered the lens on a camera pointed up at the aerostat. If the zipper did its job, then they could hold on to the element of surprise just a little longer.

"Let's go," said Conan, wedging the blanket into the webbing on her backpack. They tried to run, but the vegetation was so thick and the roots were so treacherous they could manage only a fast walk.

"Nearly there," said Finn, holding a hand over his right eye; he'd gotten jabbed by a branch. Conan stopped to catch her breath, taking a knee. The heat and humidity, even the altitude, were crushing. Finn reached down to lift her up and dragged her along, tripping over a slimy root himself.

"Why's the goddamn balloon still attached?" said Conan.

Tricky shrugged with a new recruit's look of shame. She was a fourth-generation Hawaiian and had been only seventeen years old and into her second year of surfing sponsored by Billabong when the war came. That they'd brought her along showed just how thin the Muj ranks were getting. She offered Conan an ax that was nearly as tall as she was.

"You deserve the honors," said Tricky.

"This isn't a damn ceremony, just cut the cable!" said Conan.

Tricky shook her head no, wiping sweat from her eyes. "All right, give me the ax," said Conan.

The support structure anchoring the aerostat's tether cable looked like a miniature Eiffel Tower. Conan aimed the blade at the juncture where the cable attached and brought the ax down with a grunt. The ax handle was wooden, but the blade had a nano-synthetic diamond edge. It was Chinese military issue, and they'd stripped it from the back of a supply truck a month ago. Conan brought the ax down again with a loud clang that made the rest of the insurgents tense up. Finn instinctively scanned the perimeter of the clearing.

"We better hurry," said Finn. He held out the control stick for the zipper. The light now flashed red.

She heaved again and smashed the ax into the steel cable.

"Fucker's stuck," said Conan, bending over to lever the blade out. She turned slightly as a volley of rounds hissed past the place where her head had been a moment ago. The angry sound of autocannon fire followed.

"Contact!" shouted Conan. A quadcopter drone appeared, leaping above the canopy around the site's perimeter. The strobelike muzzle flashes from its cannon lit up the plateau. The NSM insurgents took off at a run away from the cable's tether point and slid into the foliage at the edge of the clearing.

"Target the drone; it'll track your fire, and I'll go after the tether," said Conan. She sprinted back to the cable's anchor point, clutching the ax.

Finn tried to track the quadcopter but kept losing it as it ducked in and out of the forest canopy. A rapid reaction force would definitely be coming now. They might helicopter up, and if they did, it would be all over soon. If the Directorate soldiers instead drove up from the mountain's base, then they might have a few extra minutes.

Another crash of autocannon fire from the quadcopter, which emerged again from the canopy and started to close on Conan's position. There was a flash of red light to Finn's right as Tricky fired a flare gun they'd scrounged from a sailboat's emergency kit. Temporarily blinded, the drone automatically paused and stabilized itself, following its standard protocol to reset its sensors. *Dumb-ass machines,* thought Finn.

He took it out with his second shot, and the quadcopter spun off into the trees. Then a dark shadow passed overhead: the aerostat, its plump belly faintly lit by the flare's dying red light, a light wind taking it west.

They ran to the tree line, joining the other insurgents. Already, they could see three sets of headlights coming up the Mount Ka'ala road to the plateau.

Above them, the first stars were already out, joining the array of lights from Schofield Barracks in the distance. Conan could see all the way to the sweep of lights at Diamond Head, and she allowed herself to wonder what those who hunkered down over there thought of the far-off solitary balloon, lifting off into the night.

Then Conan heard another buzzing in the distance. It was another quadcopter, scouting ahead of the Directorate trucks in the dark.

"Let's move," said Conan. "Remember, we stay together this time."

USS *Zumwalt*, Gulf of the Farallones, California

Captain Jamie Simmons walked forward past the rail-gun turret and stood at the very tip of the ship's bow. The chisel-like bow narrowed to a fine point, but there was enough room that he could stand on steady legs and take in the view while he went over the ship's systems on his viz.

The Z had sliced through the oddly still water of San Francisco Bay at just over ten knots, accompanied by seventeen other ships from the Ghost Fleet, most of them old transport and amphibious ships. They'd left in the foggy darkness. No sendoff with dignitaries and officials. Most of the tearful goodbyes had been wrapped up a day ago, and those who'd thought they could avoid difficult face-to-face conversations by saying goodbye online found themselves with no connection to the rest of the world. The ship was at full EMCON A emission control, running dark, electronically speaking, without the connectivity that the U.S. military had taken for granted for decades. Even if Directorate satellites or spies had seen the ships leaving the Bay, they would have gleaned little information, as the fleet was not leaving a trail of data and information in its wake. The ships wouldn't even form a local network connection. Mostly, as Admiral Murray insisted, they would use signal flags and lights, old-school nautical communications methods, to help conceal the fleet's position and course.

The ships passed silently under the Golden Gate Bridge, lit only by the few cars on the road. The scaffolding, ostensibly put up for a construction project, prevented anybody from driving by and taking a close-up viz of the departing fleet. In an age of ubiquitous video capture and Directorate spy satellites, it was a desperate throwback to the early Cold War years.

Jamie watched as, off to port, the sea stacks of the Farallon Islands emerged from the water twenty miles off Point Reyes. Closer in were the remnants of a faint series of triangular wakes left by the three ships leading the way, the USS *Mako* and two sister ships. The stealthy unmanned surface vessels looked like they belonged in orbit, not on the ocean. But the tiny ships were predators, no question about it. With the fleet operating on radio silence, the fifty-seven-foot-long carbon-fiber *Mako*-class ships were in full autonomous mode, programmed to hunt and destroy anything made of metal that moved counter to the currents underwater. All the prewar concerns about setting robots loose on the battlefield didn't seem to matter as much when you were on the losing side. Plus, there was no worry about collateral damage underwater, no civilian submarines that might accidentally get in the way. The worst the ships could do was torpedo a great white shark that had eaten too many license plates.

A flash of movement caught Jamie's eye and he peered down into the bow wave. A pod of dolphins surfed along with the *Zumwalt*. Instead of watching them play, he focused on the map layout and saw that the *Mako*-class ships racing ahead had not detected any mines or signs of the Directorate's quiet diesel-electric submarines.

"All clear ahead?" said Mike. Jamie turned his body slowly to acknowledge his father but kept looking at his screen.

"So far, so good," said Jamie. "That won't last, will it?"

"Probably not," said Mike. "Look, I need to talk to you for a minute."

Jamie turned off the glasses, not wanting this conversation recorded. "Let's head over to the turret."

In the lee of the rail-gun turret, well out of the wind, Mike spoke first. He braced his back against the rail-gun housing with the kind of effort that betrays exhaustion. His coverall seemed to flap looser, Jamie thought, as if his father'd lost weight.

"We have to solve this," said Mike. "We don't have the time to work together, blow up, work together, and then blow up again. Two steps forward and all that."

"Agreed," said Jamie. "We can't have an argument every time we spend more than a minute or two with each other. It's got to stop. The ship can't have that. Cortez has already brought it up, suggested you transfer to one of the other ships in the task force. But I kept you with this ship. You know why?"

"I would have stowed away anyway," said Mike.

Jamie cracked a smile. "I don't like having to keep the civilian techs onboard, but the ship needs Dr. Li," said Jamie. "And she needs you."

"What are you talking about?" said Mike.

"Dad, you can't bullshit the captain on his own ship. You taught me that," said Jamie.

"Vern's less than half my age —" said Mike.

"It's Vern now?" said Jamie.

"— and got twice the years in school."

"Whatever you want to tell yourself. It's your business, not mine. But I need you to keep her safe," said Jamie.

"She's doing it to show the rest of them that they can't question her . . . well, her right to serve, I guess," said Mike. "One of the guys got after her and —"

"I heard. Is your hand okay?" asked Jamie. "You should have just brought him to me; we could have replaced him."

"That's the thing — now he's going to be the best behaved sailor on this cruise," said Mike. "In my Navy, we handled things up front and got it over with. All this bullshit about diversity and the new Navy, and still Vern has to deal with this?"

"I know. And if anyone is going to protect her on this ship, it's you," said Jamie.

"You've already made your point. Would it be hard on you, me with Vern?" said Mike.

"Actually, this might be difficult for you to hear, but, no, it wouldn't be," said Jamie.

"You still hate me," said Mike. "When's that going to stop? That officer's uniform's not going to fix things between us. Times like this I don't fucking understand why you even went in."

"So this is our chance to have it out? Okay, then. You left us, Mackenzie died, and it all ruined Mom. But that's not even it. It made me a better man than you. And I prove it every single day."

"Jesus, now we're back to square one," said Mike. "I'd tell you to quit being a martyr, but you're not that wrong. I should have been there, and I live with it every single day too . . . And that anger to prove you're better than me may have gotten you to this point. But you need to get it out of you. There is nothing personal about war. Purge it. Now. Before it poisons the captain you ought to be."

Jamie paused and looked off into the distance and then back at his father. "I hear you . . . Chief," said Jamie, still not able to address him by the name he swore he'd never use again the day his father left. "Let's get back inside. I need to check in with the mission center to make sure we don't run over one of the *Makos*."

The two walked carefully along the starboard side of the ship, staying out of the wind and dodging the spray from the growing Pacific swell.

"You know I'm right on this, Jamie. And I know you're trying. We can talk more when we get to Australia," said Mike.

Jamie leaned in close to his dad's ear, cupping it against a gust of wind.

"Going to be a long wait, then," he said. "We're going somewhere else."

As his son walked away, the ship made a slow, lazy turn, and Mike noticed the faint hint of the rising sun peeking through the fog. Oddly, it was off to starboard. They were headed north.

Directorate Command, Honolulu, Hawaii Special Administrative Zone

Colonel Vladimir Markov looked across the room and winced as Lieutenant Jian yawned. The boy did not even try to conceal his fatigue, which to Markov was one of the many reminders of the young officer's weakness, and just when he finally needed his aide/minder actually to do something.

"Is the model ready?" the Russian asked.

"I'm working on getting the last of the data to load," said Jian. "Some of these weren't meant to be put together, so the system is —"

"And that's why we're doing this," said Markov. Being a hunter required more than guns. He'd learned that over two decades ago. He needed data. "If there's one thing I am going to teach you, it's to stop thinking that things can work only the way you've been told they're supposed to. You can't win a war that way. Nobody ever has."

"Will it be stable enough?" asked Lieutenant Jian, ignoring Markov's advice, as usual.

"We'll find out, won't we?" said Markov. "Besides, even if it doesn't work, nobody is going to see. You're not going to tell the general on me if it doesn't, are you?"

Lieutenant Jian avoided Markov's look.

"Of course you are," said Markov. "Just do your job and don't get in the way of me doing mine. When this is all over, they are going to ask you what you did in your war. I bet you thought you would get to do something heroic. It's your first war, and that's what everyone thinks. Well, that's not going to happen. But instead of being some dumb underling, give yourself something to be proud of. At least make me proud. There's still time."

Lieutenant Jian gave him a sideways glance, as if the Russian had said something treasonous. Maybe he had.

"Yes, Colonel, as you say," said Lieutenant Jian. "The model is ready now."

"Start it," said Markov. "Let's go hunting."

The lights went off and all was dark. Then the projectors arrayed around the spherical room's perimeter blinked on in sequence.

The holographic model wrapped itself around the bodies of the two men. For a moment, Lieutenant Jian gazed at Markov in disbelief, but the face looking at the Russian was melded with the holographic image of the face of the young Directorate marine who'd had his throat gouged in the stairwell of Duke's Bar on Waikiki Beach. *Another horrific image to forget,* thought Markov. Then a different dead body was overlaid on the map; the system had been directed to pull from the casualty list all the Directorate personnel who had gone missing or been killed by any method other than firearms or explosives.

"Now overlay with the movement analysis."

A spread of small pictures seemed to spray across the room as if from an imaginary tube. The software allowed the capture and processing of hundreds of thousands of hours of multiple-image-viewpoint recordings simultaneously. The American military had gotten the idea from the way media companies covered the Super Bowl and had first used it in Iraq. You could saturate a city with drone cameras flying overhead and record everything, but all those images were useless unless you could process the embedded information. That was where the artificial intelligence came in: it found patterns in the noise of daily life.

As the small dots filled the room, the faces of the dead soldiers began to flicker.

"It's crashing," said Markov. "Fix it."

Lieutenant Jian barged through the holographic image, leaving a wake of warped faces and streaming video dots behind him.

"There, okay," said Lieutenant Jian. "It was the overhead tracking feed from the drones; it does not want to sync up with the traffic cameras."

Markov waded into the middle of the model, hands raised slightly to the level of his heart, as if he were inching into an icy pool.

"Drop the topography now, set to bird's-eye view."

As he stood there, faces and names, numbers, and grid points were overlaid on a 3-D map of Honolulu.

"Here, here, and here." He indicated points on a map of the city and its environs. "This is where your personnel were found. Here and here too, this is where these unlucky gentlemen went missing. No women, note."

"What's the relation? Insurgents are everywhere, they can attack at any time," said Lieutenant Jian.

"Watch," said Markov. "Set the system to correlate with known insurgent activity." A series of red lines began to appear between the various points, forming a random cluster around Markov.

"I don't see the pattern," Lieutenant Jian said.

"That's the point," Markov said. "These deaths were not consistent with any pattern of normal insurgent activity."

"What about insurgent activity is normal?" said Lieutenant Jian. "They don't follow any rules."

Markov laughed and walked through the model that now connected the body icons with rainbow-like arcs. From each arc dangled a holographic image, akin to a driver's license, of every person whose DNA had been tracked in the area.

"Lieutenant, I have seen the work of plenty of killers. Insurgencies bring out the truly savage side of humanity. Hands used to kill despite fingernails having been ripped out only days before. Broomsticks topped with shotgun shells. Rusty blades dipped in shit to ensure an infection," said Markov. "And yet, they all followed a simple rule: anything goes in the name of freedom."

"You sound like you admire them, these assassins killing our troops one by one," said Lieutenant Jian. "They are just monsters, all of them."

"I don't admire them, but I seek to understand them," said Markov. "However, this is something different. Lieutenant, you may finally be right about something. I think we are indeed looking for monsters. Just not the kind or number you think. Pull up the file of Ms. Carrie Shin."

"The woman from the hotel?" asked Lieutenant Jian. "If you're playing another joke on me, this is not the time."

Carrie Shin's face appeared on a wall screen. The photo had been taken by the Directorate security teams for the special ID used by the workers at the Moana hotel. Stunningly beautiful, her tan face beamed. Yet to Markov, something was not right with her eyes; they were almost dead in their expression.

"Now remove the insurgent activity." The swirl of red lines disappeared.

"And now populate for all facial-recognition traces of Ms. Shin."

Images of Carrie appeared in tiny flashing pictures and video-stream dots, the viz screen spiraling through still shots from traffic cameras, videos of drone coverage overhead showing her crossing a street, checkpoints where she had shown her ID badge. A person's entire life couldn't be recorded, but it left traces. As more and more data was fed through, lines of the patterns of her life formed, all of them crossing again and again with the victims' locations.

"Do you see the spider's web?" said Markov. "She is who we have been looking for."

"You can't be serious," said Lieutenant Jian. "Just one girl? It's only because she works in the same areas. I will reboot the system."

"Why? Because you don't like the answer?" said Markov. "You don't understand what you're looking at, do you? This is something special, Jian. A true killer hiding in the death of war. A rarity to be observed and understood."

This was indeed something new, thought the Russian. It seemed like this war wasn't going to be such a waste after all.

He reached into the hologram on his tiptoes and pulled the photo down, expanding Carrie's image to larger than life-size.

Markov began pacing around the perimeter of the model, trying to remember the lines from his tattered book of poetry, speaking quietly to himself in Russian.

Calmly he contemplates alike the just / And unjust, with indifference he notes / Evil and good, and knows not wrath nor pity.

He changed back to English. "Pushkin should have said '*she*,' Lieutenant," said Markov. "The hallmark of a true professional is the ability to admit when one is on unfamiliar ground, and that is where we are now."

"Colonel, I have to ask, have you been drinking?" said Lieutenant Jian. "I cannot tell the general that we think this woman, this American beach babe, not only killed the minister's son but also has been brutalizing all our forces."

"You coward, all you can think about is what you're going to tell your master. Look into those eyes," said Colonel Markov. "She is what you should fear."

Lieutenant Jian's mouth puckered with dismay, but his eyes showed he could not find the right disapproving words, much less the courage to say them.

"You and I, we can put on a uniform, but we will always be prey. Mere bodies to be sacrificed by our leaders. She, though, she is a huntress and she wears — what, a bikini? A cocktail dress?" said Markov.

Jian looked annoyed and queried the system for her current location. The last image had been her stepping off a city bus a few blocks from her apartment.

"You just asked the wrong question. The question we should be asking is not where is she now, but what is she doing? If she is what I think she is, she is likely hunting right now . . . Or is she coming down, grasping at normalcy?"

"Colonel, it is late, and this is a waste of time," said Lieutenant Jian. "There is no way this one woman has killed so many men. We can pick her up, but first I must report your waste of valuable resources to the general."

"Yes, go run to your master," said Markov. "But have a squad ready in thirty minutes. And you had better hope we find this black widow before . . ." — he paused for dramatic effect and then laughed — "she finds you!"

USS *Triggerfish,* Task Force Longboard

The USS *Mako* raced past the *Zumwalt*'s stern in what looked like a reckless game of chicken. A fifty-seven-foot trimaran, it had a main hull and two thin outriggers attached by lateral beams. The design, often used in racing yachts, was lighter and faster than a standard single-hulled boat's, having a shallower draft, a wider beam, and less surface area underwater. For the racing yachts, it meant minimal crew space inside the thin hulls, but that wasn't a concern for a robotic warship.

The autonomous sub hunter sped away to the far edge of the fleet and began to patrol in a racetrack figure-eight pattern with a sister ship, the USS *Bullshark.* It had been a controversy when ships with no crews had received names at their commissioning ceremonies four months earlier. It was an important cultural shift, and ultimately the secretary of the Navy herself made the decision: these were not disposable robots but warships the fleet could count on to save lives. Nobody questioned the naming on this day as the high-speed vessels worked to keep Directorate and Russian submarines at bay.

The *Mako* bolted in a straight line to the east, its speed rising past forty-five knots. The *Bullshark* slowed, its chisel-like bows diving slightly in the Pacific swell, then took off on a different heading to the west. The pair located a Directorate Type 39A submarine six miles away. Following an algorithm developed from research done on the way sandtiger sharks cooperated in their hunting, the two ships coordinated and began to box in the fleeing nuclear submarine. The Chinese sub didn't know that a third *Mako*-class ship, the USS *Tigershark,* lay silently drifting in its projected path.

The *Tigershark* launched a Mark 81 rocket-powered torpedo from a range of three miles. The supercavitating design allowed the torpedo to reach underwater speeds of almost two hundred knots, giving it just enough time to get up to full speed before it punched through the sub, entering the hull from one side and exiting through the other.

The sounds of the submarine's hull collapsing were captured by the *Mako*-class hunters and relayed to the *Zumwalt,* as was the burst-transmission distress message from the buoy that had been automatically ejected by the sinking Chinese sub. The task force ships were now safe from the undersea threat, but they were leaving a trail of crumbs behind them.

Mount Ka'ala, Hawaii Special Administrative Zone

Conan pressed her cheek deeper into the wet mud beneath the hapuu ferns. A moment ago she'd thought she heard the buzz of a small rotary-powered drone. Yes, there it was. The sound ebbed and flowed in the damp air.

She curled her knees into her chest and pressed them tighter, hoping the wool blanket would shield her from the thermal sensors. These were the moments when you were truly alone, when you had to face up to all the things you could have done after the invasion instead of taking up arms. The camps at Schofield Barracks weren't that bad, people said. The Red Cross visited regularly, as the whole world saw via images collected and broadcast by Directorate social media teams.

The buzzing intensified and Conan held her breath, smelling orchids and damp mud. She felt the prick of a mosquito's bite near her jaw. Then another. The buzzing stopped. Was that it? Just a pair of fucking bugs?

Conan had expected to be killed within a few moments of setting off down the mountain. Yet here they were. They'd been moving in the dark as quickly as they dared until they'd heard the sound of the pursuer overhead, and then they'd sheltered under their woolen blankets, diving under ferns and into furrows in the forest floor. That was all that was between them and a fléchette rocket or autocannon round. Just a half an inch of wool that hid their heat signatures.

They'd gotten the idea from the Taliban, who used them to elude American drone searches. Finding wool blankets in Hawaii had been the hard part. They'd had to sneak into a frozen-fish processing facility off North Nimitz Highway, where Nicks traded the foreman a captured pistol for the blankets. Conan hoped that gun would be on their side someday. Lots of people said they were waiting for the right moment. A podiatrist in Kaneohe who had hidden Conan and Finn in his garage one night had even shown them his great-grandfather's *newa*, an old Hawaiian wooden war club with shark teeth embedded in it. He'd sworn that his ancestors would see him smash it into an occupier's skull one day soon.

Soon. Would that day ever come? Conan lifted the edge of her blanket and listened. Nothing mechanical moved; she heard only the sounds of the forest at night. She raised her head and clicked quietly and saw the spectral shapes of insurgent forms rise up and circle around her. She waited five minutes and then hissed softly, and they began to move with soft steps down the mountain.

"Beautiful night," whispered Finn. She could tell he was close by the sweetly vile smell of ammonia and musk.

And then the world went white.

The first explosion lifted her off her feet and launched Finn into a tree trunk. A second explosion followed an instant later, shredding trees with hundreds of dart-like metal-fléchette rounds.

Conan tried to look around but couldn't focus, as white static seemed to fill her eyes. When her vision cleared, she looked through the infrared scope on her sniper rifle and saw a dozen Directorate soldiers bounding down the trail. In the distance came the low growl of a quadcopter. Then all the soldiers flicked on their flashlights at once. Confident bastards.

She peered out from behind the protection of a koa tree trunk and pulled the trigger. The shot hit a soldier squarely in the middle of the protective faceplate on his helmet. She panned for another target, but a volley of shots ripped through the leaves to the left and right above her and forced her to dive into the dirt and roll to the base of a tree ten feet away. Turkey-peeking around the trunk, she saw the first soldier, now with a shattered visor, back up and advance, firing steadily.

Let them come. She needed them close so the quadcopter couldn't fire at the Muj from above the forest canopy without also killing the Directorate soldiers. She waited, her back to the tree trunk, wiping sweat from her forehead with her hand.

This was it.

"Montana! Montana! Montana!" she shouted over the irregular bark of assault rifles. She fired wildly around the trunk, not even looking, and then immediately tossed the cumbersome sniper rifle. She took off running, knowing there was no way they could catch her loaded down with their helmets and armored tac-vests, just like the old mujahideen in the 'Stans had run circles around the U.S. troops hauling eighty pounds of gear up and down the mountains. After a hundred feet of running, she ducked behind a tree, took off her backpack, and tossed it onto the path.

Then she took off sprinting downhill again, more agile now without the weight of the backpack, bounding over stumps and rocks. Branches and leaves slashed at her right arm, which she was holding up to protect her face.

The explosives in her backpack detonated on the trail above her. The back blast tossed Conan down, but the two hundred pea-size ceramic ball bearings shot up the trail in the direction of her pursuers. At her insistence, all the Muj patrolled with the homemade mines strapped to their backpacks, what Finn called, appropriately, death insurance.

She lifted herself up and started running down the trail again. The crack of another explosion meant Finn's charge had gone off as well. It didn't tell her whether he was still alive or not, but the explosion did illuminate the trail ahead of her, and what she saw sent her stumbling to try to slow her descent.

She hardly saw or heard the third explosion, maybe Tricky's, because she tripped and started to cartwheel down the trail. Conan clawed at the mud, rocks, and branches trying to stop her acceleration. The speed of her tumbling picked up as the slope steepened.

A fourth explosion.

She snatched a glance at a horizon split between the last few feet of overgrown slope and a black void decorated with twinkling lights. Whether they were stars or buildings below, Conan couldn't tell. For some reason, she relaxed and fixated on that question as she felt her body lose contact with the ground.

Kakaako, Honolulu, Hawaii Special Administrative Zone

Colonel Vladimir Markov nodded once at the Directorate commando. He was a bit surprised General Yu had let the mission go forward. It could have been the prospect of writing yet another letter to a Directorate senior official who had sent his boy off to get a safe war for his résumé only to receive in return a body unfit for an open-casket funeral. Or perhaps the possibility that a woman might be doing the butchering had affronted his warrior's sensibility.

The commando affixed what looked like a ridged black plastic cup to the apartment door's handle. He gently pressed the white button on the back of the device, and there was a faint hum, followed by a hiss. The electromagnetic charge in the breacher device silently shook the lock apart. There was a faint pop as the commando removed the cup, and he waved Markov forward with an exaggerated bow that showed the Russian the sinister skull painted on the top of his assault helmet. Markov thought it silly, knowing they'd gotten the idea from that video game they all liked to play in their off-hours.

The team already knew she wasn't home. An external thermal scan of the one-bedroom apartment had shown it was empty. He'd made them confirm it with a second painfully long search done by a two-inch creeper that wormed under the door and checked every room for carbon dioxide levels.

Even though Markov had to bring the commandos with him, he would enter alone. Their commanding officer didn't mind. He knew what they were thinking: If the Russian wanted to blow himself up in a booby trap, so be it. This war was dragging on, and only the Russian seemed to be in a hurry to lose a limb.

Markov was indeed in a hurry, but his careful movements did not show it. He removed his shoes in the hallway and covered his feet in a pair of surgical booties.

"Your shoes, sir?" said the Directorate commando in English. "Shall I shine them during your stay with us?"

"Just make sure they're good enough for General Yu," said Markov over his shoulder as he stepped through the doorway. The laughter in the hallway followed him inside.

He headed first for the kitchen. He'd never understood why, but people loved to hide things in the kitchen. Explosives in the freezer. Shells in the breadbox. False papers and ID tags among the recipes.

He found nothing. No heads in the refrigerator or fingers drying on the windowsill, which part of him had thought was a possibility.

It was a depressing apartment, bare of any personal items. Just a collection of build-it-yourself furniture, much of it apparently bought used. There wasn't a single photograph anywhere.

Markov sighed and reached into the satchel. He put on a pair of thick, green opaque goggles that looked like the heavy-duty night-vision gear worn by infantry. He powered them on, and the room appeared before him as clearly as he had seen it moments before. A signal meter showed he was connected to the router in the armored vehicle outside where Jian waited, as ever.

He murmured a series of commands in Russian and the room began sparkling with mosquito-size points of light. The flickering consolidated, giving the floor and furniture a green-blue shimmering hue, like a boat's phosphorescent wake in the moonlight.

Each streak represented the DNA trail that she'd left during her daily patterns of life. Each was a tiny piece of her that she would never get back.

Ending up in the bedroom, Markov followed the shimmering trail around the bed and over to the wide closet. Of course the trail would lead here. A woman should be close to her clothes, he thought, especially this woman. He then smiled at his own sexism.

The lights showed a cluster of activity toward the back of the closet, mostly concentrated on a faded red-and-white shoebox. The box was for a pair of Puma flip-flops, men's size 11. Whose, he did not know.

He carefully lifted the box slightly with a pen, testing the weight. It was light, making it less likely that it was booby-trapped. *Less likely* was not *impossible*, though. Still using the pen, he gently raised the lid, teasing it up to see if there was any resistance from tape or a wire. There was none, and he took the box's lid off fully, finding inside a hairbrush in a plastic sandwich bag and a green piece of paper folded into a small envelope. He carried the box over to the bed and sat down.

The envelope was addressed to *My Love*. He slowly opened it, fold by fold. More writing, some kind of anniversary note, and then, with the final unfolding, a small razor blade. It gleamed even in the low light, bright with DNA traces. He folded the blade back into the envelope and laid it on the bed.

He looked at the hairbrush, curious about why it was stored inside a plastic bag. What was so valuable about it? He took the brush out of the bag and eyed it more closely, turning it in the light.

He slowly shook the brush just above the green envelope; strands of hair fell out. He pulled out his pen and ran it across the brush slowly; a few more hairs fell down. Using the pen, he began to separate them, holding his breath so as not to disturb any. The hairs were all short, none longer than an inch, a few straight, a few curled, all of varied thickness. There were twenty-one hairs in total.

Lotus Flower Club, Former French Concession, Shanghai

Sergei Sechin sat at the edge of the bed and stared at the strands of Twenty-Three's blue hair sticking out from under the sheet. Against the pink fabric, the hair looked like something found on a coral reef, beautiful and fragile. Then, as the weight of his body pressed down on the mattress, bright red blood started seeping toward him.

He stayed seated as the blood came closer and closer. Had she done it herself, or was this a message to him?

In either case, it meant he was blown. Did he have time to destroy his devices and get a back-alley body scan to see if they had tagged or chipped him? Or should he just run? And yet, what he found himself thinking was that now he'd never know Twenty-Three's name.

The knock on the door snapped him to attention, and he returned to being the intelligence professional he'd been before he entered the room. Why knock? Perhaps to unsettle him further? See how he would react?

His eyes moved to the corner, where there was a small writing table. He quietly opened the desk drawer and found a pen. It had an ivory inlay set with eight brushed-metal bands and a gleaming silver nib, reflecting the recent fad that had many of China's most powerful writing letters by hand for the first time in decades. It would have to do.

Aware that he was being watched, Sechin scribbled a note. They would give him time to write it, he knew, thinking it a confession. But it was just a message in Klingon directing them to where they could stick something.

He went back to the bed and sat down, then felt her warm blood seeping into the seat of his pants. He leaned over and kissed her through the wet sheet. As he kissed her, he brushed her hair with one hand and felt his neck for the pulse of his carotid artery with the other. With closed eyes, he tensed up and prepared to jam the fountain pen's nib into his artery as far as he could and then rip it out.

The door exploded in a spray of fine wooden particles, and the concussion from the blast lifted Sechin off the bed. He crashed face-first into the mirror.

He slumped over at the foot of the mirror, then rolled onto his side, frantically looking for the pen, his ears ringing too loudly for him to hear the faint hum of rubber treads on the floor. The breacher robot rolled up to him, and the gun mounted at its end pointed at Sechin's neck and fired.

Tiangong-3 Space Station

When they retold the history of this war, no one would believe just how boring the space part of it had been.

They were the true "Warriors of China's New Century," as the unit's commendation letter from the Presidium itself put it. Colonel Huan Zhou had read it to them as they shared a celebratory meal of dehydrated roast pork and mooncakes the day after Tiangong fired the war's opening salvos. But since then, in a metal box two hundred miles above all the action, little had happened for months.

And for that Chang was thankful. If it was boring, Chang dared not mention it. Huan kept riding them hard, conducting training drills as if they had to shoot down the whole cosmos. *There's nothing left!* Chang wanted to shout. *All the targets have been serviced!*

The only real threat they had faced came from a U.S. Air Force jet — an F-15, Huan said later, flying at its maximum altitude — that had fired an antisatellite missile at the station. The Tiangong's laser-defense system turned the missile into more space junk and would have lased the plane if it hadn't had some kind of high-altitude mechanical failure first.

The worst part about that action was that it was all automated. Chang wanted his son to think he was a hero, but the onboard systems had handled the targeting while Chang slept.

He ate another mooncake and gazed longingly down at the blue Pacific.

"Chang," Huan called. He sounded even more on edge than normal, which perhaps reflected the fact that they'd run out of stims three days earlier. The pace of war in space was so slow, they'd gone through them faster than planned, trying to stay alert. "What is the MAGIC array status update?"

"Operative at one hundred percent. No anomalies," said Chang. Hainan had ordered them to shift the geosynchronous orbits of the surveillance satellites from their position above the central Pacific to an area over the Arctic region. It hadn't made any sense until the new readings came in.

"It's still tracking the American East Coast squadron coming from the North Atlantic. Two nuclear-ship readings, all data confirmed received. It seems whatever intel they had was right. The Americans are making one more push, this time up north."

"I almost admire them. They have to know it won't work, but the sacrifice is still worthy," said Huan. "Near space clear?"

"Exclusion zone intact. The German comsat launched out of Sudan last week made sure to stay extra-wide. I think it's a broadcast bird," said Chang. "I can check the intel reports again."

"Make sure you do. We want no surprises," said Huan.

The Directorate had declared a two-hundred-kilometer zone of exclusion around Tiangong. The Germans had apparently learned their lesson three weeks ago after a Belgian weather satellite had wandered into the zone and been lased into a molten ball of junk.

"Today's traffic?" asked Huan.

"A slow day. Intelligence reports two launches expected: an unmanned Russian replenishment vehicle for the ISS and one of those space-tourism flights from the European spaceport in French Guiana," said Chang.

"War-zone tourists. In space! Such idiots. Let me check with Hainan to see if we can service that target, maybe make their trip even more exciting," said Huan, laughing.

Huan's braying laugh was one of the most trying aspects of life aboard the station for the entire crew. Was it bloodlust or boredom that drove Huan?

"And I will inquire about the resupply. You know, Chang, there may be fresh crew coming."

Home.

"I'll leave only when you leave, sir," said Chang, hoping those words would be enough. If Huan thought he wanted to leave, Chang knew he would be the last to get off the station.

"Naturally," Huan replied.

Chang closed his eyes and waited. He was good at waiting. He thought about his son: What was he doing at this moment? Were his eyes closed too? Chang began to hum a song he used to sing to his son when he was a baby.

A steady *ping* snapped him to attention. The station's flight-tracking systems had detected a change of course by the tourists' space plane.

Chang wiped his eyes with the back of his hand and stared hard at the screen again. No. That couldn't be. It was heading straight toward the exclusion zone.

USS *Zumwalt*, North Pacific Ocean

"All stop!" shouted executive officer Horatio Cortez.

As the USS *Zumwalt* slowed, the black smoke coming up from the bow section of the ship blocked out the view of the nearly flat Pacific Ocean.

"Who gave the order to stop?" asked Captain Simmons, wanting to yell but producing more of a wheeze, as he had to catch his breath. He'd dashed up from the engine room, where he had been talking to the crew about how to get a few more knots of sprint speed out of the ship. "What the hell is going on, XO?"

"It's some kind of internal explosion," said Cortez, eyes flickering behind his glasses as he watched the ship give an automated damage report. "Fire-suppression system is working, should be under control any moment."

The smell of burning plastic started to waft through the bridge.

"No sign of an attack. ATHENA says battery fire," said Cortez in the clipped voice he used during high-stress situations.

"Then we can start moving. We have a schedule to keep!" said Simmons. He turned and left the bridge, and there was no doubt in any-one's mind that he was headed to find the source of the problem.

As he rushed below decks, the calls of "Captain!" and "Make a hole!" echoed down the ladder wells and passageways. He could never catch up to the crew's warnings to the others that he was on his way and they should look shipshape.

As he got deeper into the ship, the calls ended. Damage-control teams rushed back and forth, focused on their work. A caterpillar-like fire-suppression bot crawled past, and Simmons tucked in behind it as the crew made way for the machine's steady slink toward the rail-gun battery.

Simmons felt a hand on his shoulder pull him back.

"Captain, they've gotten it extinguished," said Mike. "I mean, she's gotten it extinguished. The Z's fire-suppression system took care of it. If only one thing works right on this ship, I guess it's good that it's the sprinklers."

"I need to talk to Dr. Li, help her light a fire under the power team's asses," said Simmons.

"Son — I mean, sir — let me handle this," said Mike. "Not much you can say to her or any of the crew to make them move faster. This one's for me and Vern."

"Chief, it's my ship, my mission," said Simmons.

"I told you to stop personalizing it. It's the Navy's ship, not yours. That's what the best captains learn," said Mike. "You think anybody's going to go easy on themselves now? You keep everyone busy upstairs and let me get my hands dirty down here. You're going to have your hands full soon enough."

Jamie didn't answer. He didn't want to admit his father was right.

Tiangong-3 Space Station

"Turn off the damn alarm," said Colonel Huan. "I can see them."

Chang saw him searching the shoulder pocket where his stim tabs had been before they'd run out.

They'd just given the third warning to the space tourists, and again no response.

"Should I try Hainan control center again, Colonel?" said Chang. This was clearly a civilian target, and the shuttle belonged to a European nation that the Directorate had hundreds of billions in trade with. More important, that nation was a former ally of the United States that had so far stayed out of the war. But that wasn't what was troubling him. Destroying satellites was one thing, but blasting a shuttle full of rich tourists was not the war he wanted to tell his son about some day.

Huan grunted his approval. The long-range communications appeared to be jammed, the transmissions digitally hopping across each of the frequencies they tried.

"It doesn't matter. We don't need Hainan's approval. The jamming only proves they are a threat," said Huan. "Proceed with station defense protocols. Set them to begin firing at two hundred kilometers."

"Wait, wait. I've got a transmission coming through," said Chang. "It's . . . music?" He set the transmission to play on the station's speakers: first there were the strums of a single guitar, then a beating of drums, and then a gravelly voice singing in English.

> Out of the blue came a kill-crazy crew,
> Whose motto was stomp on the weak,
> With bones in their hairs,
> They were as hungry as bears,
> And their leader was the King of the Freaks.

"What? What does that mean?" said Huan. For once he seemed to have no ready answers.

Chang directed the computer to match the lyrics to all records of codes and transcripts, even military anthems, thinking it might be a unit's marching cadence. The system's answer made the music even more confusing. There was nothing in the classified files, but an open-source search had found a match. It was a song performed by a twentieth-century musician called Alice Cooper.

"This is Directorate space station Tiangong calling unidentified spacecraft ordering immediate course correction to avoid our exclusion zone," said Chang. "You will be fired upon if you advance further. Answer to confirm receipt."

The order was met with more blaring rock-and-roll.

> *Death on their hips,*
> *There was foam on their lips,*
> *And behind them a shadow of blood,*
> *They was Space Pirates.*

The rock-and-roll song continued on to describe a sort of bizarre savagery that barely made any sense in the highly engineered confines of the space station.

"They can't even bother to turn off their awful music?" Huan said. "Now I am certain they are Americans. What an expensive way to commit suicide."

"They will cross into the exclusion zone in ten seconds," said Chang.

"Good," said Huan. "Then we won't have to listen to this racket for much longer."

Chang noted that Huan pressed down the red firing button almost a full second before the target crossed the imaginary line in space. Either the music had gotten to him or the bastard just couldn't wait to kill real people.

But then — nothing.

"Are the lasers functioning?" said Huan. "There's no damage."

"Sensors are properly tracking the target, showing a hit at the aim site," said Chang.

Huan pressed the red button again, jabbing it hard, as if the added pressure would make it work this time.

Again, the target showed no damage. It was as if they'd never fired a shot.

"Full systems reset. Now," Huan commanded.

"Target is decelerating," said Chang.

"I want to see it up close," said Huan, pointing toward what he thought was the space plane, although actually his finger was aimed at the station bulkhead. The virtual image of the targeting goggles did that to some people. They simply forgot where they were.

The screen shifted from the radar-targeting icon to a visual from the station's telescope. As it focused, Chang thought the shuttle was the shiniest thing he'd ever seen.

> *And behind them a shadow of blood,*
> *They was Space Pirates*

The song continued repeating. He'd lost track of how many times it had played.

"System rebooted. Back online."

Huan fired again, and they saw a quick bright dazzle at the target point but no burn-through.

"It's got some kind of a reflective coating that's causing the laser energy to bounce off," said Chang.

"We'll see how many shots it can take as it gets closer," said Huan.

"Sir, the range is making it dangerous for us. The closer they get, the more likely that one of our shots will reflect back and hit us," said Chang.

Huan didn't answer, he just pressed down on the red button. The laser fired once more.

There was no effect, and the beam fortunately didn't angle back at them. The plane began to decelerate and came to a stop three kilometers away. It fired its maneuvering jets, tiny bursts of flame, setting itself in a parallel orbit to the station, out of the laser's firing angle. As the shiny plane lazily rotated, the wings came into full view.

"What is that?" said Huan, though he recognized what he was seeing.

"A skull," said Chang. "And two bones crossed beneath it."

> *They was Space Pirates*
> *Sack a galaxy just for fun.*

Then the music stopped, and the station went silent.

A voice with a strange accent came on, sort of a cross between an Indian's and a British noble's from one of those old shows Chang's wife loved, about the servants living downstairs in the manor.

"Tiangong, Tiangong. I have the pleasure to be Sir Aeric K. Cavendish, captain of the legally registered privateer *Tallyho*," said the voice. "And I demand your surrender."

Ehukai Beach, Oahu, Hawaii Special Administrative Zone

He'd grown up in a twenty-two-story apartment building in Chengdu, but the booming surf always made Bo Dai homesick. It reminded the big Directorate sergeant of the New Year's fireworks when he was a child. He could never admit this to the others in his unit, but he wished he were back home. The fun of this so-called tropical paradise had long since worn off, right around the time they'd found poor little Xiao Zheng dead in the bar, his neck stabbed through.

The bulky marine walked carefully at the edge of the lapping ocean water, placing one foot in front of the other right where the fresh sand was wiped clean with each pulse of the ocean. He looked over his shoulder to be sure that nobody caught him in such a forlorn mood. Even in the dark, the sag of his shoulders would have been a giveaway to the other marines, who feared him.

It was the beauty that did it. For somebody who did not spend much time reflecting, he'd come to understand that Hawaii's best weapon against any occupier was its beauty. It made you let down your guard.

He had told his men living out of the beachfront houses near Ehukai Beach that he needed to make sure the guards at the far point weren't sleeping during watch. This was a rest-and-relaxation assignment after the past few weeks of tough urban patrols, his men not knowing if that kid in the alley was just taking out the recycling or getting ready to toss a Molotov cocktail their way. The beach, known as the Banzai Pipeline to the local surfers, was too rough for landing craft and too open for any of the damn insurgents to use as a hideout. He knew it was safe ground. But the men knew these facts also, and Bo worried his unit would become slack. He would find out in a few more minutes if he had to dole out another beating in order to encourage better attentiveness.

A few paces behind Bo and about thirty feet from shore, a pair of straw-like antennae emerged from the choppy water. They twitched and then disappeared.

As Bo walked on, lost in his thoughts, the antennae reappeared ten feet from the shore, then quickly vanished again. They emerged again at the water line, attached to a small black lobster. It advanced by alternating between crawling along the ocean's bottom on its eight legs and using the force of the water's swell to help it glide toward the shore.

Bo continued to walk along the beach, his body armor, weapon, and helmet a dark silhouette against the sky. The lobster began to stalk its prey, starting and then stopping again, the water covering it.

Bo thought he heard something and pivoted on his heel. He flipped down his night-vision goggles but saw nothing moving in the tree line.

As the lobster made a final sprint to close in on its prey, Bo instinctively turned, swinging his rifle out toward the dark ocean. Nothing but the water splashing around his boots. He brought the rifle down and cursed himself for being so jumpy.

The water receded, revealing the small lobster a few feet away, its body covered in matte, sandpaper-rough, purple-black ballistic carbon. Before Bo could react, the robot fired a small dart into his leg, dropping him instantly. The poison was a synthetic derivative of a sea snake's venom and had him unconscious within a second.

As he lay face-down in the water, drowning, six dark figures emerged at the waves' break line and bodysurfed their way ashore. They slowly eased past Bo, crawling on their stomachs and elbows to the water line. Then they waited, scanning the beach for threats, holding suppressed HK 416 rifles. They wore ultrathin wetsuits that matched their heat signatures to the ambient temperature of the water around them. They were almost invisible to the naked eye, lacking the telltale humps of rebreathing units. They had made the hour-long swim to shore without oxygen tanks, their bodies flush with trillions of micron-size nanoscale devices that provided far more oxygen than normal red blood cells. The technology had first hit the mainstream at the Tour de France three years ago, causing the race to go on indefinite hiatus but piquing the interest of DARPA program managers working on human-performance modification.

After waiting for ten minutes in the surf, the six dark figures slithered one by one into the trees. Two of them dragged Bo's body deep into the thick undergrowth of mangrove trees.

The lobster scurried along the beach, following Bo's path, darting back to the water when the moon broke through the clouds in order to avoid the splash of light on the sand. Then the machine crept carefully forward as a single figure emerged from the forest at the turn in the shoreline.

The robot beamed the image back to the six who'd taken cover. Even on the small view screens of their tac-glasses, they could see the fatigue of the person coming out of the trees. The figure wore torn clothes and walked with an obvious limp.

The robot scuttled forward and then paused ten feet behind the figure. One of the hidden commandos hissed a challenge through a tiny speaker set in the robot's carapace.

"Sugar Bowl Resort."

"Best skied in February," responded the figure, slowly turning, pointing a Chinese-made QBZ-95 automatic rifle at waist level and then noticing the tiny robot below.

Fifty feet away, one of the dark figures stood, two open hands in the air, and remained motionless until the rifle was lowered.

"Aloha and welcome to paradise. I'm Major Doyle, Twenty-Second Marine Air Group but more recently, ah, detailed to what we call the North Shore Mujahideen."

"We're familiar with your work. Hell, you're a celebrity back home, Ms. Die Screaming," said the man, who was clad in a green, gray, and black tiger-striped wetsuit. "I'm Duncan, proud member of the Dam Neck Canoe Club. It is an honor to meet you."

Conan considered the reference to the U.S. Navy base in Virginia and the fact that he hadn't given a last name or rank.

"SEAL Team Six for an extraction team? I guess it's me that should be honored."

"I believe there may be some confusion, Major Doyle," said Duncan. "Who said we were your extraction team? We're the advance party."

Tallyho, Low Earth Orbit

Sir Aeric K. Cavendish stared at the helmet in his lap and then bounced it on his knee like a soccer ball. The helmet floated away slowly and then rebounded against what would have been the ceiling if there were an up or a down here. It was his first time in space, and he was enjoying it far more than his time in goal in the match with Leeds, heretofore the peak of his pleasure-rich existence as a tycoon. Zero gravity was remarkable. His body, always a source of secret disappointment, was no burden to him here.

The *Tallyho* had originally been called the *Virgin Galactic 3*, a space plane designed to take off like a conventional aircraft and then blast into orbit. Cavendish had bought it for a song after the original owner had gone missing in a balloon accident. It was partly out of admiration for the man and his inspirational lifestyle, and partly because it was a good deal he couldn't resist. Even a billionaire should not be above a bargain, particularly when it involved a one-of-a-kind aircraft.

He looked out at the space plane's wing. The only time he had ever seen anything so brilliant was that necklace he'd given to Miss Ukraine after forcing the manager of the Harry Winston in London's Mayfair to open at three in the morning. The look on her face when he'd fastened the necklace around her swanlike neck and then simply walked away had been priceless, though the tabloids had reported it cost fourteen million dollars. He was pretty sure that story would be in his obituary, which hopefully would not appear anytime soon. What wouldn't be in it was how Miss Ukraine's visit two nights later had turned his extravagant gift into a worthwhile investment.

No, this was more brilliant, in every sense of the word. The *Tallyho*'s surface was coated with nano-manufactured diamonds, baked into the aircraft's composite skin. The bet, and Cavendish's engineers swore the science was sound, was that the diamonds would render the Tiangong's laser weapons useless against the *Tallyho*. The coating would work only briefly, though, as each time the laser beam lashed the spacecraft's surface, it would ever so slightly fuse the composite material and the diamonds. Totally impractical for the military, of course. It was a one-off trick. But as with Miss Ukraine, it was a bet worth taking.

The inspiration for the diamond idea he'd kept secret, like Miss Ukraine's visit, but in this case because it was so mundane. He'd come up with the concept at the bankruptcy auction of a famous rapper turned fashion mogul. Blinging an entire Cadillac Cascade SUV was certainly in poor taste, but the image had stuck with Sir Aeric.

Cavendish studied his reflection in the helmet floating in front of him for another instant, and then he checked his watch again and smiled.

"It seems they are not going gently into that good night," said Cavendish. "Gentlemen," he called, "I would like to request your help in evicting those squatters from my property."

"You heard the Sir, boys," said Best. "Time for a walk."

Corner of Mission and Kawaiahao Streets, Honolulu, Hawaii
Special Administrative Zone

Twenty-one kills. Twenty-two if you counted the single brown hair from the American officer who was listed as missing in the Directorate records. Had he been her first kill? Or was he a casualty of the war? Was that all it took to unleash this inside her? A single death? Or was there something more?

Markov looked out the car's window into the night at the vague outline of the complex of low-slung buildings. His eyes tracked to the faint silhouette of a steeple, like catching a glimpse of a dagger in the night. The power had been out in this area for a few days now. Insurgents had destroyed the transformer in the neighborhood, and the replacement parts from Shanghai would not be ready for another week, at least. The people here would think it a victory, though, hurting themselves out of spite just to make the other side work harder to win a love that would never come. That was the essence of insurgency.

He wondered if she really was in there. A Directorate mini-drone on an automated-presence patrol had recorded her walking down the street and entering the small wooden building. The drone's small size limited its onboard processing, meaning that it had to send its video feed back for analysis as it continued on its sweep. Carrie Shin's facial-recognition match had come seven minutes later, which was a lifetime in a hunt.

He needed to talk to her. If anyone was worth understanding in this war, it was her. What did he hope to find? That they were alike? Hunters, both of them?

Markov stepped out of the Geely sedan, keeping the vehicle between him and the target. The Directorate commandos crouched behind their civilian-style Great Wall pickups looked tense. *They'd better be,* he thought, *they're about to raid a church.*

"Everyone ready?" said Markov. "And remember, Carrie Shin comes to us alive. You know what she looks like." He paused and tapped the sizable opaque visor atop the assault helmet he wore. "I'll be in on the tac-view with you, so cue her up on contact."

"All are in position, sir," said one of the commandos. "We'll await your go order."

Before Markov could respond, squealing tires made the men twitch, and the entire assault force turned and trained their weapons on the oncoming vehicle. It was a convoy of armored Geely SUVs, bookended by two APCs. The men noticed the flags flying from the front fenders of the third vehicle.

Of course, General Yu would want everyone to know it was him, confusing personal bravery with stupidity. The faint rhythmic thumping of attack helicopters circled overhead. A platoon of bodyguards exited and took up positions as General Yu jumped out of his vehicle, waving his pistol in the air like he was leading a cavalry charge. One of his aides knelt a few feet away, filming the general from below, which was meant to make the man look even taller in the video clips sent back home. He truly was a giant, the kind that didn't bother to think about where he stepped.

"Colonel, get everyone back. Across the street," said Yu, taking charge of the scene as if it were his birthright, his command voice sounding like he was about to lead an army of thousands into battle.

"Sir, the men are already in position," said Markov. The general looked down at the cameraman and scowled, putting away his pistol. Markov looked at him innocently and asked, "Would you like to give the attack order, General?"

"No, Colonel. I said pull them back. We're going to destroy the entire nest. My dead boys deserve their due," said General Yu. Then a helicopter pilot's voice came over the headsets of the assembled commandos.

"This is Green Dragon Six. Target acquired, engaging in thirty seconds," he said.

"General, I must strongly advise against this," said Markov. "We need her alive. We need to know what she's done. Does she have a network? Is she operating alone? What are her ties to the insurgents? I need to speak with her. If you blow everything from here to Shanghai, we lose that chance."

"I don't need to know. I don't need a date," said Yu. "The threat needs to be eliminated. Entirely. When the smoke clears, we will learn all that we need to know: that she's dead."

The thumping approach of the attack helicopter changed pitch as it began to dive toward the church.

"This will only backfire in publicity terms, flattening a church so soon after the school raid killed all those children. We're going to lose the entire population. You don't kill like this, not for one person. That's a card the losing side plays."

"It's not for one person. It's for the twenty-one boys of mine she butchered. I am not writing another damned letter because of her. And what happened at that school is exactly why we're not going to go in and lose any more of my men. You wanted me to understand the foe? Well, they need to understand me," said General Yu.

Markov tried to shout a further protest, but nothing could be heard over the deafening arrival of the twin-engine helicopter.

He cast a glance at the church and watched a young girl, maybe thirteen years old, towing two small toddler boys from an outbuilding and into the main parish hall, seeking its sanctuary. As they entered the wide wooden doors of the church, one of the little boys looked back at them and stared at the hovering helicopter until he was pulled inside.

Markov turned to confront Yu and saw that the man had already clambered back inside the SUV, which was now pulling off in reverse. He slapped the side of the vehicle's window in anger. At least the general would hear that.

One after the other, two missiles flashed from beneath the helicopter's stunted wings. All Markov could do was quickly duck behind the nearest pickup for cover. He sat facing down the street they'd driven up, turned away from the explosions erupting behind him. He'd seen so much carnage before in war, but for some reason this time he couldn't watch. There was no point. The hunt had been lost, the lessons he'd learned over his career of no value to anyone.

Research Facility 2167, Shanghai

The fact that he couldn't feel the drill going into the back of his skull made the noise all the more terrifying.

Sechin's eyes darted around the room. He tried to turn his head, but he couldn't move. A computer display in front of him was all that he could see; the screen showed a surgeon drilling into a shaved skull. A puff of bone dust smoked up from the metal boring through the skull on the screen. Then the screen itself was covered with a fine white powder that wafted in from behind him. His vision blurred as some of the powder fell in his eyes. He tried to blink but couldn't. Someone outside his field of view squirted a liquid into his eyes and dabbed the corners as the liquid dripped out.

A second and third time, the drill bored through the skull on the video screen, sending more puffs of bone dust wafting over. He wanted to close his eyes to stop watching, but he couldn't. After the second squirt of liquid into his eyes, he realized it was because his eyelids were no longer there. He couldn't do anything, in fact, but watch as the surgeon began to insert thin fiber-optic wires into the three holes in the skull. He knew the wires were filled with over five hundred electrodes, each as thin as a human hair, that would link with the electromagnetic signals of his brain's neurons.

The surgeon, if one could call him that, then disappeared from the computer screen. Sechin heard the sound of metal wheels scraping on the tile floor, coming closer. Then the surgeon was there in front of him, pushing a cart with a small box on top, fiber-optic wires stretching out from it and wrapping around the back. Also on the cart were two robotic hands; other wires linked them to the box.

Sechin knew who the man was even before he removed his surgical mask.

"General Sechin, it is a pleasure to meet you." Dr. Qi Jiangyong stood with the practiced upright posture of a university lecturer, which he had been before his neuroscience research had led him to be reassigned to the Public Security Ministry.

Sechin didn't reply; he was trying to take his mind elsewhere, lock his thoughts away in a place of complete intensity beyond, just as they'd taught him in training. He thought of Twenty-Three's touch, losing himself in the exact moment of his imagined release.

"Well done, General, exactly as you should," Dr. Qi said. "So, it seems you recognize the Braingate technology. Just a few more seconds and I will complete the modulating test."

He felt Twenty-Three's breath hot on his neck, then blowing slightly in his ear; his body spasmed.

"Now, there it goes. Hookup confirmed. General, I must apologize, as it does seem you are enjoying yourself, but we must begin."

Suddenly Sechin was thrown back in the moment, and he noticed the two metallic hands in front of him moving, as if caressing something that was not there.

"Yes, there we are."

The two hands stopped their rhythmic motions and then tried to reach out. The fingers stretched, grasping, their attempt to strangle Dr. Qi futile, as the robotic hands each ended at a wrist affixed to the cart.

"Let us start, then, shall we, General?"

Qi then began a lecture he had given hundreds of times, first to his students, then to the Directorate officials who had paid for the research, and now to his subjects. It was as much a ritual as a requirement that he felt obliged to follow. He still felt the desire to teach even as he learned.

"The human brain is the most powerful computer in the world. And if we want to unlock its secrets, we must treat it as such. The neurons we have in our brains fire to communicate, each signal beaming out on a different frequency. These are the so-called brain waves. Already in electrical form, these waves convey what we believe to be our thoughts, both conscious and unconscious. They carry memories, instincts, and the body's operating systems, everything from your deepest fears to your brain's command to your lungs to keep breathing. They are all but simple electrical signals."

Sechin could only watch as the two hands before him balled up into fists, clenching in anger.

"The challenge is not just transforming these electrical signals into something that can usefully connect to a machine but isolating the ones we want from all the trillions of other signals going through the brain. One way to achieve the brain linkup is noninvasively, by tapping into these brain waves from the outside. An electroencephalograph, or

EEG, for example, is what's used by most researchers. It essentially listens in on the electrical signals that leak out through your skull. Such systems, however, remain limited by the fact that the technology is not directly connected to the body; it merely allows someone to watch from the outside. The EEG provides such an unsatisfying representation of what the brain is doing. Have you ever worn glasses? Ah, I see you have not. Well, I will tell you, then, that using the EEG is like seeing the world not only without the clarity of optical correction, but with lenses of the wrong prescription."

The fists unballed and just hung in the air. Sechin again tried to lose himself in thoughts of Twenty-Three, in his mind running his finger along her tattoo.

"When I was coming out of graduate school, the cutting-edge brain-interface research focused on direct links. The idea of such a jack into the brain originated in the West. Not from a scientist's lab but, aptly, from the mind of an artist. We know that you are an aficionado of science fiction. Are you then familiar with William Gibson's 1984 novel *Neuromancer*? If not, I highly recommend it. Not so much for the plot, but for the vision. In the imagined future, hackers plugged wires into their brains to link up with a virtual world of computers that Gibson termed *cyberspace*. Yes, the very word we use today to describe its fruition."

The hands began caressing something in the air.

"Now, this concept remained theoretical, of course —" Dr. Qi noticed the hands, paused in his lecture, and entered a command into the keyboard. "Please pay attention." The robotic hands stopped moving and balled up into clenched fists again. "Until American military researchers found willing subjects among the paralyzed. With Braingate, they implanted a computer chip in a young paraplegic and recorded the neurons that were firing electric signals. It was a remarkable discovery. It was like putting the right prescription to the lens; they now could see everything that had eluded them. Soon, they were not just recording the signals but isolating those that were leaving the brain when the boy thought about moving his arms or legs, even though the pathways to those limbs were now broken."

Dr. Qi paused and dabbed a cloth over Sechin's forehead, blotting the beads of sweat that had gathered just above where his eyelids had once been.

"A mere three days into what was supposed to be a twelve-month research study, there was a breakthrough. Just by thinking about it, the young man moved a cursor on a computer screen. And with the ability to move a cursor, a new world opened up. The paralyzed boy could move a robotic hand, surf the web, send e-mail, draw, and even play video games, just by thinking it. This work became the basis of modern-day prosthetics. Indeed, what your 'hands' are experiencing right now is exactly the kind of link first forged between man and machine years ago. I find it to be a useful test, as it provides evidence that the system is working, evidence for me and, more important, for you."

Sechin tried to focus on Twenty-Three but found that he couldn't pull up her memory. Then he felt himself wanting to move the robotic hand. But why? He didn't want to move the hand.

"Ah, you are now likely asking, What does this mean to me? Let us pause for a second as the calibrations begin to take hold."

Half of Sechin's brain tried to focus on Twenty-Three, her breath, her skin, her hair, anything, while the other half seemed to want only to move the fingers on the right hand and then the left.

"Well, that is where my research comes in. You see, in addition to real-time monitoring analysis of neuron patterns to relay movement, we began to explore other options for such brain interfaces."

Sechin watched as all of the fingers on the robotic hands began to wiggle, his mind now simultaneously telling them both to move and not to move with all his focus.

"Data that can be monitored can also be changed. Just as in a computer, so too in the signals in your brain — we can change your commands for movements, your memories, and, most important, your will."

Corner of Mission and Kawaiahao Streets, Honolulu, Hawaii
Special Administrative Zone

For almost an hour, the church burned, no matter how much fire suppressant they sprayed. The flames crackled and snapped, lashing out at the sky and at anyone who came close enough to feel the blaze.

So the first to enter the site was a machine. The five-foot-tall spider-bot, each of its legs painted matte black, looked ominous, but its original purpose had been all about saving lives. Japanese engineers had turned to the insect form as the most fit for climbing over and sifting through rubble for survivors after an earthquake or tsunami. In Hawaii, Directorate techs found they could also use it for BSE, or biological site exploitation. That was the euphemism for sifting through the aftermath of a manmade disaster in order to pick up scraps of people and figure out who they once were.

Markov donned his sensor-laden helmet and virtually followed in the wake of the spider-bot's advance. As the scout robot patiently stalked the ruins, Markov watched its readouts on his heads-up display. He coughed and spat out acrid phlegm. Even from a distance, the smoke and smell were almost overwhelming. The commandos wore respirators, but he didn't have one. A white handkerchief bunched over his mouth was all he had to keep the stench of burned flesh, plastic, and wood out of his throat.

The spider-bot picked its way through the ruined church. It moved each of its eight legs with a steadiness that no human could have managed in such a scene. Each leg ended in a flat pad that opened to a delicate-looking eight-fingered claw. While the spider-bot balanced on five, four, or even three legs, depending on its angle, the other legs would pick through the rubble like a prospector turning over stones. Occasionally, a claw would quickly withdraw inside the body and then return to hunt again. Inside the bot's belly, the pieces of found bone and flesh would be scanned for their DNA profiles and then stored for deposit and reassembly later in the morgue.

It was all so rational and smart. Markov wondered if someday they would make a spider-bot smart enough that it too would have nightmares. His head pounded and he needed water.

Then a message flashed across Markov's visor screen. A DNA match. A pop-up showed the item and its owner's identity.

A charred finger, belonging to a Carrie Shin of Honolulu, Hawaii.

Tiangong-3 Space Station

Chang couldn't see his hands.

The designers of the thin orange survival suit had made it strong enough to withstand an emergency depressurization, but they had not considered how scared the suit's wearer would be. The suit's environmental system could not keep up with Chang's rapid breathing and the rivulets of sweat trickling down his back and arms, and his faceplate had slowly but surely fogged over. That made him breathe even faster.

Chang tried to steel himself, gripping tighter the firm, familiar handle of his HEXPANDO wrench. As Huan had ordered, he'd smashed at the smooth glass of the laser-weapon control panel as best as his atrophied muscles could in the zero-g confines of the station. But now he could no longer see what he was striking at, and his heart rate was spiking again. He was going to drown in his own sweat.

He had to take the helmet off.

Tiangong was still pressurized, so it was not suicidal to pop the suit's seal. He sucked in the stale air, the familiar fragrances of food, sweat, and electronics giving him an odd comfort.

Then he saw the small tears in his right glove at the knuckles where he had struck the weapon station's control system. There had to be pressure tape in the emergency kit, Chang thought, and he struggled to unbuckle himself so he could look for the bright yellow box. It was gone. So was Colonel Huan.

How had he missed that? He craned his head to see if the escape pod was activated. No, the egg-shaped craft remained attached to Tiangong.

A voice came over the communications bud Chang wore in his left ear. "Are they here?" said Huan.

"No, they are not. Neither are you, Colonel," said Chang.

"I know," said Huan. "The rest of the crew and I will get in the EVA suits and attack them. You stay there and continue to destroy any classified materials. Chang, if we don't succeed, they must not be allowed inside the station. Do whatever it takes."

Research Facility 2167, Shanghai

"What we observe is not nature itself, but nature exposed to our method of questioning."

Dr. Qi continued his lecture. "Werner Heisenberg was, of course, thinking in the realm of physics and string theory, but the lesson also holds true here. In any interrogation, there is an observer effect, where the mere act of someone watching has an effect on the subject."

Sechin felt part of himself eager to cooperate, hungering to answer, while another part of his mind tried to imagine a clock. Both he and his interrogator were in a race against time.

"This is all the more true when the subject is a set of electromagnetic signals in the brain. The longer the interface, the more we corrupt the very thing we study. To put it simply, General, if you want to remain you, I advise you to let your mind relax."

A part of Sechin's mind began to calm, while another part screamed to resist, knowing that the longer the interface lasted, the less his interrogators could trust its findings. Truth, fear, and drugs would create a cocktail of new memories and new fictions.

Qi asked his first question in a soft, unhurried voice, as if quizzing a student. In any other circumstance, it would have been reassuring.

"We know you have been passing information to the Americans. What have you given them?" asked Qi.

"Just some technical information," said Sechin. The part that wanted to resist thought the best way to do so was to appear to cooperate, to extend the clock. Or was that the part that actually wanted to cooperate tricking him?

"About?" asked Qi.

"Space," said Sechin. "About satellites."

Sechin's mind raced. Which part had said that?

"We are losing time. Both of us," said Qi, leaning in closer as if admiring the texture of Sechin's skin. "Based on the documents you accessed, it would seem you have provided them information on how we can track their submarines. Is that correct?"

Yes. No. What had he said?

"Excellent. Thank you for your cooperation." Had he really answered, or was that one of Qi's tricks?

"What I need to know is what they are planning to do with that information. What other information had they asked you to gather? What was the meeting today to be about?"

Sechin tried not to answer, to take his mind somewhere else again, imagining Twenty-Three's face, running his hands through her blue hair. Or was he telling Qi that he had passed the file to her?

Qi displayed a photo of Twenty-Three on the view screen, her body laid out on a stainless-steel morgue table, the bluish pallor of her skin a faint echo of her blue hair. Sechin tried to imagine her in bed with him but couldn't bring back the image. "This is who you were to meet today. I show you her not to provoke bad memories but to let you know that while I am in a hurry, the ultimate truth I seek is more important than your own truths. If you want to save them, you must cooperate."

Suddenly the image of Twenty-Three in the morgue disappeared. Was it gone from the screen or from his memory?

"Now, tell me, why the meeting today?"

He tried to hold on to something, anything. Her hair was blue. Yes, her hair was blue.

"Today?" said Sechin. "Today was about many things."

After not feeling his body for most of the interrogation, Sechin became acutely aware of his skin burning, as if every single cell were on fire. His nose involuntarily sniffed the air for the scent of smoldering flesh.

"I am sorry to do that, but you must understand there is no tolerance here," said Qi. "No tolerance for your lies and no tolerance for your pain, when the very experience of it is merely signals in your brain. It can last as short or as long a time as we want you to feel it, or, rather, perceive that you feel it. Now, please tell me, what was the primary goal of the meeting today?"

"Sex," said Sechin.

At the base of his skull, Sechin felt a tingling, almost purring sensation that then exploded in another wash of fire across his body. Why? He had told the truth! Or had he?

Qi shook his head and paused. Or was there actually a pause? Had someone talked, and then they'd rewound back to this moment, his sense of time now manipulated?

"Only one last set of questions, then. Why did the Americans want you to provide them information about our northern defenses? Does it have to do with their fleets now on the move?"

Sechin saw only blue. He heard someone talking but wasn't sure who it was. What had been said? Had he answered? He could see only blue.

"Thank you. You have done very well." Sechin heard Qi order the information be relayed to an admiral as fast as possible and then felt Qi's hand gently cup his face. It was soft, the effect almost soothing.

"I am not the monster many think me to be. This is far more humane — dare I say refined — than their old ways of forcing information. More important, what has been taken can be restored. And that, General, is my farewell gift to you."

Qi then lightly patted him on the cheek and exited from his field of view. Sechin thought he heard the whirring again of a drill, but then he saw her. Twenty-Three. She truly was beautiful. He began to caress her, running his hands through her blue hair, stroking her skin from her neck down, and then his body spasmed over and over again in the exact moment of his imagined release.

It was all Sergei Sechin could think of as the fiber-optic wires were yanked out of his brain.

Directorate Command, Honolulu, Hawaii Special Administrative Zone

General Yu held the plastic bag up to Markov's face. The finger looked like it had been seasoned with pepper and tossed in flour. It was unmistakably a burned finger, though: Carrie Shin's entire left ring finger.

"The fingerprints match," said Yu. "So does the DNA. It seems I got your girl before you did."

"Where's the body?" said Markov.

"Mixed in with the rest of them," said General Yu. He tossed the bagged finger to Markov. "Make a necklace out of it."

Markov snatched the plastic bag out of the air with his left hand without breaking eye contact. His right hand rested loosely at his side, meaning he could draw his Makarov and fire two rounds in just over a second. Tempting as it was to think of himself holding the severed finger of a serial killer in one hand and his two-rounds-lighter pistol in the other, he centered himself with a steady exhale and said nothing.

"You can take it back to Moscow with you," said Yu. "You're done here. But to show you that I am not as terrible a man as you think I am, you will use my jet for the return trip. Let your last glimpse of Hawaii be from my seat."

Markov shook his head. "You're in that much of a hurry to get rid of me, General? Do you know what they call her? The Black Widow. Your spider-bot may have found her, but your stupidity creates more like her every day." He threw the plastic bag at the general, who flinched as it bounced off his barrel chest and back onto the desk.

General Yu started to tremble, his eyes bulging in anger, but then he calmed himself by running his hands over his freshly shaved scalp.

"On second thought, Colonel, my plane is no longer available," said Yu. "We have a resupply ship departing for Yangshan tomorrow evening. Its voyage should give you sufficient time to contemplate what punishment awaits you for striking your commanding officer. Guards!"

Tiangong-3 Space Station

Without his helmet, Chang felt far calmer. He knew he was still trapped, but he did not feel like it for the moment. He felt his pulse start to slow until a flash of movement at one of the observation windows caught his eye. A deranged face with a tongue sticking out hovered outside the observation hatch. Then someone tapped a gleaming short sword on the shatterproof glass.

Chang switched to the camera view that monitored that section of the station for tiny space debris and micro-meteor impacts. He panned the camera and saw a man in a jet-black EVA suit, the helmet and face-plate apparently painted with some kind of strange design. He watched as the astronaut began to attach a device to the outer hull of Tiangong.

Then the radio speaker on the console in front of him chirped to life.

"Tiangong crew, this is Sir Aeric, er . . . Captain Cavendish here. Righto. My men have just attached a pair of auxiliary thrusters to your station. You will now surrender the station to us. If you do, we will treat you as prisoners of war, following the rules set by the Geneva

Conventions. If you do not comply, the station's rotation will cease, and my scientists tell me the temperature inside will slowly but surely rise, cooking you to a temperature of eight hundred degrees, all thanks to our comrade in arms the sun, who is always on the side of the righteous . . . This is our last communication. Grant us access, and do not resist. Or you will die. Your choice, really."

A burst of static hissed through the speakers, so loud that Chang turned off the sound. He peered at the monitor to see what Huan was doing. All Chang could tell was that the rest of the crew members were arguing with Huan, their EVA suits not yet on.

A jolt made Chang return to the window. He craned his neck to see if that specter had returned. He saw nothing. Then a faint telltale distortion of the stars behind the station chilled the sweat pooling in his suit. It was one of the pirates' auxiliary thrusters beginning the gradual slowing of the station's rotation.

A steady alarm honk started, indicating that the station's position was shifting from its preprogrammed orbit.

They had promised to treat the taikonauts fairly, hadn't they? Wasn't it better to live as a prisoner than die as a — what, a pig roasted to death in a box of coals?

There was no other option. Huan could keep arguing with the others about some foolhardy attack, but in the command center, Chang now had the power. He disarmed the Tiangong airlocks. He didn't care whether his son would be proud or not, he just wanted to see him again.

Sundown Lounge, Honolulu, Hawaii Special Administrative Zone

Colonel Vladimir Markov swallowed an ice cube that had been slowly dissolving in his vodka over the past few minutes. He hadn't been this drunk in years. Not since the aftermath of that debacle in Yalta. He was irretrievably drunk but thinking with such clarity that he wondered how many days he had squandered not seeing things as plainly as he did now.

He delicately turned another page in his treasured book of Pushkin's poems, ignoring the footfalls closing in behind him and the faint chill working its way from his toes up to his fingers. He knew it wasn't the bartender, whom he had ordered to leave.

"Jian, my shadow, I have missed you. What brings you here?" Markov said, still not looking up from the pages.

Ruin was a gradual process, just as Pushkin had foreseen. The poet's financial fall and then humiliation by the czar must have stolen so many words and passages from the great man's mind. Or had it? Maybe it had given him his real voice. Was it courage, then, that made the poet agree to fight a duel that he knew he could not win? Was the choice whether to die gradually or accept it all in a sudden blow? As he heard Jian's footsteps cross the room, Markov put his hand on the empty pistol holster at his hip, his fingertips brushing where the weapon's metal slide would have been if his pistol had not been taken away, back at the base.

"Colonel! General Yu ordered me to find you," said his former aide.

"And so you have. But for what purpose? That is the real question," said Markov. "Let us reason this out, Jian. He cannot fire me again, and I doubt he is a man who would change his mind about the final objective of the long slow journey to an inevitable death sentence he has sent me on. Ah, that is it. He lacks the patience to await the natural course of what he has set in motion for me."

He looked up to see that the aide had already drawn his pistol.

"Yes, finally you answer something correctly, Jian. Well done. That is it, I see. General Yu calmed down and now wants certainty. Far better for him if I die in an unfortunate incident here — perhaps another insurgent attack. That way he does not risk my speaking truths to the wrong ears."

"I do not question my orders," said Jian. He stepped two paces back from Markov, as if unsure how close he should be to the man he was about to shoot.

"Have a drink, at least," said Markov, reaching to grab a bottle. "Might be the last one for both of us."

The aide stepped back again to ensure he was outside the Russian's reach and extended his arm with the pistol, aiming it right between Markov's eyes rather than targeting his body mass. *Yet another amateur move,* thought the Russian. He smiled at Jian and saluted him with his glass of vodka. Jian looked confused for a second, and then shocked, as a knife blade shot out of his throat from behind.

As drunk as Markov was, the details suddenly were very important to him. She had waist-length ebony hair and wore green contacts. But he knew it must be her from the way she didn't even give Jian's blood pooling around her bare feet a second glance as she pulled the long knife out of his throat. She stepped right over the aide's body, never taking her eyes off Markov. He saw also that the slender hand now pointing a pistol at him was missing the left ring finger.

She sat on the barstool next to Markov, dressed in a loose summer skirt and a linen shirt. Up close, he saw that her eyebrows were gone, replaced by delicate brushwork. She slowly pulled back her hair and peeled off a wig. Her head was razor-shorn down to the skin. There was no stubble, just a bald white dome that gleamed like ceramic in the mirror above the rows of bottles behind the bar. She would truly be a ghost, leaving no trace other than the bloody footprints.

He smiled and raised his glass in her direction, a salute.

"It is a pleasure to see you again, Ms. Shin. You continue to surprise me. Or should I call you what the others call you?"

"Black Widow," said Carrie. "It is more appropriate than they know. Do you know why I'm here?"

"Yes. I can guess," said Markov. "What happened at the church was an atrocity. You cannot kill like that and win this war. Other wars, maybe, but not this one. I tried to tell them, but they wouldn't listen."

"Wrong!" she snarled, slamming the knife into the bar; its blade quivered an inch from his hand. It was a Type 98 bayonet knife, the kind the Chinese commandos carried, and the pistol was a Chinese-made QSZ-92. Well, that answered another question regarding the whereabouts of Jian's escort; Markov doubted the aide would have come here alone. She still held the pistol on him, pointed at his center of body mass. Someone had taught her well. Or was it natural? That question could be asked for so many things about her.

"It doesn't matter anymore," he said. "Before we get on with this, let me finish my drink." He turned back to the bar to finish off his glass of vodka, closing his eyes and savoring the simultaneous burn of the alcohol and coolness of the ice cube he had tucked in his cheek.

He felt her hand around his neck. She gasped as the meaty rawness of the remains of her burned finger pressed into his throat. But it wasn't a cry of hurt, Markov realized. She was savoring the pain.

"I want my hairbrush!" she whispered in his ear.

In that instant, his vodka wore off with a chill.

Tiangong-3 Space Station

"Sir, I know you are excited to seize your prize, but you need to let Tick go in first," said Aaron Best in the practiced tone of a commander used to dealing with very difficult situations. He was tethered just outside the main airlock of the Tiangong, trying to stay out of view of the porthole next to it. The airlock access panel glowed green, indicating it was safe to enter the purgatory between the vacuum of space and the oxygenated confines of the Chinese station.

"But it is my mission, isn't it?" said Sir Aeric Cavendish.

"Affirmative. But once we exited the vehicle, mission execution became my responsibility. Sir. We did not drill for you to join the boarding party, so we are going to need you to hang back outside until things settle in there. Highest probability for success that way. We can do the breach with fewer men, but not more." He pointed toward the hatch with a gleaming silver dagger that caught a flash of the sun and momentarily blinded Sir Aeric. "But we're honored to have you as part of the assault crew, Sir Aeric."

Best's logic was as obvious as his sarcasm. Cavendish nodded his assent.

"Stack up," said Best. The commando called Tick was first inside the airlock, which was soon crammed with four men.

Once inside, the men stopped and paused as the airlock depressurized. Immediately, they took off their helmets, stripped out of the bulky EVA suits, and secured them to the airlock wall.

The men wore slash-proof, formfitting, tiger-striped gray-and-black bodysuits that covered their heads, making them look like evil speed skaters. They put on ballistic masks, motocross-style eye-and-face protection that was resistant to bullets up to nine-millimeter rounds, each painted over to give its wearer a savage look. Another of Sir Aeric's ideas, but the men had taken to it with relish. Tick's black facemask had been overlaid with a *ta moko,* the facial tattoo of a Maori warrior. Hugger, who hunched behind Tick, had used a metallic gold to create hyena-like fangs beneath deeply sunken eye sockets. Hook wore a black mask with almost abstract white brushstrokes to indicate eyes and mouth, like a savage Kabuki actor. Best was the fourth and final commando of the first wave. His mask was airbrushed a gleaming bone white in the style of an old-school hockey goalie's mask. He'd seen it once in an old horror movie; the lack of expression on the killer's face made him somehow more menacing. The effect was that these men, while obviously human, looked immune to reason and appeal. The sense was reinforced by the fact that each had a Taser X26 pistol in his hand and one of Sir Aeric's foot-long titanium-handled steel-bladed brass-knuckled trench knives strapped to his hip.

The first thing Tick noticed when the airlock groaned open was the smell of piss. Floating weightlessly, he pulled himself one-handed inside the main research bay and looked at the three taikonauts there. They had apparently been trying to get into EVA suits.

"Do you surrender?" he asked them in Mandarin.

The three taikonauts stared back at Tick.

Tick repeated himself as the three other commandos made their way into the room, each holding on to the wall with one hand and pointing a Taser with the other.

"Do you surrender?" he asked yet again in Mandarin.

The three taikonauts stayed silent; there was no real movement, just darting eyes and dry lips being licked. Then a hatch to their side opened.

"Contact," said Best. "Head on, Tick."

Tick pushed off the station's wall and rotated his body, turning to parry. But the taikonaut moving through the hatch closed in on him with far more speed than he'd expected given their training. Then he saw why. The man wore a pair of orange exoskeleton boots from an EVA suit, their micro-rockets firing. He had a titanium-mesh frame on his back, and attached to it were the bulky robotic gloves designed for repair jobs in space. One of those exo-gloves wielded a massive wrench.

Tick fired his Taser; the compressed air in the chamber shot out the electric dart on a thin wire, but it pinged off the bulky gloves and then floated weightlessly in the air.

The two men collided, and the taikonaut's momentum knocked

Tick into the bulkhead. The impact broke Tick's right forearm; he'd been trying to pull out the short sword but had to release it. Screaming, Tick attempted to grapple with the taikonaut using his legs, but one of the taikonaut's exo-boots drove into his left foot with a crunch of flesh and bone.

Tick's agony was muted due to the pain pump implanted in his abdomen. Triggered by a sensor in his spinal cord, it released a massive dose of opiates so he could keep fighting. The tiny actuators of the taikonaut's powered exo-glove now gripped him, and though Tick writhed and flexed, he was unable to escape from its grasp. As the two wrestled, the other commandos closed on their opposites, and the sounds of grunting and stabbing filled the air. Tick tried to wrench his body to the right when he saw his sword float by, mere inches from his uninjured arm. But he was unable to break free to reach it, and then he spun off in another direction, bounced against the far bulkhead, and cracked the back of his helmet. The last thing Tick saw was the wrench smashing into his faceplate.

Ehukai Beach, Oahu, Hawaii Special Administrative Zone

The SEALs and Conan eased deeper into the thick trees. The robot lobster sat idle at the feet of one of the frogmen until he picked it up and put it on his back; its claws wrapped around him like straps.

"Butter's pretty creepy, right?" said Duncan.

"At this point, nothing's creepy to me," said Conan. "Any more gizmos we've added since I've been living under a rock?"

"Just this," said Duncan, tossing a small nylon bag the size of his fist to Conan.

"What is it?" said Conan, unwrapping it to reveal a poncho.

"You remember Harry Potter? It's his invisibility cloak," said Duncan. "Well, it doesn't really make us invisible, but it does fuzz the Directorate sensors. Metamaterials in it fuck with the EM spectrum, kinda like how a magician uses mirrors in a trick."

"We've done all right with these," said Conan, drawing her wool blanket around her shoulders. It was so stiff with sweat and dirt in places that she seemed to be donning a mantle of armor.

"But this doesn't smell like a dead goat," said Duncan. "We have others for the rest of your unit."

"No need; I'm it now," said Conan.

Duncan knew not to ask anything further. It was not the time for that kind of conversation. From the way Conan's voice dropped with her response, he knew she would be trying to figure out her own war for the rest of her life.

A rustle in the scrub at the seam of the beach made Conan fling off her blanket, drop down, and put her weapon to her shoulder. Duncan dove down behind her. She saw a figure advancing slowly, staying in the shadows. The silhouette of an assault rifle showed it to be armed. Conan looked over to Duncan and motioned with her finger for him to follow her lead. He shook his head.

Screw it, this was her turf and her war. She leaped up and smashed the figure full in the face with the butt of her rifle.

"Co kurwa, do kurwy nedzy!" the man hissed from the ground, blood coming from his apparently broken nose.

A Russian. She knew they'd been aiding the Directorate with advisers. Conan leveled the rifle at him, pressed it to his forehead.

"I don't know if you understand me," she whispered, "but you need to shut the fuck up or this will be the last thing you see."

Conan felt something cold and sharp at her neck. "Major, you need to stand down." The man who'd called himself Duncan was holding a knife to her throat.

USS *Zumwalt,* North Pacific Ocean

Mike wiped his forehead with the back of his hand. It was hot in the rail-gun turret. The cabling that snaked through it seemed to be choking the air out of the space. But that was not what was making him sweat.

"Please take it," said Mike. He was embarrassed, never having heard himself plead like this before. "It's a float vest." This flotation vest was not like the others aboard. It was a dark green inflatable model, the kind issued to Navy aviators, not the bulky vest in bright orange that just made it easier for the sharks to find you. The aviator's vest had more than a dozen pockets stuffed full of essentials, as much to put a pilot's mind at ease as to enable him or her to make it in the wild or survive ditching in the ocean. The detachable pockets were hooked with Velcro straps onto horizontal lanyards stitched into the vest and they opened in various directions, each holding a mystery, like an aviator's Advent calendar.

"Pilots wear them," Mike said. "So do some of the SEALs. You've got these here pockets that—"

She did not let him finish. "Where did you get this? Nobody else is wearing this, are they?" said Vern. "It's just me in this . . . straitjacket?"

"It comes from the captain, who knows you're the most important person on the ship."

At least part of that was true. He'd actually gotten it from a supply contractor at Mare Island whom he'd served with in the Venezuela campaign, no questions asked about why he wanted the best life vest in the warehouse, size small.

"It inflates automatically if you don't pull this tab first. Now, here's the smoke hood, this is the locator beacon, here's the strobe . . ."

He had kept the float vest out of sight, waiting until he knew she really needed it and, more important, until she finally realized she might need it. That moment was now.

Vern put the vest on, moving carefully, as if it weighed ten times more than it did.

"Well, thank him for it," she said. "And thank you."

"Don't thank me yet," he said with a wink. "It's government issue, meaning it's made by the lowest bidder in order to get some overpaid jet jockey to think the Navy actually gives a shit about what happens to him."

She smiled. "I mean it. Thank you, Mike."

She wrapped her slender arms around him with surprising force.

A call to general quarters battle stations prevented either of them from saying anything more. They stepped back and looked at each other at arm's length, then took off in opposite directions, unsure if they would ever see each other again.

Tiangong-3 Space Station

Chang screamed into the monitor as he watched the battle play out, but none of them were able to hear him.

At first, seeing Huan floating above the limp commando with the crazy mask, Chang thought that Huan's madness just might have worked.

But behind Huan, the monitor showed the three other taikonauts had not fared as well. One floated unconscious, knocked out by the commandos' Tasers. The other two had their faces against one of the station walls, each with a commando floating astride him, their suits streaming red blood globules into the air.

Huan pushed the unconscious commando back toward the airlock, which opened as if to swallow him up. But instead, another commando slipped into the station. This one, much slighter than the others and wearing no mask, appeared shocked for a brief second, his eyes wide. Then he batted the floating commando's limp body away and fumbled with something at his side. He pushed toward Huan with a diver's kick of his legs against the airlock door, his entire body formed into a spear, the short sword at its tip.

Huan pushed forward off his side of the wall with his arms in an attempt to kick the commando with his feet first. The bulk of the exo-boots smashed into the blade, and the force sent the two men careening off in opposite directions. Huan bashed into the hard plastic of a food station, his exo-glove ripping open the rehydration unit, while the slight commando banged headfirst into the wall.

Before Huan could pull his arm out of the mess of the food unit, the commando with the blank white mask was on him. He jabbed the foot-long sword into Huan's leg, straight through his suit and into the bulkhead's insulation. Huan, his body now diagonally pinned to the wall, tried wrenching free, to no avail. Chang watched as the white-masked commando drew a six-inch-long metal stake from a bandolier on his assault vest and drove it into Huan's chest, puncturing his lung.

Chang could see Huan looking up at him in the monitor, his face imploring, as if Chang could do anything to save him now. Then Huan's head lolled to the side, lifeless.

The man in the white mask removed the sword and stake from

Huan's body and slapped tape over the holes in the suit to keep them from leaking more globules of blood into the station's atmosphere. The rest of them began to tape up the other bodies. Sheng Hu, the tai-konaut who had been shocked unconscious, jerked slightly when the white-masked commando thrust another metal stake into her.

They truly were monsters, Chang thought. The most disturbing of them, though, was the small, maskless commando. He had a tiny cut over his right eye but was smiling and wildly gesticulating, replaying the battle that had just ended. He seemed to be enjoying it all.

The men conferred briefly, and the one in the white mask slowly drifted over to the camera and tapped a bloody stake on the screen. He held up three fingers and began counting them down. Three. Two. One.

Alone, Chang didn't know what else to do. He let the monsters in.

Honolulu, Hawaii Special Administrative Zone

"It itches, right? That's the thing with amputation, they say. Not the pain, but the itch."

Markov was doing exactly what she wanted. As far as Carrie could tell, he would have been happy to oblige her, even without the muzzle of the pistol that she'd lifted from the guard pressed against his kidney. They drove slowly through the dark night in his mottled green-and-gray Geely SUV, the Russian glancing over at her whenever the road straightened. It was not lust or fear; she knew those looks well. It was more a sort of scientific curiosity.

They drove past a parking lot full of Directorate vehicles. It looked familiar, and she recognized it as where she'd listened to jazz in the APC.

"You're taking us the long way," Carrie hissed. "If we're not there soon, I'll—"

"You'll what? Kill me with that gun because you're in a hurry?" said Markov. He drove on, stopping briefly at the corner of Queen and Ward, just across from the Alto Café.

"I am sure you don't want to kill me just yet, especially with that gun. That wouldn't feel right, yes? So if you can give me a little bit of your time, I will take you to what you really want. Or, rather, *who* you really want."

He drove on, humming to himself. They passed by Addiction, the nightclub attached to the Modern, the hotel where she had strangled that naval officer in the bathroom three weeks ago. At the next intersection, he turned to look at her.

"Where to next? Maybe the hotel? Or did you kill any at your home?" He laughed. "My, how that would surprise your neighbors. You know they all think you are a traitor who enjoys our company."

"Whatever. They can think what they want," she said.

"So, if you're not a traitor, then you're a predator? You kill only the healthy? A wicked insurgent princess of the night wearing a red, white, and blue cape?"

"The flag's got little to do with me," she said. "I just want everything back the way it was."

"You mean you want to be back the way you were? Before the war?" said Markov. "What was that like? All I know is the pictures from your file. There's nothing of Carrie Shin's heart or soul there."

"You're not looking hard enough," she said.

"I doubt that," said Markov, chuckling.

She put her pistol on her lap and watched him with a slight twist of her head, as if sizing up a target.

"You should put the safety on if it's just going to sit there," said Markov. "For both our sakes."

"I guess you're a professional," said Shin. "Through and through?"

"You stick with something long enough and it's what you become. But you're certainly no amateur at this," said Markov. "This war was waiting for somebody like you. Or were you waiting for the war? Did it make you, or was it already there, just waiting to be released?"

"You talk too much. You said it yourself, we are all changed by war," said Carrie. "Some more than others."

"The war is all about you, then? Did it take something important from you?" asked Markov. "There are many who feel that way. Maybe you are not as unique as I thought."

He slowed the car to a walking pace as they passed by Duke's, overflowing with drunk sailors, marines, and soldiers. He slammed the brakes to avoid running into a short, stocky sailor who'd dropped to one knee to throw up in the intersection.

"Perhaps we can test it. Should I let you out here, perhaps?" said Markov. "I think you'd quickly make new friends again, maybe visit old ghosts?"

She didn't reply, but she adjusted her wig in the side mirror as if slightly tempted by his offer. As she did so, Markov spotted the cut marks on her forearms.

"The cutting, did it start before or after your loss?" said Markov. "You know, the hunger won't stop, even if all of them go back home. What are you going to do then?" He winced as the pistol's muzzle pressed into his rib cage.

"Your little tour is over," she said. "The next stop better be where we agreed or you really will be dead. I won't enjoy it, but I'll do it."

He nodded and kept driving, humming to himself as they headed through the night. After ten minutes, he made another turn and pulled the car to the side of the road.

"We're here," he said, pointing to the first security checkpoint outside the Directorate headquarters complex. "You sure you want to do this?"

Carrie nodded and climbed into the back seat. She pulled out a pair of metal handcuffs.

"Cuff me," she said. "Gently."

Ehukai Beach, Oahu, Hawaii Special Administrative Zone

"Peaches, I think you better introduce yourself to Major Doyle," Duncan said, still holding the knife to Conan's throat. Conan kept the rifle pointed at the forehead of the man in the dirt.

"Major, I am introduced to be Lieutenant Pietor Nowak of Jednostka Wojskowa Formoza." He reached up a hand to shake, but Conan kept the rifle trained on him.

"Polish navy special operations. He's our ride," Duncan said, slowly pulling the knife away from her throat.

"I must compliment you on your tradecraft, Major," the figure in the dirt said. "Now could you remove, please, the gun?"

"I'm not buying this shit," Conan said, keeping the gun on him. "Why the mind games? There's no one left in the NSM. Just kill me and get it over with. But he's going to die with me." She jabbed the figure with the tip of the barrel.

Duncan walked over and knelt beside the figure on the ground, sheathing his knife and putting himself in Conan's line of fire.

"No mind games, Major; a lot has changed. The Directorate cracked how to track our nuke subs. So we had to find a new sub. Or, rather, a shitty old rust bucket that runs on diesel."

"You should not make the fun of the *Orzel*," said the man in the dirt. "She is wonderful ship; she got us here, did she not?"

Duncan turned to him.

"Wonderful? I know you had it hard here, Major," he said, looking back at Conan, "but try spending two months on an old *Kilo*-class sub transiting from the Baltic to the Pacific. God, the smells. Not the diesel, mind you; the fumes from the crew eating only borscht, pierogi, and smoked cheese. Worst cruise of my life. Going to have words with the travel agent when I get back to Dam Neck."

"I thought NATO imploded and wouldn't give us help. That's what the Directorate propaganda said," said Conan.

"It did. The Poles, though, didn't like how things were playing out and came to a private agreement to loan us the services of their shitty little ship and stick it to the Russians along the way."

"And what did the Poles get in exchange?" Conan asked, her body starting to ease, the rifle lowering.

"A very good deal," Nowak said.

"Major, you're looking at an officer in the world's newest nuclear power. That's what they got. We got the services of a crappy old diesel-powered *Kilo*-class submarine that's untrackable from space and shows up on sonar as Russian. And Peaches, of course. All that in exchange for ten B-eighty-three one-point-two-megaton nuclear bombs. The Nuclear Lend-Lease is what the planners call it."

The Polish officer smiled. "We live in very dangerous neighborhood. But now our neighbors will think twice about looking our way again in future."

"And what was that you said when you went down?" Conan asked.

"You surprise me, and so I curse in Polish — not at you, but myself. Duncan would say it translate as 'WTF.'"

Conan lowered the rifle completely and reached out her hand to help the Pole to his feet.

"How do you say 'thank you' in Polish?" she asked.

"*Dziękuję.*"

"That, then."

Directorate Command, Honolulu, Hawaii Special Administrative Zone

During most of his drive with the Black Widow, he had still been partly drunk. Now, as Colonel Vladimir Markov stared down at the nineteen-year-old Chinese corporal questioning him, he realized he was finally sober. *I should be,* he thought, *it's the third checkpoint I've had to get her through.*

"You know who this is?" said Markov to the corporal. "Quite a prize."

He hadn't been certain they'd make it past even the first checkpoint. But she'd gone through the body scanner and been searched by the two marines for weapons, and then they'd been waved on. At the second checkpoint, he'd been more worried about himself, unsure whether his ID badge would still work and wondering if the guards would just shoot him on the spot if it didn't. But as they waited, a call came in from General Yu's aide-de-camp, a major who had been alerted to Markov's presence by the base's automated security system, and eventually they were buzzed through. But first the major had the guards scan them again, to ensure that they carried no weapons.

At the third checkpoint, Markov stood next to his prisoner and yanked on her handcuffs, trying to eke out a sign of submission from her. On cue, she whimpered and lowered her eyes. The corporal looked closer, attempting to reconcile the stories he'd heard about the woman who'd killed so many with the timid figure before him.

"She's for the general," said Colonel Markov. "Kids like you just get to watch." His eyes started to sting and his bladder throbbed as his dehydrated body began to come to grips with his looming hangover.

The corporal's face reddened beneath his high-crowned riot helmet and he pursed his lips. In his left hand, he held his radio close to his mouth, as if he were pausing before taking a bite. His right palm rested on the pistol in his thigh holster. He had the tense posture of somebody who was totally alone in a moment of crisis.

"You need to wait," said the corporal. "I have to do another security scan."

"Fine. And while we wait I will call the general and tell him why you're delaying his special delivery," said Markov. "I am going to get a medal for what I've done. For what you're doing, you'll be lucky not to get shot."

The hand on the corporal's gun flashed up to his neck, where he scratched a patch of flesh just behind the jawbone, an inch in front of the stim-plant node that was scabbing over. The brief scratch seemed to soothe his anxiety, and he nodded up at the black sphere on a pole behind him.

"No, Colonel, they know it's you. That's why they're watching us now. For all I know, the general's watching too," said the corporal.

"Hope so," said Shin under her breath. "I want him ready."

"Shut up!" shouted Markov. "Or I'll tape you up." Carrie bowed her head and shuffled forward through the scanning booth. After another search, the guard motioned them on.

"That was the last checkpoint," Markov said. "Be on your best behavior."

"As long as I can," she said.

Shanghai Jiao Tong University

Hu's commanding officer wouldn't say why the orders had changed, so she'd hacked his access point to the command network. The Americans were apparently on the move and, more important, had acted in a way that had taken Hainan by surprise.

So now America would be put back in the box with a devastating strike designed to teach its public a lesson once and for all. The target list was displayed in the system library. Hu entered the 3-D representation of the university's library, where the target files were laid out on what appeared to be wooden bookshelves, and ran a search of current temperatures, marking any below freezing. There, glowing in blue on a wooden bookshelf to her right: a power company in Akron, Ohio. That would be her starting point.

It was too easy, not worthy of her skills. The backdoor into the target had been created before she had joined the unit. Now it was just a simple matter of inserting new programming. Modeled after the Americans' Project Aurora malware, which had first been tested in 2007, the attack program would use the power companies' own generators as weapons. The malicious software would cause them to rapidly connect and disconnect to the electrical grid, all of them out of phase. This would wreck not just the generators, leading to the collapse of the electric grid, but also the synchronous induction motors, which ran the machinery everywhere from factories to oil-pipeline facilities.

Her fingers flicked in tiny motions, the smart-rings on each sending commands to initiate the attack protocols while also bringing up her personal photo album. She cued it to scan and add any images geo-tagged in the Akron area. She wanted to capture the Americans' last enjoyment of warmth.

But then the photo album turned white. Just as Hu was starting to flick her fingers to reset the system, the white cover of the album began to shrink, pulling in to show black edges. The fingers on her right hand continued with the attack protocol while she watched, fascinated, as an image started to form in the album. It began as a blank mask of white against black but then slowly filled out to show arching eyebrows, a wide mustache upturned at both ends, and a thin, pointed beard. The face had an oversize smile that somehow appeared horribly cruel.

Hu's armpits flooded with sweat, and her stomach tightened. She blinked to make sure it was real and not a hallucination. It had to be a prank. She'd learned about them in the training courses, but they had been offline for over a decade.

She lifted up her visor and cast a glance to the auditorium floor below to see if her commanding officer saw what she was seeing. No;

he was engrossed in the slow unwrapping of a stick of gum. The others seated around him were equally oblivious, a symphony of helmets and fingers bobbing up and down and back and forth as they proceeded with the attack-prep command.

Hu pulled her visor down, projecting herself back into the virtual world. Her fingers began to dance again, each ring in action, a force command overriding the album's operating system and terminating the program while simultaneously starting a full-system verification.

Hu violently punched and pulled the space in front of her as the multiple commands spun out. She felt angry but exhilarated, her stim pump kicking in when the new commands initiated. A wash of euphoria came over her, stronger than she'd ever felt before.

As the album closed at her command, another white-masked avatar appeared, this time hovering over the Akron file she had pulled from the target library. Hu's fingers danced, another wash of euphoria coming with each command movement.

Just as her counterattack made this new mask disappear, the technical specifics of the Akron target re-emerged. Then the mask morphed and divided into two identical masks. Fingers dancing in midair, she attacked again. As the masks split into four, Hu felt another pump of stim kicking in; such intense happiness. Ah, that was it. Each action just created more masks, her mind realized. She knew she should stop, but the smiling mask was taunting her. Whoever was behind it needed to be taught a lesson, plus, her body craved just one more wash of the stim that came from each command.

Soon there were thousands of the white masks washing out the once-beautiful digital landscape. It was as if the entire virtual world had risen up in revolt. But Hu had never felt so wonderful.

The commanding officer below was just starting to chew his gum when he noticed that the helmets above him in the amphitheater rows were not swaying in their usual patterns. Some were tilted in evident confusion; others rocked back and forth violently. He panned the room and saw one helmet tipped to the side, its wearer's head lolling.

Hu's body slumped off the chair, and her helmet bounced on the wood floor; the officer didn't know whether to run to her or the system control station. Before he could decide, the auditorium's projector lit up the center of the room. A massive white blaze of light crystalized into a holograph, the pinpricks of light forming a smiling black-and-white mask.

A digitized voice boomed across the room's speakers and into each of the linked helmets:

> "We are Anonymous.
> We are Legion.
> We do not forgive.
> We do not forget . . .
> And we are back!"

Then the room went dark.

Directorate Command, Honolulu, Hawaii Special Administrative Zone

So the Russian had really done it. General Yu's aide-de-camp had seen them on the security camera, and her identity had been confirmed, but he hadn't been truly sure until he saw them up close.

The thought knotted the major's stomach as he led the two of them into the general's office. He watched, his hand on his pistol, as the Russian pulled out a key and handcuffed her to one of the wooden office chairs in front of the general's desk. It made the major doubt again whether it really was her, whether the tests had placed the right person at the scene of those horrors. She was curled up tightly in the seat, knees pulled up to her chest, her posture that of a girl who was truly broken. The Russian ripped her wig off with a flourish, revealing her bald head, and tossed the fake hair onto her knees. She just studied the floor in submission.

This made the aide worry. When radioed the news of the Russian's unexpected arrival with the girl, General Yu had ordered them brought to his office. But now the aide was uncertain how the general would react to her in person. She didn't look the way he or, he guessed, the general would imagine.

"Can you get us some water?" asked the Russian. The woman kept herself curled up in a fetal position in her chair. She seemed scared out of her wits, literally.

"I'm sorry, Colonel, but that is not possible. General Yu will be here any minute; there's no time."

"Damn it, she's about to pass out from dehydration. We need to get some water and stims into her."

The aide thought it over, eyeing Markov, who looked like he might be a bit drunk, or at least battling a hangover, as he leaned against the wall. The aide was still mulling it over when he heard loud footsteps in the corridor and turned, ready to greet General Yu. He could hear the general bellowing at a young communications lieutenant to recheck the connections to Hainan; they had been problematic all day. The general blamed his underlings' incompetence, but the aide assumed it was insurgent sabotage yet again. He also guessed the general wanted the young officer's eyes and ears to be somewhere other than at this meeting.

When the general entered, the Russian spoke first; a mistake. "I've done it," Markov said with a note of weary triumph.

Yu nearly exploded, just as the aide had feared he would. "You've done it?" he said. "How many of my men died because you failed to catch her sooner? And now you want credit for her capture. You think we will give you a medal, that it will somehow save you?"

The general started to laugh. "Let me take a look at this killer you have brought in, and then we can discuss exactly what you deserve."

He dropped to one knee in front of the girl, who kept her gaze on the ground.

"Look at me, girl," ordered Yu as he leaned in closer. The girl moved slightly in her seat and then her head rose. The sight of her made the aide lose his breath. Her expression shifted instantly from meek to primal, her pupils almost eclipsing the irises of her eyes. She stared directly at General Yu, who studied her quizzically, their faces inches apart.

Then the mass of black hair on her knees stirred, and the wig flashed up as she wrapped it around the general's neck and tipped her chair over onto its side, using its weight to topple the general's bulk. They went down in a tumble of arms and legs. General Yu staggered up with the girl's feet pressed against his side and both of her arms pulling on the rope of hair she'd wrapped like a noose around his throat. The wooden chair she was still cuffed to swung like a pendulum, adding its weight to the pull.

Before the aide could rush over to help the general, he felt a press of cold metal on his temple. He turned to see the Russian holding an American-made SIG Sauer pistol, the general's trophy from the cabinet.

"No, no. Leave them be. I'm quite curious to see how this plays out," Markov said.

Tiangong-3 Space Station

"He could be lying, sir," said Best.

"It is the truth," said Chang. "We need to leave. There are maybe five rotations until the station orbit deteriorates enough to burn."

"You are telling me that I am about to lose a lot of money!" Cavendish screamed. "Why did you do it? Why destroy *my* station?"

For ten seconds, the only sound in the station was the zipping up of the last body bag. The others were already sealed and affixed with tape to the station's wall.

"It was my duty. I had to do it," said Chang quietly, speaking now to Best, who was clearly a soldier of some sort. He had the bulk for it, but it was more in how relaxed he looked after the battle, his eyes closed as he savored a stick of gum he chewed with steady precision. The slight one — Sir Aeric, he called himself — must be something else. He screamed more like an angry shopkeeper than a soldier.

"Sir, we have met the objective," said Best. "It's a shame about the prize. But you know, we can do it all over again."

"Yes, perhaps the Russians will be more reasonable," said Cavendish, calming down. "And I'll offer to hire them, not just ask for their surrender. Carrot *and* stick this time. How about that?"

"It's worth a try, sir," said Best. "But we need to get off the station now. This part of space is going to light up as the American ASAT missiles start knocking down the Chinese and Russian birds. Then they'll try to launch their satellites, and the Directorate will do the same. With no one commanding space, each side will just knock the other's satellites down as fast as they're launched. Pretty soon any orbit above the Pacific is going to be one big cloud of space junk."

"Makes you wish you worked for someone who had the foresight to invest in the rocket-fuel business," said Cavendish, starting to calculate a new set of gains. "To the *Tallyho*, then! Mr. Tick, are you up for it?"

"I'm feeling no pain, sir," said Tick. The commando's forehead was swollen and his eyes were bloodshot.

"You're a good man, Tick," said Cavendish, now studying Chang. "Best, get the men through the airlock. I will be the last to leave."

"Yes, sir," said Best. "And, sir, I think we finally have your call sign. How does Zorro sound?"

"Splendid," said Cavendish, smiling. "Absolutely splendid."

A flash of relief washed across Chang's face. It felt like the tension in the room had completely lifted. Chang started to float toward an emergency suit, but the slight one in charge, the shopkeeper, shook his head. In his hand was one of their electric pistols.

"No, not you. I warned you that if there was any resistance, you all would die. I didn't get so far in business without being a man of my word."

Chang didn't have time to protest that it hadn't been his decision to resist, that it had all been Huan's fault, before the 7.5 million volts from the Taser dart entered his body.

USS *Zumwalt*, Gulf of Alaska, Pacific Ocean

Captain Jamie Simmons stood in the lee of the helicopter bay and scanned the blue sky. Even with the chill that grew as they moved farther north, the rhythmic rise and fall of the following Pacific swell made the moment wholly pleasant. It was the kind of beauty that unexpectedly wormed its way into the experience of war.

"Captain, visual IFF signal just confirmed it's ours," said Seaman Eric Shear. Simmons took the oversize binoculars. There was an electronic icon in the viewfinder that prompted him to turn to the port side and look slightly up toward the incoming plane, three miles out and closing quickly. A repeating triple dash of lights confirmed the IFF —the identification, friend or foe— signal.

"We'd be dead by now if it wasn't," said Simmons. "Get the recovery crew ready."

"Already standing by, sir," said Shear.

The form of a gray General Atomics Avenger stealth drone appeared behind the lights. It moved fast and low, lower than any human pilot would dare take a plane, fifteen feet above the sea, the splash from the highest waves licking at its underbelly. The pilotless jet's autonomous flight was nearing its terminus. With no other way to securely communicate with the fleet, Pacific Command had resorted to using what was essentially a twenty-million-dollar carrier pigeon. The drone's first pass over the *Zumwalt* crossed the stern fifty feet off, far too close for Simmons's comfort. As it pushed past, the jet waggled its wings slightly. At least somebody among the mission's programmers had a sense of humor.

Tracking the next pass, Simmons saw the doors covering the internal weapons bay open. The jet slowed and ejected two bright yellow canisters, then it powered away to the east and dropped canisters to the rest of the ships in the task force. After that it went to full power and dove straight down into the Pacific. The drone disappeared in a violent splash, the sound of its impact lost in the faint wind.

The canisters gleamed as they were hauled aboard the *Zumwalt* and carried into the hangar bay, where a pair of techs disarmed the scuttle devices that would have melted the contents into a toxic mess with a chemical spray if someone had used the wrong access code.

"Ever think it would come to this, Captain?" said Cortez, eyeing the stack of foil packets.

"Never. When's the last time you opened an actual letter, XO?" said Simmons, tearing open the foil and beginning to read the cover memo outlining the ops plan. "If Congress had known this war was coming, I bet they never would have shut down the U.S. Postal Service."

"Some of these kids, I doubt they've ever held a letter, at least one written by another person," said Cortez.

"I like how you refer to them as kids. Shows how far you've come, Horatio. Shows why I know you'll do the right thing in whatever comes next." Jamie paused, letting that sink in. He looked back down and read further, leaving Cortez standing awkwardly in silence. Then he folded the paper and returned it to the envelope.

"Pep talk's over. We need to get to the bridge."

Cortez looked back quizzically.

"PACOM reports Directorate space-based ISR has been neutral-ized, meaning we just disappeared from their overhead surveillance. There's a new set of mission orders and a new destination. You can let the crew know they can put their mittens away. Full sprint south. It's time to see if this ship is as stealthy as they say."

Kahuku, Oahu, Hawaii Special Administrative Zone

The hike from the beach was just as long as some of the previous treks Conan had done with the NSM, but it took only a fraction of the time. The SEAL fire team moved with confidence rather than the stop-and-go of the insurgents. Where the NSM would have waited and watched for an hour to ensure an intersection in the trail was free of guards, the SEALs moved right through, the tiny robotic lobster they called Butter scurrying ahead, clearing the way.

Conan thought their noise discipline was terrible. It wasn't that they were loud; they were quiet, at least for predators. It was that they clearly had never been prey. They announced themselves with the small things, like the way they tightened a harness or wiped a hand across a sweaty forehead. They also took too many risks. Instead of steering wide of Directorate positions, they seemed to seek out every place the NSM had learned the hard way to avoid.

She didn't understand why until they got to the first site, a cluster of houses being used to barrack a Directorate infantry platoon. She and Duncan went prone and wiggled to the lip of a small creek about seventy-five yards from the houses. She suspected they were prepar-ing an ambush, which worried her. Even if they took out this unit, it would do nothing but bring the rapid-reaction force down on them. She'd heard stories about the SEALs' arrogance, but this was going to get them all killed.

Conan was preparing to pull back and leave them on their own when Duncan set down his rifle. Using a flexible tablet strapped to his forearm, he compared the location to the map scrolling on the screen and then dropped a digital pin on the site.

"We've got the old GPS coordinates of almost everything on the island from before the war down to the inch — not that we can use it for navigation," he whispered. "But we didn't know where all their forces were located. Now we do. Where to next, Major?"

The hike took the whole day, and Duncan slowly filled his digital map with pins. Conan didn't feel at ease until they slipped into trails of the Pupukea-Paumalu Forest Reserve, away from any population. Their journey ended with a hike up a stream in the East 'O'io Gulch to the old Kahuku training center. The hundred-acre site had been built to train construction workers away from the view of tourists. Tucked into the back of a hill were a few buildings, a sixty-three-thousand-gallon water tank, and space for union apprentices to drive around excavators and loaders. It was now abandoned, the jungle rapidly closing in around it.

But what mattered to the team was the other side of the complex. *Kahuku* translated into English as "the projection." The finger of the hill rose three hundred feet above the surrounding landscape. Laid out below them was the Kamehameha Highway with a golf course on its other side, still maintained as if the war had never come. Beyond lay a complex of three low-rise buildings set on a peninsula that had open views to the ocean.

"Just like the Chinese to take the best real estate, huh?" Duncan said.

"Turtle Bay Resort, the only major hotel on the North Shore," Conan said. "And now headquarters of their regional quick-reaction force." She pointed out the row of helicopters and small drones parked on the tennis courts west of the resort complex.

Duncan motioned for the team to set up a hide site and lay out the nylon shield bags. Conan still kept her wool blanket close. She watched as Peaches picked up the robotic lobster, placed a tiny cylinder on it, and then set it back on the ground and gave it the kind of gentle pat you would use to encourage a puppy. Duncan tracked his finger across the flexible tablet screen and placed another pin on the Turtle Bay complex. The tiny robot scurried off and disappeared into the bush.

"After all we've been through together, not even the courtesy of a wave goodbye," Duncan said.

"So he's not going out on perimeter patrol?" Conan asked.

"No, Butter's traveling a little bit farther than we can this time. He's the key to getting our intel out."

On the screen they watched as the tiny robot's icon closed in on the Turtle Bay complex, its advance painfully slow, but steady. The three-dimensional view showed it skittering over the highway and then entering the main hotel complex through a six-inch-wide drainage pipe that ran under a barbed-wire fence the Directorate had put up around the hotel. The robot crossed various gardens and paths, staying in the brush whenever possible. At an open field in front of the hotel, the site of many a wedding in years past, the lobster paused, scanning both directions for movement.

"That's right, be careful," Duncan said, voicing a command to Butter from afar, even though the system was set on full autonomous mode.

The robot sensed movement, two Directorate officers walking down the pathway, and buried itself in a pile of mulch that lined the bordering garden. After they passed, it emerged from the mulch pile and crossed quickly, finally edging itself next to the main hotel building's concrete wall. The tiny robot angled its front four legs up and attached them to the wall. Dry elastomer adhesive in its tiny legs made them twice as sticky as a gecko's feet and allowed it to hold fast to the concrete. Those four legs then pulled up the rest of the robot, and it climbed up the side of the building, one tiny step at a time, at a rate of two inches per second. When it reached the rooftop, the robot scanned again for human presence and, finding none, scurried over to a radio-transmission tower mounted amid the air-conditioning units. It climbed the tower and attached itself to the top rung. And then it waited.

"There you are, Butter. Good boy," Duncan said, picking out the robot poised atop the radio tower with his binoculars. He motioned to Peaches, who began setting a metal tube the size of a thermos on a small tripod.

"Laser designator? Is that the strike site?" asked Conan.

"Maybe later, but for now it's how we communicate without them tracking us. Laser bursts to Butter, who'll then beam out using their own transmission tower. That way, we sidestep any triangulation protocols they have set up; their scans will show only their own signal locales. And when we decide we don't want to share their wonderful comms setup anymore, well, Butter can be quite the little terror."

While Peaches finished rigging the metal tube and linking it to the flex tablet, now unfolded out on the dirt like an old road map, Conan leaned in to Duncan. "You have any stims? We ran dry a while back."

"That's rough. We did that in BUD/S, going cold turkey to show we could be SEALs, but now? I couldn't imagine going without them even for a day," said Duncan. "Digger there, he can sort you all out. Hammer, we good?" said Duncan as Conan took a handful of packets from Digger, evidently the team's medic.

"Online already, boss," said Hammer, a rail-thin man with gray stubble and a scarred scalp who looked to be at least fifty. "All frequencies are green."

"Let's make connection, then."

Conan found the SEALs' confidence unnerving. They were professional, but not wary enough, which made her even more on edge. She cocooned herself in the wool cloak and inched forward to the edge of the perimeter they'd set to track for any threats. She worried about an ambush even more now that the little gadget the SEALs depended on as their eyes and ears was gone.

As she scanned the perimeter one more time, a tap on her boot heel sent a shot of adrenaline up her spine. She started to swing her rifle around and then realized it was Nowak, the Pole, smiling, redeeming himself in his own mind by getting the drop on her. He motioned her back and took her position watching the perimeter.

"So, are you ready to see what it was all for?" Duncan asked as she edged over.

"Impress me."

He handed her a lightweight tactical-glasses rig. It was an updated version of the ones she'd first trained with years back. It looked a bit like a hockey helmet, with pinkie-size antennas running over the crest and a trio of golf-ball-size sensors embedded just above the forehead. The device's conforming battery pack was worn in a harness across Duncan's chest. She put it on and felt for the power button at her temple. Her body reflexively jerked as the heads-up display changed the darkness around her into daylight.

Conan panned her head about, visually traveling over the island's topography, seeing it overlaid with bright icons on each of the sites they had marked and on known Directorate bases; flashing icons denoted active ground-based radar and missile sites.

She felt a hand on her shoulder. "The view's much better that way." Duncan slowly guided her to look toward the sea. At the edge of the horizon, she saw a cluster of bright blue dots blinking against the dark of the ocean. She focused, and the system tracking her eyeballs automatically began to zoom, taking her farther and farther out to sea. As she closed in, the ball of blue began to separate, becoming a dozen small triangular blue icons dancing along the horizon. Friendly forces. A lot of them. The tab associated with the cluster winked at her: *TF Longboard.* As she zoomed out from the cluster of blue, she noticed that a single blue dot was a few hundred miles ahead of it; it had a *Z* for an icon.

Admiral Zheng He, Four Hundred and Fifty Miles Southeast of Kamchatka Peninsula

The *Admiral Zheng He* pushed through the Pacific swell, each wave slapping the flagship of the joint Directorate-Russian task force, almost like slow applause.

The ship's namesake was the second son of a lowly rebel captured by Ming Dynasty forces and castrated at the age of eleven. The young eunuch had been trained as a soldier. But by navigating the perilous politics of the age, he rose to distinguish himself, eventually becoming *taijian,* grand director of the palace servants. Zheng He was remembered for none of this, though, for it was at sea where the eunuch reshaped Asia and went on to become one of history's greatest admirals.

Starting in 1405, Zheng He set out on a series of tours of the world then known to China. His fleet carried twenty-eight thousand soldiers and sailors in over three hundred ships, with his nine-masted flagship being the largest ship ever built in the age of sail. As it traveled from Asia to Arabia and Africa, the massive fleet cowed some kingdoms into submission and defeated the few that chose to fight. By the end of the voyages, Admiral Zheng He had created the first transoceanic empire, a ring of some thirty vassal states with China at the center.

Subsequent emperors would turn away from the sea, preventing future voyages. Imperial China grew progressively weaker and eventually suffered the indignity of becoming a vassal to others. The greatness of the age became an embarrassment, as did the memory of Admiral Zheng. Not anymore.

At 603 feet, almost as long as the *Zumwalt,* the ship was officially classified as a cruiser, but it was a battleship by any of the old measures. Initial work on the vessel had begun back during the Communist Party days, and Americans had first learned of it when a picture leaked on Chinese Internet chatrooms showing a massive mockup ship being built hundreds of miles inland at the test range in Wuhan. But the Directorate had seen the effort to completion. There was no attempt to be stealthy, so the ship lacked the *Zumwalt*'s strange, sleek lines. Instead, carrying 128 missile cells, 64 fore and 64 aft, the twenty-first-century *Admiral Zheng He* was all about projecting power, actual and perceived.

The symbolism of it all was not lost on Admiral Wang as he sat in his stateroom just below the *Zheng He*'s combat information center. Normally, cruisers were named after cities, but he had successfully lobbied to have this ship, the largest surface vessel built in Asia since World War II, named to honor the admiral who had once ruled the sea, back when his homeland was truly great. And if that ship just happened to be his flagship now, all the more appropriate. The symbolism would not be lost on others either.

As he mused on the old admiral, Wang absently ran his thumb along the spine of a small book in his lap. At least this meeting could be done remotely so he would not have to suffer through General Wei's briefing to the rest of the Presidium. Wei was trying to dance around the fact that so far the land forces had failed to put down the insurgent activities in Hawaii.

"General," the admiral said, "I certainly do not question the effectiveness of our counterinsurgency campaign, but for now, let me confine myself to discussing the impact on our naval forces. The recent attack on our main aerostat radar station outside Honolulu has resulted in lost long-range coverage from the island. We can help you compensate by providing additional reconnaissance planes for aerial patrols if needed —"

"Help us 'if needed'?" said General Wei. "No, I think you need not trouble yourself with concern over the loss of one balloon, Admiral. In the real wars we fight on land, loss is to be expected, not like the clean wars you wait for at sea. Space-based sensors on the Tiangong are, of course, continuing to provide theater-wide coverage. Let us worry about the land while you focus on the sea, most especially on what you intend to do about the U.S. task force of old ships that recently left San Francisco."

Never rush to give big news, because your foe might display his ignorance of it in front of the group first, Wang's mentor had once told him regarding the strategy of staff meetings. Wang's hands lay still on the small, leather-bound book as he leaned forward. The screen projection before him showed a dozen men and women wearing suits and glasses sitting in a semicircle. Whether they were really weighing his remarks or just tracking the Shanghai market's stock prices was hard to tell.

"Thank you, General. Yes, the American squadron mostly consists of older vessels from their reserve fleet station on their western coast. American command network intelligence intercepts and analytics of their fuel load project it as reinforcement for Australia. A Marine unit, their Second Expeditionary Brigade, moved from their East Coast, as did an Army unit, their Eleventh Cavalry, still named after horses but a tank unit now. This squares with the mining of social networking data, where several correlative mentions were made by family members of known task force officers."

"All the better," said Wei. "Let them send more forces to wither on the vine with the Australians."

"Yes, General, that would seem the best route" — and now to teach Wei in front of the others what he did not understand of managing modern war — "if we are to believe that is their actual destination. However, the fleet is moving north, not south. Simultaneously, the latest space-based surveillance shows that a task force of their remaining modern and capable warships left in the Atlantic is moving toward the Arctic. If they are able to navigate the Arctic passage, they could then make a dash through the Bering Strait and down into the North Pacific. Notably, the Cherenkov sensors indicate that this group includes their remaining capital ships, the older *Nimitz* aircraft carrier and the *Enterprise,* their last *Ford*-class carrier that they rushed out of construction. This would seem to be connected to the information just in from Dr. Qi's Shanghai 'research' facility of their captured agents' interest in our northern defenses."

Wei looked flustered for a moment at the mix of data and sources that Wang had introduced into the meeting and the dots that he had connected, but then he collected himself.

"Then, it seems, Admiral, you finally have the storm that you were so happy to lecture us on, and without our needing to expand this war into other oceans. Simply establish a blocking position with our Russian partners in the Bering Strait and let them come to you. Stonefish will rain down and your fleet will only have to fish out the bits and pieces. Or as the great *General*" — Wei made sure to emphasize the word — "Sun-Tzu whom you are so fond of quoting would argue, 'If you wait by the river long enough, the bodies of your enemies will float by.'"

"Indeed, General Wei, a wonderful reminder. And yet war at sea is more fluid. As Master Sun himself wrote, 'Water retains no constant shape, so in warfare there are no constant conditions.' There is much in motion here. I believe that the combined risk of —" Admiral Wang stopped. They had all disappeared.

Wang sighed and opened the book on his lap, determined to wait out productively whatever gremlin had decided to run around inside the signal feed.

After a few minutes, a warning klaxon blared, and the hatch to the room swung open with a clang. His aide came in, announcing breathlessly, "Admiral, we have lost our satellite communications and overhead coverage. First it was just Tiangong offline. Then all space assets just went dark. Just like that! We've tried to bring Hainan up and are getting only interference there too."

Wang began to speak before he even knew what he would say.

"Battle stations, then," said Admiral Wang. "I will be on the bridge momentarily."

He hated to be right about something like this, but at least he was ready. Bad news, indeed. What would General Wei or the others in the Presidium say? Nothing, and that was what Admiral Wang had wanted for a very long time. Now he had the independence of decision and action that every great strategist craved.

So much was in motion, perhaps the last grand battle he had foreseen as necessary, but the question was, what exactly were they planning? The Americans had sortied two fleets, but toward which targets?

He flipped through the book in his lap and read a passage aloud. "'Should the enemy strengthen his van, he will weaken his rear; should he strengthen his rear, he will weaken his van; should he strengthen his left, he will weaken his right; should he strengthen his right, he will weaken his left. If he sends reinforcements everywhere, he will everywhere be weak.'"

For once he grew angry with the ancient strategist's guide to the art of war. He needed firm answers now, not vague sayings that could be pondered for days.

Wang stood and placed the book on the conference table, then headed to the bridge. He would have to make this choice alone.

Kahuku, Oahu, Hawaii Special Administrative Zone

Her mind wanted her to sleep, but for the first time in weeks, her body wouldn't let her. The stims lasted longer than normal because she'd been without them for so long.

It was so damn frustrating. Before, it had been her body that craved sleep and her mind that couldn't allow it. More frustrating was the fact that Duncan had told her to catch some sleep. Conan knew he was trying to be kind, that the team clearly admired her for making it this far, but it just reminded her once more that they didn't need her. Every minute, every hour, every day since the attack, she'd been necessary. She'd had to produce the next op plans, give the final orders, and make the toughest calls, some of which meant that sleep would bring back ghosts who would haunt her forever. But now she knew she was useless, just excess baggage for the SEALs.

So she waited under her blanket, sweating, with nothing more to do than pick pieces of the gummy stims from her teeth.

She heard a slight rustle and swung her rifle; no one would get the drop on her twice. It was Duncan this time. He motioned her to follow him to the observation post the team had set up on the perimeter, just on the edge of the brush. It had a clear view out, overlooking the golf course and the resort beyond. Oblivious to their presence, a threesome played on the fourth hole of the Fazio-designed course; clearly they were high-level officers or dignitaries, as two armed escorts followed in a second electric cart commandeered from the resort.

"So this was the unit that got your guys?" said Duncan, hooking her up into the tactical-glasses rig.

Conan nodded, taking in the full-enhanced scene as the system filled the panorama with red and blue icons, this time many more of them. The team had certainly been busy while she was picking her teeth.

"We never learned which unit, but they were good," she replied. "Too good," she added, giving credit where credit was due.

"You're owed some payback, then."

"How soon?"

"Three minutes good enough for you?"

"Typical man, but it'll have to do."

She watched and waited as the team finally started to show their nerves, checking and rechecking their weapons. Duncan kept his binoculars trained on the little robot still affixed to the tower that would be their relay station.

"Okay, mission clock is good, open the comms link," said Duncan.

A voice came through their earpieces, modulated from the digital encryption, but recognizable as having a slight Latino accent. "Nemesis, this is Longboard. Authenticate Zulu, One, Bravo, Two, Three, X-Ray, Four, Two, Golf, Golf, Five, Seven, Papa, Delta, Mike, Six, One, Eight, Mike. Counter-authenticate with match code Polski."

Peaches began the receipt code, speaking in Polish. The language's unique combination of Latin and Greek diacritics gave it thirty-two letters in total, and the letters that were modified with glyphs were almost incomprehensible to computer-decryption algorithms.

"Ś, jeden, pi, ą, ź, ztery ń, siedem, ę, szesna, cie, pi, ł, dwana, cie, ż."

"Roger, Nemesis, match code received. Quick hit human confirm, query mission commander: Best pizza near your home, over?"

"Gino's, New York–style, over," Duncan said quickly into the comms net. He turned to Conan. "They give you five seconds to outrun any algorithm guessing. Good thing they didn't ask favorite Mexican or we'd have been cut off. Too many choices."

"Confirmed, Nemesis," the voice said. "We'll order out for you, over."

"We'd prefer your special delivery today, over," Duncan replied.

"Affirmative. Any updates to the targeting data, over?"

"None, all active and confirmed," Duncan said. "We have a small unit out golfing near us, but we don't think they're worth your while. We can take them on our own if it comes to match play, over."

"Roger that, Nemesis. Standing by for authorization, over."

Duncan looked at Conan, his expression and tone serious for once. "Major, I can't even begin to understand what you've been through, but . . . I just wanted to say how much we respect it, what you had to do."

Conan's face remained impassive.

Duncan, knowing not to go any further, changed tack. "You know why we chose Nemesis as the call sign?"

"Greek god of trouble," she replied.

"Almost. A goddess. Technically, the goddess of vengeful fate; her name translates as 'to give what is due.' That's us, but in this case, I think you're due the privilege of giving the order."

Conan just nodded and said into the microphone, "Longboard, this is Nemesis, you are cleared hot . . . and may all our enemies die screaming."

Duncan smiled, but then he saw her face. It was no longer an expressionless mask. She truly was Nemesis.

Admiral Zheng He, Four Hundred and Fifty Miles Southeast of Kamchatka Peninsula

At this moment, Admiral Wang felt that the flagship's windows on the bridge had the best view of the war. And he could see nothing except the line where the blue water met the horizon.

Everything was happening beyond that horizon, out of sight. He had enemies waiting for him well beyond that horizon but no sure way to find them. He had weapons that could reach well beyond that horizon but no sure way to aim them.

He could sense the crew was discomfited by the absence of vital information; they had expected it would always be there, as certain as the stars. The satellite signals had gone down, the long-range radio was jammed, and the network-data links were worse than severed — they were feeding the crew information and navigation positions that were clearly in error. All the more reason for Wang to exude calm.

It was as it should be, part of him felt. This was naval warfare as it had been for centuries, not as it had been imagined for the past few decades, an organized and predictable exercise with defined and computable odds. If he was going to measure up to his ship's namesake, it would be on a day just like this.

"Show me the last reported positions and scenarios three and four for distance traveled since contact lost," he instructed a young officer.

The screen displayed the potential locations of the enemy task forces. For their Arctic force, there were not many choices. At some point, they had to come down through the Bering Strait. Yes, they could certainly continue on to the Chukchi Sea and harry the Russians on their northern coast, but then it wouldn't be his problem.

"'Ponder and deliberate before you make a move.'"

He recited the instructive quote from *The Art of War* aloud, more for himself than for the bridge crew, though it was good for their morale, he thought, to see their commander in conversation with the great master. They kept silent, knowing not to interfere with his thinking.

The real question was about the southern force of older ships. By this point, they could almost be off their port of Anchorage. Would they lie in wait there? Or would they risk darting down the Aleutian Islands, perhaps to effect a linkup?

Mentally, he went through the priorities, stating out loud Sun-Tzu's rankings once more.

"'The highest form of generalship is to balk the enemy's plans; the next best is to prevent the junction of the enemy's forces.'"

That was certainly what Hainan would want. The integrity of the force and, indeed, the alliance with the Russians would be held by keeping his task force positioned to block that passage and prevent the juncture of the two small American fleets.

"'The good fighters of old first put themselves beyond the possibility of defeat, and then waited for an opportunity of defeating the enemy.'"

He preferred this advice about patience to General Wei's quote about waiting by the river. It was like Wei to choose the less apt quote, but he was still right. The Bering Strait was not a river, but the effect would be the same. They could simply wait for the American forces to enter the strait and be channeled into their arms.

And yet patience was like any other weapon: it had to be used properly or it would backfire on its owner. And patience was not the weapon his foes would be using; he was sure of that. It was the one thing he could be certain of concerning the Americans somewhere across that horizon. That, and that they had to know their moves north had likely been tracked up to this point.

"'All warfare is based on deception . . . When we are near, we must make the enemy believe we are far away; when far away, we must make him believe we are near.'" Deception, he realized, would be the Americans' weapon of choice.

He turned to face his aide so that what he said next would be captured for posterity by the aide's glasses. These words would decide how history would remember him. He would be either the fool who abandoned his post and was shot for it or the great admiral who divined the enemies' ruse and ended the war by appearing out of nowhere right behind them.

"We shall head south, full steam. The surface task force shall proceed in a sweep arc forward, keeping the carriers protected. I want passive sensors only, though. If we are blind to their presence, I want them to be blind to ours. When in range of Hawaii, the carrier's attack squadrons shall launch with anti-ship strike packages even if targets are not yet acquired," Wang said. He smiled to show his confidence in what he knew was a gamble. "As Master Sun advised, 'Never venture, never win'!"

He hoped the great strategist of old was right one last time.

Kahuku, Oahu, Hawaii Special Administrative Zone

The tactical view showed Conan a blinking yellow light on the blue *Z* icon out to sea. They waited several minutes for whatever it was indicating to arrive.

Then there was a sudden roar overhead, almost like an airborne locomotive. A massive explosion erupted miles away, almost certainly at the old Wheeler Army Airfield, where the Directorate had a mobile search radar the SEALs had marked coming in. Her tac-view showed one of the red icons flash with a yellow overlay. Then another wink, and another round of explosions: a mobile Stonefish ballistic-missile launch site in Waialua to the west, the firing pattern prioritizing any mobile targets before taking out the fixed sites.

They watched below as the golfers stood confused; one stopped in midswing and threw himself to the ground. After figuring out the fire wasn't aimed at them, they piled into the electric cart and drove off toward the resort complex.

"Yes, that's it, boys, pack it in. You're shit golfers anyway," Hammer said.

The firing continued above them, a whooshing sound every six seconds, some followed by an explosion close, others in the distance. More and more of the array of red icons began to blink yellow. Below them, the base became a beehive of activity. Two of the helicopters on the tennis court began to spin their rotors.

"Come on, come on," Duncan whispered, starting to grow antsy.

"Nemesis, this is Longboard," the comms link crackled. "Verify friendly position Augusta, over."

"Longboard, Nemesis, affirmative," said Duncan. "And don't leave a scratch on that comms tower or there'll be hell to pay, out."

Again, a wait of minutes. The rail-gun rounds moved at 8,200 feet per second, but they had almost two hundred miles to travel. Then another whooshing sound came in, this time almost upon them, and the tennis courts disappeared in a massive cloud of dirt and fire. Several smaller explosions followed as helicopters and vehicles just beyond the blast site began to cook off. Then another whoosh, and a series of tents set up around the golf course's clubhouse as a command complex disappeared. Six seconds later, a third rail-gun round hit the parking lot, leaving a gaping crater where the unit's motor pool had been. The team was well beyond the strike zone, but they still felt the pressure in their eardrums change and their stomachs turn at each of the explosions.

Duncan scanned the complex with his binoculars and saw that the tower was still standing, the tiny robotic lobster still clinging on.

"Longboard, Nemesis Six. Confirm targets serviced and communications link strong. Nice shooting, over."

"Thank you, Nemesis. We aim to please, out."

The strikes began again, the locomotives rushing by every six seconds like clockwork, some directly overhead, some at a distance. Then the intervals between strikes began to shift, first to twelve seconds, then to eighteen. Conan panned her view and saw icons on neighboring islands starting to flash. Maui, then the Big Island, even Lanai. She'd been so focused on her own fight, she hadn't known what was happening on the other islands.

Duncan brought her attention back. "Time for the seaside fireworks." He pointed off to the coast just as a flash of light about five miles away rose from the ocean and streaked into the clouds. A few seconds later there was a flash above, followed by the sound of a distant explosion, and debris started to rain down.

Conan's visor said those were AIM-9X Sidewinder missiles fired by the *Orzel* using a system developed by the Navy's Littoral Warfare Weapon program; it allowed the heat-seeking missiles, which were normally carried by fighter jets, to be ejected underwater from the submarine's torpedo tubes using gas pressure and a watertight capsule and then launched into the air.

"That's our ride," said Duncan. "Never a good idea to park your combat air patrol above a submarine full of pissed-off Poles who haven't won a war in a few hundred years."

Lieutenant Nowak, lying prone in the dirt just a few meters away, smiled at Conan, gave her a thumbs-up, and then flipped a middle-finger salute at Duncan.

Two more streaks shot up from the water, and another shower of flame and sparks appeared behind the veil of the clouds. The visor registered them as formerly being Chengdu J-20 fighter jets.

The waiting stretched into almost an hour. They watched as the Directorate troops began to sift through the rubble, pull out bodies.

"Don't get too comfortable," Duncan whispered. "Peaches, tell Butter that sharing is no longer caring."

"Sir?" Lieutenant Nowak asked.

"Switch the lobster to jamming mode."

There was no immediate change in the activity below, but soon Directorate troops paused, awaiting instructions that would not come.

Another cluster of blue appeared in the tac-view on the horizon. As it grew closer, icons branched off.

"Major, I think it's time you stopped being the only Marine in this island paradise," he said.

She tried to say something flip back, but she couldn't. All she wanted was to see them. As the icon grew closer, she flipped up the tactical rig. Duncan waited for her to tear up or something, but her face had returned to its usual impassive mask.

With the naked eye, they looked just like dots in the distance. Then the faint chop of blades could be heard. The flight of six low-flying Marine Corps Osprey tiltrotors slowly drew into view. They were flying incredibly low to the ocean, far below what Conan had been taught to do as a trainee back at New River. Clearly, they were trying to stay below the radar to the bitter end.

Now the Directorate would feel real fear. She wondered what Finn would have thought of the scene, and then she pushed that idea away.

"Shit," Duncan said. "They're waking up."

He pointed to a small quadcopter taking off from Kuilima Bay, apparently protected from the first rail-gun strikes by the shadow of the hotel buildings.

"Break-break!" Duncan said into the radio, telling everyone on that frequency this was a priority message. "Ares Flight, Ares Flight, this is Nemesis Six. Heads up, they have a quad drone in the air."

They heard only a crackle of radio static.

"Longboard, this is Nemesis, we can't raise Ares Flight," Duncan said into the secure link to the ship hundreds of miles away. "Can you let them know a quad drone is headed toward them from the east, over."

"Wilco, Nemesis," replied the radio, both parties knowing the jury-rigged game of telephone likely wouldn't work in the heat of battle.

One of the Ospreys splashed down on its belly into Turtle Bay, a few hundred feet from the beach, then flipped across the water, parts breaking off.

"I didn't see any weapon strike," Conan said. "Their propellers just started to feather; fuel or engine trouble of some sort."

The rest of the flight kept going, beginning to hover above the fairways on the far side of the golf course complex, the section designed by Arnold Palmer.

"Shit, they still don't know about the drone," said Conan.

As the lead Osprey touched down over the green of the first hole, the Chinese quadcopter popped up from the swirl of smoke around the destroyed tennis courts and fired a missile. The tiltrotor aircraft pulled up quickly, trying to dodge the missile. A Marine cartwheeled out of the open rear ramp from forty feet up, clutching his rifle the whole way down until he slammed onto the second hole's men's tee box. The quadcopter's missile hit the Osprey's aft fuselage near the horizontal stabilizer, causing the heavily loaded aircraft to swing wildly and then crash into one of the condo units overlooking the fairway.

The second Osprey in the flight, hovering just behind, pivoted. As the aircraft turned its back to the quadcopter, a gunner fired a .50-caliber machine gun mounted in the Osprey's rear ramp. The aircraft turned in its hover, and the arc of red tracers edged closer and closer to the quadcopter and then shattered it in a small explosion. The Osprey then pivoted back and touched down on the golf course. Marines poured out the ramp onto the fairway grass. They immediately started to take small-arms fire from the porch of a townhouse that Directorate troops had been billeted in. As the Osprey's propellers tilted forward and pulled the aircraft out of its hover, a missile arced in, fired from the main resort. The aircraft's defensive flares fired, decoying the missile's seeker head and triggering its proximity fuse, causing an explosion a few hundred feet away, but shrapnel slashed the right engine. One of the massive blades broke off and knifed into the Osprey's fuselage just behind the cockpit, and an explosion broke the aircraft in two.

Conan tracked the missile trail back and saw two Directorate troops just at the edge of the main resort's pool complex reloading an FN-8 man-portable missile system.

"Time for us to get down there and help out," said Conan, checking her rifle and rig.

The fourth Osprey in the line exploded; machine-gun fire from another townhouse had hit a fuel tank. The Marines on the ground popped smoke grenades and the swirling white smoke added to the confusion.

Duncan shook his head. "No, Major, that's not our fight. We're to stay put and coordinate fires. I know it's not what you want to hear, but those are the orders. Mission comes first."

"Not this time, not for me," Conan said.

She took off toward the resort at a jog. Duncan let her go. She was no longer essential to the mission.

USS *Zumwalt* Ship Mission Center, One Hundred and Eighty Miles Off the North Shore of Oahu

The view was majestic in a way, the columns of black smoke rising above the green landscape, the peaks of the Waianae mountain range in the distance. Then the image fizzled and the screen in the ship mission center went blank.

Captain Jamie Simmons swore under his breath. The live video feed from the SEAL team labeled Nemesis had to be considered a luxury, not a requirement.

"Did we lose them or just the connection?"

"Jamming, sir. We're working it," responded the communications officer.

Simmons took in the scene around him. It was a sign of how different this ship was that the best place for a captain to be in the midst of battle was not on the bridge but in a windowless room. Looking down from the second level of the ship mission center, he could see each of the LCD screens that paneled the walls displaying the various systems' status while in the middle of the room, a holographic map projected the topography of the island of Oahu, the various targets and suspected enemy formations overlaid with constantly updating digital red dots and triangles.

He checked the screen for the SEAL fire team's footage of the strikes, but it was blank. Still, the mission moved on smoothly without it. The anxiousness he felt at that one missing piece of data flow was a reminder of how quickly people took for granted the sea of information they floated in. He only hoped that being thrown back into the dark would be even more disorienting for the Directorate generals and admirals who had enjoyed a war of such data dominance so far.

"ATHENA, display task force with projected time to point bravo."

The holographic map pulled out, shrinking the island and projecting the rest of the task force several hundred miles behind them. The system predicted just a few hours of steaming time before the forces would tactically link, but those hours could make all the difference, not just to the success or failure of the assault but to getting the Z back under their air-defense umbrella. It was an honor to be the tip of the spear, but very lonely.

"We've got it back, sir." The footage from the SEAL fire team at Turtle Bay Resort reappeared on the screen. Then the video feed began to cycle through the other imagery sent from teams inserted around the island chain.

"Fidelity?" asked Simmons.

"We're at forty percent," said the communications officer.

"Not good enough. I don't want to risk any more civilians than we have to," Simmons said, knowing that some would become casualties in any event, "and I damn well don't want to stay powered down any longer than we have to if we're just shooting wild."

That was the more disconcerting part, having the ship essentially motionless, the engines at minimal turns solely to hold steady. Conceived as Drift Ops, this approach was meant to both maximize power to the rail gun and make the Z an even more difficult target to detect. Ships were always moving, it was assumed, so a radar signature the size of a dinghy just floating with the current would be filtered out by automated sensors. That was the hope, at least.

"Captain! One of the recon teams, Erinyes, outside Wheeler Army Airfield, is requesting another salvo," said a weapons officer from the bullpen of desks below.

"The hangars were taken out as planned, but the runway strike was off target by a few hundred meters." Simmons winced, hoping they hadn't put one of the rail-gun rounds into the POW compound they suspected was on the base.

"ATHENA has updated the firing solution," said Cortez, looking over at Simmons, who nodded. "Main gun, batteries release," said Simmons. The weapons officer's hands flicked at the touchscreen in front of him, giving ATHENA control over the rail gun's targeting. The intelligent system did more than just aim the barrel of the rail gun at the target; it also interfaced with the ship's propulsion and navigation systems to ensure that it stayed on target.

"Commencing power transfer," said Cortez. "In five, four, three, two —"

The tactical action officer broke in. "Viper, Viper, Viper. ATHENA is reporting two, no, there's three YJ-12 cruise missiles in the air."

The YJ-12 supersonic anti-ship missile carried a four-hundred-and-fifty-pound warhead and could go Mach 4. More important, in addition to their radar, the missiles had imaging seekers, so they could be fired off blind and sent on a hunt for targets in a radius of two hundred and fifty miles, roughly the same range as the rail gun.

"Cease fire," said Cortez.

"No, proceed with the firing plan, XO," said Simmons emphatically. "Either they'll find us or they won't. In the interim, we need to get in as many hits as we can."

"Aye, Captain," said Cortez. Simmons noticed him tapping the heel of his prosthetic foot, which he did when he got anxious. His voice boomed throughout the ship. "This is the XO. Batteries release. Switching to auxiliary power in three, two, one. Mark."

A warning siren blared throughout the ship. "All hands, the ship is on auxiliary power."

The room's LED lights flickered twice then returned to life, powered by their own local batteries. But screens throughout the ship mission center went dark as key ship systems shut down. A low whine followed, giving the crew a sense of dread as the ship powered down.

"ATHENA, bring the tactical map up to air-defense view." The holograph moved upward, displaying icons for three missiles now performing a search pattern, each moving back and forth across a sector farther and farther out from the island.

"Viper one and two are projecting away from us," said the tactical action officer. Simmons and Cortez locked eyes. Their unspoken question was how much fuel the third missile would burn up in a search pattern before it found them.

"Viper three inbound, sir. I think it's tracking us." They watched as the curving search pattern of the missile shifted to a line running directly at the Z.

The ATHENA battle-management system began its targeting solution as it tracked the missile approach, and Simmons watched the crew at the desks below steal glances at one another, wondering how long it would take the captain to power back up and activate the defenses.

He answered their concern, but not as they'd hoped. "Immediately after the final rail-gun shot, transfer power to the laser-point defense systems," said Simmons.

"Firing sequence beginning in ten, nine . . ." said the weapons officer. He stood up in his chair, bracing himself slightly against the console he had been tapping feverishly.

"Viper three down!" said the tactical action officer. "Right in the wet. Looks like it ran out of fuel." As he spoke, the ship began to hum, at first an almost imperceptible vibration, like you'd feel if you laid your hand on a track just before a train appeared.

A flash of movement caught Simmons's eye in the darkened room. It was Vern, entering the mission center, eyes fixed on the screens showing the thermal image of the *Zumwalt*'s bow section and the rail-gun turret pointing accusingly at the shore. Then there was a series of sharp cracks, every six seconds, as six rounds raced toward the targets. With each shot, a flash engulfed the front of the ship in 1,100°F flames.

All eyes shifted to the video feed from the SEAL fire team targeting Wheeler. At the airfield, a pair of fighter jets raced down the runway. From the design, twin-engined and twin-tailed, they appeared to be J-31 Falcon Hawk strike fighters, each wing loaded with a YJ-12 anti-ship missile. The rail-gun rounds were moving too fast for the camera to pick up from afar, but the evidence of the rail-gun rounds' arrival was immediate. So massive was the force of the explosions that even though the first fighter made it into the air, the shock wave tossed it onto its side and it fell back onto the runway, adding a fiery secondary explosion to the devastation.

"Sir, Erinyes reports target destroyed," said one of the crew. "Says good hits. Moving to site Torrey Pines and will report back."

"Now the real test," said Vern.

Cortez looked over at her quizzically, somewhat lost in the information on his viz glasses. "Turning the system off is easy," said Vern, smiling. "Getting it back on is the part that always worried me."

Highway 99, Oahu, Hawaii Special Administrative Zone

Brigadier General Gaylen Adams tried to focus on the taste in his mouth, the familiar mix of bile, dirt, and blood. He hadn't tasted anything like that since Kenya.

"Nearly there, sir, this one piece is a bitch," said Lieutenant Jacobsen. They were huddled in a culvert just beside the concrete roadway. The young officer was new, pressed into duty after Adams's executive officer had died in the crash. The saniband liquid he had sprayed on Adams's wound would set in sixty seconds, creating a hard but porous membrane over the wound site. It also contained a long-acting local anesthetic. But the lieutenant needed to work quickly to debride the wound before the spray set or the wound would seal around the dirt.

Adams kept silent, both cursing himself for wanting to be the first Marine to land and counting himself lucky for surviving the fall that had made that wish come true.

Using a pair of tweezers from his med kit, Jacobsen worked out one last piece that had been lodged just under the general's lip.

"Got it," said the aide, proudly holding up in his tweezers a sliver of a wooden golf tee the size of a matchstick. Adams could only think that it made the young officer look even younger, like one of his sons playing the board game Operation.

Fortunately, the numbness from the anesthetic had set in by this point. As the general rubbed his jaw, testing the edge of it, a helmetless Marine jumped off the roadway and into the culvert.

"Sir, Colonel Fora sent me back to let you know that we've got enemy armor coming," said the Marine, trying to catch his breath. Adams couldn't read his name, a scarlet slash of blood painted across the body armor, just his insignia. A corporal.

"How fah ut, Cupril?" Adams asked, his speech slurred by the anesthetic. He looked over in anger at Jacobsen.

"How far out are they, Corporal?" the general's aide translated.

"Scouts tracking them about a klick away from our position, headed out from the old Schofield Barracks," said the corporal, unfazed. It was the first time he'd ever talked to a general up close; for all he knew, they always had their aides translate for them. He handed the general a muddy map he'd been given to deliver; the units had been ordered to stay off networks as much as they could.

"Knew ur luck run ut ventually," Adams said, mostly to himself. Except for his falling out of the back of an Osprey and onto a golf course, the operation had gone about as well as could be expected. Stealing a play from the Russians, they'd launched from the fleet almost four hundred miles out, the maximum range they could fly without refueling.

They had cut it close, all but one of the tiltrotor aircraft making it in on fumes. The strikes from the Z and the Poles had given them a lane through the air defenses, and even better than expected, the initial reaction from the ground defenses had been fierce but localized. It was as if the various Directorate units were operating without any leadership from the top. Adams didn't know if it was due to the jamming or a lucky hit from the shore bombardment that had killed a Directorate general. He didn't care; he would take a confused enemy every time.

The downside of their long-range method of infiltration was that his units were fighting lighter than normal. While each of the Ospreys that had landed at locations all up and down the North Shore could carry twenty-four combat-loaded Marines, they couldn't carry the unit's complement of artillery or vehicles. The Marines had commandeered civilian vehicles to stay mobile, but they would have to wait for the landing craft to bring them their own armored firepower.

"Colonel Fora said to tell you that he can bring them under fire to delay," said the scout, "but he is requesting to blow the two bridges just north of town, sir."

Adams studied the cracked screen of his tablet computer, matching the map to the locations he knew by heart. They could blow the bridges over the Anahulu River, but that would leave his forces on the wrong side of the little harbor in Haleiwa. And he wanted that harbor. As dinky as it was, hosting mostly deep-sea fishing charters before the war, Haleiwa had the only pier on the entire northern side of the island. His Marines could cross the beach, but that little harbor would make offloading the Eleventh Cavalry far easier. And, more important, he didn't want to lose momentum. Never give an enemy the opportunity to catch his breath; instead, grind your boot down hard on his neck.

He pointed on the map to the juncture of Highways 83 and 99 and the section just beyond Haleiwa, where the main road was raised on concrete pillars above the marshy land and small streams.

"Tell da Z to hut huh and huh."

He looked over at the young marine corporal, who was waiting to be dismissed.

"Num, son?" said General Adams.

"Name, Corporal?" the aide asked.

"Snyder, sir," said the corporal.

"Gut joh, Sny-drr," Adams said slowly, trying to enunciate each word. He nodded at the aide to get to work.

Jacobsen pointed a baseball-bat-size antenna out to sea and set up a directed microwave-burst transmission to the task force; the signal's frequency hopped with each transmission, allowing it to slip through the Directorate jamming.

"Longboard, Longboard, this is Ares, requesting fire at Fo-wer, Quebec, Delta, Kilo, Zero, Tree, Niner, Ait, Tree, Tree, Zero, Six, Two, Niner, and at Fo-wer, Quebec, Delta, Kilo, Zero, Fo-wer, Wun, Two, Fo-wer, Tree, Zero, Two, Niner, Zero. Confirm, Longboard," said the aide, using the military's phonetic pronunciation for the grid coordinates to ensure distinct sounds.

"Ares, this is Longboard Actual. Copy all, but what's the situation? Where is Ares Actual? Over." Adams recognized the voice as Admiral Murray's.

"Longboard Actual, I've got Ares Actual right beside me, but he is, um, verbally incapacitated. I'll be speaking for him, wait," Jacobsen said.

"Tull er dat —"

Before Adams could finish the young officer started. "Longboard Actual, present status strong but precarious. Enemy armor column advancing down Route Ninety-Nine. We'll need fire support to block threat. But not just yet. It'll cost us, but we want to wait for max effect . . . I will relay fire order to time for exactly when their column crosses Helemano Stream."

Adams eyed the young lieutenant with newfound respect. He was crap at surgery, but he was a bloody-minded killer, just the way they'd taught at Quantico.

Highway 99, Oahu, Hawaii Special Administrative Zone

"Snyder, are you sure this is what the general said to do?"

Lance Corporal Ramona Vetter fired off another ten-round burst from her M240 machine gun. The bullets bounced off the lead tank, a Type 99 whose brown-and-green camouflage paint stood out on the highway's black asphalt. It was belching smoke from where its engine used to be after a direct hit from a Javelin shoulder-fired rocket. Their machine-gun fire wouldn't cause any damage, but it would keep the crew from exiting.

"Well, not exactly this," said Snyder, pointing his M4 rifle at the next tank in line, which was pushing the damaged tank off the road. Through his tactical glasses, he could see the Directorate tank designated with a bright green halo. With the road cleared, the tank began to advance toward them again. Another Javelin missile was fired off, but it was deflected by the tank's active protection defenses, which shot down the incoming missile with a small rocket that detonated the threat fifty meters away.

When the tank finally reached the small stream, Snyder did just what the lieutenant had instructed him to do. Normally, he knew to ignore what lieutenants said, but the general beside him had nodded his approval.

He toggled the glasses menu with a controller mounted on the forward rail of his M4. The connection relayed back to the young lieutenant's transmission out to sea, and after a few seconds, the system began to push data to Snyder's glasses, detailing the incoming fire's expected blast radius.

"Damn. You should see this, Vetter," said Snyder. He panned his head left and then right. Hundreds of meters out from the projected impact point on the tank, his glasses showed all red, with a warning signal overlaid in bold: *Danger Close.*

"Whatever they're firing, it isn't in the system. Figured it would be a five-incher, but it's something else."

"Bigger than a five-incher? You promise?" said Vetter.

"You know, your dirty mouth is going to ruin our Hawaiian honeymoon," said Snyder. He yelled to the rest of their platoon strung out along the road: "Incoming fire, danger close. Get your asses down!"

"Probably just can't shoot straight. Typical Navy," said Vetter. The two of them lay prone in a muddy ditch.

"Yeah, well, you know who the colonel is going to blame when this kills us all? Me," said Snyder.

He'd barely finished speaking when the roadway before them vaporized in a bloom of orange and white flame. The blast wave lifted Snyder and Vetter a few inches off the ground and then dropped them back into the ditch. Their ears ringing so loud they couldn't hear anything, they edged back up to the lip. The roadway was now a massive crater where the two lead tanks had been. Even tanks farther away in the column had been flipped onto their backs like turtles.

A second wave of rail-gun fire came in, lifting Snyder and Vetter up again. The effect on the roadway was like scattering hot coals with a sledgehammer. A few seconds later, another two rounds landed in the traffic circle just to the west; now both roads into town were blocked.

Vetter was saying something, but Snyder couldn't hear her over the ringing in his ears. He scanned across the scene of destruction with his eyewear, tagging each smoldering crater and piece of smoking wreckage with a red circle. The message to the *Zumwalt*'s ATHENA system was simple: *Targets destroyed*.

USS *Zumwalt* Ship Mission Center

The battle had settled into a rhythm, a steady monotone patter of queries and replies as the ship and its crew carried out fire-support missions onshore. The only physical indicator that they were at war was the sound of the room's cooling fans, which seemed to be working extra-hard.

The holograph map now showed the Z joined by the rest of the task force, an arc of escort ships surrounding a convoy of transport vessels, all moving closer to shore. A blue bubble overhead extending almost a hundred and ten miles out indicated the air-defense range provided by the USS *Port Royal*, the Aegis cruiser accompanying the task force. Beyond it, small moving icons indicated the *Mako* ships sweeping for underwater threats and a small combat air patrol of six F-35Bs overhead. They were from the USS *America*, the amphibious assault ship at the center of the task force. The *America* also served as Admiral Murray's flagship and so was marked by a bolder icon.

The *America* lacked an aircraft catapult launch and arrestment recovery equipment, which meant it could carry only those aircraft that could take off and land vertically, like F-35Bs, helicopters, and Ospreys. But for all other purposes, it was essentially a forty-five-thousand-ton aircraft carrier that could also load twenty-five hundred Marines, and, most important, it ran on non-nuclear engines. The mission planners had swapped out its normal heavy helicopter complement for the bulk of the first Osprey wave, which were joined by other Ospreys that had flown off the accompanying *San Antonio*– and *Austin*-class landing ships brought out of retirement in the Ghost Fleet. The arrival of so many of the big, slow, non-stealthy ships meant Task Force Longboard's presence would now be much more evident to any Directorate sensors, but being surrounded by other ships felt comforting to all in the Z.

"Captain, we have an incoming drone from the north," a sailor announced. "Its squawking code says point of origin is Shemya?"

Cortez started to read off his glasses. "Shemya . . . Aleutian Islands. There's an old Air Force weather station there that has an emergency-landing airfield. Not so great for that; says the wind never drops below sixty miles per hour and there's a ten-foot visibility fog three hundred days of the year. That explains it; robots don't mind the weather. Op plan has it used as a relay station for secure drone comms. A Pony Express–style handover."

"Allow download. It is about time we finally get some news on what's happening up north," said the captain.

Within a minute, Cortez appeared at Simmons's side with a tablet screen. It showed an animated map of the current and projected locations of the U.S. forces making their way through the Arctic passage. Noticeably absent was the Directorate battle fleet that was supposed to have been drawn north.

"Shit," said Simmons.

Cortez nodded, and he winced slightly as he read the message aloud.

"'No contact Directorate battle fleet. Undetected from searches in Bering and off Aleutians. In absence of further information, must assume strong substantial attack force proceeding towards your area of operations. In carrying out the task assigned in operation plan twenty-nine–forty-two, you will be governed by the principle of calculated risk, which you shall interpret to mean the avoidance of exposure of your force to attack by superior enemy forces without good prospect of inflicting greater damage to the enemy. Given communications link delays and uncertainty, decision authority is now with task force commander. COMPACOM will support. But priority is to protect the fleet in being.'"

"Sir, we have Admiral Murray on the localized net for you," Cortez said. The video link opened, and the admiral appeared.

"You've seen the message?" she asked.

"Yes, ma'am."

"Then you know what it means?" she asked.

"Yes. PACOM is not going to say it, but they're giving us the option to withdraw if the situation turns too hairy," he responded. "Which would hang the Marines onshore out to dry."

"That is indeed what it means, Captain," she said. "That's the trade-off. Instead of being puppeted from afar like in the last war, we get the kind of command freedom our predecessors dreamed of. But it also means the hard calls get piled on our shoulders."

Simmons's eyes flashed up to the monitor bank showing the array of system updates and videos of Marine combat footage. How many hours had it been since he'd seen the sea? It should have been easy to follow a cold-hearted, calculated order like this because he was devoid of any physical contact with the war and was essentially playing a video game in this floating box. It wasn't.

"We will proceed as planned," said Murray. "But be aware of the option if needed. I'll give General Adams the bad news myself."

No more than ten minutes after she had signed off, another urgent transmission came in.

"It's the bird on the northwest patrol," Cortez said, pointing to the icon on the holographic tactical display.

"Let's hear it," said Simmons.

"Big Bird, Double Down Four," said the female pilot. "You have an incoming flight of sixty-plus enemy jets. I repeat, six-zero-plus enemy jets, coming from the northwest. They've got carriers out there somewhere. Double Down Four is engaging, but . . ." The pilot trailed off.

They all knew. It was best left unsaid. Her F-35B was one of the handful of jump jets squeezed onto the USS *America* to form the task force's combat air patrol. Given what had happened to their predecessors, all the pilots had been volunteers. Their planes had been scanned and rescanned and as many of the suspect chips swapped out as possible, replaced with chips scavenged from donated commercial gear. But there was no certainty they'd removed all of the Trojan horse hardware. The technicians likened it to trying to find a particular needle in a haystack made of needles. But finding bad chips was actually even harder than that, as they activated only in the presence of a combination of an unknown frequency and an encrypted transmittal message.

Her voice sounded strained as she braced against the increasing g-load that went with her aggressive tactical turn toward the threat in the northwest. The flight suit fought the physics of the maneuver but it was always a losing battle. "We'll do what we can, but expect incoming within fifteen minutes. Double Down Four out."

Double Down 4 stopped transmitting and fired a salvo of joint dual-role air dominance missiles at the squadron of Chinese Shenyang J-31 fighters that had entered the defense sector. The Chinese planes were almost her jet's twins, having benefited during their development from F-35 blueprints stolen by hackers in 2009. Her incoming-missile warning alerted her that the closest one had counterfired a PL-21D. Powered by ramjets, it closed quickly, so she banked hard and up to get some altitude. Then she activated the broadcast protocol. To counter the risk of some traitor chip signaling out, the whiz kids had dreamed up the idea of flooding all the frequencies. All stealth was lost, but the theory was that whatever homing beacon the missiles were trying to ride in on would be overwhelmed by all the other signals broadcasting.

She rotated the plane so she was inverted, catching a glimpse of the incoming missile exhaust streaking toward her as she did. The F-35 automatically fired off a dozen flares, and she put the plane straight down into a dive that made it crack the sound barrier. The missile kept climbing past her, seemingly fooled for the moment. Double Down 4 turned again, visually hunting for another target, her search radar rendered useless by the mix of the enemy's and her own jamming. In the distance, she saw an explosion. At least one of her missiles had made contact.

All of this was invisible to the *Zumwalt*'s crew, still haunted by the clipped tone of her transmission. Jamming made it impossible for them to hear anything more. This spared the crew from hearing Double Down 4's choked scream as 30 mm cannon fire from a Russian Su-33 gutted her plane's belly. The only indication of her fate came when the all-frequency jamming stopped and ATHENA changed the F-35 icon from blue to gray and then moved it off the screen.

"Ladies and gentlemen, it seems we have found the rest of the enemy fleet," said Simmons. "You know what to do."

Wolf Flight, Pacific Ocean

Some 120 miles away from the *Zumwalt*, Captain Second Rank Alexei Denisov swept the sky again, craning his neck to look past his MiG-35K's twin tails. He wanted to confirm what his cockpit displays and flight communications told him: the last of the American combat air patrol had been shot down. He looked around his plane; all that remained was a faint haze of smoke from the dogfight.

This was a perfect coda, he believed. He had been there at the beginning and would be there at the end of it all. How many decades had the Americans claimed the world's skies? No more.

"White and Red Squadrons, this is Dagger-Three-Thirty-Four. Sky looks clear of any enemy planes." He checked his radar screen again; still no targets acquired. Both sides were jamming each other, and neither could cut through the electronic fog until they closed.

"Begin your attack, Formation Wolf Hunt," said Denisov.

Denisov pulled back on the stick and slowed, allowing the aircraft to reposition itself into the attack formation. Within seconds, the Russian MiG-35Ks and Su-33s of White Squadron and the Chinese J-31s of Red Squadron were neatly arrayed in a line extending two hundred kilometers, just as they had trained on the simulators for weeks. Like wolves on the Siberian plains, they would sweep forward until some part of the line made contact, then all the others would close in a circle. It was simple but brutally effective.

USS *Zumwalt* Ship Mission Center

"Damn it to hell," said an angry voice, not bothering to keep her frustration in check. The sailor was just out of Simmons's line of sight, but her frustration was clear.

He walked down the stairs to the sailor's workstation. "Patience, Richter, just have patience," said Simmons in a calming voice.

"Aye, sir," said Operations Specialist Angelique Richter, a bit surprised to find the captain leaning over her shoulder to look at the three screens at the workstation she was using. A diminutive twenty-five-year-old radar systems operator, she wore a matte-black eyebrow stud like the ones many of the female Marines wore. "Might as well turn the damn thing off, sir, jamming's only getting worse."

"Ebb and flow, Richter, that's how this is going to go," said Simmons. "You get a glimpse, then you use what little you have. Don't forget: they're just as confused as we are."

The girl nodded, running chewed fingernails over her shaved head.

"Richter, you've been in three years now, right?" said Simmons.

"It will be four years in two months, sir," she said.

"That's a lot of Navy in your blood," said Simmons. "Makes you one of the sailors I'm counting on today. There's nothing here you can't handle. What we know is all we know. Got me?"

"Aye, sir."

He was walking back up the stairs to the observation floor when the radar operator called him.

"Sir, we've bogeys coming in from the northwest. They're strung out in a long line," Richter said. Then, in a lower pitch: "ATHENA counts sixty-two in total.

"Shit," the radar operator continued. "It's worse than that. ATHENA is now showing something coming in from the east. It's patchy, but at least a hundred bogeys . . . we're right square in the middle."

As the information from her screen began to populate the central tactical hologram where all could see it, the room seemed to grow more quiet. A brief groan from the ship's engines welled up through the hull, as if the *Zumwalt* had just accepted its fate.

Then a voice rang out over the speakers arrayed around the room. It had a gravelly, Southern twang: "Longboard, this is Boneyard Six

Four. You seem to have some party crashers on the way. Can we be of assistance? Over."

Boneyard Flight, Pacific Ocean

U.S. Air Force Colonel Roscoe Coltan ended the transmission and re-checked his position. The twelve-by-nineteen-inch glass-panel Garmin AeroScreen was bolted on shock mounts over the F-15C jet's original flight instruments. He had rimmed the screen with duct tape for good measure, which showed the level of confidence he had in the technology. It was effective, but it still didn't seem right, which basically captured just about everything so far in this mission.

Roscoe's jet had been among the 256 F-15s and F-16s the U.S. Air Force had early-retired in 2014. The argument was that the fourth generation of fighter planes couldn't keep up with twenty-first-century threats, but the real reason was that retiring the planes created an artificial fighter gap, which helped make the case for keeping the spending up on the F-35, the fifth-generation plane, whose cost had spiraled. The old but still flyable planes had spent the past years stored out in the dry Arizona air of Davis-Monthan Air Force Base, better known as the Boneyard, the aircraft equivalent of the Ghost Fleet. Alongside some four thousand other retired planes dating back to World War II, Roscoe's jet had been waiting its turn to be harvested for scrap metal and spare parts.

But now, the age of the planes in Boneyard Flight worked to their advantage. They were crude, but they could be trusted. First flown in the 1970s, the F-15s needed only rudimentary electronics to operate; they had less computing power than his grandson's talking toy bear and were steered by about twenty million fewer lines of code than the F-35. Most important, the chips in their flight systems had been produced long before hardware hacking or even the Directorate itself had been conceived.

His fuel gauge showed he had about two hours of flight time left if he just nursed the plane along. Unfortunately, the dogfight he expected would shave his time aloft down to a fraction of that.

Boneyard Flight had taken off with two dozen desert-worn KC-135s that had also been pulled out of retirement. Those things were tougher than cockroaches. First flown back in the Eisenhower days, the 707 passenger-jet derivatives did not have a modern chip anywhere, unlike the new KC-46s, which had turned out to be missile magnets like all the other Chinese-chipped gear.

The plan was that another flight of old Stratotankers would be waiting to refuel them on the return leg. He looked down at the rippled sea surface. It was a profoundly deep azure dusted with white lines that reminded him of a light snow on tree branches back home in North Carolina. The tankers would be there, the briefer had promised, and if not, he said, the sea would contain only friendly ships they could ditch near.

After two wives and twenty-four years in the Air Force, Roscoe knew when he was being bullshitted. He also knew when not to care.

"Oscar, Roscoe. You picking up the same fleet data I am? Over," said Roscoe.

"Roger that, Roscoe," said Oscar, an F-16 pilot flying the other element of the escort. The pilot had gotten his call sign back when he was a new lieutenant, a way to put him in his place after he'd been hot-dogging it in flight school. "Sky is clear over Oahu, but the squids look like they are in for some major rain, over."

"I'm thinking we need to give them an umbrella. I'll take Eagle and Wall-E elements of the escort to mix it up. You take Viper element on with the big boys to keep 'em safe and give the ground pounders some support, over."

"Understood, Roscoe. Just like an Eagle driver to steal all the glory," Oscar responded. "We'll get them through. Good hunting, over."

"Eagle Flight, I know you heard that conversation. Form up on me." Then he paused, and when he spoke again, he made sure to enunciate his words. They said the voice-recognition software would work anyway, but he wanted to be certain.

"Wall-E Flight. Authorization Roscoe. Voice authenticate Eagle, Two, Eight, Alpha, Delta. New mission order. Autonomous hunt. Air-to-air weapons authority release. Execute."

He turned his head to see if they would follow the order or just start shooting down all the American jets close to them, like some bad movie. But the twelve F-40A Shrikes in the escort all took a smooth, literally perfect turn with a precision that would make a flight instructor orgasm and then formed up on the flanks of Eagle Flight's F-15 fighters.

To Roscoe, it was one of the war's many ironies that the jets they most needed to come through today were the very ones his service's leadership had done its best to fight for years. Unmanned planes had proved their worth in the Afghan war and then in the various counterterrorism campaigns from Pakistan to Nigeria. But the early models had been remotely operated by pilots on the ground, and they were propeller-powered by four-cylinder engines taken from snowmobiles, meaning they had performance capabilities that even a World War I pilot would laugh at. The generals had always made sure to tell the public that while they were fine for killing terrorists, the early drones wouldn't be able to survive in any kind of denied airspace. That was true enough, but oddly, behind the scenes, the critics did everything possible to make sure future models would have those very same flaws. The Pentagon bureaucracy, which had begrudgingly started using armed unmanned aerial systems only after the CIA got into the business, consistently slow-rolled any attempts to make the next generation of drones faster, stealthier, and more lethal.

In the lean years after the Afghan war, the research budget for unmanned systems was slashed four times as much as any other program. The rationales for opposition included everything from worries about pilots losing jobs to defense contractors' concerns that the better the new technology became, the more it would threaten their already signed multitrillion-dollar weapons contracts. It got to the point that, in 2013, when a test drone successfully took off and landed on an aircraft carrier by itself, the Naval Air Systems Command tried to send the cutting-edge technology not out to the fleet, but to the Smithsonian. There, in a museum, one of the most advanced planes on the planet could be "celebrated," and, more important, it wouldn't be carrying out any further tests that might make people rethink the existing order of things.

The F-40 Shrike program had been proposed by a maverick colonel who'd risked his career by publishing an article about it in the U.S. Air Force's professional journal. He argued that instead of replacing its workhorse F-16 Fighting Falcon jets with the heavy and expensive F-35s, the Air Force should go with a similarly lightweight, cheap, and durable plane. The only difference was that it would be unmanned. It would get a small radar signature from having a thin, tailless, bat-wing shape that the absence of a cockpit made possible. Its software would match capabilities that had already been proven effective in the civilian market, autonomous flight and navigation, with weapons software that would follow the same identification-friend-or-foe protocols as missiles.

While the idea was anathema to leadership at the time, the concept of a cheap, useful combat drone struck a chord with the researchers at DARPA. A prototype was funded and it flew right about when Roscoe was starting his second marriage. But just like what had happened to the Predator drone a generation before, the little Shrike languished in what was known in the Beltway as the "valley of death," never rising to full program status with the Air Force or the major contractors.

The program had received new life when all the agency's old prototypes were reevaluated for their utility in a new war. There, the DARPA connection proved critical again, as the Shrike's computer chips had been made through the agency's trusted-foundry program, not sourced from the marked-up Chinese-made chips that the major contractors' weapons programs used. Initially, the old guard in the Air Force had wanted to strip out the chips and use them as part of a plan to ramp up production of the very same manned planes that had failed at the war's opening. But when Secretary of Defense Claiburne fired the Air Combat Command general who had proposed it and said she would use Navy planes exclusively for future missions if anyone came to her with any more such backward-looking ideas, the rest of the service got onboard. It wasn't only because of that proposal that the general was fired; Claiburne had already been planning to fire him, but she had held back until she could do it in what she called "a teachable moment."

"Roscoe, one last thing," Oscar called over as he watched the drones form up beside the old F-15s. "You better shoot down more bogeys than those damn robots do, or you and I are truly going to be out of the business."

Pua'ena Point Beach Park, Hawaii Special Administrative Zone

Standing on the concrete slab that had been the foundation of the old radio tower, General Adams admired the controlled chaos. The last time this field had seen such a buzz of activity had been the original "day of infamy" itself.

Back in 1941, the Haleiwa fighter strip had been a satellite landing field away from the main U.S. Army Air Corps base at Wheeler airfield. As soon as the attack started, without waiting for orders, two young fighter pilots, Lieutenants George Welch and Kenneth Taylor, had jumped in a car and raced to the secondary field. They made the twisting sixteen-mile drive in under fifteen minutes. When they arrived, the crew chiefs told them that instead of flying out, they should disperse the aircraft on the ground. "The hell with that," said Welch.

Ignoring the usual pre-takeoff checklists, each pilot climbed into a P-40 Warhawk fighter plane and took off down the airstrip. Only once they were in the air did they figure out they were about to take on over three hundred enemy aircraft. Undeterred, Welch and Taylor plowed straight into the second wave of the Japanese attack. They didn't stop the attack, but they did manage to shoot down six planes before they ran out of ammunition. More important, the two pilots put up enough of a fight that Japanese planners assumed there were far more defenders in the air. They decided against sending in a final, third attack wave designed to pummel Pearl Harbor's fuel storage, maintenance, and dry-dock repair yards, an attack that would have set back the American war effort at least another year.

The airstrip stayed in use up to the 1960s and was then turned over to the locals. Eventually owned by Kamehameha Schools and renamed Pua'ena Point, the real estate remained undeveloped, the concrete tarmac becoming cracked and gradually overtaken by the jungle. The only human presence for the past decades had been a squatters' camp and an occasional rave party.

This real estate was now priceless to Adams. All the other active airstrips on the island, even the small civilian fields, had been used by the Directorate for basing and drone-landing strips, and they'd been taken out by the Z's bombardment. A platoon of his Marines had been tasked to prep the old field as best they could, clearing away the squatter shacks, bushes, and concrete fragments that blocked the field. When word of what they were doing spread, civilians had started showing up to help. Retirees with garden tools, surfers with their bare hands, the now truly homeless squatters, all filling in holes in the tarmac and hacking away at the jungle. That had been unexpected good fortune. A corporal was now directing eighty of them in the cleanup of a helicopter-landing site, over where the hangars used to be. That would mean Adams could keep the runway clear and still bring his attack helicopters off the ships ahead of schedule. Even better, a SEAL fire team had appeared out of the jungle with two bulldozers and a Polish navy officer driving a massive yellow roller. He couldn't even begin to fathom where they had found construction equipment in the middle of a battle, but he'd take it.

"Sir, they're here," his aide Lieutenant Jacobsen said.

"Dank you, 'Tenant," Adams responded, his jaw still numb. "Clear um ut."

Jacobsen ordered those still on the runway to clear as an F-16 buzzed low and waggled its wings. Typical pilot hot-dog bullshit, thought Adams. Despite all the work, the runway was still far too rough for any plane to land on. He forgave the pilot as the F-16 flew on toward the front, where it could do some actual good.

What Adams cared most about were the big lumbering planes that were appearing in the sky, the massive C-5 Galaxies that could carry over two hundred and seventy thousand pounds of payload, the sleek C-141 Starlifters that had ferried troops to Vietnam and the First Gulf War, and even some of the more modern C-17 Globemasters. He knew they were the early production models, built before the full reliance on electronics.

Three missiles arced up toward the planes from the east, somewhere behind enemy lines. The spray of countermeasure flares distracted one missile, but the other two smashed into a C-5 and sent it careening into the ocean. Adams could see the F-16s in the escort, 20 mm Vulcan cannon firing, swoop down to punish whoever had committed the transgression of harming their flock.

Undeterred, the other big planes moved closer, the first wave filling the air with tiny dots that blossomed into parachutes, each C-141 dumping a string of 123 paratroopers as it flew overhead.

As they landed on the airfield, Adams blessed those civilians yet again. Every filled pothole in the tarmac meant one less twisted ankle or sprained knee taking a soldier out of action. Marines ran out to help the paratroopers stow their parachutes and find their rally points.

At each unit rally point, a line of civilian vehicles waited on the road leading out to the main town. Just as World War I French troops had been ferried to the Battle of the Marne in Parisian buses, the Third Brigade Combat Team of the Eighty-Second Airborne Division would join the Battle of Kamehameha Highway in a mix of pickup trucks, SUVs, and even a few minibuses from the local tour companies.

The next wave of cargo planes came down low, almost at sea level, staggered out in a long line, one behind another. As each plane raced down the length of the runway with its rear door open, a drogue parachute deployed out the back, caught the air, and then yanked out a large pallet. The plane then pulled up, its wheels never having touched the ground, and the pallet slid and bumped down the runway at over a hundred miles per hour before friction caused it to grind slowly to a stop. Teams of civilians directed by a paratrooper then swarmed over the pallet, tearing at thick belts strapping down everything from aviation-fuel bladders to combat vehicles. With all that extra manpower, the offloading went at least twice as fast as anticipated, and it freed up more forces for the frontlines. Adams heard Jacobsen yelling at the workers to prioritize the M1128 Stryker mobile-gun systems. Damn, that boy was good. The eight-wheeled armored fighting vehicles each mounted a 105 mm tank gun, which meant Adams could soon start punching back, hard.

The most lethal supplies to come in on the pallets, though, were what looked like two ordinary fuel-tank trucks. In fact, the tanks were filled not with fuel but with a mix of resin-based binders. When sprayed down and smoothed out over the base of the old runway, the substance would form polyurethane polymer concrete. After just thirty minutes of drying time, he would own the only operative airfield on the island.

Adams smiled at the thought, the first smile he'd allowed himself in months. It quickly died, though, when Jacobsen reached over with a handkerchief to dab away a thin trickle of drool dripping from the corner of the general's still-numb mouth.

Boneyard Flight, Pacific Ocean

Roscoe fired a pair of AIM-120E AMRAAM air-to-air missiles well before he could see the enemy planes. The twelve-foot-long missiles came cleanly off his plane's fuselage stations and disappeared into the blue sky ahead. With so much radar and communications interference, these were the long shots. Shoot two, hope maybe to hit one. More usefully, they'd create a cover of fast-moving death for his jets to come in behind, throwing off whatever formation the enemy had planned.

He pushed the plane to afterburners, noticing a faint vibration in his ejection seat as his F-15C's speed passed Mach 2. With no stealth features, the older planes would be at a disadvantage until they made this an up-close-and-personal knife fight. Plus the F-15C's speed meant they could start their kill count before the slower Shrike drones arrived.

It all happened in seconds: a few explosions in the distance and closer alongside him as some of Eagle Flight were hit by the enemy's counterfire, and then a swirl of smoke and contrails as fighters from three nations mixed it up.

Roscoe could focus only on his part of the fight, quickly firing a pair of AIM-9X Sidewinder missiles at two Russian MiG-35Ks less than a mile away, both of them banking hard as they tried to get inside the turn circle of another F-15. One missile went astray but the second smashed into the trailing jet's tail section with an explosion that pitched the MiG's nose skyward and then left a smoky scar in the sky. The other MiG fighter jet turned to escape, Roscoe following. As he turned, a faint puff of tracer rounds crossed in front of him; a Chinese J-31 fighter was boring through the chaos, its nose trained on Roscoe's F-15. Before Roscoe could evade, one of the incoming rounds blew off the top of his left vertical stabilizer.

The F-15 shuddered and buffeted as the J-31 bird-dogged Roscoe, staying on his rear. Instinctively, the experienced pilot unloaded the jet. While one way to gain speed was to max engine power, the most effective way was essentially to trick physics into working for you. Roscoe slid the stick forward and put the aircraft into a shallow ten-degree dive. As the plane dipped slightly, it created a zero-g condition, essentially "unloading" weight from the plane, akin to going over the crest of a small hill in a bicycle and coming out of your seat. Acceleration is a matter of thrust and weight, and in that weightless moment, Roscoe's F-15 powered ahead rapidly, leaving his attacker behind.

As Roscoe saw the airspeed indicator approaching the plane's structural design limits, he felt a sharp shudder, the damaged tail wing starting to crack. The jet's designers hadn't counted on the effect of a 30 mm cannon. As Roscoe pulled the stick up to lose speed, his radar-warning receiver howled: the J-31 was catching up to finish him off.

He pushed the throttles all the way forward, rolled the plane onto its back, and pulled the stick back into the seat pan. He hoped that the Directorate pilot would get greedy, cut across his turn circle, and provide him a reversal opportunity. It was a classic move, which, unfortunately, meant it was one the J-31 pilot had been trained to counter. Roscoe snuck a look over his shoulder and saw the Directorate plane stabilized at his deep six o'clock, between his tail.

Roscoe swung the plane back and forth, straining against the force of the turns, trying to ruin the J-31's firing solution but knowing his bag of tricks was empty. His plane groaned with the turns. If a Chinese missile didn't kill him, his jet would.

His flight suit compressed and fought the g-forces just as Roscoe pulled into another tight turn. The tunnel vision started, the perimeter of his field of vision beginning to shade inward from the massive pressure on his body. A gray form entered on the right side of his line of sight, just above his canopy, and then disappeared as the tunnel around him grew smaller and smaller. He was blacking out; he knew it.

Roscoe pulled out of the turn; the tunnel widened, and the heavy weight on his body lifted. His plane's radar-warning receiver abruptly went silent. He craned his neck to see where the J-31 was. He couldn't find it at first, and then he saw the matte-gray-and-blue Chinese fighter falling end over end toward the ocean below, trailing a thick plume of smoke and flame. Flying away was a Shrike. The wedge-shaped drone pulled an insanely tight turn that would have knocked out any human pilot, firing a missile at a MiG-35K in the midst of it. Even before that MiG exploded, the Shrike was already off hunting its next target, its autonomous programming relentless in its computerized efficiency.

"Little bastard didn't even stop to see if I was okay," said Roscoe, silently thanking the drone's designers.

He checked his radar display, which was momentarily free of jamming strobes. He felt sick when he saw how empty the sky was of aircraft. In less than a minute, at least a hundred lives had been lost.

"Longboard, Longboard, this is Boneyard Leader. We've serviced most of your visitors, but I show eight leakers made it through our picket line. MiG-35Ks," he said, trying to steady his voice as his plane bucked. "We're going to run them down, but it looks like some bogeys are going to make it to you first, over."

The four F-15s remaining in Eagle Flight took off in pursuit at almost nine hundred miles an hour, their maximum at low altitude. The low-fuel warning flashed in Roscoe's cockpit. Going to afterburner so much would cost him the chance to get home, he thought, but that was beside the point at this stage of the game.

He visually picked up the Russian MiGs by the telltale signs of their missile launches. The remains of Eagle Flight had arrived too late.

"Jesus, that's a lot of hurt," said Roscoe to the other three pilots. "I count at least two dozen missiles."

"At least thirty," said Squiggle, the pilot in the F-15C flying off Roscoe's right wing.

"Fire everything you have left. Use 'em or lose 'em!" Roscoe ordered.

He fired off his remaining AIM-9X, visually following it as it locked on one of the MiGs trailing the formation. The MiG was breaking upward, climbing for more altitude after launching its anti-ship missiles, when the Sidewinder exploded just aft of the jet.

"Eagle Flight, I'm Winchester," Roscoe said, letting whoever was left know he was down to guns only.

He pushed his jet past the MiG flat-spinning into the waves below, maxing the power to try to run down the cruise missiles starting to accelerate into the distance. Above him, the Russian and American jets grappled in a final violent confrontation that took six Russian missiles and two more MiGs out of the sky but also resulted in the destruction of three of the four American F-15s.

He'd hoped to catch one of the missiles with a lucky shot from his guns, but his luck had run out; the F-15's damaged vertical stabilizer broke away like a shingle in a hurricane. "So there's me," said Roscoe to himself as he struggled with the bucking plane.

He eyed the ocean below, looking for the driest spot to ditch in. The left engine began to sputter. His war would end now. Roscoe took his left hand off the stick and reached for the yellow metal bar by his knee on which his crew chief had jokingly written *Do not touch!* in felt-tip marker. The plane's violent pitching made getting a grip on the ejection handle far harder than he'd expected.

USS *Zumwalt* Ship Mission Center

"Twenty-six missiles incoming, sir," said Richter with the kind of detachment that often accompanies extreme fear. "ATHENA shows *Port Royal* counterfiring."

While not of the same design, the *Port Royal* was a sister ship of sorts to the Z. She had been the youngest of the Navy's *Ticonderoga*-class cruisers, and one of the first with the ability to shoot down ballistic missiles as part of the Navy's Linebacker program. But in 2009, when it ran into a coral reef about half a mile from the Honolulu airport, the ship earned a new, cruel nickname. The *Port Coral*, as it became known, didn't sink, but the extensive damage to the ship's hull, propellers, and sonar dome put the U.S. Navy's then youngest cruiser on the target list for early retirement to the Ghost Fleet.

The *Port Royal* fired a wave of SM-6 air-defense missiles that sped upward from the vertical launchers embedded in its deck. The missiles arced up and then pitched down toward the low-flying cruise missiles. A wave of RIM-162 Evolved Seasparrow defensive missiles followed.

The collisions were almost instantaneous, showering the ocean surface with flame, fuel, and metal shards.

"I count that as fourteen hit, sir. We have twelve still incoming," said the sailor.

"Full countermeasures and launch the *Utah*," said Simmons.

A large metal canister that had been affixed to the *Zumwalt*'s stern separated from the ship with a loud bang. It popped thirty feet into the air and then dropped into the water with an anticlimactic splash, bobbing up and down.

Vern, who had been out on the deck checking a power-cable connection during a lull in the rail-gun fire, stopped to watch as the massive gray form the *Z* was leaving behind began inflating.

Mike ran up to her yelling, "We need to get back inside!"

Vern gave him a puzzled look and then returned her attention to the growing form, the words USS *Utah* unfurling on its side in white paint as it inflated. "What is it?"

"Now, Vern, move!" Mike half carried her roughly back to the shelter of the main superstructure. He steered her below decks and talked at the same time, occasionally pausing to catch his breath. "USS *Utah* was an old World War One battleship. By the time of the first Pearl Harbor attack, it had been turned into a floating naval target ship for our own gunners to practice on. But when the Japanese attacked in '41, their pilots saw what looked from above like a real battleship. The old *Utah* was sunk, but not before she soaked up a ton of bombs that the enemy could have used on other, better targets. Our *Utah* is supposed to do the same."

As they descended deeper into the ship, the matte-gray bag behind the *Z* continued to expand until it formed the silhouette of a small warship, with metallic reflective squares on it enhancing its signature. With a jerk, the towline finally paid out a quarter mile behind the ship, and the *Utah* now followed the *Zumwalt,* matching its speed.

"Sir, ATHENA says the incoming missiles are selecting targets. Twenty seconds out," said the sailor in the mission center.

"ATHENA, full autonomous mode! Authorization Simmons, Four, Seven, Romeo, Tango, Delta," said Simmons quickly.

The ship's laser-point defense fired first. There was no noise or visible light and only faint, almost delicate movements as the solid-state, high-energy laser fired. It was a moment of faith for the crew, as the weapon lacked the certainty of gunpowder. The ship's laser-gun camera showed a small flame spark on the target as the hundred-kilowatt beam came into contact with it. The missile caught fire and sank into the water. Then ATHENA automatically directed it to track and fire on a second missile.

At the same time, two Metal Storm computerized machine-gun turrets on the *Zumwalt's* port and starboard sides came out of sleep mode. The weapons started to move back and forth, tracking the incoming cruise missiles with what looked like a predator's patience. Then they locked targets and fired. The brief electronic zipping sound the guns made when they fired was as anticlimactic as it was effective; thousands of bullets shot out all at the same instant.

The Russian Zvezda KH-31 missiles were programmed to feint and dodge as they flew just above the ocean surface in order to complicate a defense's firing solution. That tactic was of no use against the Metal Storm, as the missiles flew right into what was almost literally a wall of bullets.

"Seven missiles left," said the tactical action officer.

"Activate *Utah*'s radar beacon," said Simmons.

The remaining seven missiles' ramjets kicked in, accelerating them to nearly three times the speed of sound as they closed on the task force, flying just fifty feet above the rippling sea surface.

As another missile was plucked away by a laser fire, the missiles broke formation like a startled flight of birds. Their targeting program picked out the largest ships in the task force. Two missiles vectored off toward the *Zumwalt*; two turned for the USS *New York*, a twenty-five-thousand-ton amphibious transport dock ship; two homed in on the USS *America*.

Aboard the *Zumwalt*, the Metal Storm turrets zip-fired again, and one of the incoming missiles turning toward the *America* disappeared with a spray of shrapnel.

Simmons held his headset mike close to his mouth with one hand and braced himself against the railing of the ship mission center's second story with the other, looking at the sailors below him. "All hands, all hands. Incoming missiles, prepare for impact."

As the two missiles sped toward *Zumwalt*, one appeared to twitch. It broke off and slammed into the *Utah*, the missile's electronic brain registering what a human brain would have felt as satisfaction when it found its supposed target. The decoy ship exploded with a massive eruption of air and water.

The second cruise missile stayed true to its targeting-software designer's intent. It made a final course correction and then enveloped the *Zumwalt* in a bloom of orange flame. The explosion rocked the ship, sending a shock wave through the mission center and tossing the captain over the balcony's railing.

When he came to, Simmons found himself on the lower level of the ship mission center. He pulled himself up by the arm of the radar operator's chair. Richter reached over and gave him a hand and then turned back to her screens. His back ached, but otherwise he seemed fine. Less so the room. Two of the wall screens had fallen off their mounts, one hitting the tactical action officer, who looked to have a broken collarbone. Acrid smoke made Simmons's eyes water.

"Somebody get the air back on," he shouted. He looked for Cortez. He had been beside him a second ago, but now he was gone.

"XO! Damage report!" said Simmons.

The air started to clear in the room as the fans switched on, but the stink of fire and plastic remained. If they made it through, they were going to smell like this for weeks, Simmons mused.

"EV system back online, sir," called Cortez. He tracked the ship's self-diagnostics on his glasses. "Working on the damage report."

The voice came from the room's upper deck. Simmons raced back up the steps and saw Cortez kneeling, helping a sailor into his chair.

Cortez stood, straightened his glasses, and gave Simmons the battle-damage update as far as he knew it. The missile warhead had detonated just fore of the superstructure. The good news was all the fires were contained to the impact site, and ATHENA, propulsion, and radar were online.

The rest was bad news. The only operative external camera showed smoke and flame shrouding the ship's forward superstructure, blackening the whole surface. The laser turret on that side had evidently popped out of its mount before it settled back into place. The shock of the explosion had knocked loose power cables across the ship.

"Damage-control team is already on the way," he said. "Fire-bots and ship's suppression system are operative." Two more of the monitors flickered back on as more of the ship's external cameras rebooted. The faces of both officers fell at the images.

The *New York* listed over on its port side, almost at a forty-five-degree angle to the water's surface. The image zoomed in on the two smoldering holes in the sides of its hull, which were sucking more and more water into the bowels of the ship, dragging it down. Sailors leaped from the superstructure into the flaming waters around it, only to disappear as the ship rolled over on top of them.

Better off was the *America,* but not by much. The missile had apparently gone into the opening of its elevator lift. A delicate-looking mushroom cloud hung above the hole ripped in its flight deck. Secondary explosions from aviation fuel stored below punched jets of flame out into the air. Yet for all the smoke and fire, the ship looked steady in the water.

"How many?" said Simmons.

"*New York* had already disembarked most of their Marines, so ATHENA is reporting five-hundred-plus KIA or missing. *America,* another eight hundred and twenty-five. Those numbers will change as data updates," Cortez replied softly.

"I meant our ship," said Simmons.

"System shows seven dead, twenty-two wounded," said Cortez. "Four missing."

"My dad?" asked Simmons, lowering his voice. He squinted, suppressing something he did not want to feel now, or ever.

"No, sir. He's registering as active with the damage-control team below decks," said Cortez, placing his glasses on top of his head, transfixed by the sight of the hull of the now-capsized *New York* slipping under the waves.

Simmons didn't allow himself to feel any relief at the news. He gripped the railing until the tendons in his hands surrendered to the pain. The discomfort cleared his head and focused his attention.

"Helmsman, move us over parallel to the *America,*" said Simmons. "They're going to need our help fighting those fires."

USS *Zumwalt,* Below Decks

Mike followed the caterpillar-like fire-bot down the smoky passageway, knowing it would lead him to where he was needed most.

"Hit it over there," he heard Davidson say, his voice muffled through a smoke hood. Already the blaze was nearly under control. Brooks wielded an extinguisher, spraying foam and coolant on the seared metal and melted composite. Davidson gave the Mohawked kid a thumbs-up, the kind of silent compliment that meant the most to the young man. The fire-bot scooted ahead and detonated its fire-retardant-chemical payload near the Russian missile's impact point.

As the smoke cleared, daylight from the irregular oval hole in the deck above them punched through with a spotlight's intensity. Mike had Brooks spray the walls again, and he climbed up carefully to put his head through so he could see the deck-side damage. The missile appeared to have struck as the ship rolled, which deflected its blast skyward, not into the hull. The heat, though, had seared the entire superstructure, melting the composite material into something that looked more like cooled lava than the creased lines of the radar-deflecting design. He took in the wider view beyond, the Z edging closer to the burning USS *America*, two of its fire hoses spraying toward it. Mike looked down and spotted a figure splayed out on a litter being rushed somewhere by another sailor and a corpsman. It was Parker; the big sailor was crying as he tried to move a blackened arm. Mike rested his head on his forearm briefly, suddenly fatigued, and then began to climb down.

"Superstructure's all melted to shit," said Mike, pulling off his smoke hood. Davidson did the same, coughing slightly. Brooks left his hood on.

"Take off your hood, Mo, surgeon general's orders. It's not the smoking that's going to kill you today," said Mike, inhaling deeply.

Brooks reluctantly pulled the hood off and blinked bloodshot eyes.

Mike turned to Davidson. "We need to seal and reinforce that material up there; if we get into any kind of seas, it's going to get wet down here fast."

"When's that going to happen?" said Davidson. "Chinese missiles don't care about whatever sea state we're in."

"No," said Mike. "But I do. Take care of the ship, and it'll take care of you. You should know that by now."

"We can slap some epoxy and Kevlar ply up there, then brace it. Sound good?" asked Davidson, digging in his right ear, trying to clear it.

"It'll do," said Mike. "Your ears okay?"

Davidson nodded and said, "Everything's tinny-sounding. But don't worry, Chief, I can still hear you if you need to chew my ass out."

The radio slung over Mike's right shoulder started to squawk. "Chief? This is the captain," his son said, as if he needed to identify himself to his own father. "What's your status? Over."

"I'm okay, but we're counting multiple wounded, mainly burns and broken bones and burst eardrums. We've got a hole about twelve foot wide and some fire and heat damage. You can kiss whatever stealth signature we had goodbye. Fortunately, the missile didn't dig too deep. No structural damage that I can see. Main laser turret is going to need some major repair hours to get back into alignment, but we look to still be in business with the rail gun. I've got a damage-control party working on the hole. It's above the water line, but I want it sealed up."

"Thank you, Chief. I knew I could count on you," his son said. Mike could hear the relief in his voice, and he wasn't sure whether it was for him or for the role he was filling. Today, either would do.

USS *Zumwalt* Ship Mission Center

Captain Simmons felt a tap on his shoulder: Cortez letting him know they had finally gotten the link to the task force command network back up.

The video image filled the display screen, and Jamie looked at a grim-faced officer, Commander Alexander Anderson. Years ago, when he and Jamie were both just out of ROTC, they had served together onboard the USS *Chafee*. Anderson now had command of the *Port Royal*, which had pulled to the other side of the *America* and was adding the water from its fire hoses to help beat down the flames.

"Jamie, it's good to see you in one piece," said Anderson. The officer had a slim face and narrow shoulders, and his uniform always looked slightly oversize. It was as if any extra calories his body had went to fueling his legendary brain.

"Same here," said Simmons. "Ship's holding together. Crew too. We're still in the fight. Any word from Admiral Murray?"

"She's gone, sir," said Anderson, shifting back to a formal tone now that he saw his old friend was unhurt. "Confirmed by the *America*'s quartermaster, a petty officer who seems to be all that's left in command there. Reports all power out. She had to yell over to us with a bullhorn." He paused. "Captain Simmons, you know what this means. If that petty officer is right, and we have to assume she is, at this point . . . with Admiral Murray dead, and Captain Brookings on the *America* . . ."

"I'm task force commander . . ." Simmons said, realizing what Anderson was saying.

"Yes, sir," said Anderson. "Longboard is yours. We're in good hands, I know it."

The two of them went silent for a few seconds as the moment sank in, and then they turned to business.

"With your permission, sir, I'd like to begin evacuating the *America*'s crew."

Simmons nodded even as he was trying to make up his mind.

"I don't like the idea of scuttling a ship still afloat," Anderson continued, "but I like the idea of towing a forty-thousand-ton weight with an enemy fleet coming in behind us even less."

Simmons finally realized what Anderson assumed their next course of action would be.

"We are not leaving behind either *America* or the Marines onshore," said Simmons. "We will evacuate the wounded off the ship, but hold this line of position until our main fleet or the enemy's arrives, whichever happens first."

Anderson shifted slightly sideways, as if he did not quite believe what he was seeing and hearing. His eyes squinted and his brow wrinkled in what Simmons recognized was an eloquent objection forming, the kind of argument they might have had back in the *Chafee*'s wardroom when they were young officers. Then the look washed away, and Anderson nodded with an exaggerated bob of his head.

"Yes, sir," he said.

"We have to locate the enemy," said Simmons. "It's that simple. I'm ordering *Orzel* out on picket duty and deploying all our Fire Scouts to maximum range. And God help us if they don't find what's out there coming for us."

Vicinity of USS *America*, Pacific Ocean

He'd been close to greatness, thought Denisov. And yet now here he was, wondering whether he should try to take off his flight boots for added buoyancy. He slowly kicked his legs, knowing he was too far offshore to do anything but drift until something ate him or one of the

American ships in the near distance plucked him from the water.

He lay back against the collar of his inflated life vest, watching the strange, thin, wedge-shaped American drones circle high overhead. They were now flying a combat air patrol against an airstrike that wouldn't come. "I was it, you stupid *abtomat*, there's no more!" he screamed. Mindless machines, but lethal; he had to give them that.

A tingling at the back of his neck made him spin around. Seen from thousands of feet in the air, the Pacific looked inviting. But floating in it, he thought these waters were as dark and foreboding as his worst nightmare. Something was nearby, he could feel it.

An enormous black shape slowly moved through the sea maybe thirty yards beneath him. It surfaced a few hundred feet away, puffed a blast of air, and then went back under. No shark could be that big. He sighed with relief. A humpback whale, perhaps, content to eat krill, not Russian pilots.

He was alone for a little while longer. He was close enough to see the still-smoking USS *America*, and he was confident the little aircraft carrier had been the one his missile had hit. He watched the chiseled form of a massive destroyer pull alongside it; sailors appeared to be tethering the ships together. He recognized it as a *Zumwalt*-class ship and decided instead that had been the one his missile had hit; far better to have hit the more exotic creature with his last shot.

With his eyes stinging from the salt and sun, Denisov watched the litters of wounded men and women being passed off the burning *America* via ziplines strung between the two vessels. The sailors were bound up like mummies as they traveled from their dying ship to another with an uncertain future.

From the stern of the strange-looking ship, three small forms lifted off. When they formed up, he identified them as MQ-8 Fire Scout drones, scaled-down helicopters with pinched noses that looked like they had never made it out of aviation adolescence. Another two lifted off from the ship tethered to the other side of the *America*; some kind of cruiser or destroyer, he couldn't tell.

The drone helicopters paused in formation and then each set off in a different direction, looking like foraging steel wasps. They flew low, hugging the waves. One of the Fire Scouts flew almost directly overhead, the drone oblivious to Denisov as the force of its rotor's downdraft pushed him under the waves. At that moment, Denisov realized that maybe the Americans wouldn't come for him.

USS *Zumwalt* Ship Mission Center

The tactical holograph still hadn't come back on, so the fuzzy image was carried across the entire bank of monitors on the wall. Given how the holographic projectors seemed to get knocked offline in every fight, Simmons wondered why they even bothered with the finicky high-tech contraptions. The grainy image they were watching looked like one of those old low-resolution YouTube videos.

"Sir, the task force is a mix of Chinese and Russian ships," said the *Zumwalt*'s intelligence officer. "And ATHENA agrees, based on the EM signatures the Fire Scout is picking up."

The live image kept shaking as if somebody were swatting at the drone, but the shaking was only the drone's autonomous-flight software keeping the rotorcraft as low as possible to the waves, dipping into the troughs between them for cover.

"Freeze that for me," said Simmons. The image on the screen locked, and the officer zoomed in on the superstructure of a large ship that the long-range camera had picked up on the upward ride of a wave.

"What a beast. That's gotta be the *Zheng He*."

"Yes, sir. Looks like it," said the intelligence officer. He moved the still image of the massive Chinese capital ship off to one screen and resumed the live camera view. The video feed began to jiggle and shake, and the Fire Scout picked up speed, giving up its cover, as the wind shifted and the troughs of the waves grew shallow. It was a panic move, the robot's algorithms having run out of good options to evade detection.

The shaking image then showed a series of smoky trails lifting up from the task force and flying toward the camera.

"Uh-oh" was all the intelligence officer could say before the image blanked out.

Cortez spoke up, reading from his glasses, as Simmons watched the replay of the Fire Scout's frantic final moments.

"Between the visuals and SIGINT collection, ATHENA is reporting

it as seven surface ships: three *Sovremenny*-class anti-surface destroyers, two Type Fifty-Four frigates, one *Luyang*-class guided missile destroyer, and a battle cruiser, most likely the *Admiral Zheng He*. They're
making twenty-five knots. They're likely coming at us off a loose fix
they got from the air attack."

Simmons took in the small amount of information he had and realized he needed to think like an admiral and consider the entire Longboard task force, not just his own ship.

"But where are their carriers?" said Simmons out loud, mostly to
himself.

"No further information, sir," said Cortez. "ATHENA can run some
models to guess where they are, but it'll essentially be throwing the
same darts at the wall as we are."

"We'll take what we can get. We need to hit that task force while we
can. Release Puffin batteries," said Simmons.

Cortez barked out the orders. The lines linking them to *America*
were fed out to give space between the two ships. Then the deck
hatches for the *Zumwalt*'s vertical launch cells all flipped up simultaneously, revealing a line of dark openings, each twenty-eight inches
wide. One after another, a series of thirteen-foot-long cruise missiles,
eighty in total, popped out from the vertical launch cells, like unte-
thered jack-in-the-boxes.

Originally known as the Naval Strike Missile, the Puffin was a
stealthy replacement for the old Penguin missile. Though it flew under
the speed of sound, the Norwegian-designed missile could evade radar detection and had a range of more than 180 miles, which made it
lethal, especially when fired in great numbers.

The missiles seemed to hang in the air for an instant as their solid-
fuel rocket boosters ignited, and then they arced off into the sky. When
their boosters burned out, they were jettisoned in a rain of metal that
bombarded the water below. The missiles then raced through the sky
powered by turbojet engines that took them at just over five hundred
miles per hour to the general vicinity of the Fire Scout's last known
location. Each Puffin then began autonomously hunting, using its own
imaging infrared seeker to match anything it saw against an onboard
database of authorized targets.

It was a ship's wake that gave the enemy's fleet away. A Puffin missile at the far end of the spread detected the faint V-shaped lines of white foam on the ocean surface and began to circle in the area. An FL-3000 Red Banner short-range air-defense missile rose up to knock it down, but not before the Puffin had shared its data with the rest of the flock and beckoned them to join in.

One by one, the other missiles began to converge on the area. Three more Puffins were sacrificed to defensive missiles, establishing the perimeter of the task force's defenses. The robotic swarm then circled, just out of range, with machine patience as more and more missiles joined. While they waited, though, the task force below fired off its own volley of cruise missiles at the Puffins' point of departure.

Admiral Zheng He Bridge

Admiral Wang now knew his gamble had been the right one; the instant that the garbled radio calls from Hawaii had burned through the Americans' jamming, his staff had looked at him with new esteem. He truly was the equal of the ancient strategist with whom he had seemed to be conversing before them.

Yet he also knew that the way history would remember this moment depended on all the powers and tools now beyond the realm of human plans. Even the great leaders of old could not have understood this era.

"How many of our cruise missiles were we able to get off at their force?" he asked his aide.

"Sixty-nine, sir," said the aide, nervously looking at the gathering swarm of American missiles, blurs on the horizon, as they circled the task force. Then, seeming to make up their machine minds, the swarm of American missiles began to approach at sea-skimming level from all directions of the compass. The missiles operated in unison, all turning inward simultaneously, but each individual missile made small, slight hops up and down, randomized maneuvers designed to throw off targeting locks.

"It should be sufficient," said Wang calmly. "More than enough to make this our day in the end."

Another wave of Red Banner missiles was loosed at the Puffins, which were now coming within range, followed by the machine cannon opening fire. The *Zheng He* mounted three Type 1170 close-in defense systems, each with an eleven-barrel 30 mm machine cannon. But the cannon were now indistinguishable from one another, merging into a single tearing sound as all thirty-three gun barrels fired at once.

Wang offered a look of calm and put his hand on his aide's shoulder as if to reassure him, buying himself a few seconds to take in the scene.

Three angry red fingers pointed out from the ship, followed by scores more. The tracer rounds from the other 30 mm gun systems throughout the fleet were visible even in the bright of day. The way the lines waved and weaved through the clouds of white smoke exhaust left by the defensive missiles reminded Wang of his grandchildren playing with flashlights in the dark. He didn't need to monitor the count on the display screen to know its hard truth: not all of the enemy's swarm could be shot down before they began diving toward their targets.

The Puffins came in low, designed to detonate their 275-pound warheads just at the water line of the targets. A sickening series of booms began, one after another, in quick succession. Wang watched a pair of missiles disappear from sight as they slammed into the *Huangshi,* a Type 54A frigate, rupturing its bow with a fiery spout. The open bow filled with water as the ship plowed forward, its momentum ensuring its demise. As the bow went deeper into the waves, the frigate's stern lifted, flashing its spinning props. Then the *Huangshi*'s steel hull shook from an internal explosion, likely a detonation in its engine room.

"'If one is not fully cognizant of the evils of waging war, he cannot be fully cognizant either of how to turn it to best account,'" he quoted Sun-Tzu aloud. No one heard him above the noise.

His eyes caught a blur of movement, and then the entire *Zheng He* shuddered and the klaxons rang out. A damage-control display showed a strike in the far stern. He walked the bridge deck to assess, his view obscured by smoke. Then the wind shifted and blew the smoke in the other direction, revealing a ten-meter hole of twisted metal and a small fire burning in the deck below. Not sufficient to take them out of action.

Wang turned away from the scene to see how the fleet's other ships were faring. His role was to stay above it all, to maintain his wits while others let the moment consume them.

As he panned his binoculars, the *Admiral Ushakov*, one of the massive *Sovremenny*-class destroyers the Russians had sent, was settling in the water, four open holes along the portside water line. It would not survive, he knew.

But Wang also knew that its missile batteries were already empty, eight of the cruise missiles in the counterbarrage already on their way to the American fleet. He walked back to his ready room. The human decisions had been made; all he could do now was wait with composure.

USS *Zumwalt* Ship Mission Center

Simmons silently observed the video feed on one of the wall monitors displaying his father's damage-control party rushing to apply what was essentially a bandage to the composite superstructure, covering up the missile impact point near the laser turret with epoxy. He knew what his father was thinking, that it was fortunate the stinging chemical binders were more powerful than whatever smells were wafting over from the sad stink of the *America*.

"Sir, we've got sixty-plus targets incoming," said the radar officer. "Flight profile of cruise missiles. Arrival within two minutes."

On another monitor, Simmons watched as a wounded sailor in a litter being carried across the void between the two hulls started to scream and wave his arms. The litter stopped and then reversed direction, pulled back toward the *America*. He couldn't blame them. They knew what was coming for all of them, and he would have wanted to end his days on his own ship too.

The *Port Royal* tossed lines and began to pull away from the *America* at flank speed.

"Detach lines from the *America*?" asked Cortez.

"No, we're staying here. *America* can't take another hit; that's our job now," said Simmons. "That's why I placed our damaged side on the interior."

The screen showed the *Port Royal* firing a long series of SM-6 missiles and then disappearing behind a cloud of brown smoke from its own weapons fire.

"Captain, she fired off her entire magazine," said the *Zumwalt*'s tactical action officer. "First intercept in twenty-five seconds."

"We're back where we started, it seems," said Simmons to Cortez. The XO knew he was referring to the attack they'd weathered together at Pearl Harbor.

"Maybe they need to put us on different ships next time, sir," said Cortez, offering a smile.

"I'll make sure of it," said Simmons. "You'll get your own ship after this."

"Splash seven bogeys," said the radar officer, narrating the *Port Royal*'s progress in whittling down the enemy cruise missiles. As he spoke, he made gentle waving movements with his right arm, using a cuff on his forearm to switch between the system's radar bands to cover all the incoming data.

As the enemy's missiles advanced closer, the various assault ships in range fired off medium- and short-range Seasparrow and Rolling Airframe missiles in hopes of plinking more of the cruise missiles.

"Eleven enemy missiles left," the radar officer reported.

"ATHENA, full autonomous mode! Authorization Simmons, Four, Seven, Romeo, Tango, Delta," said Simmons.

The smallest weapons became the most important once again. On the *Port Royal*, the revolving 20 mm Gatling guns of the ship's close-in weapons system added the metallic roar of a chainsaw biting into metal.

On the *Zumwalt*, the undamaged laser-point defense turret fired steadily. The twin Metal Storm guns tracked the incoming missiles and fired another wall of bullets into their path. They pivoted, reactivated, and again fired off thousands of rounds in the time it took to clap your hands once.

"Metal Storm magazines emptied. We're out," said the weapons officer. "Five incoming missiles left: two at us, two at *Port Royal*, and one's split off for the *San Antonio*," he said, indicating the closest of the amphibious ships they'd been trying to screen.

"We could get your dad out on deck and have him throw up a screen of foul language," said Cortez.

Simmons looked at Cortez, taking in his relaxed demeanor. The XO became more poised as the situation worsened. Simmons realized that

Cortez was the kind of officer he himself had always wanted to be.

He reached out and gripped the young officer's artificial arm. "It's been an honor."

North of Oahu, Pacific Ocean

Roscoe Coltan cursed at his raft for the hundredth time as it nearly swamped when he tried to get on his knees for a better view of the ships. He recognized the big one that looked like a jagged piece of metal as the *Zumwalt*, the fleet's ugly duckling, he'd heard. It was tied up next to a mini–aircraft carrier that poured smoke into the air.

In the distance there was the shriek of engines coming in low: cruise missiles. A flash of light as a Gatling gun of some kind fired from one of the other ships, an Aegis destroyer of some sort. Then the water all around him burst into hundreds of ripples. He didn't know whether to cheer the weapons on or curse them until one of the missiles exploded.

"Splash one, assholes!" Roscoe cheered.

He stared at the silent *Zumwalt*, willing the ship to offer up some defense. "C'mon, brothers, do something!"

Suddenly there were two simultaneous explosions on the aft and bow sections of the *Zumwalt*. The sound of the twin detonations reached him a moment later.

Another thundering crash in the direction of the Aegis ship followed.

Seeing the smoke pouring from the ships was as painful as seeing his own jet spiral into the ocean after his ejection. Roscoe felt his eyes well up and held his head in his hands. His entire Boneyard Flight was gone. Nobody remained under his command. And now the ships they had given their lives to protect were on the verge of going under. He was alone.

Except he wasn't. He took off his helmet and ran a finger over the red-and-black lightning bolts that lined the crest.

Then he braced himself, leaned over the side of the raft, and scooped up a helmet full of water. Then again. And again.

The paddling was slow going, but he told himself he wasn't going to stop until he reached the *Zumwalt*. The Navy clearly still needed his help.

USS *Zumwalt*, Below Decks

The unconscious sailor outweighed Vern by at least a hundred pounds, but that did not stop her from trying to drag him by his ankles away from the flames at the end of the passageway. She could manage only five feet before she had to stop and catch her breath in the dark. Gagging on sharp smoke, she strained to put more distance between them and the fire. She hoped she was going toward safety, but anything was better than where she was coming from.

As she struggled on, coughing, she watched two fire-bots worm their way past her and advance into the swirl of flames and toxic smoke ravaging the room. They detonated their fire retardant and began tagging the bodies they found with strobes, giving the room a disorienting celestial look.

"Here, Dr. Li," said Brooks, coming up from behind her. "We're gonna do this together."

She nodded and continued to strain against the weight of the limp body.

"On three, here we go," said Brooks, lifting the man under his arms. "You keep on the feet there."

In the light of the strobes, she could see the unconscious man was wearing coveralls, seared black in places so that the fabric had melted against the pale skin on his legs. She could not yet see his face.

"Shit, is this the chief?" said Brooks.

Vern blinked a tear as she knelt forward and caught the smell of leather and bay rum mixing with burned plastic and singed hair.

USS *Zumwalt* Ship Mission Center

Simmons tried to focus on the face staring at him from the wall screen.

The man spoke before Simmons could remember his name.

"Jesus, Jamie, I'm looking at the Z. Half the ship is on fire!" the man said.

"Still afloat," said Simmons slowly, still not sure who he was talking to. "Give me your situation."

"We took one amidships. Fires are contained, but we're down to fifteen knots, maximum. More important, we shot our wad in that last volley," the man said. "Our missile magazines are spent. I've got the CIWS, which have only a few more fires left. After that, spitballs is all we've got to shoot down missiles."

The fog lifted. Anderson. The USS *Port Royal*.

"Well done, in any case. Tell your crew they saved a lot of ships today," said Simmons.

The *Zumwalt*'s fire-control officer shouted: "Sirs, we have an incoming target. It looks to be a surveillance drone. We're jamming its radar, but it'll be in visual range in four minutes. I'm tasking the Shrikes to shoot it down."

Simmons opened his mouth to speak, then pursed his lips in thought.

"Belay that order. Let it see us," said Simmons.

"Say again, sir?" said Anderson, worry showing in the crow's-feet around his eyes.

"They already know where we are. I want them to see us this way," said Simmons.

Admiral Zheng He, Admiral Wang's Stateroom

The door to his stateroom shuddered, but fortunately not from another explosion, just his aide's knock.

Admiral Wang's aide entered, carrying a tablet computer.

"Sir, I am sorry to disturb you during your contemplation, but we have new reconnaissance information. One of the Soar Eagles launched from Guam at your order has finally entered the area. It is beaming back information line of sight to us."

The Soar Dragon was a derivative of the U.S. Global Hawk unmanned aerial spy plane. The original American drone was a large spy plane, its wingspan greater than a 737 jetliner's, built to replace the manned U-2.

Chinese designers had added a few flourishes, sweeping the wings back to attach to the tail. Looking like a plane crossed with a kite, their version had a better lift-to-drag ratio and less complex flight controls. But the tradeoff was that the engine had to be mounted above the tail, as in a commuter jet, giving the Soar Eagle a slow cruising speed.

As he scanned the images of warships smoking and sinking, Wang thought the wait was almost worth it. The only ships unscathed were the slow, toothless American transport vessels now waiting to be scooped up.

"Show me this one," said Wang, tapping the image of the largest warship in the task force. It was immediately recognizable as their novel *Zumwalt* class. So the Americans had indeed brought back their strange experiment, just as the intelligence reports had claimed. It confirmed all his assumptions that this was the last victory the Directorate would need, just as he had argued to the Presidium. Using a ship like that was simultaneously an act of innovation and of desperation. Indeed, the same was true of the Americans' entire operation today.

The image zoomed in on the massive ship, tied up next to one of their stricken small helicopter carriers. The warship was indeed sleek and lethal-looking, but it was now dead in the water, smoking from what looked to be at least three missile strikes. Smoldering steel debris littered its deck, blocking its main gun turret.

He walked toward the bridge using the exterior gangway. Taking the longer route gave him the chance to breathe in the fresh air, to savor the salinity and the moment itself. He fished in his pants pocket for a stim tab and unwrapped it, then tossed the foil bubble into the wind. He had resisted taking one at the beginning of the battle, the need to exude calm being paramount. Now was the time for energetic aggression.

"'Prize the quick victory, not the protracted engagement,'" he quoted to the aide. "Signal to the task force for all ships to advance at flank speed. It is time to close in for the kill and end this war."

USS *Zumwalt*, Below Decks

Mike peered into the dark hallway, inhaling deeply from the firefighting breathing unit. Until they could vent the unit, the air was too toxic for anyone to spend time here, but the louvered covers on the vent openings had melted shut and it was going to take some doing, or at least a few minutes with a crowbar, to get those back open.

"Bridge, this is damage-control team. Bridge, this is damage-control team," said Mike. His voice echoed inside the firefighting mask.

"Glad you're okay, Chief," said a familiar voice. "What do you have for me?"

"Good to hear you too, son . . . sir. The news isn't good. Multiple casualties, more than I can keep track of. Starboard-side superstructure is melting; the composite just can't handle the hits and the heat. It's still a mess at the laser turret, and debris is blocking the rail gun's movement. That's not the real problem for the gun, though. Those shots took down the whole auxiliary power network. We've got break points across the ship," said Mike. "The VLS, well, we're not going to get our deposit back. Most of the cell hatches look like they got peeled back with a rusty can opener. But there's something worse away from the impact points. We've got reports of leaks below decks, and the superstructure and hull seam look iffy on the starboard, right below the helo deck."

"What's the good news?" said Simmons.

"Ship's afloat, and we're still breathing, you and I," his father responded.

"We need the ship in the fight. How long before I can get the laser and rail gun back online?" said the captain.

"Martin will be graduating college before that laser's back in business. Ninety minutes at least on the rail gun to clear it, and even then, who knows. But I'm not sure you heard me . . . sir. We're taking on water below. Even if it works, we can't shoot the rail gun and keep the ship afloat with no auxiliary power. We gotta have power for the pumps."

"Chief, just get the rail gun back online," said Simmons.

"Aye, Captain," said Mike. He paused and then added, "Or should I say Admiral? Heard you got a promotion."

"Not really," said Simmons.

"Well, congratulations either way," said Mike. "Wear it proud. I am."

"Just get the rail gun ready, Chief," said Simmons. "We're counting on you all down there."

Mike turned to address the crew, most of whom were working slowly, unable to shake their dazed looks.

"You heard the captain. Take stim tabs if ya got 'em, and then let's get to work," said Mike. "Brooks, have your team concentrate on getting this debris cut away topside. Dr. Li, you're with me, we're going to unfuck this wiring. Captain wants us back in the fight, and we're not going to let him down."

The crew scattered, foraging in their pockets for whatever stims they had left, not thinking about the last time they had had something to eat or a stretch of calm to sleep.

Vern, her hair matted with sweat, began to head down the passageway toward the rail-gun turret, but then she stopped and turned, her face angry.

"I thought I found you — your body," said Vern.

"Doesn't seem like it," said Mike.

"It was Davidson," said Vern. "He's gone."

"You confused me with that reeking tub of guts?" said Mike, knowing his old friend wouldn't want him to answer any other way.

She reached into a pocket on her vest just below her heart and pulled out two square foil packets. "This thing's stocked like a pharmacy," she said, handing one of the stim tabs to Mike.

He shook his head. "Not sure my heart can take it. I think, though, when we get back to shore I'll have a stiff drink. I think we've earned it."

"It's a date, then." She smiled.

USS *Zumwalt* Ship Mission Center

If it was possible to be calm aboard a sinking ship, the Z's crew was managing it. There was a studiousness in the mission center, as if the hull breaches below decks were the least of their problems. And to the captain of the *Zumwalt*, they were.

Cortez was below decks, checking on the largest breach. One of the monitors near the captain's chair, which Simmons still hated using, showed the view from Cortez's glasses. It was just aft and below where the superstructure joined the hull, a foot-long opening two inches wide. The worry was that it had ripped open on its own, almost like bark peeling from a tree. There were sure to be more such breaches soon.

"Sir, we've got a homing-pigeon drone coming in. It's from the *Orzel*," said the communications officer.

"Let's have it," said Simmons, feeling his stomach knot. If the Poles, safely hidden away beneath the ocean's surface, had broken cover to pass along a message, it had to be bad news.

"'Three enemy carriers detected,'" the officer read. "'Quadrant seventy-four X, fifty-six G. The *Shanghai* and two *Admiral Kuznetsov*–class carriers, one believed to be the Russian original and the other the *Liaoning*, accompanied by five escort ships. Will engage after communications drone launches.'" The communications officer stumbled through the next sentence. "'*Za wolność Naszą i Waszą*. For our freedom and yours.'"

"Anything more?" said Simmons.

"That's all we have, sir," said the officer. "Database has the closing lines as something from their history, a saying by doomed Polish resistance fighters."

Simmons was silent, thinking not of the Polish sailors, he shamefully realized, but of the need to decide the next course of action.

"Order the combat air patrol to that quadrant," said Simmons.

The tactical action officer cleared his throat before speaking in a parched voice: "Sir, they're armed only for air-to-air. They'll be able to engage the remaining enemy planes, but that's it. They're not carrying any bombs or anti-ship ordnance."

"You neglected to mention that tasking out our combat air patrol will also leave us naked without overhead cover," said Simmons.

"Yes, sir."

"Good; don't be afraid to challenge me when it is needed. Just not too often," said Simmons. "I understand your concern, but they're an asset we have to use, in this case just like the original designers of drones intended. Deadly, but disposable. Order them out, command protocol Divine Wind."

Fifty-Five Miles Northwest of the *Zumwalt*, Pacific Ocean

The remaining Shrikes climbed steeply up to sixty-five thousand feet and raced toward the coordinates provided by the *Orzel*. They flew in a tight stack of wedges, each pilotless aircraft programmed to hold itself exactly seventeen inches away from the next. The distance had been chosen by the Shrike software designer after reading that the closest that human pilots would risk was the eighteen inches of distance that Blue Angels pilots put between their planes during their Diamond 360 maneuver. The effect was to blur the drones' already small radar signatures into one.

Within minutes, the formation crossed the white wakes of the Russian and Chinese surface-ship formation, arced out in a wide curve.

They relayed the image back to the bridge of the *Zumwalt*.

"Sir, we have a video burst from the flight. They've got visuals on the enemy surface task force. Looks like the Puffin missiles took out three of the smaller ships, but four biggies, including the *Zheng He*, are steaming in our direction at flank speed, fifty-five miles out," said the tactical officer. "We're in their missile range now. I'm not sure why they haven't fired again."

"They're likely as low on missile stocks as we are," said Simmons. "Looks like they're planning on making it personal, finishing us off with guns."

"Redirect the drone flight at them?" said the tactical officer.

"No, taking out the enemy's remaining carriers is more important than even us," said Simmons. "Proceed as planned."

The drones flew onward past the surface ships, indifferent to both the tension that this bypass caused the American fleet and the relief it gave to the surface ships below.

Admiral Zheng He Bridge

The shouting on the bridge of the *Admiral Zheng He* subsided as the aircraft flew on. It had not been visible, but radar had initially picked it up at over thirteen miles overhead. They tried to shoot it out of the sky but it was impossible to get a radar lock. That it had not come in low pointed to its being one of the Americans' surveillance aircraft, perhaps one of their rumored high-altitude drones. They passed on the information to the aircraft carrier element's combat air patrol and ordered a pair of fighters to intercept.

A single surveillance plane would confirm the surface screening force's position to the Americans. But they would also know it didn't matter. His force was closing in on the remains of the U.S. task force to finish them off. Any kind of follow-up attack from the American mainland would come too late. They were alone, soon to be cut off, and as vulnerable as any enemy commander could hope. It would be an absolute victory, the kind Sun-Tzu had written about but never achieved in his own career.

Wang considered for a moment that perhaps, once his staff reviewed his command footage and records, he should write his own book.

USS *Zumwalt*, Forward Rail-Gun Turret

It was like being back on one of those road trips, the kids in the back seat of the station wagon constantly asking the same question over and over.

"Damage crew, how much longer?" said Captain Simmons into the radio.

Yet it also nagged the old man that it had taken this kind of moment for him to see his son at his best.

Mike took in the showers of welding sparks raining down onto the crew below decks frantically trying to repair the rail-gun loading mechanism and the power cable connections.

"Twenty minutes," said Mike.

"You have ten. That battle cruiser mounts one-hundred-thirty-millimeter main guns with a fifteen-mile range. You taught me boxing, so you know that I need that rail gun to be punching at them before we get inside their swing."

"If we're going to fight the rail gun, Vern says we really are going to need to power down the bilge and auxiliary pumps. We can't do that, sir, not now. This ship wasn't designed to take hits. Big, top-heavy design like this, we risk taking on too much water and we'll roll."

"Chief, I understand. Just focus on your job and I'll do mine."

The little bastard is even starting to talk like me, thought Mike.

USS *Zumwalt* Ship Mission Center

The display on the far wall showed the rail-gun turret free of the debris, but then a spray of sparks shot out from one of the holes punched in the deck. Out leaped Brooks; his work overalls were already singed at the legs, and now they were blackened about the shoulders. He was literally smoking. He threw an acetylene cutting torch down on the deck and cursed, first at the malfunctioning tool, then at the hole in the ship, and then at something in the distance, evidently the enemy fleet. Then the young sailor picked up the tool and went back into the hole. In that action, Jamie saw his father's influence.

"Sir, we've got a contact burning through the jamming. It must be close," Richter at the radar station said. "Yes, I have the enemy task force at forty miles out. Four ships, one capital-ship size. That must be the *Zheng He*."

The rail-gun turret tried again to swivel, but it just shook back and forth like a muzzled dog. Sneaking peeks up from their workstations, the crew whispered, getting visibly anxious.

Simmons cued his headset again, leaning forward to get a better look. "Damage control, how much longer is it going to take?"

"Jamie, I am not trying to assemble your goddamn bicycle on Christmas Eve! Just leave us alone and we'll get it fixed," said Mike.

A few of the crew stifled laughs as the conversation played out on the room's speakers. Simmons grimaced in exasperation and shook his head, throwing the headset at the deck.

"Radar's picked them up, sir. Thirty-nine miles now," said Richter. "I'm guessing they've developed the same tactical picture we have. They're now closing directly at us at flank speed."

138 Miles Northwest of the *Zumwalt*, Pacific Ocean

The two Chinese J-31 fighter jets from the task force's combat air patrol elevated to follow the incoming target and then went to afterburner to close for a firing solution.

The pilots were angry. They hadn't been sent on the strike mission against the enemy fleet, which had most likely kept them from dying, but it left them furious at their impotence, all the more so when their wing mates didn't return. And now, twenty thousand feet below, the *Liaoning*, the carrier they had launched from, their home for the last two years, had smoke spilling out of its stern. A submarine had somehow snuck close enough to fire off a torpedo before the destroyer escort had sunk it. They had been bystanders yet again, powerless against an attack that had left their home listing badly to starboard. They were unsure if they would be able to land on it at the end of their patrol or if they would have to divert to one of the other carriers. That was a question to be answered later, though. Now, at least they could vent their fury on the American drone.

The lead pilot radioed that the radar signature of the surveillance drone coming in above them at seventy-seven thousand feet was strange. It didn't fit any profile in the recognition software, which conformed with the report from the surface-fleet element. He fired a long-range PL-12 air-to-air missile at it, and then a second one, just for good measure.

Moments later, there was an explosion above in the distance, followed by another. And yet the radar signature stayed on his screen. Still climbing altitude to close for visual range, his wing mate fired off a PL-10 short-range heat-seeking missile as added insurance.

As the fighter jets reached their maximum altitude of sixty thousand feet, they saw what looked like the silhouette of an arrowhead falling from the sky, a triangular drone of some sort diving back down to their level. At sixty-two thousand feet, when the third missile reached the target, its proximity warhead exploded a spray of metal shrapnel a mere hundred feet away. The arrowhead was clearly hit, showing a burst of orange flame and then smoke trailing as it fell toward them.

Yet as the arrowhead passed by them, the damaged drone seemed to shed a layer; a smoking plane peeled off. The rest of the triangular drone continued to dive at maximum speed at the task force below. As the two pilots pushed their fighter jets down to follow, straining against the g-forces as they lost altitude, their threat warnings began to sound. Somehow in the midst of its steep dive, the drone below had fired off six Sidewinder missiles, which turned and raced back up at them. They attempted to pull out, but it was too late.

The air-defense systems on the ships below tried to pick up a radar lock, but while the fighter pilots had had a silhouette view of the drones, the systems were faced with only thin, sixteen-inch wing edges coated with radar-absorbent material. At thirty thousand feet, a firing solution finally crystalized, but just as the system locked, the target seemed to dissolve. The Shrike drones spread out from one another, a closed network among them sharing a targeting algorithm that ensured they did not all select the same destination point. Lookouts on the ships began to visually pick out what looked like seven thin lines falling down toward them. At twenty-three thousand feet, one of the lines disappeared in an explosion, hit by a rising air-defense missile.

When the drones were at twenty thousand feet, the task force's machine cannon opened up, and their tracer bullets tried to connect with six thin, sixteen-inch wedges from miles away. The drones maxed their power, creating sonic booms that fell behind them as they accelerated well past the speed of sound.

Another drone was hit at a range of six thousand feet, leaving the five remaining Shrikes to reapportion their targets in the final seconds of their terminal fall. Flying down at maximum speed from almost directly overhead, an arrowhead slammed into the flight deck of each of the two undamaged carriers. The speed of the dive combined with the drone's mass drove each robotic kamikaze deep into the bowels of the ship. From five decks below, fiery explosions shot out through the gaping holes they had left. Then the explosions traveled across the length of the carriers, turning them into massive fireballs.

The listing *Liaoning* turned out to be the lucky one. The remaining Shrike hit its flight deck at an angle. It punched straight through the tilted flight deck and then went out through the hangar deck and into the sea below. The drone felt no disappointment at its failure to completely sink its target, just as its wing mates felt no pride at their success.

USS *Zumwalt* Ship Mission Center

"Sir, *Port Royal* is requesting to be released from escort duty so it can advance on the enemy force."

"Permission denied. That battle cruiser's main gun range is two miles longer than the *Port Royal*'s gun. They'll just stand off and pound the *Port Royal*, especially at that reduced speed. You heard the old man on the radio. Let's give him a little more time before we play the martyr," said Simmons, sounding confident for the crew but inside hoping he was right to trust his father.

"Range is now twenty-eight miles," said Richter, tracking the four ships of the enemy surface task force in, since the two fleets were now too close for radar jamming to be effective. When the ships were roughly thirteen miles away, they would come into visual range and her job would become redundant.

"Are they following the amphibs?" Simmons had ordered the transport ships in the task force to position themselves where they could support the troops ashore but were as distant as possible from the brewing battle between the surface ships.

"No, sir. Still steaming toward us," said Cortez. "They want to finish this."

"So do we," said Captain Simmons.

USS *Zumwalt*, Forward Rail-Gun Turret

Vern dried her palm on her pant leg again and then picked up the plastic soldering gun by its greasy handle. This was the last section of wiring to lock back down, which she was thankful for because she could not take any more of the smoke, the smell, and the confinement inside the rail-gun turret. As for the fear, she had long since set that aside, balled it up somewhere next to the nausea in her stomach.

"Almost there," she said, knowing that Mike was less than a foot from her and could see it just as well. The radio on his tool harness squawked and she heard the captain's voice.

"All right, damage control. Time's up. Clear out."

Vern pulled the trigger on the soldering gun again and ran it smoothly over the surface of the insulated coupling for the rail gun's high power line; the plastic of the fitting liquefied and melded together.

She heard Mike curse under his breath. He cleared his throat and keyed the microphone with an aggressive click: "*Zumwalt* Actual, we need one more minute. That's all. Vern's literally down to the last wires here."

"If he doesn't give us more time, we're going to get a cold weld. It's not going to fully fuse, and the bond might snap right at the seam line if it gets any added force on it," Vern said.

"Damage control, repeat, clear decks, copy!" said the captain.

"When I say we're almost there, you know damn well I mean it," said Mike. "Hold for just one minute. Do you copy?"

Klaxon horns sounded an alert across the ship.

"All hands, this is the captain, clear decks; rail-gun battery preparing to fire. Powering down main systems."

Vern looked up at Mike and then went back to soldering, a wisp rising from the soldering gun's hot tip. Mike grabbed her around the waist and carried her out of the turret and through two hatches. At last, he set her on her feet.

"Your son is really a pain in the ass. Where did he get that from?" said Vern, wiping the sweat from her glasses with the inside of one of her pants pockets.

"No idea at all." Mike shook his head as he caught his breath.

The red wash of the auxiliary lighting gave the hallway a surreal glow. They leaned against the bulkhead next to each other and waited.

Then the lighting in the hallway darkened as the power system began to transfer. In the pitch-black, Vern felt a rough hand reach to hold hers. She squeezed it.

There was a crack from the rail-gun turret above. But it was not the triumphant sound of one of the rounds being propelled toward a target. It was the terse clap of an electrical problem. The auxiliary lights went dark and then turned back on with a series of disconcerting strobelike pulses.

Mike felt Vern's hand slip from his grasp as she started down the hallway, running back toward the turret.

USS *Zumwalt* Ship Mission Center

"Sir, we've got power failures across the ship. Engineering reports engines not powering up. The misfire caused some kind of surge," said Cortez.

Simmons stared at the systems feed, and he could feel everyone in the cavernous room looking up to see how he would respond. He kept his face blank and set his jaw. Inside, though, he cursed himself, hearing his dad's voice in his head. If he'd just shown a little patience and listened, they would already be engaging the enemy fleet.

"We can worry about the engines later. ETA to get the gun back online?" said Simmons.

"Don't know, sir. The chief and Dr. Li are already back in the turret, working the problem again," said Cortez.

"Range to the enemy?" asked Simmons.

"Twenty-one miles," Richter responded. On one screen, ATHENA mapped out estimated locations of the enemy task force based on their jamming emissions and radar sweeps of the area. A second screen showed the status of the Z's weapons systems; a red sphere over the rail gun indicated it was offline.

"Get me *Port Royal*," Simmons said.

Captain Anderson appeared on the screen, replacing the weapons-systems view.

"Captain Anderson, bad news, our main gun is still offline and we've got engine power loss. We're not going to be able to contribute to the fight the way we planned. But we're still going to play our part. As the larger target, we're the one they're going to focus their fires on. I want you to position the *Port Royal* and the *America* behind us to ensure that. When they open up, that's when I want you to make your attack run. There'll hopefully be enough smoke and confusion from what's happening to us to get you in range."

"Understood," said Anderson. "We'll do our best to make them pay."

"Thank you. It's been an honor. *Zumwalt* out."

Simmons turned back to Cortez. "Damage-control parties standing by?"

Cortez nodded and offered Simmons a stim tab from his uniform's breast pocket. "Last one," said the XO.

Simmons tore open the foil with his teeth and began to chew the gum, eyes fixed on the monitors. He tried to ignore the lost looks that more than a few of the youngest sailors had as they snuck peeks up at the main screens, which were back to showing the tactical map and weapons-systems status, all glowing red.

"Two minutes until the enemy has us within range," said Richter, her voice steady, professional.

Then the red sphere representing the rail gun pulsed green.

"Rail gun back online! Updating the targeting solution," said the tactical action officer. A cheer went up in the room and the crew leaned into their workstations.

Mike's voice echoed through the two-story-high room.

"Bridge, we've got the fix, and the rail gun is ready. It's an ugly solution here in the turret, but it should work."

Jamie cued up the line to his father.

"Did you say here in the turret?"

"That's affirmative." His father's voice sounded softer than he'd ever heard it.

"Damn it, Dad, what are you doing in there? Clear out! We have to fire now. We're sitting ducks."

"Jamie, the power coupling won't stay in without a little help. The impact shook loose the mountings and cracked the last repair job we did even wider. We've patched it again," said Mike. "But the thing is . . . just another weld on a gap like that isn't going to hold unless we get at least another half hour at it. Vern and I are kind of wedging the power line into the coupling so that the heat will fuse the plastic of the fitting fully this time."

"What heat? You mean the heat from the rail gun firing? That won't work; we can't fire it with you in there."

"Yes, Jamie, you can and you will. Vern and I understand the consequences," said Mike. "You know what you have to do."

"Thirty seconds until enemy contact," said the tactical action officer, focused on his task, paying no attention to the conversation behind him. "ATHENA's targeting solution is online. Ready for rail-gun release on your order, sir."

"Jamie, just take care of those kids. Be there for them. Be better than me," said Mike. The channel went quiet.

After a second of silence, Cortez cleared his throat. "Sir, we have to act," he said, eyeing his captain with concern. "If it's needed, I can take over, sir."

Simmons blinked away tears and spoke.

"Battery release . . . do it. Fire the rail gun."

Admiral Zheng He

Water from the spray over the bow soaked his uniform jacket as the flagship cut through the water at almost thirty knots, the rest of the task force arrayed behind it.

Wang knew he should be waiting calmly in his ready room, but his blood was up. It was not just the stims; it was the moment. On deck was where a sailor should be, especially for a fight that was ending like this. It was also the kind of image his sailors needed to see. Their fleet had felt the sting, but now they would gain their revenge and taste victory, all the more sweet up close.

Beside him, one of the main 130 mm gun turrets began to swivel, its turn aligning the barrel with the enemy's largest ship. The ship was not yet visible in the distance, but small plumes of smoke indicated it lay directly ahead.

Wang took the groan of the gun turret moving as his signal to go back to the bridge. He turned quickly, not wanting to wait anymore, and the next thing he knew, he was splayed out on the slick deck, flat on his back. Of all the times to slip and fall.

His aide helped him up with the care he would show a withered old woman who'd fallen while feeding pigeons in the park.

Wang nodded his thanks and took the stairs up to the bridge, aggressively, fast, two at a time, to show them he was not such an old man as they thought. His left knee cried out with every step as his aide rushed to keep pace behind him.

On the bridge, the tactical map was projected into the center of the room; the sailors went silent when the admiral entered. He wondered if they had seen him fall. No matter — the moment would be forgotten amid the glory.

The hologram showed the American task force, blue icons indicating each one's suspected class, name, and status. What was more important, though, was the parallel series of dotted red lines that steadily drew ever closer to the blue. The lines represented the targeting envelopes of the various weapons in the force; the Zheng He's main battery of 130 mm guns were the closest red line to the American fleet. All that was needed was for the red line to cross the blue icon of their primary target.

He stood before the screen, not engaged in his usual contemplative pacing but instead trying to take the weight off his aching knee. He willed the line closer so that this would all be over sooner.

There!

"In range, sir. On your orders, we are ready to engage," said his aide. He held up the tablet screen, ready for Wang to press the icon to clear all ships to fire.

Wang extended his trigger finger and then paused, holding it in the air six inches from the screen. It sounded like a freight train was racing right past the bridge. The very steel of the superstructure seemed to vibrate, tickling the soles of his boots. A giant splash erupted on the port side of the *Admiral Zheng He*, the water spray rising higher than the ship itself. A few seconds later, another erupted to the starboard side, sending water hundreds of feet in the air in a sharp fantail of white and blue.

He felt rivulets of sweat track their way down his back, and then chastised himself, whispering, "'Pretend to be weak, that he may grow arrogant.'"

He jabbed his finger down, but it never touched the screen. The rail-gun round entered the *Admiral Zheng He*'s superstructure approximately thirty feet beneath where Admiral Wang stood. The strike transferred its kinetic energy with such force that the metal superstructure was literally peeled apart as the round plowed through. The ensuing explosion amidships sent a ball of flame hundreds of feet into the air as the ship's hull cracked in two.

USS *Zumwalt* Ship Mission Center

"Fire again," said Captain Simmons. He stood with the weight fully on the balls of his feet, willing the ship to make every shot count. The steady explosions of the rail gun releasing rounds continued. One round every six seconds, with a metronome's precision.

With all auxiliary power dedicated to the weapons systems, the ship continued to drift, but ATHENA had that under control, adjusting the fire solution.

In the distance, small bright flashes and then black plumes began to appear, the only visual indicators of the steady rail-gun shots working their way through the enemy task force.

Cortez approached Simmons and kept his voice low. "Sir, water level's rising below decks. We need to get those pumps back on before we lose her," he said.

Simmons stared at him briefly and then responded. "Continue firing. We don't know if the gun will work once we stop. We just need to trust the ship."

He could hear his father speaking through him.

EPILOGUE

Remember those not here today,
And those unwell or far away,
And those who never lived to see,
The end of War and Victory.

— WILLIAM WALKER, "ABSENT FRIENDS"

SR-216, McCain Senate Office Building, Washington, DC

The fifteen senators stared at the piece of parchment folded into a square and covered with what looked like nineteenth-century English script.

"You see, ladies and gentlemen, this is the actual letter of marque. The one your president signed. There is a copy in one of my vaults and a third, as you might know, has been donated to your Smithsonian Institution for its historic significance." Sir Aeric Cavendish then playfully tapped the paper to make it spin weightlessly in front of the view screen. "It is a binding legal document. What you are asking of me is not based on, my legal team informs me, any law, terrestrial or otherwise."

"Nobody is questioning your contribution to the war effort," said Senator Bob Courtenay, the California Republican who chaired the committee. He tried not to show his frustration. Witnesses at congressional hearings were supposed to be intimidated, not showboating on a video screen from two hundred and fifty miles overhead. And they were supposed to be in clothing appropriate to the occasion, not in a baby-blue jumpsuit with the name Zorro embroidered on it. "But the past notwithstanding, you have to understand the present seriousness of our position."

"What I understand is that I delivered on all terms of a business agreement, and now my partners seek to change that agreement," said Sir Aeric. "Highly disappointing, but to be expected of politicians."

Senator Courtenay leaned forward, twirling a ballpoint pen in his hand. It was his signal for the media cameras to focus tightly on him because he was about to drop the hammer on a witness.

"Let me be explicitly clear about what the legislation this committee is considering means: You will agree to give the space station you now occupy back to its rightful owners," said Senator Courtenay, raising his voice. "Or, *Mr.* Cavendish, your properties inside the United States will be seized, and a warrant for your arrest will be issued."

"Senator, it seems you are having trouble with a great many things, from the nuances of business to the basic matter of getting my title correct." Sir Aeric Cavendish floated up and then steadied himself in front of the camera.

"So let me simplify this for you. You can make all the empty threats that you desire. I rather like it up here and I don't expect to come down there in the foreseeable future."

San Diego, California

She stayed to the shadows on the edge of the woods. They provided good cover, were familiar, comforting. They were also cool and didn't make her sweat as much in the wool blanket she'd cut a poncho slit into and wore in order to break up her heat signature.

From her vantage point, she could see the children in the field. Only children could be so brave, so oblivious to it all, running about in the open like that. An adult was pulling soccer balls out of a bag as the children lined up.

Suddenly, the back of her neck tingled, a sixth sense telling her that something wasn't right. She heard it before she saw it. It was one of the new electric versions. Lightweight and cheap, but largely autonomous, able to pick up and track human signatures on its own. A shot of adrenaline, almost like an electric shock, pushed through the handful of calmers she'd taken that morning. Her pores opened up and she began to sweat profusely.

At first, she thought it would track her, but then the drone locked in on the children in the open field. She focused on the child closest to her, a little boy around six years old. He didn't notice the drone at first. It stalked him, just thirty feet in the air, hovering at the corner of the field and then slowly moving closer until it was right above him. Then, finally, he saw it.

Her jaws clenched, locking, teeth pressing hard against each other. She wanted to run out there. But she couldn't. Every instinct told her not to move.

The little boy was now running, the other children following him, all screaming. As fast as they were running, the drone easily kept pace.

She knew she shouldn't stay there in the woods. She should be out there, among them, doing something. But she couldn't. Her body wouldn't let her move.

The drone pulled ahead of the running children and then stopped and raised a few yards to get a better shot. It steadied, fixing its position, as the children continued to run, screaming as loud as they could.

She felt cold. In the space of just a few seconds, she'd sweated through her clothes underneath the wool blanket; the rough fabric was starting to absorb the wet and stick to her. *Damn it, get your ass out there,* she could hear her old drill instructor screaming. But she couldn't move.

She closed her eyes. She couldn't watch it all anymore. Her head began to pound, the noise of the children screaming combining with the drone's rotors. Then it was all drowned out by the dull roar of white noise that began to build in her eardrums, the blood rushing in. She couldn't move.

And then she felt it. Conan opened her eyes and saw the little boy. Her little boy. Liam was standing there, holding her hand, squeezing it, tears in his eyes.

"Mommy, please won't you come play with us? You said you'd try this time."

Moscow, Russian People's Republic

Markov shook the snow from his thick jacket's shoulders. As he began to peel off his layers of fur and wool, he caught a whiff of butter and onions. The widow upstairs cooked nonstop. For whom, he did not know. She clearly did not eat it; she was an elderly little wisp of a woman.

The smell made him feel trapped in the small apartment. The main living space contained only a heavy pine chair, a matching footstool, and an unsteady-looking wooden cabinet. With only enough room for him to read and pace, it was a retreat in both meanings of the term.

They had acknowledged his effort in Hawaii with a medal and then had made it clear that the episode was best forgotten by all, the various old alliances no longer seeming so wise after the coup had toppled the old spy. He'd traded the medal at the flea market for a 130-year-old book of Mikhail Lermontov's poems, including "Death of the Poet," about Pushkin's demise, and told his bosses he would like to be discharged so he could become a policeman. They thought it was a joke at first. *The pay is terrible. Nobody is good for bribes anymore. You'll have to drive a dented Lada, and even the little kids will throw rocks at you.* Better that than strutting around the Alpha Group compound like an old cock with tattered feathers and nothing to do. Three months later, he walked out into a cold Moscow evening with a badge and an ID identifying him as a junior-grade detective on the city police force. It meant a life of small apartments filled with the smell of neighbors' cooking, but also a constant supply of mysteries that made life worth living.

The thin wooden door shuddered as a fist pounded on it three times. Barely a second passed, and the door visibly flexed inward again from another round of pounding.

His first instinct was to draw the SIG Sauer pistol in the cracked leather holster on his left side. But then he thought of the old woman cooking upstairs and the tumbling children across the hall. He wasn't going to go out with his last act on earth being the death of some innocent from a stray round fired through a flimsy door.

Markov knelt, staying just outside the door frame, and drew the serrated five-inch boot knife he carried in a sheath at his ankle. Old habits die hard. He paused in a crouch, noticing the snow on his boots melting at his feet. The fist hammered the door again. Before it could finish the rest of the three-knock pattern its owner was so enamored of, Markov flung open the door and seized the extended hand. He twisted the arm and spun his own body, throwing the man onto his back in the middle of the room. A quick look in the hallway. Empty. And so Markov gently closed the door behind him and locked it.

The man on the floor wore a helmet and bulky protective gear. Still on his back, he reached out with his hands up, heavy padded gloves with carbon knuckles pointing at the ceiling in surrender. Motorcycle gauntlets, not military issue. His dark blue jacket and pants were covered with a spider-web pattern of reflective segments and pads at the elbows and knees. The uniform that Markov saw buzzing past him on the streets every day.

"Delivery," said the RusGlobal Delivery courier, almost in a whimper.

"You know you're going to get yourself killed with a knock like that," said Markov.

Markov flipped the knife in his left hand, concealing the point along the length of his forearm. He offered his right hand to the man, who was really a wide-eyed boy, likely not even twenty years old.

"I hate Moscow," the courier said as he swung a satchel across his chest and pulled out a padded silver nylon envelope covered with the company's angular black double-headed-eagle logo. The courier tossed it to him, and Markov unlocked the door and let him out.

Markov set the package on the scuffed hardwood floor and knelt before the envelope. He poked at it with the knife tip. He leaned over it and listened. Then he simply sat with it and waited. After a few dozen deep breaths, he lifted it up and slightly bent the stiff envelope.

With the knife now lying alongside the package, he carefully positioned his phone and held it steady for fifteen seconds. The phone's signal didn't waver, meaning no interference from active circuitry inside. It could still be chem, bio, or even radiological. Yes, a slow death that last way that would be classically Russian. At least the manner in which he died would help reveal the sender.

He sliced the knife through the envelope along its long edge. If you wore white gloves all the time, then all you'd get was clean fingernails when you finally put your pistol to your temple, he thought.

Inside was another package: a slightly smaller cardboard envelope with a FedEx logo on it. Its origin showed it had gone through the shipping hub in Abu Dhabi.

With the tip of the knife, he carefully slit the cardboard envelope open along its longest edge, listening for a click or a hiss of a switch.

Another package. This one was an inch smaller and only slightly thinner. This FedEx envelope had an American flag covering one entire side of it, as was the company's practice these days, and on the other side was the faint LED display of the tracking tag. He activated it and it showed the package had journeyed from Honolulu to Abu Dhabi.

He broke the button-size capsule that released the envelope's seal, and the material parted when the envelope's magnetic seal broke. A flat, brown butcher-paper-wrapped package tumbled to the floor. It landed with a familiar thump. Only one thing made a sound like that.

He smiled as he tore off the paper that wrapped the Pushkin book. Inside, tucked next to the tea-stained opening page, was a three-by-five-inch card of solid white. Only two words — *With gratitude* — were typed on it.

He didn't know whether to smile or shudder at the realization that she somehow knew where he lived. So he just opened the book and began to read again: *I live in lonely desolation, And wonder when my end will come.*

Waikiki Beach, Honolulu, Hawaii

"You need to be careful right now. See that set? See the way it's breaking? You're too far forward on the board, so slide back and paddle!"

Mario Giordini was not paying attention to the waves. He found it hard to look at anything but his instructor. When she arched her back to see how the next set of waves was shaping up, it was impossible to consider anything but the curve of her breasts beneath the long-sleeved black rash guard.

The Italian banker from Milan would be turning thirty next month, and he knew his mother would soon force him to finally settle down and get married. Thank God he was not married now.

"Mario, stay with me," she said. "You're going to have to dive under when this wave comes, okay? All the way under this time."

He'd actually arrived the day after the final prisoner exchanges between China and the United States had been completed, the U.S. forces taken in Guam swapped for the Chinese forces who'd surrendered after the Americans had taken back the island. The two nations had shown they could pound each other into a weakened equilibrium, but having sunk most of each other's fleets, neither wanted to take it to the next level. So the deal was *status quo antebellum,* a term Mario thought funny for its naive suggestion that anything could go back to the way it was before the war. And that was the opportunity for those who had been smart enough to sit it out. Half the hotels on the island had some kind of battle damage, but location had a permanent value. As did beauty, he thought, looking at the woman he'd picked up on a site visit to the Moana Surfrider hotel.

The question was, how was he going to make this particular investment pay off? Maybe ask her out to dinner and then try the tactic of testing a bottle of Italian prosecco against a California sparkling wine, which they ignorantly called champagne? It had worked enough times here, the girls grateful for a free meal and the chance to peek at luxury, even for a night. Or was she the kind of girl who needed a little narcotic persuasion?

"Now!" she shouted. Mario leaned forward on the board just as the wave approached. He meant to shove the board's nose deep under the water and arch his back to drive it deeper still, but he froze. He just stared up at a blue wall closing in on him.

The wave sucked him up and launched him into the air, spinning him underwater. Salt water filled every cavity, worked its way into his nose and ears. He surfaced with a desperate gasp but the board kept racing toward the beach, locked in the wave's rushing white water. The tug on his leash dragged him back down. He flailed harder, thrashing with open hands.

The next thing Mario knew he was on the beach, coughing as if he had just smoked two packs of cigarettes. She stood over him, backlit by sunset. He felt completely disarmed and at peace in the presence of such beauty.

"You know, you really are starting to get the hang of it," she said. "But you have to learn to trust me. How about we go back out tonight? The moon will be full. It's so amazing, like nothing you've seen back in Italy," she said.

He nodded, already thinking of which bottle to bring.

"I know just the place," she said, "quiet, just the two of us. And there's not a better break for teaching. But you gotta promise me you'll look out for that leash next time; it can be a real killer."

Vallejo Yacht Club, Vallejo, California

"Tacking now, Dad!"

Martin Simmons held the sailboat's tiller in his right hand and the jib sheet in his left. The little boy stopped calling his father Daddy ever since he'd come back. The breeze picked up as the small Lightning sailboat edged closer to the Mare Island pier.

"Don't let go of the jib just yet. Feel it fill, then . . . okay, now, now!" said Jamie Simmons. He sat hunched as low as he could, ducking the aluminum boom.

The sailboat tacked to starboard, and Jamie carefully shifted his weight across to the port side. Lindsey and Claire screamed with delight as the boat began to tilt. He watched his son, now eight, try to transfer the line and the tiller between his hands as the hull shifted underneath him. All the while, they were closing in on the barnacles.

"My turn next, Daddy!" Claire said from the bow. At least she still called him that.

The channel was so changed from a year ago. Much of the old Ghost Fleet was gone; some of the vessels were still at sea until the shipyards could complete their decades-long work of rebuilding the American Navy, and some were lost forever. And on the ships that were back, fresh paint covered the rust and bloodstains while welders daily worked over their new scars.

Simmons reached over and nudged the tiller. There was so much to do, but this was exactly how he wanted to spend the day before the change-of-command ceremony. He was going to make the most of all of this.

The sailboat kept edging closer to the pier, about two hundred yards astern from the sleek metal box-cutter bow that still looked to him as if it were going in the wrong direction from the water.

"Watch your speed; I don't think the Z could take a ramming even from us," said Simmons.

Martin yanked the tiller, turning the sailboat into the wind. With no air flow over the sails, the sheets luffed and hung limp. The young boy searched frantically for the next puff of warm breeze to fill the channel, losing track of the sailboat's momentum carrying them onward.

"Shit!" said Martin when he realized how far they had drifted, too late trying to turn the rudder. The sailboat bumped into the pier lightly; Jamie pushed off with his hand.

"Martin Simmons, who taught you that word?" said Lindsey.

"Grandpa," said Martin sheepishly.

"Well, that's appropriate," said his father.

Jamie could see the boy was blushing even under his sun hat. He drew a cooler to his feet and opened it up. He got out a can of Coke, took a sip, then passed it to his son. "You're doing great; your grandpa would be proud of you . . . and of your new vocabulary. We'll just wait here for him to send us some wind."

The sailboat slowly floated past the *Zumwalt*. One of the sailors onboard recognized the captain and snapped a salute. Claire saluted back first, then Martin, and, finally, Jamie, smiling.

The jib stiffened, and Martin took up the slack in the line as the wind picked up and the sailboat took off.

ACKNOWLEDGMENTS

Writing a book is a team effort, which is what made this partnership such a rewarding experience. But the members of the team went well beyond the two of us.

Thank you to the DC defense-policy community and the Washington Metro system for leading us continually to cross paths at meetings, interviews, and subway stops and strike up a friendship and, now, a writing partnership.

We were drawn into trying our hand at fiction by our shared love of authors who had thrilled, inspired, and addicted us as readers. They range from Arthur Conan Doyle and Herman Wouk to William Gibson and John le Carré to Tom Clancy and George R. R. Martin. Part of the fun of this effort was revisiting old memories of reading books like *Red Storm Rising* on the way to the beach in the back of the family station wagon, and then going back to read them again decades later, this time to look for tips from the masters but enjoying them just as much.

The research for the book encompassed not just the references you'll find in the endnotes section (a bit of an anomaly for a novel, but we hope it will be useful for readers who want to learn more, as well as demonstrate the story's grounding in reality), but also interviews, meetings, and conversations with a real-world cast of professionals who are reflected in the characters found in this book. We chewed through scenarios and lingo with U.S. Navy ship captains and Air Force fighter pilots, learned worldview and strategic thinking from Chinese generals, and tested out ideas with everyone from Special Forces veterans and computer hackers to Harvard scientists. We are deeply grateful to all of them. A special thanks goes to the group of expert readers who powered their way through the early texts and made the final product so much better, including Kenneth Eckman, Nathan

Finney, Allan Friedman, Mark Hagerott, John Jackson, Mark Jacobsen, D.K., Greg Knepper, Jeffrey Lin, Fernando Lujan, Aaron Marx, Rich McDaniel, Ian Morrison, and Tammy Schultz, among others.

Our agents Dan Mandel, Bob Bookman, Ike Williams, and Katherine Flynn helped with everything from setting up the meeting that was the original spark for the book idea to finding the manuscript a home with a great editor.

Eamon Dolan took a risk on us as first-time novelists and then not only provided valuable edits and big ideas but also continually challenged us along the way to try harder and be better at the craft. He is also even more brutal at eliminating characters than the Black Widow herself. RIP, Kyle and Dorothy. We would also like to thank Tracy Roe, MD, whose double-barreled copyediting prowess and medical knowledge were ably brought to bear on the manuscript.

Finally, we'd like to thank our families for their love, for their support, and, most of all, for convincing us that we could and should take this leap.

ENDNOTES

Foreword

Page

viii *He reached down for his*: John Bishop, "HEXPANDO Expanding Head for Fastener-Retention Hexagonal Wrench," NASA Tech Briefs, August 1, 2011, accessed August 16, 2014, http://www.techbriefs.com/component/content/article/10720.

ix *cloud of smog stretching from Beijing*: Global Bearings, NASA image, December 12, 2013, accessed December 12, 2013, https://twitter.com/Global_Bearings /status/411174216596074498/photo/1.

Part 1

3 *The screens inside the Jiaolong-3*: "Manned Sub Jiaolong Completes Deep-Sea Dive," CCTV.com, June 17, 2013, accessed August 16, 2014, http://english.cntv .cn/20130617/106712.shtml.

deep below the COMRA: Qian Wang, "China Bids for Rights to Search Seabed," *China Daily*, September 6, 2012, accessed August 19, 2014, http://usa.chinadaily.com.cn /china/2012-09/06/content_15737233.htm.

4 *Tianjin University developed the submersible*: Phil Muncaster, "China Seeks 'Oceanauts' for Deep Sea Exploration," TheRegister.co.uk, December 24, 2012, accessed August 16, 2014, http://www.theregister.co.uk/2012/12/24/china_ocean_exploration_plans/.

6 *P-8 Poseidon's recent engine upgrades*: "P-8 Poseidon," U.S. Naval Air Systems Command, February 2014, accessed August 16, 2014, http://www.navair.navy.mil/index .cfm?fuseaction=home.display&key=CFD01141-CD4E-4DB8-A6B2-7E8FBFB31B86.

7 *"U.S. Exclusive Economic Zone"*: "Ocean Facts: What Is the EEZ?," National Oceanic and Atmospheric Administration, accessed August 19, 2014, http://oceanservice.noaa.gov /facts/eez.html.

"as designated by the Mariana Trench": Dan Vergano, "Bush to Make Pacific's Mariana Trench a National Monument," *USA Today*, January 6, 2009, accessed March 14, 2013, http://usatoday30.usatoday.com/tech/science/environment/2009-01-05-mariana -trench_N.htm.

"drop a Remora": "Remora — Fast Reconnaissance AUV," L-3 Ocean Systems, accessed August 16, 2014, http://www.l-3mps.com/oceansystems/remora.aspx.

9 *viz glasses*: Chris Smith, "2020 Vision: The Future of Google Glass," *TechRadar*, October 19, 2013, accessed February 22, 2014, http://www.techradar.com/us/news/world-of -tech/2020-vision-the-future-of-google-glass-1190832.

10 *"stuck in the Ghost Fleet"*: "National Defense Reserve Fleet," U.S. Department of Trans-

portation Maritime Administration, accessed August 16, 2014, http://www.marad.dot
.gov/ships_shipping_landing_page/national_security/ship_operations/national_
defense_reserve_fleet/national_defense_reserve_fleet.htm.

Aegis cruiser: "The U.S. Navy — Fact File: Aegis Weapon System," U.S. Navy, November 22, 2013, accessed August 19, 2014, http://www.navy.mil/navydata/fact_display
.asp?cid=2100&tid=200&ct=2.

"something like five hundred ships": Craig Miller, "Suisun Bay 'Ghost Fleet' a Shadow of
Its Former Self," *KQED Science* (blog), November 25, 2013, accessed August 16, 2014,
blogs.kqed.org/science/2013/11/25/suisun-bay-ghost-fleet-a-shadow-of-its-former-self/

11   *"DD(X) is what they":* "Navy Designates Next-Generation Zumwalt Destroyer," U.S.
Navy, April 7, 2006, accessed August 19, 2014, http://www.navy.mil/submit/display
.asp?story_id=23064.

"Navy was going to build": "Cost to Deliver *Zumwalt*-Class Destroyers Likely to Exceed
Budget," U.S. Government Accountability Office, July 31, 2008, accessed August 16, 2014,
http://www.gao.gov/products/GAO-08-804.

12   *the USS* Coronado's *wardroom:* "Littoral Combat Ship Class — LCS," U.S. Navy, accessed August 16, 2014, http://www.public.navy.mil/surfor/pages/LittoralCombatShips
.aspx#.U-_P_Ej6L6A.

remote-piloted MQ-8 Fire Scout: "MQ-8 Fire Scout," U.S. Naval Air Systems Command,
accessed August 16, 2014, http://www.navair.navy.mil/index.cfm?fuseaction=home
.display&key=8250AFBA-DF2B-4999-9EF3-0B0E46144D03.

13   *where a pirate attack:* MarEx, "Petro-Pirates Plague Busy Shipping Lanes," *Maritime
Executive,* July 9, 2014, accessed August 17, 2014, http://www.maritime-executive.com
/article/PetroPirates-Plague-Busy-Shipping-Lanes-2014-07-09.

"More than half of the world's shipping": "World Oil Transit Chokepoints," U.S. Energy
Information Administration, August 12, 2012, accessed August 16, 2014, http://www.eia
.gov/countries/regions-topics.cfm?fips=wotc&trk=p3.

ever since Chinese special operations forces: Dean Cheng, "The Chinese People's Liberation Army and Special Operations," *Special Warfare* 25, no. 3 (July–September 2012),
accessed March 18, 2014, http://www.dvidshub.net/publication/issues/10629.

14   *renminbi, the Chinese currency:* Xinhua, "RMB to Be Global Reserve Currency by 2030:
Economist," *China Daily,* April 9, 2014, accessed August 19, 2014, http://www.chinadaily
.com.cn/china/2014-04/09/content_17420923.htm.

"sail with our own oil": Mark Thompson, "U.S. to Become Biggest Oil Producer
— IEA," CNN, November 12, 2012, accessed November 12, 2012, http://money.cnn
.com/2012/11/12/news/economy/us-oil-production-energy/index.html?iid=HP
_LN&hpt=hp_c2.

15   *"heightening regional tensions":* CNN wire staff, "Obama Announces WTO Case Against
China over Rare Earths," CNN, March 13, 2012, accessed March 14, 2012, http://www
.cnn.com/2012/03/13/world/asia/china-rare-earths-case/index.html?hpt=hp_t2.

"depend on rare-earth materials": "What Are the Rare Earths?," Ames Lab, U.S. Department of Energy, accessed August 19, 2014, https://www.ameslab.gov/dmse/rem/what
-are-rare-earths.

"Their big mistake": Edward Wong, "China's Communist Party Chief Acts to Bolster
Military," *New York Times,* December 14, 2012, accessed December 14, 2012, http://www.
nytimes.com/2012/12/15/world/asia/chinas-xi-jinping-acts-to-bolster-military.html.

"just like back in '89": Jeffrey T. Richelson and Michael L. Evans, "Tiananmen Square,

1989: The Declassified History," *National Security Archive Electronic Briefing Book No. 16,* National Security Archive, George Washington University, June 1, 1999, accessed August 19, 2014, http://www2.gwu.edu/~nsarchiv/NSAEBB/NSAEBB16/.

"saw the problem differently than they did": Edward Wong and Jonathan Ansfield, "China's Military Seeks More Sway, Worrying Communist Party," *New York Times,* August 7, 2012, accessed March 18, 2014, http://www.nytimes.com/2012/08/08/world/asia/chinas -military-seeks-more-sway-worrying-communist-party.html.

"those 'little princes' ": Cheng Li, "Rule of the Princelings," *Cairo Review of Global Affairs,* February 10, 2013, accessed August 19, 2014, http://www.aucegypt.edu/gapp/cairoreview/ Pages/articleDetails.aspx?aid=295.

16   *British trading routes:* "First World War: A Global View," UK National Archives, accessed August 25, 2014, http://www.nationalarchives.gov.uk/first-world-war/a-global-view/#.

"Some say we're fighting": Wang Jisi and Kenneth G. Lieberthal, "Addressing U.S.-China Strategic Distrust," Brookings Institution, March 30, 2012, accessed March 14, 2014, http://www.brookings.edu/research/papers/2012/03/30-us-china-lieberthal.

lingering image of CVN-80: Thomas J. Moore, "USS *Enterprise:* Past, Present and Future," *Navy Live* (blog), U.S. Navy, December 1, 2012, accessed August 19, 2014, http:// navylive.dodlive.mil/2012/12/01/uss-enterprise-past-present-and-future/.

"Ford-class carriers taking so long": "Lead Ship Testing and Reliability Shortfalls Will Limit Initial Fleet Capabilities," U.S. Government Accountability Office, September 5, 2013, accessed August 16, 2014, http://www.gao.gov/products/gao-13-396.

"You're right that the DF-21E": Otto Kreisher, "China's Carrier Killer: Threat and Theatrics," *Air Force Magazine,* December 2013, accessed December 3, 2013, http:// www.airforcemag.com/magazinearchive/pages/2013/december%202013/1213china. aspx?signon=false.

17   *"What will it be next":* Harry Kazianis, "Is AirSea Battle Obsolete?," *Diplomat,* June 21, 2012, accessed March 18, 2014, http://thediplomat.com/2012/06/is-airsea-battle -obsolete/.

"Air-Sea Battle concept": Jonathan W. Greenert and Norton A. Schwartz, "Air-Sea Battle," *American Interest,* February 20, 2012, accessed February 20, 2012, http://www.the-american -interest.com/article.cfm?piece=1212.

21   *"a brilliant Russian scientist":* "Pavel A. Cherenkov — Biographical," *Nobel Lectures, Physics 1942–1962* (Amsterdam: Elsevier, 1964), cited on NobelPrize.org, accessed August 16, 2014, http://www.nobelprize.org/nobel_prizes/physics/laureates/1958 /cerenkov-bio.html.

22   *"nine trillion dollars' worth of our debt":* "The Budget and Economic Outlook: 2014 to 2024," Congressional Budget Office, February 4, 2014, accessed August 16, 2014, http:// www.cbo.gov/publication/45010.

"Britain's biggest trading partner": "The First World War: Look Back with Angst," *Economist,* December 21, 2013, accessed August 19, 2014, http://www.economist.com/news /leaders/21591853-century-there-are-uncomfortable-parallels-era-led-outbreak.

24   *The four-engine Y-20:* Andrew Erickson and Gabe Collins, "The Y-20: China Aviation Milestone Means New Power Projection," *China Real Time* (blog), *Wall Street Journal,* January 28, 2013, accessed August 16, 2014, http://blogs.wsj.com/chinareal time/2013/01/28/the-y-20-china-aviation-milestone-means-new-power-projection/.

25   *largest submarine and air base:* Notes from webcast lecture by Alexander Neill, Shangri-La Dialogue Senior Fellow for Asia-Pacific Security, International Institute for Strate-

gic Studies, Washington, DC, October 28, 2013, http://www.iiss.org/en/events/events /archive/2013-5126/october-8493/chinas-5th-generation-leadership-7fb9.

27 *Their liquid body armor's exterior:* "Case Study — Liquid Armour," BAE Systems, accessed August 19, 2014, http://www.baesystems.com/article/BAES_020435/liquid-armour.

28 *"'On terrain from which'":* Sun-Tzu, *The Art of Warfare*, trans. Roger T. Ames (New York: Ballantine Books, 1993), chapter 11.

29 *"PLA National Defense University":* "National Defense University PLA China," *ASEAN Regional Forum*, November 17, 2011, accessed August 19, 2014, http://aseanregionalfo rum.asean.org/files/Archive/13th/9th%20ARF%20Heads%20of%20Defence%20Univer sitiesCollegesInstitutions%20Meeting/NDU%20China.pdf.

"Alfred Thayer Mahan": "Biographies in Naval History: Rear Admiral Alfred Thayer Mahan, US Navy," U.S. Naval History and Heritage Command, accessed August 19, 2014, http://www.history.navy.mil/bios/mahan_alfred.htm.

"'Americans must now'" : "The Price of Freedom: Americans at War — Spanish American War," Smithsonian National Museum of American History, accessed August 19, 2014, http://amhistory.si.edu/militaryhistory/printable/section.asp?id=7.

30 *"daring us to act":* Bernhard Zand, "Power in the Pacific: Stronger Chinese Navy Worries Neighbors and US," *Der Spiegel Online International*, September 14, 2012, accessed March 18, 2014, http://www.spiegel.de/international/world/strengthening-of-chinese -navy-sparks-worries-in-region-and-beyond-a-855622.html.

"However deep the water": Jane Cai and Verna Yu, "Xi Jinping Outlines His Vision of 'Dream and Renaissance,'" *South China Morning Post*, March 18, 2013, accessed August 17, 2014, http://www.scmp.com/news/china/article/1193273/xi-jinping-outlines-his -vision-chinas-dream-and-renaissance.

31 *"'Those who know'":* Sun-Tzu, *The Art of Warfare*, trans. Roger T. Ames.

32 *the 788th Regiment:* John Pike, "8341 Unit — Central Security Regiment," FAS.org, May 22, 1998, accessed August 17, 2014, http://fas.org/irp/world/china/pla/8341.htm; fictional unit.

"Our population demographics are not optimal": Andrea den Boer and Valerie M. Hudson, "The Security Risks of China's Abnormal Demographics," *Monkey Cage* (blog), *Washington Post*, April 30, 2014, accessed August 19, 2014, http://www.washingtonpost .com/blogs/monkey-cage/wp/2014/04/30/the-security-risks-of-chinas-abnormal -demographics/.

"Our trade routes": Sean Mirski, "How to Win a War with China," *National Interest*, November 1, 2013, accessed August 19, 2014. http://nationalinterest.org/commentary /how-win-war-china-9346.

"Our need for outside energy": "China: Analysis," U.S. Energy Information Administration, February 4, 2014, accessed August 19, 2014, http://www.eia.gov/countries/cab .cfm?fips=ch.

Part 2

37 DEFENSE INTELLIGENCE AGENCY: "Defense Intelligence Agency — About," U.S. Defense Intelligence Agency, accessed August 19, 2014, http://www.dia.mil /About.aspx.

38 *A compact HK G48:* "G36C — Das ultrakurze Sturmgewehr," Heckler and Koch, ac-

cessed August 17, 2014, http://www.heckler-koch.com/de/produkte/militaer/sturm
gewehre/g36/g36c/produktbeschreibung.html; fictional version.

using covert radio signals: Geoffrey Ingersoll, "The NSA Has Secretly Developed the 'Big-
foot' of Computer Hacks," BusinessInsider.com, January 15, 2014, accessed August 19,
2014, http://www.businessinsider.com/nsa-has-the-bigfoot-of-computer-hacks-2014-1.

39   *SIPRNet classified network:* Sharon Weinberger, "What Is SIPRNet?," *Popular Mechanics,*
December 1, 2010, accessed August 19, 2014, http://www.popularmechanics.com/tech
nology/how-to/computer-security/what-is-siprnet-and-wikileaks-4085507.

air-gapped: Peter W. Singer and Allan Friedman, *Cybersecurity and Cyberwar: What
Everyone Needs to Know* (New York: Oxford University Press, 2014).

faintly glowing metallic smart-rings: Darren Quick, "Ring Puts the Finger on Gesture
Control," *Gizmag,* March 4, 2014, accessed August 19, 2014, http://www.gizmag.com
/logbar-smart-ring-bluetooth/31080/.

nicknamed the Eastern MIT: "Shanghai Jiao Tong University," *Times Higher Education*
World University Rankings 2012–2013, accessed August 19, 2014, http://www.timeshigh
ereducation.co.uk/world-university-rankings/2012-13/world-ranking/institution
/shanghai-jiao-tong-university.

Hainan Island incident: "Interview with Lt. Shane Osborn, U.S. Navy," *Frontline,* accessed August 19, 2014, http://www.pbs.org/wgbh/pages/frontline/shows/china/inter
views/osborn.html.

40   *hacker militias became crucial hubs:* Singer and Friedman, *Cybersecurity and Cyberwar.*

China's J-20 fighter: Feng Cao, "China Unveils More Capable Stealth Fighter Prototype," U.S. Naval Institute, March 19, 2014, accessed August 20, 2014, http://news.usni
.org/2014/03/19/china-unveils-capable-stealth-fighter-prototype.

41   *her circulatory system:* David Axe, "This Scientist Wants Tomorrow's Troops to Be
Mutant-Powered," *Danger Room* (blog), *Wired,* December 26, 2012, http://www.wired
.com/2012/12/andrew-herr/all/.

42   *randomize signals:* Ryan W. Neal, "GPS Terrorism: Hackers Could Exploit Location
Technology to Hijack Ships, Airplanes," *International Business Times,* July 29, 2013, accessed August 19, 2014, http://www.ibtimes.com/gps-terrorism-hackers-could-exploit
-location-technology-hijack-ships-airplanes-1362937.

43   *Tiangong ("Heavenly Palace"):* "China's First Space Lab — Tiangong 1," China.org.cn, accessed August 19, 2014, http://www.china.org.cn/china/special_coverage/node_7125458.
htm.

44   *chemical oxygen iodine laser:* William H. Possel, "Lasers and Missile Defense: New Con-
cepts for Space-Based and Ground-Based Laser Weapons, Occasional Paper No. 5,"
Center for Strategy and Technology, Air War College, Air University, Maxwell Air Force
Base, U.S. Air Force, July 1998, accessed August 19, 2014, http://www.au.af.mil/au/awc
/awcgate/cst/csat5.pdf.

converted 747 jumbo jet: "Airborne Laser Test Bed," Missile Defense Agency, accessed
August 19, 2014, http://www.mda.mil/news/gallery_altb.html.

45   *The first target was WGS-4:* "Fact Sheet: Wideband Global SATCOM (WGS)," Los An-
geles Air Force Base, U.S. Air Force, February 11, 2014, accessed August 19, 2014, http://
www.losangeles.af.mil/library/factsheets/factsheet.asp?id=5333.

46   *known as the X-37:* David Axe, "A Year Later, Mysterious Space Plane Is Still in Orbit," *Danger Room* (blog), *Wired,* March 7, 2012, accessed March 7, 2012, http://www
.wired.com/dangerroom/2012/03/spaceplane-year/?utm_source=feedburner&utm

_medium=email&utm_campaign=Feed%3A+WiredDangerRoom+%28Blog+-+Danger+Room%29.

Geosynchronous Space Situational Awareness: Amy Butler, "USAF Chief Outs Classified Spy Sat Program," *Aviation Week and Space Technology,* February 21, 2012, accessed August 19, 2014, http://aviationweek.com/defense/usaf-space-chief-outs-classified-spy-sat-program.

47 *Ultra High Frequency Follow-On:* "Ultra High Frequency Follow-On (UFO)," Program Executive Office Space Systems, U.S. Navy, accessed August 19, 2014, http://www.public.navy.mil/spawar/PEOSpaceSystems/ProductsServices/Pages/UHFGraphics.aspx.

48 *sipped his awful coffee:* "Don't Wash That Coffee Mug," Naval Historical Foundation, November 25, 2013, accessed August 19, 2014, http://www.navyhistory.org/2013/11/dont-wash-that-coffee-mug/.

49 *"Deploy REMUS":* "Autonomous Underwater Vehicle — Remus 100," Kongsberg Maritime, accessed August 17, 2014, http://www.km.kongsberg.com/ks/web/nokbg0240.nsf/AllWeb/D241A2C835DF40B0C12574AB003EA6AB?OpenDocument.

    The handheld video-game-style controller: Jacqui Barker, "Navy PCD Designs UxV Controllers with Users in Mind," Naval Surface Warfare Center, Panama City Division, March 16, 2012, accessed August 17, 2014, http://www.navy.mil/submit/display.asp?story_id=65928.

50 *submitted the required DNA:* Axe, "This Scientist Wants Tomorrow's Troops."

51 *They had said Tokyo was big:* Visible Earth catalog, "Tokyo at Night," NASA, accessed August 17, 2014, http://visibleearth.nasa.gov/view.php?id=8683.

    Major Alexei Denisov's MiG-35K: "Products — Military Programs: MiG 35/MiG-35D," MiG Russian Aircraft Corporation, accessed August 17, 2014, http://www.migavia.ru/eng/military_e/MiG_35_e.htm.

    launched from the Admiral Kuznetsov: Ben Farmer, "Russian Carrier Sails into the English Channel," *UK Telegraph,* May 8, 2014, accessed August 17, 2014, http://www.telegraph.co.uk/news/uknews/defence/10816463/Russian-aircraft-carrier-sails-into-English-Channel.html.

52 *The Patriot IV missile batteries:* "Patriot," Raytheon, accessed August 17, 2014, http://www.raytheon.com/capabilities/products/patriot/; fictional version.

53 *RIMPAC war games:* Sam LaGrone, "China Sends Uninvited Spy Ship to RIMPAC," *U.S. Naval Institute News,* July 18, 2014, accessed August 19, 2014, http://news.usni.org/2014/07/18/china-sends-uninvited-spy-ship-rimpac.

    a volley of Sokols (Falcons): Randy Jackson, "CHAMP — Lights Out," Boeing, October 30, 2012, accessed August 19, 2014, http://www.boeing.com/Features/2012/10/bds_champ_10_22_12.html; fictional weapon.

    RBK-500 cluster bombs: "RBK Cluster Bomb Family," HarpoonDatabases.com, accessed August 26, 2014, http://www.harpoondatabases.com/encyclopedia/Entry2809.aspx.

    F-35A Lightning II: "F-35 Fast Facts," Lockheed Martin, accessed August 19, 2014, https://www.f35.com/about/fast-facts.

54 *the $8.6 billion tab to relocate the Marines:* Travis J. Tritten, "Cost to Relocate Marines a Moving Target," *Stars and Stripes,* May 15, 2012, accessed August 19, 2014, http://www.stripes.com/news/pacific/okinawa/cost-to-relocate-marines-off-okinawa-a-moving-target-1.177261.

56 *Chinese companies that ran the Panama Canal Zone:* "The Panama Canal: Now for the Next 100 Years," *Economist,* August 16, 2014, accessed August 19, 2014, http://www.econ-

omist.com/news/americas/21612185-it-was-good-investment-america-now-china-has
-its-eye-canal-now-next-100.

58   *"closed rebreather unit"*: "Military Diving," Dräger, accessed August 19, 2014, http://
www.draeger.com/Sites/enus_us/Pages/Federal-Government/Military-Diving.aspx.
Joint Chiefs and the president: Marine Corps order 3504.2, June 8, 2007, http://www
.mcieast.marines.mil/Portals/33/Documents/Adjutant/SAPR_MCO%203504.2%20
OPREP%203%20Reporting[1].pdf.

59   *USS* Abraham Lincoln: "USS *Abraham Lincoln* (CVN-72)," U.S. Navy, accessed August
19, 2014, http://www.lincoln.navy.mil/.
roll-on, roll-off ship: "Deepsea RO/RO Shipping: Operators, Ships and Trades," Dynamar
BV, March 2014, accessed August 19, 2014, https://www.dynamar.com/system/table_of
_contents/125/original/DEEPSEA%20RORO%20Contents%20Overview.pdf.

62   *to still have an outdoor wedding:* "Kanye: A Paparazzi Drone Could Electrocute My
Daughter," FoxNews.com, August 8, 2014, accessed August 19, 2014, http://www
.foxnews.com/tech/2014/08/08/kanye-drone-could-electrocute-my-daughter/.
electric V1000 drone: Fictional drone.
a symbolic act of bravery: Julie Makinen, "Tiananmen Square Mystery: Who Was Tank
Man?," *LA Times,* June 4, 2014, accessed August 19, 2014, http://www.latimes.com
/world/asia/la-fg-china-tiananmen-square-tank-man-20140603-story.html.

63   *located on the Mokapu Peninsula:* "Marine Corps Base Hawaii," U.S. Marine Corps, accessed August 19, 2014, http://www.mcbhawaii.marines.mil/.

64   *over forty thousand pounds of thrust:* "The F-35B: First Descent," Lockheed Martin, accessed August 19, 2014, http://www.lockheedmartin.com/us/100years/stories/f35b.html.

65   *Moana Surfrider hotel:* "Moana Surfrider," Starwood Hotels and Resorts Worldwide, accessed August 19, 2014, http://www.moana-surfrider.com.
USS Gabrielle Giffords: "Keel Laid for Future USS *Gabrielle Giffords*," Program Executive Office Littoral Combat Ships, U.S. Navy, April 16, 2014, accessed August 19, 2014,
http://www.navy.mil/submit/display.asp?story_id=80409.

66   *USS* Pinckney: "USS *Pinckney* (DDG 91)," U.S. Navy, accessed August 19, 2014, http://
www.public.navy.mil/surfor/ddg91/Pages/default.aspx#.U_QZHkj6L6B.
firing an M249 machine gun: "The M249 Series," FNH USA, accessed August 19, 2014,
http://www.fnhusa.com/l/products/machine-guns/m249-series/.

67   *SAFFiRs (Shipboard Autonomous Firefighting Robots):* "Shipboard Autonomous Firefighting Robot (SAFFiR)," Office of Naval Research, U.S. Navy, accessed August 19, 2014,
http://www.onr.navy.mil/en/Media-Center/Fact-Sheets/Shipboard-Robot-Saffir.aspx.
PGZ-07 antiaircraft vehicle: "Air Defense Regiment Equipped with 35 mm Double Loading Anti-Aircraft Gun," *People's Daily Online,* February 13, 2013, accessed August 26,
2014, http://english.people.com.cn/90786/8128497.html.
The ship's 57 mm Mk 110 cannon: "57MK3 (57MM MK110), Naval Gun," BAE Systems, accessed August 19, 2014, http://www.baesystems.com/product/BAES_020040/57mk3
-57mm-mk110-naval-gun?_afrLoop=449462026735000&_afrWindowMode=0&_afr
WindowId=llgqyxgjh_1#%40%3F_afrWindowId%3DWiJ3c7DG%26_afrLoop%
3D449462026735000%26_afrWindowMode%3D0%26_adf.ctrl-state%3Dllgqyxgjh_4.

68   *TY-90 air-to-air missile:* "TY-90 Multi-Purpose Missile," China National Aero-Tech-
nology Import and Export Corporation, accessed August 19, 2014, http://www.catic.cn
/indexPortal/home/index.do?cmd=goToChannel&cid=746&columnid=1914&cpid=165
3&dataid=4298&columnType=102&likeType=view&ckw=ATAM.

70   *The AN/AAQ-37 electro-optical distributed aperture system:* "AN/AAQ-37 Distributed Aperture System (DAS) for the F-35," Northrop Grumman, accessed August 19, 2014, http://www.northropgrumman.com/capabilities/anaaq37f35/pages/default.aspx.
     the MV-22's massive engine: "MV-22 Osprey," Naval Air Systems Command, accessed August 19, 2014, http://www.navair.navy.mil/index.cfm?fuseaction=home .displayPlatform&key=60296EB4-9CAC-403A-BA7A-6A8D96DA9B53.

71   *H-250 phased array:* John C. Wise, "PLA Air Defence Radars," Air Power Australia, last updated April 2012, accessed August 19, 2014, http://www.ausairpower.net/APA-PLA -IADS-Radars.html.

72   *Type 99 tanks:* Martin Andrew, "Type 96 and Type 99 Main Battle Tanks," Air Power Australia, September 2009, accessed August 24, 2014, http://www.ausairpower.net /APA-PLA-Type-96-99.html.
     Airbus A380s: "A380 Family," Airbus, accessed August 19, 2014, http://www.airbus.com /aircraftfamilies/passengeraircraft/a380family/.
     The headquarters of Pacific Command: "About USPACOM," U.S. Pacific Command, accessed August 19, 2014, http://www.pacom.mil/.
     Chinese-made Z-10 attack helicopter: Jeffrey Lin and Peter W. Singer, "Army Helicopter, Navy Ship," *Eastern Arsenal* (blog), *Popular Science,* April 4, 2014, accessed August 19, 2014, http://www.popsci.com/blog-network/eastern-arsenal/army-helicopter-navy-ship.

73   *A Type 93A submarine:* Jeffrey Lin and Peter W. Singer, "New Chinese 039C Submarine Doesn't Need to Come Up for Air . . . in Several Weeks," *Eastern Arsenal* (blog), *Popular Science,* April 15, 2014, accessed August 19, 2014, http://www.popsci.com/blog-net work/eastern-arsenal/new-chinese-039c-submarine-doesn%E2%80%99t-need-come -air%E2%80%A6-several-weeks.
     USS George H. W. Bush: "USS *George H. W. Bush* (CVN-77)," U.S. Navy, accessed August 19, 2014, http://www.public.navy.mil/airfor/cvn77/Pages/USS%20GEORGE%20 H.W.%20BUSH%20%28CVN%2077%29.aspx.
     USS John Warner: Eric Durie, "Meet SSN 785—the Navy's 12th *Virginia*-Class Submarine," *Navy Live* (blog), U.S. Navy, March 15, 2013, accessed August 19, 2014, http://navy live.dodlive.mil/2013/03/15/meet-ssn-785-the-navys-12th-virginia-class-submarine/.

74   *"releasing Mark Fifty-Four":* "United States Navy Fact File: MK 54—Torpedo," U.S. Navy, accessed August 19, 2014, http://www.navy.mil/navydata/fact_display .asp?cid=2100&tid=1100&ct=2.
     RIM-161 SM-3 missiles: "Standard Missile-3," Raytheon, accessed August 19, 2014, http:// www.raytheon.com/capabilities/products/sm-3/.

75   *"Update from the* Stockdale's *ATHENA":* "USS *Stockdale,*" U.S. Navy, accessed August 19, 2014, http://www.public.navy.mil/surfor/ddg106/Pages/WelcomeAboard.aspx#.U _Qx5Uj6L6A.

77   *AN/ASQ-239 Barracuda system:* Dave Majumdar, "F-35 as ISR Collector," *Defense News,* November 1, 2010, accessed August 19, 2014, http://www.defensenews.com/art icle/20101101/C4ISR02/11010309/F-35-ISR-collector.

78   *not even a tiny percentage could be tested:* John Villasenor, "Compromised by Design? Securing the Defense Electronics Supply Chain," Brookings Institution, November 2013, accessed August 19, 2014, http://www.brookings.edu/~/media/research/files /papers/2013/11/4%20securing%20electronics%20supply%20chain%20against%20 intentionally%20compromised%20hardware%20villasenor/villasenor_hw_security _nov7.pdf.

79   USS Boxer: "USS *Boxer* (LHD 4)," U.S. Navy, accessed August 19, 2014, http://www.navy
      .mil/local/lhd4/.
      Fifteenth Marine Expeditionary Unit: "15th Marine Expeditionary Unit," U.S. Marine
      Corps, accessed August 19, 2014, http://www.15thmeu.marines.mil/.
      the Arizona *memorial:* "USS *Arizona* (BB-39) Memorial at Pearl Harbor, Hawaii," U.S.
      Navy History and Heritage Command, accessed August 26, 2014, http://www.history
      .navy.mil/photos/sh-usn/usnsh-a/bb39-v.htm.
80   USS Lake Erie: "USS *Lake Erie* (CG 70)," U.S. Navy, accessed August 19, 2014, http://
      www.public.navy.mil/surfor/cg70/Pages/default.aspx#.U_Q-3Uj6L6A.
81   *modafinil for endurance:* Peter Rubin, "Superhuman Performance Enhancers You Can
      Find Online," *Wired,* December 20, 2012, accessed August 17, 2014, http://www.wired.co
      .uk/news/archive/2012-12/20/performance-enhancers.

Part 3

85   *so many boys and so few girls:* Louisa Lim, "China Demographic Crisis: Too Many Boys,
      Elderly," NPR.org, April 14, 2008, accessed August 19, 2014, http://www.npr.org/temp
      lates/story/story.php?storyId=89572563.
      Duke's: "Duke's Waikiki," TS Restaurants, accessed August 19, 2014, http://www
      .dukeswaikiki.com/.
88   *what had happened to the Japanese Americans:* "Teaching with Documents: Documents
      and Photographs Related to Japanese Relocation During World War II," National Ar-
      chives, accessed August 19, 2014, http://www.archives.gov/education/lessons/japanese
      -relocation/.
89   *"major cause of degradation":* Barry Thaler, "Affordable Switches for Pulsed Power Sys-
      tems," *Empfasis,* January 2007, accessed August 19, 2014, http://www.empf.org/empfa
      sis/2007/Jan07/january%202007%20empfasis.pdf.
90   *officer's quarters in Fort Mason:* "Fort Mason," Golden Gate National Parks Conser-
      vancy, accessed August 19, 2014, http://www.parksconservancy.org/visit/park-sites/fort
      -mason.html.
94   *Mark VI patrol boats:* Valerie Insinna, "Navy Receives First New Patrol Boat," *National
      Defense,* November 2014, accessed October 21, 2014, http://www.nationaldefensemaga
      zine.org/archive/2014/November/Pages/NavyReceivesFirstNewPatrolBoat.aspx.
95   *"they sunk the* Ford": Tom Moore, "CVN-78: A True Leap Ahead for the Navy and Na-
      val Aviation," *Navy Live* (blog), U.S. Navy, July 9, 2013, accessed August 19, 2014, http://
      navylive.dodlive.mil/2013/07/09/cvn-78-a-true-leap-ahead-for-the-navy-and-naval
      -aviation/.
      "and the Vinson": "USS *Carl Vinson* (CVN-70)," U.S. Navy, accessed August 19, 2014,
      http://www.cvn70.navy.mil/.
      "Only the boomers": "Fleet Ballistic Missile Submarines — SSBN," U.S. Navy, Au-
      gust 14, 2014, accessed August 19, 2014, http://www.navy.mil/navydata/fact_display
      .asp?cid=4100&tid=200&ct=4.
97   *"fight this war as a contractor":* Peter W. Singer, *Corporate Warriors* (Ithaca, NY: Cornell
      University Press, 2003).
98   "I live in lonely desolation": Aleksandr Pushkin, "I Have Outlasted All Desire," 1821.
101   *wartime orphans "the Lost Boys":* "The Lost Boys of Sudan," International Rescue Com-
      mittee, accessed August 19, 2014, http://www.rescue.org/lost-boys-sudan.
      "principal deputy undersecretary of defense": "ACQWeb: Office of the Under Secretary

of Defense for Acquisition, Technology and Logistics," Department of Defense, accessed August 19, 2014, http://www.acq.osd.mil/.

102 *"either of the Big Two firms"*: Sandra Irwin, "Consolidation of Top Pentagon Contractors Only a Matter of Time," *National Defense*, April 27, 2014, accessed August 19, 2014, http://www.nationaldefensemagazine.org/blog/Lists/Posts/Post.aspx?List=7c996cd7 -cbb4-4018-baf8-8825eada7aa2&ID=1489.

106 *Mare Island Naval Shipyard*: "History," Mare Island Museum, Mare Island Historic Park Foundation, accessed August 20, 2014, http://www.mareislandmuseum.org/about/his tory/.

"Damn the torpedoes, full speed ahead": "Famous Navy Quotes: Who Said Them and When," Naval Heritage and History Command, U.S. Navy, accessed August 20, 2014, http://www.history.navy.mil/trivia/trivia02.htm.

107 *fifty times less visible to radar:* Clay Dillow, "The Most Technologically Advanced Warship Ever Built," *Popular Science,* October 16, 2012, accessed August 20, 2014, http:// www.popsci.com/technology/article/2012-08/ocean-power.

wave-piercing tumblehome hull: Jim Downey, "Presentation by DDG 1000 Program Manager to the American Society of Naval Engineers (ASNE): DDG 1000," American Society of Naval Engineers, April 17, 2013, accessed August 20, 2014, https://www.naval engineers.org/flagship/meetings/Documents/Downey_DDG1000_4-17-13.pdf.

108 *an integrated power system:* Greg Szepe, "The DDG-1000 Zumwalt Integrated Power System's Unique Indirect Logical Interfaces with Weapon and Sensor Systems. An Instantiation of a Federated Ship Controls Architecture," American Society of Naval Engineers, June 4, 2010, accessed August 20, 2014, https://www.navalengineers.org /sitecollectiondocuments/2010%20proceedings%20documents/emts%202010%20pro ceedings/papers/thursday/emts10_2_21.pdf.

seven billion dollars each: "Selected Acquisition Report (SAR) Summary Tables," Office of the Under Secretary of Defense for Acquisition, Technology and Logistics, Department of Defense, December 2013, accessed August 20, 2014, http://www.acq.osd.mil /ara/sar/SST-2013-12.pdf.

109 *"used a NAVSEA selection algorithm"*: "NAVSEA Naval Sea Systems Command," U.S. Navy, accessed August 20, 2014, http://www.navsea.navy.mil/default.aspx.

110 *four IEDs detonated:* Peter W. Singer, "The Evolution of Improvised Explosive Devices (IEDs)," *Armed Forces Journal,* February 2012, accessed August 20, 2014, http://www .brookings.edu/research/articles/2012/02/improvised-explosive-devices-singer.

111 *flash-bang grenade:* Marshall Brain, "How Flashbang Grenades (AKA Percussion Grenades or Stun Grenades) Work," How Stuff Works, February 23, 2011, accessed August 20, 2014, http://blogs.howstuffworks.com/brainstuff/how-flashbang-grenades-aka-per cussion-grenades-work/.

113 *the renowned artists:* "About," Christo and Jeanne-Claude, accessed August 20, 2014, http://www.christojeanneclaude.net.

a train of iRobot Majordomos: "Robots for Defense and Security," iRobot, accessed August 20, 2014, http://www.irobot.com/us/learn/defense.aspx; fictional robot.

115 *"space-based underwater detection"*: Mackenzie Eaglen and Jon Rodeback, "Submarine Arms Race in the Pacific: The Chinese Challenge to U.S. Undersea Supremacy," Heritage Foundation, February 2, 2012, accessed August 20, 2014, http://www.heritage.org /research/reports/2010/02/submarine-arms-race-in-the-pacific-the-chinese-challenge -to-us-undersea-supremacy#_ftn9.

116 *"low-level Cherenkov rays"*: John Millis, "Cherenkov Radiation: The Physics of Gamma-Ray Astronomy," About.com, accessed January 5, 2013, http://space.about.com/od /astronomytools/a/Cherenkov-Radiation.htm.

118 *the UCLA alma mater song*: "The Den Traditions," UCLA Bruins, accessed August 20, 2014, http://www.uclabruins.com/ViewArticle.dbml?ATCLID=208268269.

120 *president of the Naval War College*: "About," U.S. Naval War College, accessed August 20, 2014, https://www.usnwc.edu/About.aspx.
the congressional inquiries that had decimated the senior ranks: "Joint Committee on the Investigation of the Pearl Harbor Attack (Pearl Harbor Committee)," U.S. Senate, accessed August 20, 2014, https://www.senate.gov/artandhistory/history/common/in vestigations/PearlHarbor.htm.

122 *"the vertical launch cells"*: Kris Osborn, "Navy Upgrades Vertical Launch Systems," DefenseTech.org, July 2, 2014, accessed August 20, 2014, http://defensetech.org/2014/07/02 /navy-upgrades-vertical-launch-systems/.
Known as the Metal Storm: Tyler Rogoway, "The Seven Deadliest Naval Close-In Weapon Systems," *Foxtrot Alpha* (blog), Jalopnik.com, April 27, 2014, accessed August 20, 2014, http://foxtrotalpha.jalopnik.com/the-seven-deadliest-naval-close-in-weapon -systems-1568291678.

123 *"from the Dahlgren facility"*: "About NSWC Dahlgren," U.S. Navy, accessed August 20, 2014, http://www.navsea.navy.mil/nswc/dahlgren/default.aspx.
rail gun represented a break point: Spencer Ackerman, "Video: Navy Fires Off Its New Weaponized Railgun," *Danger Room* (blog), *Wired*, February 28, 2012, accessed August 20, 2014, http://www.wired.com/2012/02/railgun-real-gun/?utm _source=feedburner&utm_medium=email&utm_campaign=Feed%253A+WiredDan gerRoom+%2528Blog+-+Danger+Room%2529.

124 *called a Lorentz force*: "Railgun Physics," Massachusetts Institute of Technology, accessed August 20, 2014, http://web.mit.edu/mouser/www/railgun/physics.html.

126 *The original Tank*: "The JCS Conference Room: 'The Tank,'" Defense Technical Information Center, Department of Defense, accessed August 20, 2014, http://www.dtic.mil/ doctrine/doctrine/history/jcspart5.pdf.
Florida subcontractor: Fictional characters were inspired by actual events; see Guy Lawson, "The Stoner Arms Dealers: How Two American Kids Became Big-Time Weapons Traders," *Rolling Stone*, http://www.rollingstone.com/politics/news/the-stoner-arms-dealers-20110316.

128 *"A sonic boom"*: Esther Inglis-Arkell, "Cherenkov Radiation Is a Sonic Boom for Light," iO9.com, September 29, 2012, accessed August 26, 2014, http://io9.com/5947197/cher enkov-radiation-is-a-sonic-boom-for-light.

131 *their golden hour to save a life*: Chris Willis, "After the Battle: The Golden Hour," U.S. Air Force, March 14, 2013, accessed August 20, 2014, http://www.bagram.afcent.af.mil /news/story.asp?id=123340100.
These nearly undetectable vehicles: "Converting Wave Motion to Propulsion," Liquid Robotics, accessed August 20, 2014, http://liquidr.com/technology/waveglider/how-it -works.html.
Great Pacific Garbage Patch: "Marine Debris: Great Pacific Garbage Patch," National Oceanic and Atmospheric Administration, August 20, 2014, accessed August 20, 2014, http://marinedebris.noaa.gov/info/patch.html.

132 *United Kingdom's new red-and-white flag*: Matt Ford, "Will This Be the U.K.'s New Flag?,"

Atlantic, March 5, 2014, accessed August 20, 2014, http://www.theatlantic.com/international/archive/2014/03/will-this-be-the-uks-new-flag/284234/.

133 *flailed at each other:* Francis Fukuyama, "America in Decay: The Sources of Political Dysfunction," *Foreign Affairs* (September/October 2014), accessed August 21, 2014, http://www.foreignaffairs.com/articles/141729/francis-fukuyama/america-in-decay.

134 *"'To secure ourselves'":* Sun-Tzu, *The Art of War,* trans. Lionel Giles (Blacksburg, VA: Thrifty Books, 2009).

136 *"Our Weibo micro-blog":* Sign-up page, Weibo, accessed August 20, 2014, http://www.weibo.com/signup/mobile.php?lang=en-us.

137 *"a very messy manner":* John J. Mearsheimer, *The Tragedy of Great Power Politics* (New York: W. W. Norton, 2001).

139 *Sandy Beach Park:* "Sandy Beach Park," Hawaii Beach Safety, accessed August 20, 2014, http://oceansafety.ancl.hawaii.edu/v2.0/?i=oahu&shid=4&bch=sandy. The beach is known as one of the most dangerous surf spots on Oahu.

140 *787-9 executive jet:* "787 Dreamliner: Fact Sheet," Boeing, accessed August 20, 2014, http://www.boeing.com/boeing/commercial/787family/787-9prod.page.
the Studio 54 nightclub: Sean O'Hare, "Inside Studio 54: Fascinating Photographs Reveal What Stars Really Got Up to in World's Most Famous Nightclub," *Mail Online,* January 17, 2013, accessed August 20, 2014, http://www.dailymail.co.uk/news/article-2263800/The-crazy-antics-Studio-54-revealed — pictures-just-stars-got-legendary-New-York-nightclub.html.

141 *"A letter of marque":* "Marque and Reprisal," Heritage Foundation, accessed August 20, 2014, http://www.heritage.org/constitution/#!/articles/1/essays/50/marque-and-reprisal. Also see Captures Clause.

142 *"It is one of the last":* Chris Hoel, "What It's Like to Sip a Century-Old Champagne from a Shipwreck," *St. Louis Magazine,* February 22, 2012, accessed August 20, 2014, http://www.stlmag.com/What-its-Like-to-Sip-a-Century-Old-Champagne-From-a-Shipwreck/.

143 *"article one, section eight":* "The Constitution of the United States: A Transcription," National Archives, accessed August 20, 2014, http://www.archives.gov/exhibits/charters/constitution_transcript.html.

145 *the graffiti:* "Patent: Method and Apparatus for Creating Virtual Graffiti in a Mobile Virtual and Augmented Reality System, US 8350871 B2," Google, January 8, 2013, accessed August 20, 2014, http://www.google.com/patents/US8350871. Also see http://grafiti.mobi/dig-graffiti-applications-and-tools-for-smes-and-users/.

146 *first-generation Google Glass:* "Google Glass: What It Does," Google, accessed August 20, 2014, http://www.google.com/glass/start/what-it-does/.

148 *passed the SIG Sauer P226 pistol:* "Pistols — P226," SIG Sauer, accessed August 20, 2014, http://www.sigsauer.com/catalogproductlist/pistols-p226.aspx.

151 *The Versatrax 300:* "Versatrax 300," Inuktun, accessed July 24, 2014, http://www.inuktun.com/crawler-vehicles/versatrax-300.html.

157 *old Defense Production Act:* "The Defense Production Act of 1950, As Amended," Department of Defense, accessed August 20, 2014, http://www.acq.osd.mil/mibp/dpac/final__defense_production_act_091030.pdf.
representing a sovereign wealth fund: "Sovereign Wealth Funds — Frequently Asked Questions," February 27, 2008, European Commission, accessed August 20, 2014, http://europa.eu/rapid/press-release_MEMO-08-126_en.htm?locale=en.

158 *stepped out for a coffee break:* Kay Mathews, "Photo: Sam Walton's Office in Walmart

Visitor Center, Bentonville, Ark.," *Digital Journal,* June 4, 2011, accessed August 20, 2014, http://www.digitaljournal.com/image/88949.

163 *graphene was light and strong:* "The Story of Graphene," University of Manchester, accessed August 20, 2014, http://www.graphene.manchester.ac.uk/explore/the-story-of -graphene/.

164 *also known as a 3-D printer:* Bob Tita, "How 3-D Printing Works," *Wall Street Journal,* June 10, 2013, accessed August 20, 2014, http://online.wsj.com/news/articles/SB1000142 4127887323716304578483062211388072.

a manufacturing revolution: "3D printing: Second Industrial Revolution Is Under Way," *New Scientist,* accessed August 20, 2014, http://www.newscientist.com/special/3D -printing.

165 *just spoken Klingon: Klingon Pocket Dictionary,* Klingonska Akademien, accessed August 20, 2014, http://klingonska.org/dict/.

166 *"Russian Foundation for Advanced Research Projects":* "Putin Seeks to Create Russian DARPA Equivalent," *Global Security Newswire,* June 21, 2012, accessed August 20, 2014, http://www.nti.org/gsn/article/putin-seeks-create-darpa-equivalent/.

168 *the electronic ink used:* Jason Koebler, "This E-Tattoo Uses Conventional Chips, No Nanotech Required," *Motherboard,* April 4, 2014, accessed August 20, 2014, http:// motherboard.vice.com/read/this-e-tattoo-uses-conventional-chips-no-nanotech -required.

Dmitri Shostakovich's Fifth Symphony: "Shostakovich's Symphony No. 5," *Keeping Score,* accessed August 20, 2014, http://www.pbs.org/keepingscore/shostakovich-symphony-5 .html.

170 *Iliahi Elementary School:* "About Iliahi," *Iliahi Elementary School,* accessed August 20, 2014, https://sites.google.com/a/dragons.k12.hi.us/iliahiel/.

173 *community development units:* "Provincial Reconstruction Teams (PRTs)," Department of State, accessed August 20, 2014, http://www.state.gov/p/nea/ci/iz/c21830.htm; fictional unit.

174 *Directorate Z-8K assault helicopters:* "Product Information — Z8 Helicopter," Changhe Aircraft Industries Group, accessed August 20, 2014, http://www.changhe.com/english /ecpxx/ecpxx.htm.

175 *"It was always a risk":* Charles J. Dunlap Jr., "Lawfare Today . . . and Tomorrow," in *International Law and the Changing Character of War,* eds. Raul A. Pedrozo and Daria P. Wollschlaeger (Newport, RI: U.S. Naval War College, 2011), 315–25.

The bridge was illuminated: Heather Kelly, "San Francisco Turns a Bridge into Art with 25,000 Lights," CNN.com, March 8, 2013, accessed August 20, 2014, http://www.cnn .com/2013/03/06/tech/innovation/bay-bridge-light-installation/.

178 *The space was cavernous:* "US Naval Air Station Sunnyvale, Historic District (Moffett Field)," National Park Service, accessed August 21, 2014, http://www.nps.gov/nr/travel /santaclara/usn.htm.

now filled Hangar One: "Hangar 1, Shenandoah Plaza Historic District," NASA, accessed August 21, 2014, http://historicproperties.arc.nasa.gov/hangar1.html.

come up with a unique plan: "Moffett Federal Airfield," GlobalSecurity.org, accessed October 6, 2014, http://www.globalsecurity.org/military/facility/moffett.htm.

Silicon Valley: "Major Silicon Valley Companies," Google Maps, August 27, 2011, accessed August 21, 2014, https://maps.google.com/maps/ms?msid=203174842897863924 077.0004ab7eb4bb25f971c1d&msa=0&dg=feature.

NASA's Ames Research Center: "About," *NASA,* accessed August 21, 2014, http://www
.nasa.gov/centers/ames/about/index.html.

179 *Google acquired Hangar One:* Brandon Bailey, "Google to Restore Hangar One and Operate Runways at Moffett Field," *San Jose Mercury News,* February 10, 2014, accessed
August 21, 2014. http://www.mercurynews.com/business/ci_25109267/google-restore
-hangar-one-and-operate-runways-at.

The NSA had cost Silicon Valley: Danielle Kehl et al., "Surveillance Costs: The NSA's Impact on the Economy, Internet Freedom, and Cybersecurity," New America Foundation,
July 29, 2014, accessed August 21, 2014, http://oti.newamerica.net/publications/policy
/surveillance_costs_the_nsas_impact_on_the_economy_internet_freedom_cybersecurity.

human-flesh-search-machine: Celia Hatton, "China's Internet Vigilantes and the 'Human
Flesh Search Engine,'" *BBC News Magazine,* January 28, 2014, accessed August 21, 2014,
http://www.bbc.co.uk/news/magazine-25913472.

184 *his first time on the cover:* "Brad Pitt: The Sexiest Man Alive," *People,* November 13, 2000,
accessed August 21, 2014, http://www.people.com/people/archive/article/0,,20132898,00
.html.

186 *"The old MIG welder works":* "MIG Welding FAQs," Lincoln Electric, accessed August
21, 2014, http://www.lincolnelectric.com/en-us/support/welding-solutions/Pages/mig
-faqs-detail.aspx.

188 *passed Angel Island to starboard:* "Angel Island State Park," California Department of
Parks and Recreation, accessed August 21, 2014, http://www.parks.ca.gov/?page_id=468.

eBay Park's pier: "AT&T Park," San Francisco Giants, accessed August 21, 2014, http://
sanfrancisco.giants.mlb.com/sf/ballpark/.

190 *Art Hodes:* Jon Pareles, "Art Hodes, a Pianist Known for the Blues in the Old Style, 88,"
New York Times, March 6, 1993, http://www.nytimes.com/1993/03/06/arts/art-hodes-a
-pianist-known-for-the-blues-in-the-old-style-88.html.

193 *ship mission center:* Jay Sego and Jim Downey, "Life at Sea Aboard DDG 1000," *Surface Warfare,* accessed August 21, 2014, http://surfwarmag.ahf.nmci.navy.mil/feature
_ddg_1000.html.

197 *"calling it Blackwater":* August Cole, "Blackwater Vies for Jobs Beyond Guard Duty,"
Wall Street Journal, October 15, 2007, accessed August 21, 2014, http://online.wsj.com
/news/articles/SB119240518691958669.

205 *"the history of wine itself ":* Tom Standage, *A History of the World in Six Glasses* (New
York: Walker, 2006).

207 *inside the 3-D environment:* Betsy Book, "Virtual Worlds: Today and in the Future," BCS,
March 2006, accessed August 21, 2014, http://www.bcs.org/content/conwebdoc/3336.

submerged rendition of Las Ramblas: "City Visit of Las Ramblas District in Barcelona,"
Barcelona.com, accessed August 21, 2014, http://www.barcelona.com/barcelona_city
_guide/city_visits_of_barcelona/ramblas.

208 *a liver shot:* Eric C. Stevens, "Analysis of the Liver Shot: Throwing and Defending,"
BreakingMuscle.com, accessed August 21, 2014, http://breakingmuscle.com/martial
-arts/analysis-of-the-liver-shot-throwing-and-defending.

210 *"at DevGru with me":* Brandon Webb, "DEVGRU/SEAL TEAM 6," Sofrep.com, accessed
August 21, 2014, http://sofrep.com/devgru-seal-team-6/.

212 *"cognitive augmentation":* Ed Boyden, "In Pursuit of Human Augmentation," *MIT Technology Review,* September 17, 2007, accessed August 21, 2014, http://www.technology
review.com/view/408686/in-pursuit-of-human-augmentation/.

"*JSOC*": "Joint Special Operations Command," U.S. Special Operations Command, accessed August 21, 2014, http://www.socom.mil/Pages/JointSpecialOperationsCommand.aspx.

"*One Hundred Sixtieth helo drivers*": "160th Special Operations Aviation Regiment (Airborne)," U.S. Army, accessed August 21, 2014, http://www.soc.mil/ARSOAC/160th.html; the Persistent Operations Group is a fictional special-mission unit.

215 *penthouse suite number 3*: "Moana Surfrider Room Types," Starwood Hotels and Resorts Worldwide, accessed August 21, 2014, http://www.moana-surfrider.com/rooms andsuites/roomtypes/.

223 *AH-1Z Viper attack helicopters*: "AH-1Z Super Cobra/Viper," U.S. Marine Corps, accessed August 22, 2014, http://www.marines.com/operating-forces/equipment/aircraft /ah-1z-cobra.

Part 4

227 *the Republic of Kalaallit Nunaat*: "Greenland: Oil Fortune to Fund Independence," United Nations Regional Information Centre for Western Europe, accessed August 23, 2014, http://www.unric.org/en/indigenous-people/27308-greenland-oil-fortune-to -fund-independence.

228 *massive oil fields were discovered*: "U.S. Department of the Interior U.S. Geological Survey USGS Fact Sheet 2008-3049 2008 Circum-Arctic Resource Appraisal: Estimates of Undiscovered Oil and Gas North of the Arctic Circle," U.S. Geological Survey 2008, accessed August 23, 2014, http://pubs.usgs.gov/fs/2008/3049/fs2008-3049.pdf.

the U.S. Coast Guard had only one: "USCGC *Healy* (WAGB-20)," U.S. Coast Guard, accessed August 23, 2014, http://www.uscg.mil/pacarea/cgcHealy/.

230 *steadying a spotting scope*: Geoffrey Ingersoll, "New 'One-Shot' Rifle Sight Could Make Snipers Deadlier Than Ever," *Business Insider,* October 12, 2012, accessed August 23, 2014, http://www.businessinsider.com/new-one-shot-rifle-sight-technology-does-the -aiming-for-every-sniper-2012-10.

a QBU-88 rifle: "QBU-88," World Guns, accessed October 6, 2014, http://world.guns.ru /sniper/sniper-rifles/ch/qbu--e.html.

with a TrackingPoint spotter: "What the Shooter Does," *Tracking Point,* accessed August 23, 2014, http://tracking-point.com/.

231 *Hawaii's first radar defense network*: "Mount Kaala, Oahu, HI," Radomes.org, accessed August 23, 2014, http://www.radomes.org/museum/recent/KaalaAFSOahuHI.html.

235 *Gulf of the Farallones*: "Welcome to Gulf of the Farallones National Marine Sanctuary," National Ocean Service, August 7, 2014, accessed August 23, 2014, http://farallones .noaa.gov/.

at full EMCON A: "Emission Control," U.S. Navy, accessed August 23, 2014, http://www .navair.navy.mil/ibst/03_E3/emcon.html.

236 *stealthy unmanned surface vessels*: Sandra I. Erwin, "Navy Will Deploy Swarms of Autonomous Robots to Protect Warships at Sea," *National Defense*, October 5, 2014, accessed October 5, 2014, http://www.nationaldefensemagazine.org/blog/Lists/Posts/Post .aspx?ID=1628.

239 *The American military had gotten the idea*: Ellen Nakashima and Craig Whitlock, "With Air Force's Gorgon Drone 'We Can See Everything,'" *Washington Post,* January 2, 2011, accessed August 23, 2014, http://www.washingtonpost.com/wp-dyn/content/art icle/2011/01/01/AR2011010102690.html.

242 *"what you should fear"*: Jack Pemment, "Blame the Amygdala: The Neuroscience of Crime and Violent Behavior," *Psychology Today*, April 5, 2013, accessed October 27, 2014, http://www.psychologytoday.com/blog/blame-the-amygdala/201301/what-would-we -find-wrong-in-the-brain-serial-killer.

243 *the way sandtiger sharks cooperated:* "Co-Operative Hunting in Sandtiger Sharks," ReefQuest Centre for Shark Research, accessed August 23, 2014, http://www.elasmo -research.org/education/topics/b_coop_hunting.htm.

Mark 81 rocket-powered torpedo: Eric Adams, "Supercavitating Torpedo," *Popular Science*, June 1, 2004, accessed August 23, 2014, http://www.popsci.com/scitech/arti cle/2004-06/supercavitating-torpedo; fictional weapon.

247 *idea from that video game:* "Call of Duty: Ghosts," Activision, accessed August 23, 2014, http://www.callofduty.com/ghosts/home.

250 *dehydrated roast pork and mooncakes:* Gregory Mone, "Eat Like a Taikonaut," *Popular Science*, July 25, 2007, accessed August 23, 2014, http://www.popsci.com/article/2007-07 /eat-taikonaut.

fired an antisatellite missile: Peter Grier, "The Flying Tomato Can," *Air Force Magazine*, February 2009, accessed August 23, 2014, http://www.airforcemag.com/magazine archive/pages/2009/february%202009/0209tomato.aspx?signon=false.

254 *"Out of the blue":* Steve Hammond and David Pierce, "Space Pirates," *Flash Fearless Vs. the Zorg Women, Parts 5 & 6*, 1975, performed by Alice Cooper, http://www.allmusic .com/song/space-pirates-mt0011871423.

257 *Ehukai Beach:* "Ehukai Beach Park," Hawaii Beach Safety, accessed August 23, 2014, http://oceansafety.ancl.hawaii.edu/v/2.0/?i=oahu&shid=1&bch=ehukai.

a small black lobster: Maryann Lawlor, "Lobsters Populate Navy Robot Platter," *Signal Online*, May 2004, accessed August 23, 2014, http://www.afcea.org/content/?q=node/135.

258 *the lobster made a final sprint:* Joseph Ayers, "Biomimetic Underwater Robot Program," Northeastern Marine Science Center, accessed August 23, 2014, http://www.neurotech nology.neu.edu/.

suppressed HK 416 rifles: "HK416 A5," Heckler and Koch, accessed August 17, 2014, http://www.heckler-koch.com/en/products/military/assault-rifles/hk416-a5/hk416 -a5-11/overview.html.

swim to shore without oxygen tanks: "110 Predictions for the Next 110 Years," *Popular Mechanics*, December 10, 2012, accessed August 23, 2014, http://www.popularmechan ics.com/technology/engineering/news/110-predictions-for-the-next-110-years.

260 *The* Tallyho *had originally been:* "Spaceships: Virgin Galactic's Vehicles," Virgin Galactic, accessed August 23, 2014, http://www.virgingalactic.com/overview/spaceships; fictional spaceship.

Harry Winston in London's Mayfair: "Harry Winston," Bond Street Association, accessed August 23, 2014, http://www.bondstreet.co.uk/shop/harry-winston/.

the image had stuck with Sir Aeric: Thom Patterson, "Overheard on CNN: New Shuttle Needs Space Plane 'Coolness,'" CNN.com, June 8, 2012, accessed March 18, 2014, http:// www.cnn.com/2012/06/08/us/space-shuttle-overheard-on-cnn/index.html?hpt=hp_c2.

261 *a love that would never come:* Christopher Paul et al., "Paths to Victory: Detailed Insurgency Case Studies," RAND Corporation, 2013, accessed August 23, 2014, http://www .rand.org/pubs/research_reports/RR291z2.html.

civilian-style Great Wall pickups: "Wingle 5," Great Wall Motors, accessed August 23, 2014, http://www.gwm-global.com/wingle5.html.

265 *the two metallic hands:* Francie Diep, "A Mind-Controlled Robotic Hand with a Sense of Touch," *Popular Science,* February 5, 2014, accessed August 23, 2014, http://www.popsci.com/article/science/mind-controlled-robotic-hand-sense-touch.

266 *"lenses of the wrong prescription":* Emily Gold Boutilier, "Thinking the World into Motion," *Brown Alumni Magazine,* January 2005, accessed August 23, 2014, http://archive.today/hf0P9.

"William Gibson's 1984 novel Neuromancer": Ed Cumming, "The Man Who Saw Tomorrow," *Guardian,* July 27, 2014, accessed August 23, 2014, http://www.theguardian.com/books/2014/jul/28/william-gibson-neuromancer-cyberpunk-books. Also see http://williamgibsonbooks.com/books/neuromancer.asp.

267 *the five-foot-tall spider-bot:* Lance Ulanoff, "3D-Printed Spiderbot Is Stuff of Dreams and Nightmares," Mashable.com, July 5, 2013, accessed August 24, 2014, http://mashable.com/2013/07/05/3d-printed-spider-robot/.

268 *sifting through rubble:* Dan Nosowitz, "Meet Japan's Earthquake Search-and-Rescue Robots," *Popular Science,* March 11, 2011, accessed August 24, 2014, http://www.popsci.com/technology/article/2011-03/six-robots-could-shape-future-earthquake-search-and-rescue.

269 *"What we observe":* Werner Heisenberg, as quoted in Robert Pine, *Science and the Human Prospect* (Honolulu: University of Hawaii, 1999), online edition, accessed July 15, 2014, http://home.honolulu.hawaii.edu/~pine/book1qts/chapter8qts.html.

276 *a Type 98 bayonet knife:* Fan Zhibin, "Regiment in Bayonet Training," *People's Daily Online,* accessed August 24, 2014, http://english.peopledaily.com.cn/90786/7689290.html.
QSZ-92: "NORINCO QSZ-92 (Type 92) Semi-Automatic Pistol (1998)," MilitaryFactory.com, September 2, 2011, accessed August 24, 2014, http://www.militaryfactory.com/smallarms/detail.asp?smallarms_id=392.

278 *Taser X26:* "Taser X26 CEW," Taser International, accessed August 24, 2014, http://www.taser.com/products/law-enforcement/taser-x26-ecd.

279 *the pain pump implanted:* "What Is a Drug Pump?," Medtronic, accessed August 24, 2014, http://www.medtronic.com/patients/chronic-pain/device/drug-pumps/what-is-it/.
"kinda like how a magician uses mirrors": "How Do 'Invisibility Cloaks' Work?," Physics.org, accessed August 24, 2014, http://www.physics.org/article-questions.asp?id=69.

280 *"It's a float vest":* Matthew Cox, "Navy Upgrading Its Aircrew Survival Vest," *Kit Up* (blog), Military.com, December 20, 2013, accessed August 24, 2014, http://kitup.military.com/2013/12/navy-upgrading-aircrew-survival.html.

283 *corner of Queen and Ward:* "Ward Avenue and Queen Street, Honolulu, HI 96814," Google Maps, accessed August 24, 2014, https://www.google.com/maps/place/Ward+Ave+%26+Queen+St,+Ward+Farmers+Market,+Honolulu,+HI+96814/@21.2975539,-157.8542867,17z/data=!3m1!4b1!4m2!3m1!1s0x7c006de2ff5f99a7:0x5012c07f4400063f.

285 *Jednostka Wojskowa Formoza:* "Informacje," Jednostki Wojskowej Formoza, accessed August 24, 2014, http://www.formoza.wp.mil.pl/pl/index.html.

286 *"make the fun of the* Orzel": "ORP *Orzel,*" Polish navy, accessed August 24, 2014, http://www.navy.mw.mil.pl/index.php?akcja=orzel.
"ten B-eighty-three one-point-two-megaton nuclear bombs": "B83 Thermonuclear Bomb," U.S. Air Force, October 15, 2008, accessed August 24, 2014, http://www.hill.af.mil/library/factsheets/factsheet.asp?id=5708.

289 *companies' own generators as weapons:* Michael Swearingen et al., "What You Need to Know (and Don't) About the AURORA Vulnerability," *Power*, September 1, 2013, accessed August 24, 2014, http://www.powermag.com/what-you-need-to-know-and -dont-about-the-aurora-vulnerability/?printmode=1.

arching eyebrows, a wide mustache: Monica Nickelsburg, "A Brief History of the Guy Fawkes Mask," *Week*, July 3, 2013, http://theweek.com/article/index/245685/a-brief -history-of-the-guy-fawkes-mask.

291 *"We are Anonymous":* Singer and Friedman, *Cybersecurity and Cyberwar*, 80–84.

295 *General Atomics Avenger stealth drone:* "Predator C Avenger UAS," General Atomics Aeronautical Systems, accessed August 24, 2014, http://www.ga-asi.com/products/air craft/predator_c.php.

297 *Pupukea-Paumalu Forest Reserve:* "Kaunala Loop," Trails.com, accessed August 24, 2014, http://www.trails.com/tcatalog_trail.aspx?trailid=HGP040-047.

old Kahuku training center: "Hawaii Training Center," Operating Engineers Local No. 3, accessed August 24, 2014, http://www.oe3.org/training/hawaii.html.

"Turtle Bay Resort": "The Resort," Turtle Bay Resort, accessed August 24, 2014, http:// www.turtlebayresort.com/resort/.

298 *Dry elastomer adhesive:* Ozgur Unver et al., "Geckobot: A Gecko-Inspired Climbing Robot Using Elastomer Adhesives," International Conference on Robotics and Automation 2006, accessed August 24, 2014, http://nanolab.me.cmu.edu/publications/papers/ Unver-ICRA2006.pdf.

299 *"We did that in BUD/S":* "Stages Overview," Naval Special Warfare Command, accessed August 24, 2014, http://www.sealswcc.com/navy-seals-buds-training-stages-overview .html#.U_o1C0j6L6A.

a lightweight tactical-glasses rig: Jim Hodges, "More Control and Precision for JTACs," *Defense News*, February 12, 2012, accessed February 22, 2012, http://www.defensenews .com/article/20120212/DEFFEAT01/302120009/More-Control-Precision-JTACs.

300 *Zheng He:* Frank Viviano, "China's Great Armada," *National Geographic*, July 2005, accessed August 24, 2014, http://ngm.nationalgeographic.com/ngm/0507/feature2/.

301 *it was a battleship:* Jeffrey Lin and Peter W. Singer, "Learning More About China's New Massive Warship Plan (055 Cruiser)," *Eastern Arsenal* (blog), *Popular Science*, May 1, 2014, accessed August 24, 2014, http://www.popsci.com/blog-network/eastern-arsenal /army-helicopter-navy-ship.

302 *"their Second Expeditionary Brigade":* Amanda Wilcox, "II MEF Reactivates 2nd MEB as Part of Restructuring Initiative," *Jacksonville Daily News*, November 21, 2012, accessed August 24, 2014, http://www.jdnews.com/news/military/ii-mef-reactivates-2nd-meb -as-part-of-restructuring-initiative-1.53422.

"their Eleventh Cavalry": "11th Armored Cavalry Regiment," U.S. Army, accessed August 24, 2014, http://www.irwin.army.mil/CommandGroupUnits/Units/11acr/Pages/default .aspx.

304 *but toward which targets:* "Battle of Midway, 4–7 June 1942, Overview and Special Image Selection," Naval History and Heritage Command, accessed August 24, 2014, http:// www.history.navy.mil/photos/events/wwii-pac/midway/midway.htm.

305 *the Fazio-designed course:* "The Original Fazio Course at Turtle Bay," *Turtle Bay Resort*, accessed August 24, 2014, http://www.turtlebayresort.com/hawaii_golf/fazio_course/.

"Gino's, New York–style": "Menu," Gino's Pizzeria by Maurizio, accessed August 24, 2014, http://ginospizzeriavb.com/menu.php.

307 *"'Ponder and deliberate'"*: Sun-Tzu, *The Art of War,* trans. Lionel Giles, chapter 7.

"'The highest form of generalship'": Ibid., chapter 3.

"'The good fighters of old'": Ibid., chapter 4.

308 *"'All warfare is based on deception'"*: Ibid., chapter 1.

"even if targets are not yet acquired": Craig L. Symonds, *The Battle of Midway* (New York: Oxford University Press, 2013).

"'Never venture, never win'": Sun-Tzu, *The Art of War,* trans. Lionel Giles, chapter 7.

310 *Navy's Littoral Warfare Weapon program:* "Raytheon-Led Littoral Warfare Weapons Team Demonstrates Successful Underwater Launch," Raytheon, September 14, 2009, accessed August 24, 2014, http://investor.raytheon.com/phoenix.zhtml?c=84193&p=irol -newsArticle&ID=1331411&highlight=.

312 *the section designed by Arnold Palmer:* "Palmer Course," 808Golf.com, accessed August 24, 2014, http://www.808golf.com/oahu/turtle_bay_resort/Palmer_Course/images /palmer_map.jpg.

man-portable missile system: David Cenciotti, "New Video Shows Deadly MANPADS Hit on Helicopter in Syria," *The Aviationist* (blog), September 16, 2013, accessed August 24, 2014, http://theaviationist.com/2013/09/16/fn-6-hit/; fictional weapon.

315 *"YJ-12 cruise missiles"*: Robert Haddick, "China's Most Dangerous Missile (So Far)," WarOnTheRocks.com, July 2, 2014, accessed August 24, 2014, http://warontherocks .com/2014/07/chinas-most-dangerous-missile-so-far/#_.

316 *J-31 Falcon Hawk:* Jeffrey Lin and Peter W. Singer, "New Chinese 5th Generation Fighter Jet — J31 Performs More Flight Tests," *Eastern Arsenal* (blog), *Popular Science,* May 22, 2014, accessed August 24, 2014, http://www.popsci.com/blog-network/eastern-arsenal /new-chinese-5th-generation-fighter-jet-j31-performs-more-flight-tests.

318 *the little harbor in Haleiwa:* "Harbor Haleiwa," Google Maps, accessed August 24, 2014, https://www.google.com/maps/preview?oe=utf-8&client=firefox -a&channel=sb&ie=UTF-8&fb=1&gl=us&q=harbor+haleiwa&hq=harbor&hne ar=0x7c0058cb4dbb9179:0xa24ef2e2df99f0c7,haleiwa&ei=pUv6U8SaKs6VyAS2 -YDQDw&ved=0CKABELYD.

319 *"Helemano Stream"*: "Helemano Stream," Google Maps, accessed August 24, 2014, https://www.google.com/maps/place/Helemano+Stream,+Haleiwa,+HI/@21.5833329, -158.1088889,15z/data=!3m1!4b1!4m2!3m1!1s0x7c005f318cae17b5:0x3e9ad372b4590a58.

320 *M240 machine gun:* "The M240 Series," FNH USA, accessed August 24, 2014, http:// www.fnhusa.com/l/products/machine-guns/m240-series/.

a Javelin shoulder-fired rocket: "FGM-148 Javelin," U.S. Marine Corps, accessed August 24, 2014, http://www.marines.com/operating-forces/equipment/weapons/javelin-law -at-4-smaw-tow.

"it's something else": Louis Palazzo, "The Jtac Fixation," *Marine Corps Gazette,* May 2012, accessed August 24, 2014, https://www.mca-marines.org/gazette/article/jtac-fixation -taking-blinders.

321 *the USS Port Royal:* "USS *Port Royal,*" U.S. Navy, accessed August 24, 2014, http://www .public.navy.mil/surfor/cg73/Pages/default.aspx#.U_pRJ0j6L6A.

the USS America: "USS *America,*" U.S. Navy, accessed August 24, 2014, http://www.pub lic.navy.mil/surfor/lha6/Pages/default.aspx#.U_pRZkj6L6A.

322 San Antonio– and Austin-*class landing ships:* "Amphibious Transport Dock—LPD," U.S. Navy, accessed August 24, 2014, http://www.navy.mil/navydata/fact_display .asp?cid=4200&tid=600&ct=4.

"Aleutian Islands": "Welcome to Shemya!," Eareckson Air Station, accessed August 24, 2014, http://chugach-eareckson.com/.

323 *"'the principle of calculated risk'"*: "C in C, U.S. Pacific Fleet, Letter of Instructions, May 28, 1942," Midway1942.org, accessed August 24, 2014, http://www.midway1942.org /docs/usn_doc_24.shtml. The text of Task Force Longboard's orders was taken from the *Nimitz* orders at the Battle of Midway.

324 *joint dual-role air dominance missiles:* Zach Rosenberg, "USAF Cancels AMRAAM Replacement," *Flight Global,* February 14, 2012, accessed August 24, 2014, http://www .flightglobal.com/news/articles/usaf-cancels-amraam-replacement-368249/.

   almost her jet's twins: Craig Scanlan, "Chinese Spies Steal F-35 Joint Strike Fighter Data from BAE Systems," Asia Security Watch, March 12, 2012, accessed August 24, 2014, http://asw.newpacificinstitute.org/?p=10596.

   PL-21D: Wendell Minnick, "China Developing Counterstealth Weapons," *Defense News,* January 31, 2011, accessed August 24, 2014, http://www.defensenews .com/article/20110131/DEFFEAT04/101310315/China-Developing-Counterstealth -Weapons.

325 *a Russian Su-33:* "Su-33," Sukhoi, accessed August 24, 2014, http://www.sukhoi.org/eng /planes/military/su33/.

   neatly arrayed in a line: Wendell Minnick, "Is China's J-31 Stealth Fighter Going Navy All the Way?," *Intercepts* (blog), *Defense News,* January 31, 2013, accessed August 24, 2014, http://intercepts.defensenews.com/2013/01/is-chinas-j-31-fighter-going-navy-all -the-way/.

327 *Garmin AeroScreen:* "Avionics and Safety," Garmin, accessed August 24, 2014, http:// www.garmin.com/en-US/explore/intheair; fictional electronic system.

   the F-15C: "F-15 Eagle Fact Sheet," U.S. Air Force, March 14, 2005, accessed August 24, 2014, http://www.af.mil/AboutUs/FactSheets/Display/tabid/224/Article/104501/f-15 -eagle.aspx.

   the aircraft equivalent of the Ghost Fleet: Mark Wilson, "Google Earth's View of the Boneyard, Where Planes Go to Die," *Gizmodo* (blog), February 23, 2010, accessed August 24, 2014, http://gizmodo.com/5478203/google-earths-view-of-the-boneyard -where-planes-go-to-die.

   Roscoe's jet: Jon Harper, "Air Force to Eliminate Nearly 500 Aircraft in 25 States, D.C., and Overseas," *Stars and Stripes,* March 11, 2014, accessed August 24, 2014, http://www .stripes.com/news/air-force-to-eliminate-nearly-500-aircraft-in-25-states-d-c-and -overseas-1.272304.

   desert-worn KC-135s: "KC-135 Stratotanker," U.S. Air Force, September 15, 2004, accessed August 24, 2014, http://www.af.mil/AboutUs/FactSheets/Display/tabid/224/Ar ticle/104524/kc-135-stratotanker.aspx.

328 *KC-46s:* "KC-46A Pegasus," U.S. Air Force, May 4, 2011, accessed August 24, 2014, http:// www.af.mil/AboutUs/FactSheets/Display/tabid/224/Article/104537/kc-46a.

329 *even a World War I pilot would laugh at:* Robert Valdes, "How the Predator UAV Works," How Stuff Works, accessed August 25, 2014, http://science.howstuffworks.com/preda tor1.htm. See also Singer, *Wired for War.*

   tried to send the cutting-edge technology: Interview with UCAS program officer, June 2014, Washington, DC.

   proposed by a maverick colonel: Michael W. Pietrucha, "The Next Lightweight Fighter," *Air and Space Power Journal* (July/August 2013), accessed August 14, 2014, http://www.

airpower.maxwell.af.mil/apjinternational/apj-s/2014/2014-2/2014_2_02_pietrucha_s
_eng.pdf.

330 *"the valley of death"*: "Several Factors Have Led to a Decline in Partnerships at DOE's
Laboratories," Government Accountability Office, April 19, 2002, accessed August 25,
2014, http://www.gao.gov/products/GAO-02-465.

the agency's trusted-foundry program: "Leading Edge Access Program (LEAP)," DARPA,
accessed August 25, 2014, http://www.darpa.mil/Our_Work/MTO/Programs/Leading
_Edge_Access_Program_%28LEAP%29.aspx.

331 *the main U.S. Army Air Corps base at Wheeler airfield*: "Wheeler Field," Hawaii Aviation,
accessed November 5, 2014, http://hawaii.gov/hawaiiaviation/hawaii-airfields-airports
/oahu-pre-world-war-ii/wheeler-field.

"The hell with that": Patricia Sullivan, "Kenneth Taylor; Flew Against Pearl Harbor
Raiders," *Washington Post*, December 3, 2006, accessed August 25, 2014, http://www
.washingtonpost.com/wp-dyn/content/article/2006/12/02/AR2006120201162.html.

332 *massive C-5 Galaxies:* "C-5 A/B/C Galaxy and C-5M Super Galaxy," U.S. Air Force, May
15, 2006, accessed August 25, 2014, http://www.af.mil/AboutUs/FactSheets/Display
/tabid/224/Article/104492/c-5-abc-galaxy-c-5m-super-galaxy.aspx.

C-141 Starlifters: "Lockheed C-141C Starlifter 'Hanoi Taxi,'" U.S. Air Force, July 2, 2014,
accessed August 25, 2014, http://www.nationalmuseum.af.mil/factsheets/factsheet
.asp?id=3981.

modern C-17 Globemasters: "C-17 Globemaster III," U.S. Air Force, October 27, 2004,
accessed August 25, 2014, http://www.af.mil/AboutUs/FactSheets/Display/tabid/224
/Article/104523/c-17-globemaster-iii.aspx.

333 *Stryker mobile-gun systems:* "Stryker MGS," General Dynamics, accessed August 25,
2014, http://www.gdls.com/index.php/products/stryker-family/stryker-mgs.

form polyurethane polymer concrete: "Polymer Concrete and Ucrete," Prime Polymers,
accessed August 25, 2014, http://www.primepolymers.com/polymer-concrete-ucrete
.php.

334 *AIM-120E AMRAAM air-to-air missiles:* "AIM-120 AMRAAM," U.S. Air Force, April
1, 2003, accessed August 25, 2014, http://www.af.mil/AboutUs/FactSheets/Display
/tabid/224/Article/104576/aim-120-amraam.aspx.

335 *leaving his attacker behind:* Richard G. Sheffield, "Chapter 2: The Airplane," *Jet Fighter
School*, FlightSimBooks.com, accessed August 25, 2014, http://www.flightsimbooks
.com/jfs/page13.php.

indicator approaching the plane's: Richard Sheffield, *The Official F-15 Strike Handbook*,
FlightSimBooks.com, accessed October 11, 2014, http://www.flightsimbooks.com
/f15strikeeagle/03_02_Air_Combat-Related_Aerodynamics.php.

337 *ability to shoot down ballistic missiles:* John D. Gresham, "Navy Area Ballistic Missile
Defense: Coming On Fast," *Proceedings*, January 1999, accessed August 25, 2014, http://
www.usni.org/magazines/proceedings/1999-01/navy-area-ballistic-missile-defense
-coming-fast.

Port Coral, *as it became known, didn't sink:* Sam LaGrone, "Navy Changes Assessment
on *Port Royal* Damage," *U.S. Naval Institute News*, July 18, 2013, accessed August 25, 2014,
http://news.usni.org/2013/07/18/navy-changes-assessment-on-port-royal-damage.

A wave of RIM-162 Evolved Seasparrow: "Seasparrow Missile (RIM-7)," U.S. Navy, November 19, 2013, accessed August 25, 2014, http://www.navy.mil/navydata/fact_display
.asp?cid=2200&tid=900&ct=2.

338 "*USS* Utah": "USS *Utah* (Battleship # 31, later BB-31 and AG-16), 1911–1941 — Overview and Special Image Selection," U.S. Naval History and Heritage Command, April 18, 2007, accessed August 25, 2014, http://www.history.navy.mil/photos/sh-usn/usnsh-u /bb31.htm.

the solid-state, high-energy laser: "Solid-State Laser Technology Maturation Program," U.S. Navy, accessed August 25, 2014, http://www.onr.navy.mil/Media-Center/Fact -Sheets/Solid-State-Laser-Technology-Maturation-Program.aspx.

339 *the USS* New York: "About," USSNewYork.com, accessed August 25, 2014, http://www .ussnewyork.com/ussny_about.html.

341 "*registering as active*": Michael Peck, "Sailors' New Uniforms Could Electronically Track Them All Over the Ship," Medium.com, September 18, 2014, accessed October 27, 2014, https://medium.com/war-is-boring/sailors-new-uniforms-could-electronically-track -them-all-over-ship-94365277c53f.

344 "*hold this line of position*": James D. Hornfischer, *The Last Stand of the Tin Can Sailors: The Extraordinary World War II Story of the U.S. Navy's Finest Hour* (New York: Bantam Books, 2005).

345 "*you stupid* abtomat": Translation of *automaton* from English to Russian, Google Translate, accessed August 25, 2014, https://translate.google.com/#auto/ru/automaton.

347 Sovremenny-*class anti-surface destroyers:* "Hangzhou Type 956 Sov-Sovremenny," GlobalSecurity.org, May 9, 2012, accessed August 25, 2014, http://www.globalsecurity.org /military/world/china/haizhou.htm.

Type Fifty-Four frigates: Gabe Collins, Morgan Clemens, and Kristen Gunness, "The Type 054/054A Frigate Series: China's All-Purpose Surface Combatant," Study of Innovation and Technology in China, University of California Institute on Global Conflict and Cooperation, January 10, 2014, accessed August 25, 2014, http://www.igcc.ucsd .edu/assets/001/505322.pdf.

Luyang-*class guided missile destroyer:* Ridzwan Rahmat, "PLAN Commissions First Type 052D DDG, Puts Second on Sea Trials," *IHS Jane's 360,* March 23, 2014, accessed August 25, 2014, http://www.janes.com/article/35842/plan-commissions-first-type -052d-ddg-puts-second-on-sea-trials.

Naval Strike Missile: "Naval Strike Missile — NSM," Kongsberg, accessed August 25, 2014, http://www.kongsberg.com/en/kds/products/missilesystems/navalstrikemissile/.

Penguin missile: "Penguin Anti-Ship Missile," U.S. Navy, February 20, 2009, accessed August 25, 2014, http://www.navy.mil/navydata/fact_display.asp?cid=2200&tid=600&ct=2.

348 *FL-3000 Red Banner:* James C. Bussert, "China's Navy Deploys Three-Tier Defensive Weapons," *Signal Online,* July 1, 2013, accessed August 25, 2014, http://www.afcea.org /content/?q=node/11461.

The robotic swarm: Vijay Kumar, "Scalable sWarms of Autonomous Robots and Mobile Sensors (SWARMS) Project," Swarms.org, accessed August 25, 2014, http://www .swarms.org/. See also Singer, *Wired for War.*

349 "*If one is not fully*'": Sun-Tzu, *The Art of Warfare,* trans. Roger T. Ames, chapter 2.

351 *using a cuff on his forearm:* Homepage of Thalmic Labs, accessed August 25, 2014, https://www.thalmic.com/en/myo/.

Rolling Airframe missiles: "RIM-116 Rolling Airframe Missile (RAM)," U.S. Navy, November 19, 2013, accessed August 25, 2014, http://www.navy.mil/navydata/fact_display .asp?cid=2200&tid=800&ct=2.

354 *Soar Dragon:* Richard Clements, "New Photos of Chinese Soaring Dragon High Altitude

Long Endurance Drone Emerge," *The Aviationist* (blog), January 21, 2013, accessed August 25, 2014, http://theaviationist.com/2013/01/21/soaring-dragon/.

355 *better lift-to-drag ratio:* Marissa Menezes, "Guizhou Soar Eagle," DefenceAviation.com, January 26, 2013, accessed August 26, 2014, http://www.defenceaviation.com/2013/01/guizhou-soar-eagle.html.

"'*Prize the quick victory*'": Sun-Tzu, *The Art of Warfare,* trans. Roger T. Ames, chapter 2.

358 *The* Shanghai: Jeffrey Lin and P. W. Singer, "Is This a Model of China's Next Aircraft Carrier?," *Eastern Arsenal* (blog), *Popular Science,* June 17, 2014, accessed August 25, 2014, http://www.popsci.com/blog-network/eastern-arsenal/model-chinas-next-aircraft-carrier.

the Liaoning: "Chinese Aircraft Carrier 'Liaoning' Finishes Training Mission," CCTV.com, January 1, 2014, accessed August 25, 2014, http://english.cntv.cn/program/asiatoday/20140101/104882.shtml.

"*command protocol Divine Wind*": "This Day in History, August 15, 1281, Kamikaze Saves Japan from Mongol Invasion, Again," HistoryChannel.com, accessed October 27, 2014, http://www.historychannel.com.au/classroom/day-in-history/756/kamikaze-saves-japan-from-mongol-invasion-again.

359 *Diamond 360 maneuver:* Video from BLUESPAO, "2014 Blue Angels Diamond 360 Maneuver — Pensacola Beach Air Show," YouTube, July 14, 2014, accessed August 25, 2014, https://www.youtube.com/watch?v=G9J6OjBtUPw.

362 *PL-12 air-to-air missile:* Richard Fisher Jr., "China's Emerging 5th Generation Air-to-Air Missiles," International Assessment and Strategy Center, February 2, 2008, accessed August 25, 2014, http://www.strategycenter.net/research/pubid.181/pub_detail.asp.

369 "'*Pretend to be weak*'": Sun-Tzu, *The Art of War,* trans. Lionel Giles.

Epilogue

371 *William Walker, "Absent Friends":* Liam O'Brien, "William Walker, Battle of Britain Pilot," *Independent,* October 24, 2012, accessed August 25, 2014, http://www.independent.co.uk/arts-entertainment/music/features/page-3-profile-william-walker-battle-of-britain-pilot-8224117.html. Also see "Funeral of Oldest Known Battle of Britain Veteran," Royal Air Force, March 12, 2013, accessed August 25, 2014, http://www.raf.mod.uk/stclementdanes/news/index.cfm?storyid=B1ADDBB7-5056-A318-A81624170C45F8D8.

373 *Her head began to pound:* "Symptoms of PTSD," Department of Veterans Affairs, January 3, 2014, accessed August 25, 2014, http://www.ptsd.va.gov/public/PTSD-overview/basics/symptoms_of_ptsd.asp.

374 *strutting around the Alpha Group compound:* "Alpha Russian Special Service Unit Is As Strong As Ever," *Pravda,* August 20, 2004, accessed August 25, 2014, http://english.pravda.ru/russia/politics/20-08-2004/6631-alpha-0/.

Popular Library
Detroit Public Library
5201 Woodward Ave.
Detroit, MI 48202